A CERTAIN MERCY

A NOVEL BY

WILLIAM L. SILVANEUS

This is a work of fiction.
All of the characters, organizations, and events portrayed in this novel are either products of the author's imagination or are used fictitiously.

Printed in the United States of America
Published by Author Academy Elite P.O. Box 43, Powell, OH 43035
www.authoracademyalite.com

Paperback ISBN-978-1-64085-568-7
Hardcover ISBN-13: 978-1-64085-569-4
Library of Congress Control Number: 2019931458

CHAPTER 1

Quote from the Journal of a Killer:

For it would be better to die once and for all than to suffer pain for all one's life.
Aeschylus

WHEELCHAIR BOUND HOMELESS MAN COMMITS SUICIDE

The First Homeless Suicide Reported In Grand Island History

GRAND ISLAND, Tuesday May 29, 2013 – 33 year old wheelchair bound Joseph E. Riederhof was found Sunday hanging in a tree south of the McDermott & Miller PC parking lot off South Locust. Items at the location indicate Mr. Riederhof was homeless. The Hall County Coroner officially ruled the death a suicide—according to The Independent, the first reported homeless suicide in Grand Island history. Chief of Police Greywright stated the man has no known …

Stephen Brown studied the three-column picture printed below the headline. In the upper right-hand corner, he noticed a thin debris covered slab of ice or snow, odd for this time of year even if it had been a cool spring. Scattered clothes and assorted trash littered the ground.

Wonder if that's the man I bought arctic coveralls for.

Newspaper in hand, he headed toward the kitchen to see if Andy or his staff remembered Riederhof. Surely the man came for meals.

Angelina Abbott stormed through the outside dining room doors just as Stephen stepped around the corner by the black garbage cans under the dishwashing window.

Every time Stephen saw Angelina in all her 19th century regalia, lace and buttons, he expected her to pop open an umbrella. No, actually he expected her to pop him with an umbrella. He also expected her to swing her butt around to show off a huge bustle with a matching bow perched on top. She never carried an umbrella. Thank God. And she never wore a bustle and bow. But crab and bustle, and sass and boss, that she did.

An equal opportunity pest, her sass and boss leveled against Stephen felt personal—threatening.

"Why aren't these empty?" she demanded pointing to the near full garbage cans.

"Staff will do it in a minute." Stephen lifted his chin and donned a placid face.

"The diners should do it!"

Stephen recoiled from her spit as Angelina stepped forward. She'd invaded his personal space now. Eyes narrowed. Mouth in a pucker. The twelve-inch difference in their height accentuated the ever present spark of tension arcing between them.

"I don't know how many times I've told you, Stephen; get the diners to do it. It's the least they can do for a free meal."

Angelina gestured toward the flip top canning jar setting around the corner in the serving window. There was only a gum wrapper in the jar.

"I don't see any money in that donation jar and half these freeloaders are working."

At minimum wage and not making enough for rent let alone food. Stephen kept the comeback in his head.

"If Grace Abbott were around," Angelina continued, "she'd see to it that these poor souls acted proper. It was her wish that her money be used to help the poor. I intend to see that it does."

She didn't say it, but Stephen heard, "when are you going to do as I say?" plus a threat to withdraw the sizeable annual Abbot Foundation contribution. The men's shelter could not absorb such a hit. Come to think of it, how did that shelter money give Angelina any say over the feeding program?

Hands on hips, lips pursed, she continued to stare up at Stephen.

One of the staff snickered in the kitchen.

Stephen almost burst out laughing.

Of course it wasn't funny.

"Jesus said, 'whosoever will to the Lord may come.'" Stephen began to lecture. "That's the Salvation Army motto." Factually, it was "Heart to God. Hand to Man" but "whosoever will may come" was painted on the wall over the serving window and Stephen knew Angelina could see it at this angle.

Give without thought of return, he wanted to scold her, but didn't.

"The Salvation Army position is we are here to serve whoever comes into this dining room. We consider serving them to be the same as serving Jesus. If someone volunteers, their assistance is gratefully received, but the diners are not required to serve the Salvation Army, just like the Salvation Army would never require Jesus to do something if he came in to eat."

"But they are not Jesus," Angelina shot back. "'Whoever does not work shall not eat.' That's one of your precious scriptures too. If they eat, let them haul out the trash. This—" she pointed at the gross food in the can, "is disrespectful to the people who donate time and money to this feeding program. You're treating these clients like they're some kind of kings or queens."

Stephen's glare hardened.

Angelina tightened her shoulders. "Maybe I should put my money elsewhere," she mumbled, then hitched her hip to the right, turned, and marched, nose in the air, through the door towards the offices.

"You goin-ta get yourself fired." Andy's voice lilted to the left, then he let out a belly laugh that rollicked into every corner of the kitchen. "Money talks."

Stephen smiled, then wrinkled his nose at Andy and laid the newspaper on the serving counter. "You remember this guy?"

Andy, Chet, and Susan crowded around him to read the byline, scrutinize the picture, and skim the article below.

"Was this Riederhof?" Andy asked.

That's Andy, thought Stephen, *just read the headline and let someone else read the details.*

"Yeh, that's his wheelchair."

Chet pointed to the picture.

"Saybra—you know the bag lady—made Joseph that scoubidou keychain tied on the armrest," Susan said. "It's green and yellow."

Stephen's eyebrows lifted. "So Riederhof did come here for meals?"

"Yeh," the staff all answered in unison.

"I thought so," he affirmed. "I think he's the man I gave some coveralls last winter."

He glanced toward the plate glass doors where Zachary Plues, one of the homeless regulars had slipped in to pick up some bread from the giveaway table. His eyebrows furrowed.

"That's right," said Andy. "You used the Christmas money from your mom for that."

"But suicide?" Chet propped a hand to his right hip. "That doesn't sound like Joe. Are they sure?"

Susan picked up the paper and scanned the article again. "It says here he hanged himself from a tree." She furrowed her eyebrows. "Joseph could hardly move without help. He couldn't even make a slip knot. How could he get a rope up a tree? He told us he'd been unable to lift his arms over shoulder since some auto accident. Lately, someone had to feed him. He couldn't get a spoon to his mouth nor his face down to the plate. Zachary Plues's been helping him the last couple weeks."

"So when did you last see Riederhof?" Stephen looked at each person in turn.

"Oh, I guess it's been a week or two," said Andy. "I don't know. People come and go. I lose track of time."

"He was here last Tuesday," Chet stated. "That's the morning he brought in the blue columbine, his favorite flower. Said they grow in Colorado, high up in the mountain passes. I haven't seen him since."

"I figured he left town." Susan spoke up. "He always said he was going to Colorado, going to move on when he got his disability check. I just figured the columbine was his way to say he was leaving—the first was a week ago. I never figured he'd commit suicide."

Thoughtful, silent, everyone looked down.

Suicide makes a perfect cover for a murder. The thought came to Stephen unbidden, perhaps from the plot lines of the hundreds of detective novels he'd read, but just as abruptly, Susan interrupted the thought.

"Hey, did you see this article down here?" She looked back down at the second page.

"Body found in a garage on the alley behind a house on First Street," she read. "Says they found the body wrapped like a mummy. Investigating officer said it felt like entering a mausoleum."

"Wonder who that was," said Andy.

"Says victim could not be identified." Susan replied.

Stephen shrugged and shook his head. Wordless, he again shook his head and headed back to the office.

Who notified the families? he wondered as he pushed open the dining room door.

Suicide makes a perfect cover for a murder.

Again the thought came unbidden.

CHAPTER 2

Quote from the Journal of a Killer:

God of justice, God of mercy,
Make us merciful and just!
Help us see all your creation
As from you a sacred trust.
And when people cry in anguish
For their own or others' pain,
Show us ways to make a difference
O dear God, make us humane!
Jane Parker Huber

Stephen strode the twenty paces back to the Social Services Office. Laid the newspaper on the military green file cabinet next to the Food Pantry door. Relaxed into his cool black leather chair and swiveled to face his desktop computer.

He punched Ryderhof [sic] into the search bar of his Clients Served List. No entry. He knew the name would not show up as a shelter resident—the shelter was not wheelchair accessible—but it did not show up on the list at all.

How could a wheelchair bound homeless person not *be on the Salvation Army Clients Served List? Didn't Riederhof ever come ask for help? How did I know he needed those winter coveralls?*

He entered Joseph Ryderhof [sic] into the search bar again—though he knew what the result would be. No matching entry.

The man came for meals—hundreds ate in the dining room on any given day, too many to type into the Clients Served List—but never for direct services.

But the coveralls?

Then it dawned on him. Riederhof never entered in his office.

In fact Stephen never spoke to Joseph Riederhof in person. One morning he saw him sitting out front, his body jerking from the cold as he waited for breakfast. He sent an army blanket out to him. Chet tightened it around him.

At Christmas, Stephen's mom shrugged off Stephen, her only child, by only sending a card. No note, no invitation to Christmas dinner, just a card, a signature, and a check with "buy what you want" on the memo line. Stephen vowed to destroy the heartless gift. That's when the picture of Riederhof shivered through his brain again. Marching straight out of the apartment building, Stephen dropped the card in the front door trash. He cashed the check at the Second Street Overland Bank drive-thru. Sped down US Highway 30 to Orscheln Farm and Home. Bought the highest rated winter Carhartts. Stuffed the remaining $45.19 into a chest flap. Drove back to the Salvation Army. Left the coveralls and a note in the kitchen for Andy and his staff, then went home and fumed.

The next morning, Andy reported that Chet gave the Carhartts to Riederhof. Zachary Plues wheeled him into the bathroom, cut a slit to thread the catheter through, and helped him struggle into them. But Stephen had never spoken to the man. Not even then.

Not my finest hour.

"Brrrt."

The phone snapped Stephen back to the present. Still looking at the "no matching entry" on the computer screen, he answered, "Stephen Brown."

"Stephen Brown?" The voice was all business, but feminine.

"Yes."

"The Secretary said you're the Director of Social Services."

Not a question. Just a fact check.

"This is Chief Investigator Ellison from the Grand Island Police Department. What is your relationship with Joseph Riederhof?"

"Joseph Riederhof?"

"Yes."

"I never met the man."

"Are you sure?"

"Yes." He glanced at the plaque on his wall.

"Has he been a client of yours?"

"Only the meal program—nothing else."

"How can that be?"

"I'm sitting here asking myself that same question. I've checked the Client Served List two times and he's not on here."

"Can you explain, then, why there was a green army blanket marked 'GI Salvation Army, Social Services' at his campsite? You are the only employee in Social Services, aren't you?"

"Yes, and yes. I saw him out front shaking in the cold one morning. So I had one of the kitchen staff take that blanket out to him. That's how he got it."

"But you never talked to him and he's not in your client database?"

"Correct."

"Is that unusual at the Salvation Army?"

"No, we often give unsolicited help and, if we haven't done an intake, it doesn't show up in the system."

"I see." Investigator Ellison paused.

Why do I feel I'm being interrogated?

"Do you remember a red Pendleton Sioux Star Blanket marked Salvation Army?"

"No."

"Did you read about the murder scene on First Street in the alley?"

"An associate of mine just read it to us in the kitchen this morning."

Stephen's stomach knotted into a small walnut. An unseen hand held him by a rope in a black void over nothingness.

"You don't remember the blanket."

Again, a statement more than a question.

"It was found at the murder site wrapped around the body. Would you care to explain how it got there?"

Tentative, unsure, Stephen answered, "No."

CHAPTER 2

"No?"
"No. I don't know anything about it."
"Nothing?"
Silence. The black pit sunk deeper.
"Then why's your name written on it?"
"You mean Salvation Army?"
"No. Stephen Brown."

CHAPTER 3

Quote from the Journal of a Killer:

... death is but the next great adventure.
J.K. Rowling, **Harry Potter and the Philosopher's Stone**

... then why's your name written on it?

Stephen leaned in and placed his elbow on his mid-thigh, then propped his chin between his index finger and thumb. One finger pressed against his nose, he stared out the window in the wall at the doorjamb in the hallway. He thought of his grandmother. He thought of the red brick cathedral in Anselmo. He thought of the Platte River in July—wide, its sand bars split by multiple channels. His thoughts, all pictorial, clicked in a random slideshow each time he blinked his eyes. Not a word, not a verbal memory dared intrude. In a grasp for control, he closed his eyes and reviewed the line between light and darkness which replaces outward sight. In the darkness he felt a clamp tightening around his head and a sour pit in his stomach. They brought him back into the tension of the moment.

Murder ... why don't you know him ... your name ... His recall remained as random as the slideshow he hid behind.

Pendleton Sioux Star blanket.

He typed the words into his Internet search bar, hit enter, then enlarged an image from the Northwest Museum Store.

So that's what that garish red blanket looks like unfolded?

Yes. He remembered.

Joseph Running Bear, a veteran, dropped it off one January after he moved out of the shelter. That must have been in 2009 or 2010. Stephen received it with the dignity and honor its owner clearly felt toward the gift, then promptly gave it to the shelter manager. He'd not noticed his name on the label. Perhaps Joe meant the blanket as a gift for him, a sign of his gratitude. Didn't matter. Staff were not permitted to accept gifts from clients. He'd have given it to the shelter anyway.

Shelter managers gave the full size blankets to residents who needed them when they moved out. When he was a night manager, Stephen passed out more than one wool blanket to a drunk or undocumented worker he'd turned away on a bitter cold night. Perhaps that's how the blanket got to the murder scene.

Still numb, Stephen got up, walked through the commons area, and dropped himself into one of the two brown stuffed leather chairs in Captain Bramwell Higgins' office.

"Yes," Captain responded as he looked up then folded his large fingers together. His hazel blue eyes took in the younger man sitting in front of him.

Stephen shrugged...

I wish Captain was my father, he thought.

"Well you didn't come in here for nothing," Captain responded when Stephen remained silent.

He felt Captain's eyes search his own without a hint of criticism, impatience, or fear. Six foot tall, broad shouldered, but not obese, Captain Higgins's warm face creased by smile lines created a universal comfort zone.

As he visually examined Captain's broad hands and fingers—working man's hands, not an administrator's or preacher's hands—Stephen structured his thoughts and emotions. But before he started speaking, Captain said, "So you had a run in with Angelina Abbott."

"Got ran into by Angelina Abbott." Stephen shook his head. "But that's nothing. She trounces me every time." He paused, "Why does she have it in for me? Did she come blowing steam to you?" Stephen hoped not. He hated that game. "I suppose she threatened to withhold the Abbott Foundation money."

"No." Captain smiled wryly. "She wanted to know when you were going to start doing your job and what I was going to do about it." He paused then clarified. "Andy came in—laughing all the way from the time clock." He pursed his lips and gave Stephen a once over. "But I agree with her. You ain't Jesus." Captain's laugh rattled the pens in his marble pencil holder.

"She said the dining crowd—they aren't Jesus," Stephen corrected. He wanted to say Angelina wouldn't know Jesus if she bumped him in the nose, but he looked down and blushed, "Guess I got a little out of line. She didn't come for a sermon."

"You? A sermon?" Captain stretched his hand out and laid it on the table. A new chuckle rumbled in his chest. "I don't think I have to worry about that. Andy thought you did—what did he call it—handsomely."

The rumble started all over, gentle, pleasant, leaving Stephen its gift—reassurance—as it trailed off.

"And don't you worry about the Abbott Foundation grant. Angelina has nothing to with that. I've seen her puff out her chest about being an Abbott, but she's not even related to those Abbotts."

Stephen started to respond, but Captain brushed it aside.

"Yeh, yeh. She claims to be, but she's just a country girl from Holdrege. Her Abbotts came over on a different ship at a different time. The girl growls, but she has no fangs… Now, why did you come in here? Something's on your mind."

"I just got off the phone with Chief Investigator Ellison." Dejection laced Stephen's voice. The atmosphere dampened so fast you could wring water from it. "You heard about those two homeless murders this weekend?"

"I read about Riederhof in the paper," Captain paused before he continued. "Murder, huh? … The newspaper said he committed suicide…. Is he in our database?"

"No. He ate breakfast and supper here, but the diners' names don't show in the database."

"Hmmm …" Captain stroked his chin. "That's all?"

"Well, no."

At Stephen's tentative response, Captain looked up.

Stephen rested his arm on the plump back of the chair. "We gave him an army blanket one morning, but since I didn't talk to him, he didn't end up in the data base. And..."

Stephen paused.

"And ..." Captain echoed back.

"And I bought him some Carhartts—my own money."

Mercifully, Captain didn't ask for an explanation.

"I suppose that doesn't look good," Stephen continued. "Wheelchair bound homeless man commits suicide. Salvation Army has no record of serving him. Salvation Army provides care package for homeless man, but doesn't talk to him."

Captain looked at Stephen over the top of his glasses. The rebuke was gentle, but he caught it.

"But you said, 'two murders.' Who's the second?"

"The body found in the garage on First Street."

"Yeh, I read that. Didn't realize he was homeless. You have a name now?" Captain tilted his chin up.

"That's what I want to talk about," Stephen replied.

Captain's shoulder relaxed but he fixed Stephen's eyes with a probing stare. "Is this about Chief Investigator Ellison? Did he call them murders?"

"She."

"She?"

"Yes. She called to ask about both of them. She found an army blanket marked Salvation Army in the Riederhof camp and wanted to know our relationship with him. I assumed she was looking for contact information...anyway she wasn't impressed when I said he wasn't on our client served list, especially when I told her about giving the blanket, but never talking to him. She kept popping questions." Stephen lifted his shoulders and shivered.

Captain gave a knowing nod. "So it's already come back to bite you?"

"I guessed. But then she asked about the other murder scene. She didn't call it that. She just questioned me like a suspect." Stephen tilted his head to the side. "You know, Captain, a suicide's a great way to cover a murder."

Captain's eyebrows rose.

"I mean—Riederhof couldn't lift a fork to feed himself. How'd he make a noose or throw a cord over that branch? He could barely inch his chair forward; his grip was so weak. So how could he push with enough tension to drop himself out of the chair?"

Stephen stopped, took a deep breath, looked up at the cross behind Captain's desk, and slowed down as he continued. "Like I said, she asked about the First Street murder. Specifically, she asked if I remembered a red Pendleton Sioux Star blanket marked Salvation Army and if I knew about the First Street murder…"

"She thought you might know something about the murder?" Captain's heavy brows narrowed and his eyes darkened.

"No…well, maybe yes…I don't know. She asked about the blanket. She assumed I'd say I didn't remember it, so she asked if I'd care to explain how it got to the murder scene, wrapped around the body."

He checked Captain's eyes but continued without pause. "When I said, 'No,' she got quiet, then asked how my name got on it. I said, 'You mean Salvation Army?' She replied, 'No, Stephen Brown.'" He sighed and dropped his head backwards onto the chair. "What should I do?"

"What did she ask you to do?"

"Nothing. When I didn't respond she just thanked me for my time and said she had to run. Just like that."

A few seconds of silence knocked the edge off the tension.

Captain asked, "What do you want to do?"

"I don't know. I mean…" Stephen jiggled his hands then laid his fist over his heart. "…emotionally I don't know what to do. But—I know it sounds crazy—what I want to do is find Riederhof's family and let them know what's happened."

"Hasn't Detective Ellison done that? Seems that's the police's job."

"I don't know. The paper said the man had no known family." Stephen shrugged his shoulders again. "Maybe Investigator Ellison was going to ask me if we had contact information. I don't even know if she called it a murder or a suicide. She seemed pretty bright. I doubt she's missed the murder possibility. But, in either case, I'd like the family to know a little more about his life and physical condition. I'd like them to know that we did try to help him...."

"Feeling guilty?" Captain interrupted.

"No, I just think family's important. Family has a right to know."

Captain's light laugh punctured the renewed tension. "Go for it," he said. "See what you can find out." He paused then lifted his eyebrows. "Oh, by the way, The Independent called for a comment on Riederhof. Maybe you could write something up. I told them we'd do some more checking before we had something to say. Maybe you could find out a little about his life, write up a little article."

Captain looked at Stephen over his glasses.

"And, don't forget to call Chief Investigator Ellison." He grinned then continued. "You'll need your facts straight."

CHAPTER 4

Quote from the Journal of a Killer:

Sister, you'll never be raped and used again.
Hold your head high.
The Journal of a Killer

AFTERNOON, JUNE 4, 2012:

Investigator Ellison peered through the driver's side rear window and scanned the body of the young woman lying in the back of the station wagon. She hated how female bodies deteriorated fast in the heat—especially those with soft sensual breasts. Bodily fluids already stained the cut-to-fit foam mattress.

Laqueta imagined her own body, instead of the victim's lying before her in the rust and white Ford Escort, shuddered, and stepped back. Nonetheless, old station wagons made her nostalgic.

Five kids. One in the front, four squeezed in back of their wood paneled 1990 Buick Estate Wagon. The rear packed to the ceiling with luggage, gifts, lunch, and a hundred other things for the seven hundred mile trip to Summerville, South Carolina. She smiled. Those were the days.

CHAPTER 4

Laqueta was ten years old in 1993 when they made that trip in a bucket of bolts held together by baling wire.

The memories were all good. Black smiling faces. Belting out 1960's Motown tunes. Hands and faces hung out the windows to catch the sun and fresh air and dry the sweat of those hot July days. They were family. They were together. They felt safe, loved.

"Sure is easier now that Jim Crow's dead," Daddy said and nobody dared ask who Mr. Crow was.

The dead girl's face looked too peaceful. Laqueta stared at it a few seconds.

I wonder if she enjoyed riding.

She pictured the girl, nineteen, light brown long hair flowing in the wind, speeding up Interstate 75 along one of her favorite escarpments in Kentucky. Though she was Grand Island Police Department's Chief Investigator, shared with the Hall County Sheriff's Department, she believed all victims have equal worth—that meant the same worth as herself. She wanted them all to possess happy childhoods, pleasant memories, and lives free of anything that made them more than random, undeserving victims. That, however, was not true of herself. She too had been the victim of her own choices. Choices that placed her in harm's way.

She turned towards the back of the car and started a detailed inspection of the vehicle and its surroundings. Ponderosa Pines overhead cooled the crime scene much like the evaporative cooler in her grandparent's home. The car sat on a mat of crabgrass that covered an old layer of crushed rock. No crushed grass—no footprints—on the driver's side of the car. The car had not been moved for three weeks or more.

She wrote down the number from the out-of-date Missouri license plate on the rear.

Inside a hint of anise with no apparent source tinged the smell of stale air and decaying body. Curtains with a print of apple blossoms stood open on the north side allowing a clear view of the body. Matching curtains on the passenger side prevented pedestrians on the sidewalk from seeing in. Two brown bags of food blocked the rear window.

Laqueta pulled a driver's license from the body's right front pocket.

Janice Zahn. Nebraska. Issued 4-10-2012. Most likely Janice wasn't from either Nebraska or Missouri. Chances were she was from who knows where, had picked up the car in Missouri, complete with tags, then drove it to Nebraska. As Laqueta slipped the license into her black portfolio, she noticed that Janice used 1320 West Third Street, the address of the abandoned Workforce Development building in front of her, as her residence. She made a note to check for the state that issued Janice's prior license.

Janice's thumb and primary finger gripped the end of the zip tie which cut into the opposite side of her neck. *Was she trying to pull free or tighten it?*

Laqueta studied Janice's eyes. The lids were shut. Maybe she committed suicide. Surely a murder victim pleaded with their eyes open. But then again, maybe she closed her eyes to concentrate on getting free.

People began to gather. A plumpish bag lady, maybe thirty or thirty-five, stood back near a cedar bush. Her chin tucked into her cleavage, she never looked straight forward. It seemed to Laqueta she wanted to ask a question. The woman, along with two flamboyant young Sudanese girls, prostitutes by their mannerisms, were the only other females present.

Six or eight men stood on the sidewalk. Several were the homeless men often seen at Pioneer Park where they urinated while seated at the picnic tables and just sat there in the filth and smell. Laqueta wondered what had drawn them to this remote area. After all, she always drove an unmarked vehicle and had not sounded the siren. Her best bet—someone already found the body and the homeless grapevine had drawn the curious.

A man in a business suit stood off to the side.

To the north, a young man, perhaps twenty two or three, not one of the park guys, edged closer until he could see inside the station wagon. His shoulders angled forward, he searched the inside of the car as if Laqueta wasn't there. As he circled the scene, he kept an even 10 feet away. He'd done the same thing at the First Street crime scene. There, as here, his eyes fixed on the body.

"You know this woman?" Laqueta's question broke his revere, but he did not respond.

"Did you know this young woman?" she repeated.

Alert, calm, his eyes fixed on her. "Yes."

"I'm Chief Investigator Ellison. And you're...?" Laqueta smiled and reached out to shake his hand.

"Zachary Plues, Ma'am."

The handshake confident and firm.

"Pleased to meet you, Zachary."

He nodded.

"What can you tell me about Janice?"

His face softened. "Sissy? ... That's what I called her. She was shy, really wary around people. 'Cause she'd been hurt a lot. She always listened to other people's conversations—from a distance—but enjoyed them like she was a part of them. That's how we met. She'd been watching me. If she liked you, if she trusted you, her eyes really danced."

"So her eyes danced when she was with you."

"Yes—but not all the time." Zachary's head dropped.

"You two had a thing going...but you hurt her?"

His shoulders slumped forward and his chin dropped further. He shook his head, yes, but said nothing

"You said she'd been hurt a lot. By you?"

"No." He reengaged, alert. "By a lot of other people."

"Here, in Grand Island? Is that why she's dead?"

"Some here. But they wouldn't kill her." He furrowed his forehead and puckered his lips.

He thinks one of them did. She thought. *What's he hiding?*

"Even if some guy took advantage of her—you know—banged her, she always acted like she enjoyed it. Like she'd said yes." He winced, peeked quickly at Laqueta's face, and shook his head. "No, not from here."

She wasn't convinced.

"Her Dad and his brothers," he continued. "uncles and cousins, you know. Then lots of rapes by boyfriends, boys at school. She wouldn't say no. She was too afraid. They beat her and hurt her too many times."

"And she told you this?" Laqueta lowered her head to catch his eyes again.

Zachary nodded.

"And you hurt her that way too?"

"Oh, no! No, ma'am!" He snapped to full alert. "I didn't hurt her. Not physically. I hurt her by having sex when she didn't really want it, when she responded like she does. I thought yes meant yes, but afterwards she cried. That's when I learned she couldn't say no. I never got it wrong again."

Laqueta changed the questioning.

"How was Janice lately? Any problems? Sad? Unhappy?"

Zachary's shoe sounded like fine sandpaper as it scraped the dry grass. He watched the slow pendulum of his left leg as if counting his thoughts then raised his chin. His olive green eyes looked deep into Laqueta's honey-colored ones.

"After she started telling me why, she cried for three days straight. I held her and comforted her the whole time. She relaxed into my arms, but she couldn't stop crying. She wouldn't eat. I tried those crackers over there." He pointed into the back of the car. "But she pushed them away. I like taking care of people, but nothing I tried helped. She barely sipped some soda and bottled water. I didn't know what to do.... "

Laqueta held his eyes with hers. Firm, but with compassion.

"It happened that way twice—I mean the crying—she ran out of tears but kept crying, sobbing, shaking. This time, when she finally caught her voice, she just kept saying, 'I wish I were dead. I wish I were dead,' and then 'I never should've been born.' She talked about killing herself and kept asking how to do it."

Laqueta's professionalism almost crumbled. Now, she held his eyes as a prop for herself.

"Even when exhausted she never went to sleep. I kept dozing off. I felt so bad. But I kept dozing off. The third morning she shook me awake and shivered slightly in my arms. I tightened them around her and she whispered, "I need some love. Please make love to me."

Zachary let out a loud sigh.

"So I did. Gently, as if she was the most important thing in the world. Finally she went to sleep. When she wasn't moving anymore, I crawled out of her arms, folded them across her chest, and left."

"When was that?"

"The end of last week, I checked on her again Sunday morning, but she was still asleep and I couldn't wake her." Then, as if anticipating her question, he added, "That's the last time I saw her. I was afraid to come back."

Laqueta broke eye contact. *Why's he fudging the time frame? She's more decomposed than that.* She pursed her lips and turned to survey the people on the sidewalk. *I suppose with the heat she might not have been dead yet.* She decided to wait for the coroner's time of death.

She turned toward Zachary again and lifted her chin toward the small crowd. "How'd these people know to come here?" She looked back at the crowd. "I know some of them. They never leave the park."

Zachary shrugged. "I don't know. Maybe heard about her at the Salvation Army."

A question crossed Laqueta's face.

"You know…at breakfast. Rainey White told people there was a body in the car. I guess he'd been poking around last night. He likes to keep track of the women, and Sissy always parked the same place on the weekends." He motioned at the men on the sidewalk. "I s'pect they've been walking by ever-so-often just to see if anything was happening."

"You, too?"

"No, someone came by the library. Said you were here."

"And last week in the alley?" A look of surprise crossed Zachary's face. "Did you hear that at the library too?"

"No. The library's closed on holidays. I just walk down that alley most days. You know…my sort of routine."

"Thanks Zachary. Plues was it? Where can I reach you if I have more questions?"

"The library, I guess. They know me there and can get me a message. I'm usually there from 11:00 till 2:00, and then again from 3:00 till 4:30. I like to miss the early meal crowd at the Salvation Army."

When the coroner—who was also the County Attorney—arrived, Laqueta walked over to brief him on the situation.

Richard Koenig, one of the city councilmen, shuffled forward to eavesdrop. His family had been burying folks in this town for over a hundred years, and he was just stuffed shirt enough to let you know it every time you met him.

While she continued the briefing, the medical examiner arrived and set to work. She'd learned that he preferred independent investigation before accepting a briefing—wanted to form his own opinions without being tainted. When finished, he lifted the body out of the station wagon, turned toward Laqueta, and handed her a Salvation Army business card.

Stephen Brown. "Where'd you find that?"

"In her left pocket."

On the back in decent lettering she read:

Sister, you'll never be raped and used again.

Hold your head high. I'm sorry.

She slipped the card found on the unidentified boy's body out of her blazer pocket and flipped it over.

At last my brother, relief from fear.

Freedom from the past and future.

The writing matched.

Time to go visit this Stephen Brown.

CHAPTER 5

Quote from the Journal of a Killer:

To die, to sleep;
To sleep: perchance to dream: ay, there's the rub;
For in that sleep of death what dreams may come
When we have shuffled off this mortal coil,
Must give us pause ...
For who would bear the whips and scorns of time,
The oppressor's wrong, the proud man's contumely,
The pangs of despised love, the law's delay,
The insolence of office and the spurns ...
William Shakespeare, **Hamlet**

Monday, after lunch, Stephen settled into his office. Time to start writing.

And, don't forget to call Chief Investigator Ellison, echoed in his memory. His arms tensed. He stroked the stubble on his chin. Not that anyone could see it. His skin and whiskers were the same gold. A metallic, bitter taste formed in his mouth.

If you're gored by a bull you don't go back for more. An overstatement, but the best sense he could make of the emotion that clamped him down.

His eyes wandered to the Celtic cross above his monitor.

God grant me the serenity to accept the things I can and wisdom to know the difference. Only his lips moved. *I slaughtered that.* It didn't matter; it calmed his thoughts about Investigator Ellison. Still…

He just wasn't ready to take that bull by the horns.

He laid his fingers on the keyboard. Research for the article offered an escape, an excuse.

After several misstarts—mainly too many entries for Joseph Riederhof and even Joseph E. Riederhof—he typed Joseph Riederhof missing into the search bar.

He considered the homeless "missing," at least from some family's life. Often that was not the truth. Some homeless had no surviving relatives. But, too many times a homeless man would be out of touch with his family, his past, and so to someone somewhere a missing person.

Bingo. Pay dirt.

Headline News: Local Family Asks Help Locating Missing Son…

Several entries revealed annual appeals from the Riederhof family—always on February 7th, the anniversary of Joseph vanishing from the hospital.

From the handful of news articles, Stephen compiled the details. Nurses discovered Joseph's absence when doing rounds at the eight PM shift change but assumed a family member or friend had taken him on a walk. Still missing at midnight, the nurses and security staff searched the Rehabilitation Unit, the main hospital, and all attached clinics, offices, and programs but did not find him. Staff notified the Hospital Administrator then, after a final sweep of the hospital grounds and all hospital street fronts, they contacted Joseph's parents to notify them he was missing and to determine if they knew of his whereabouts or could suggest other places to look. The hospital administrator called the local police and the county sheriff for further assistance.

Joseph could not have left the hospital using his own strength. His spinal injuries left him without use of his legs. His arms had a limited range of motion and did not possess enough strength to lift him from bed nor to operate his manual wheelchair.

The Riederhofs called all the family and friends who might even remotely assist him, even those from miles—states—away. The hospital downloaded a record of all calls Joseph received during his stay and called each number. No one knew his whereabouts. He had not asked any of them for assistance leaving the hospital. They found only one clue—a security camera video from seven PM of a man who wheeled what could have been Joseph out the main entrance then down the sidewalk in front of the rehabilitation center until they entered an area out of range of all cameras inside or outside the hospital buildings.

There Joseph Riederhof vanished. Stephen found no other Internet entries except the annual family appeal for help.

Exhausted, Stephen leaned back in his chair. His breaths came shallow and light. His pectoral muscles taut, an ache shuttled across his shoulders, his stomach twisted into a knot. He had to remind himself to take a deep breath before the lightness in his head threatened a blackout. He had that problem if he let tension accumulate in the back of his neck. Eyes closed, he willed the tension to flow down his body and out through his fingertips and toes.

Refocused, he clicked on the Facebook page setup by the Riederhof family. Pictures showed Riederhof before the accident, in the ICU at the hospital, in his hospital room on the Freedom Bed—like a whole hog on a barbeque spit. The bed automatically turned as needed by quadriplegics, his by voice control. Most pictures after that show Joseph sitting with assistance for a belt to hold him erect. The last picture, however, taken two days before he disappeared, showed Joseph in the whirlpool at the Center apparently able to sit erect without assistance, his belt left in his chair.

Stephen remembered that same belt, complete with a worn happy face sticker, holding Joseph erect in his wheelchair at the

Salvation Army. The belt encircled Joseph, crossed his chest in front, and then ran up over his shoulder to latch behind the chair back. Remembering made Stephen wonder how Riederhof got from his chair to a bed, how he put on clothes, or did anything. He'd ask around. And, how did Joseph get free of that contraption in order to hang himself?

Facebook also provided a narrative of Joseph's accident. His identical twin brother, the driver, died at the scene. Family stated that Joseph blamed himself for his brother's death and felt he should have been the one driving. In bold letters, the narrative warned that Joseph's physician expected his physical condition to deteriorate unless he received regular follow-up care.

On a yellow pad, Stephen wrote basic information and pertinent details useful for Captain's assignment then typed "Joseph Riederhof accident" into the search bar.

From early news accounts of the accident, he learned that the twins, alone in Joseph's brand new MX-5 Miata, skidded out of control on wet leaves on Route 58 between Lowell and Irasburg in northern Vermont. Joseph and Jonathan purchased matching cars for delivery by their 27th birthday, September 30th. They even purchased new custom Connecticut plates: TRIDER 1 and TRIDER 2. Joseph, the firstborn, drove TRIDER 1.

The morning of their birthday they picked up their vehicles from Mazda of Manchester, dropped Jonathan's car off at their grandmother's in Hartford, and sped north up I-91 to view the fall foliage in Vermont's Northeast Kingdom. They stopped in Barton to party with old college chums. It had been a planned birthday celebration at Kelsey's house, drinking and generally acting like college boys—except no girls. Jonathan threw back some debs while Joseph stuck to his favorite birthday drink, cognac. No one was surprised when, near ten o'clock, after a call to Val Sckongnofer and Ervie Stroup, the twins left for Hazen's Notch.

Avid hikers and cross-country skiers, Hazen's Notch Bed & Breakfast became their home away from home after their first solo trip at age sixteen. Val Sckongnofer and her husband Ervie Stroup soon became friends and confidants—not second parents, a title they objected to. The couple promised to wait up and allow a late check-in.

Jonathan's speed exceeded the posted warning. A mile after crossing Route 100, Jonathan hit wet leaves going seventy miles an hour. Just as the car started to hydroplane and swerve, he struck a small rock on the road. Skid marks indicated two three-sixties before taking out a fourteen-inch maple with the driver's side of the vehicle and throwing Joseph, the passenger, another twenty feet into the trunk of a mature oak.

An hour later, Val called the Highway Patrol to see if there had been any accidents on Route 58. Despite an answer of no, a gut feeling pushed him to drive back toward Lowell then on toward Irasburg where he came on the scene about three minutes before the State Patrol. Jonathan was breathing and moaning from pain. A slight wheeze started that reminded Val of stories the Bosnians told him about people dying following torture.

Joseph proved difficult to find. The officer whose light first hit him thought he was dead. His body lay wrapped around the tree back first. Not good. A quick check revealed a pulse and light respirations. Immediately the officer called for a second ambulance, one equipped to handle back and spinal cord injuries, then everybody milled around and waited checking on the boys every few seconds.

Jonathan's moans soon stopped replaced by an eerie, heart wrenching death whistle. It sounded like a doe as she lies dying from a wound. As the lights of the first ambulance lit up the roadway, even the whistle stopped. Val checked his pulse and breathing. Nothing.

The investigation filled in the missing pieces of the story. The college chums from Kelsey's remembered Joseph trying to stop Jonathan from driving, but Jonathan, already in the driver's seat and in possession of the keys, insisted it was his right to drive—after all they had left his car at Grandma's. As usual, Joseph gave in to his younger brother. Blood tests registered Jonathan legally drunk and identified the drugs in his system – amphetamines. Joseph's alcohol level, however, was under the limit. Now he understood Joseph's struggle with guilt. A tragedy all around.

Stephen saved several articles to his computer desktop—all the background needed for the Riederhof story. It would be emotional to write. He wanted it to be emotional to read. Now he needed more information on how Joseph survived in Grand Island. Anything on his last few days. Where he lived.

Stephen would interview Zachary Plues. Last week Susan mentioned that Zachary helped feed Riederhof. Zachary's responses might provide an angle to follow. Perhaps the Independent could send him a digital copy of Riederhof's homeless nest to enlarge for more detail.

And I'll call the family to put in their response to finding their lost son and the tragedy of his death. He paused. On second thought, he decided to wait to call the family. They probably had lots of unanswered questions. He ought to provide as many details as possible.

"Stephen Brown?"

Stephen looked towards his office door. His pulse forgot a beat. She was pure ebony with a slight cast of midnight blue. Her eyes, dual amber cabochons, held the mysteries of Egypt and Ethiopia and drew him somewhere deep and enchanting.

CHAPTER 6

Quote from the Journal of a Killer:

"Who Is My Neighbor?"
The man replied, "The one who showed him mercy."
Then Jesus said, "Yes, now go and do the same."
Luke 10:29b, 37 New Living Translation

Stephen's heart found the missed beat, then tried to run off with it.

This radical response to the woman in his doorway floored him. Old clichés proved worthless. Stunned. Mesmerized. Enchanted. Elegant. Wistful. Amazing. Nothing sufficed to describe this presence. Nothing had grabbed him like this before.

"Chief Investigator Laqueta Ellison. Do you have a minute?" she said.

"Yes."

No, it couldn't be!

Stephen shuttered his mind and took a deep breath. His brain spasmed lightly as it connected this vision to the threatening voice on the phone. Off kilter, he must take care not to accidently give her unintended evidence that could put him in jail.

Assertive, not reactive. His new mantra—his determination to mature his affect—would be tested by this conversation. By this woman.

As he stood, he inhaled deeply. Without breaking eye contact, he gestured towards the chair across from his desk.

"Stephen Brown!"

Angelina!

Stephen's chin dropped. How would she try to get him fired today? At last week's board meeting, one of the members already parroted her complaints.

Angelina brushed Investigator Ellison's elbow. She threw back her head and fixed the dignified figure with a who-are-you face. Or was it the what-are-you-doing-here or out-of-my-way-you-ignorant-inconvenience face?

Stephen winced. He grasped for control and his mind said a silent, *Excuse Me,* before he jutted out his chin.

"Angelina, what can I do for you?"

Investigator Ellison rolled her eyes. He flicked his own toward the ceiling and shrugged

"That makes three," Angelina declared in an accusative voice.

"Three?" Stephen repeated with a partial scowl.

"Yes, three."

"Three what?" His voice remained controlled, commanding.

I'm not going to let her bully me, he asserted to himself. Not because Officer Ellison stood there—he was just tired of it.

"Three homeless people," Angelina retorted.

"Three homeless people?" Stephen flipped his palms upward. "Three homeless people what?"

"Dead." Angelina nailed the word to the floor.

"Angelina. I don't read minds. You need to tell me what you are talking about."

"That's just like you Stephen Brown." Her anger flashed. "Standing around like an ostrich with his head in the sand. How can you help these people if you don't even know what's going on with them?"

"I'm sorry, Ms. Abbott…" *I can do this,* Stephen thought. "… accusations don't tell me what you mean. Again, please, what are you talking about?"

"The three homeless people found dead in our city and I'll bet you didn't help a one of them."

Stephen cringed and blushed. He could feel the venom from Angelina's mouth. Maybe it was spit.

"Can you name them for me? I can't answer you specifically." He remained calm.

"You trying to impress this woman?" Angelina's arm swept back towards Investigator Ellison, but she continued, "You know. That Riederhof guy."

"Yes, we fed him." Stephen wasn't about to tell Angelina that Joseph Riederhof was not on the client served list—not even under the corrected spelling of his name. "And we gave him some blankets, winter coveralls, and, though I don't usually, even some money."

"Well." Angelina faltered, her head dropped. "He should have been in the shelter, not in some trash pile out in the trees."

Angelina's loss of vocal control amused Stephen. He chose not to address the need for handicap accessibility. In the impending remodel that would be taken care of.

"And how about that kid murdered over on First Street? What's his name?" Angelina asked.

"I don't know what his name is." Stephen lowered his gaze and looked directly into Angelina's eyes. "The paper talked about a body being found, but I didn't think it had been called a murder yet. I don't even know if he was homeless. In any case, I can't say if we did or did not serve him until I have a name."

"Of course he was murdered. How else do you think he got zip tie burns on his neck?" She stopped and gave Stephen a hard stare. "You served him," she declared. "He had a blanket with 'Salvation Army' on it."

Stephen noticed Chief Investigator Ellison's eyebrows arch. Apparently, this was not public knowledge.

"Where'd you hear that?" Stephen asked.

"Chief Greywright told me."

"Did he have a name?" He referred back to the young man again.

"No."

He looked down at his desktop. "Then I'm sorry. I still can't help you."

Stephen felt a blush of compassion for Angelina. It must be hard to live intense and uptight all the time and then stand here and have to take it for the first time because of his new self control.

"And what's this third person's name—Janice Zahn?" Again' Angelina spoke clipped and confident, but Investigator Ellison's face registered a five star alarm.

"Janice Zahn?" Stephen repeated.

"Yes, the girl found dead in the car over on Jefferson behind Workforce Development." Angelina cocked her head.

Eyebrows lifted, Investigator Ellison inserted herself into the conversation. "Who told you about that body?"

"Who are you?" Angelina asked beady eyed, lips flattened in a frown.

"I'm Chief Investigator Laqueta Ellison of the Joint Grand Island Police and Hall County Sherriff's Investigative Unit."

"Well, it sounds like she committed suicide if you ask me," Angelina retorted.

"Who did you say told you about the body?" Investigator Ellison leaned in as she asked the question again.

Defiant, Angelina tilted her head up.

"Councilman Koenig. He was there. You know him?"

"Yes, we've met."

Cat fight, thought Stephen as he interrupted the two women.

"I'll have to get back to you on that, Angelina. Now, if you'll excuse me, Ms. Ellison just stepped in the door when you interrupted—rudely if I may say so." Rough words but he'd remained calm.

Without so much as an "I'm sorry," Angelina turned and stormed out.

CHAPTER 7

Quote from the Journal of a Killer:

Death - relief from fear,
freedom from the past and future.
The Journal of a Killer

LATE MORNING, DECEMBER 26, 2009:

Zachary looked up at top floor loft window in the Masonic Temple Apartments. If Stephen Brown had been sitting there painting or meditating, he would have seen him wrapped to invisibility in layers of warm clothes scurrying about on errands of compassion.

The downtown air, crisp and dry, left winter rouge marks on Zachary's cheeks. No wind, the textured gray sky of St. Stephen's Day wrapped the world in softness and comfort. The clouds, however, held the biting cold near the ground. Zachary preferred a nip on the cheek to the earlier crystal daggers in his eyes.

Behind the old Blue Moon Coffee Shop, he pulled a plastic ZipWall from the construction waste container. With temperatures already dropping, he appreciated his Carhartt coveralls, Caterpillar Hiking Boots, and insulated work gloves—gifts from Rupert Stone of Stone Demolition and Recovery. He'd appreciate them more in January when he returned to finish removing the remodeling debris from the unheated building.

He struggled against the large plastic sheet. Each time he smoothed and folded another thirty inches, the plastic popped and cracked like hailstones on a vinyl tarp. Despite the sounds, upon inspection he found no breaks.

Thank God there's no wind, he thought as he hurried home.

Home. Call it mental, but Zachary's lungs warmed at the comforting site of his "winter villa" in the alley behind the green two story Victorian house at 1218 West First Street. An old garage, the villa's Canadian split-face blocks, a soft green, reminded him of pictures he'd seen of hammered stone buildings from Tuscany. He'd never seen Tuscany, but, like most homeless men in Grand Island, he read several hours a day when the library was open.

Zachary called his winter home *My Rent Free Italian Villa.* It came complete with a raised wooden floor and a single bulb hanging from 1930's electrical cable with a ceramic switch by the door. Zachary smiled. The small dusty electric heater attached to the outlet on the north wall made the shed comfortable, even toasty when he turned it up.

The double wooden door, just wide enough for a Model A Ford, had been boarded shut long ago. However, a small handmade door less than five and a half feet tall allowed entry for a short man. Zachary assumed the main entrant was a man based on the pegboards and cupboards that lined the walls. As he thought about it, however, it could have been a washhouse. He pictured a postcard he'd seen of a wringer washer plugged into a wall socket. Two wash tubs in their stand by the door, for rinsing. A fair-haired shapely woman in a brown cotton dress with a prim and proper bustle bent over the washing machine pulling wet clothes up and sending them through the electric wringer, its small waterfall tinkling as it drained back into the agitator. Of course, he'd never used a wringer washer.

Inside, Zachary laid the plastic in the northwest corner, plugged in the heater, and dialed it back to low. Just enough heat to soften the plastic. He looked wistfully at the body wrapped in the Indian blanket lying against the opposite wall, but he still needed more supplies to properly bury his "baby brother'.

CHAPTER 7

To minimize fatigue and cold, Zachary decided to take his longest trek next. From canvas shopping bag, he pulled out a pair of blue jeans, an aging tee-shirt, and a faded blue long sleeve Van Heusen. These he stuffed into a couple plastic Super Saver bags.

The lime and salt on Zachary's needs list were stored at the old sugar beet factory about a mile down Old Highway 30. According to an old postcard at the Railroad Towne Antique Mall, Oxnard's Sugar Mill, built in 1890, was the first sugar beet factory in the United States. The history brochure he picked up at the visitor center also called it the first. But, as turned out, that wasn't true.

Zachary, like every good history hound, looked it up on the web. A factory operated in California several years before Henry Oxnard built the one in Grand Island. Still, old man Oxnard's factory was certainly the first sugar beet processing plant east of California and, as far as Zachary could find, the first one built on the Prairie.

Near the entry off South Avenue, the site appeared half bulldozed. Nevertheless, several businesses operated on the property including the Sunrise Trucking Company to his left. Straight north, then a bit to the right, stood a two-story metal bin elevated on legs with an auger and supply lines feeding into a half demolished red brick building. There, last fall, in the southeast corner, Zachary found a pile of white lime with only a slight crust from exposure to humidity.

Somewhere he'd read that lime cut the smell of putrefying bodies.

He set down his bag and nested the two grocery bags together. Using a tin can from the ruins, he scooped up two gallons of lime, returned the bright yellow grocery bag to the canvas bag, and took the tin can with him.

No cars were parked in front of Sunrise Trucking so Zachary checked for unexpected traffic then sprinted across the open lot. He ducked through a hole in the chain link fence separating the trucking firm from the Department of Roads Winter Salt Storage Arena.

Zachary slipped through the pedestrian door in the back of the building. Inside, near the back of the salt cone hidden from prying eyes, he felt secure.

He removed the bag of lime and set it aside then he filled the canvas bag three-quarters full of rock salt. Done, he nested the yellow Super Saver bag on top of the salt and put the tin can on top.

Zachary skirted the salt pile, checked for prying eyes, scurried out the front gate of the Highway Storage Arena, and headed south on Webb Road. He crossed South Street then turned left to walk along the north side of the Grand Island Cemetery. The reds, whites, and winter greens on a fresh grave caught his attention. He left the heavy bag on the sidewalk to inspect the flowers. Funeral sprays always attracted him. He considered flat sprays the most pleasing form of memorial flowers.

There would be no spray on his brother Autry's grave. There would be no grave. The best he could do was make a mausoleum out of his winter villa.

He surveyed the white chrysanthemums and red roses lying on the headstone—Joe Zininski—then turned, picked up one of the half dozen long stem roses lying across the heart of the grave and continued on his way.

After walking less than a block, Zachary's breath plumed upward like steam rising from a hot spring. The weight of the salt and lime tore at his arm. He took the yellow bag of lime off the salt, clenched the rose in his teeth, grabbed one bag in each hand, and started home again. This eased the pain, but the rose meant he couldn't take a deep breath without stopping. So, once every block he paused, set down the bags, took three deep breaths—hoping not to freeze his lungs—pirouetted, grabbed the bags in opposite hands, and started counting his steps till the end of the next block.

Three blocks from home, after setting down the bags again, Zachary popped himself on the forehead.

Duh! Lay the rose on top of the rock salt. It's a little late for that thought now!

Even without the rose in his mouth, both arms ached. His shoulder muscles burned from being stretched, and he couldn't wait to drop both bags and himself on the floor inside the shed.

CHAPTER 7

Zachary sat down by his brother and cried. Was it the pain, the cold, the exhaustion? He didn't know. His arms hurt. His back ached. His eyes wanted to close, but they couldn't. Maybe he was just grieving. Autry's death, an escape from a ravaged body, relief for a broken soul, felt like a victory, a good thing. Why would he grieve when Autry's death resolved so many problems, so many issues? Aeschylus said, "It is better to die once than to suffer pain for all one's life?" Somehow even that philosophy failed him now.

His sobbing quieted at last, Zachary unwrapped the Prairie Star Pendleton blanket covering his brother. He'd begged that blanket off the night manager at the Salvation Army shelter the first time Rainey White beat Autry and tossed him naked into the snow.

"Here's a blanket to keep you warmer," Tom had said.

He still couldn't believe someone gave away a Pendleton. It must have cost three-hundred dollars.

Zachary and Autry both loved the rich red and bright blues of the Sioux Star. It reminded them of the Iroquois Turtle blanket, their favorite, which their mother took when she left.

He turned to the task at hand. A deep gash on Autry's shoulder lay buried in dried blood. Straight up 2:00 AM, Christmas Eve, Autry had stumbled into the Rent Free Heated Italian Villa, collapsed onto the wooden floor beaten, slashed, devastated, bleeding… a plastic laundry bag grasped in his hand. A strip of cloth, torn from his shirt, tied around his neck.

Remembering, Zachary's anger boiled towards Rainey White, Autry's pimp and lover. Then he mentally beat himself again for leaving Autry behind when he himself left home. Autry had been barely twelve and Zachary sixteen.

Twelve—that was Zachary's age when their father started abandoning them for days, even months at a time. He thought Autry would be okay. On his sixteenth birthday, how could he know Autry would leave six weeks later? It was Zachary's fault. He was supposed to be the steady older brother, but he left.

Back then, he didn't know what a bed and a ride from a trucker cost, especially if you're sixteen or a prepubescent twelve. How could he know?

Dropping a shield on that part of his brain, Zachary picked up the five-gallon bucket that served as his sink and bathtub. He poured the greywater outside the door. It was time to find the final supplies. He started to leave then stepped back inside for another Super Saver bag before he headed out and latched the door.

From the dumpster behind Sherwin-Williams on Third Street he filled his Super Saver bag with paint rags. He also found some nylon rope but not enough to bind the body, so he stepped around the block and sliced the rope off the Post Office flagpole on South Front Street. He still carried the small Swiss Army knife his uncle gave him when he was ten.

At the Relax Inn, Zachary noticed a maid's cart on the second story walkway. The laundry room door would be open. Quickly, he entered from the rear, stuffed two white bath towels into the bottom of his bucket, then filled it with washcloths. Emptying the paint rags on the floor, he replaced them with four white hand towels then, beginning to shake, he disappeared down the alley.

He swung north around the Salvation Army at Third and Eddy and lifted the padlock off the driveway gate. Normally an open padlock without a key was useless. Today it was a golden treasure.

Back home he dumped the towels and washcloths on the floor then stepped across the alley to the faucet at Casey's. Thankfully, it wasn't frozen. The water weighed a ton. His arms screamed, but he managed to hold on until he set the bucket inside near Autry's head.

Every body needs to be washed before burial, or so it seemed from the websites Zachary searched before the library closed on Christmas Eve. He held his arms stiff in front of him. Undressing a man, even a teenage brother, felt awkward. First, Autry's shirt stuck to his wounds. Zachary's nerves jerked with sympathetic pain as it pulled free. Next, his anger flared as he cut the blue jeans and boxers off the body, both ripped open in the seat. Cutting them off felt more sanitary, more respectful. Autry's feet were already bare. His shoes and socks, originally left behind in Rainey's room, sat beside him on the floor. Zachary found them Christmas Eve behind the Relax Inn thrown into a snow bank with Autry's other possessions.

He washed Autry's face and dabbed at the choke burns around his brother's neck. Gingerly, with a clean wet rag, he washed Autry's wounds beginning at his slashed shoulder. The wounds finished, he paused and examined the body then carefully washed it one more time from head to feet.

Washing his brother turned out to be a mystical experience. From his conversations with Bosnians at the library, he knew that among Bosnian Muslims this preparation for burial was an honor bestowed on close family or genuine friends. Enveloped in a sense of the sacred, every bruise, every cut, even Autry's torn anus was a gift to touch. An ointment of love flowed from Zachary into each mark of desecration, an after death healing stream.

At last, after washing, drying, and combing Autry's hair, Zachary sat cradling his brother's head in his lap and started the final rite of passage.

"Baby brother." Tears coursed down his cheeks. "I'm so sorry. This should never have happened. I didn't know. I didn't know. I was so selfish. I just wanted to get away. Stop having to care for you. Stop being angry at Dad. I should have known. I should have known."

In his funeral soliloquy, Zachary blamed himself for abandoning his young brother, leaving him to also flee, a minor without ID, without a birth certificate, without knowledge of how to survive. He stroked Autry's arm, speaking each name he knew, as he asked him to forgive him for all the pimps and predators Autry had depended on for survival, depended on for what dredges of belonging and love he could find.

Sick to his stomach, tears burned away by shame, he imagined that first night in a truck—Autry shocked, terrified, and bleeding. He remembered Autry's first violent rape and beating by Rainey White here in Grand Island. Zachary struck out and bloodied his fist on the wall as he apologized for not pushing Autry to report that abuse to the Police or Human Services. Yes, they were afraid of foster care, but foster care would have been better than this—had to have been better than this.

He spoke his regret for not insisting that Autry come bunk with him at the Villa. The next time Autry had been beaten and savaged by Rainey was all Zachary's fault. He could not stop the earlier abuse, but Rainey's second abuse; that Zachary should have prevented.

•——•⁘•——•

Zachary woke up, Autry's head still cradled in his arms. His soul at last quieted.

He unfolded the ZipWall and spread the two bath towels about three feet from the edge then sprinkled a bed of salt and lime on top. Gently, he laid Autry's body face up on the bed of chemicals. He considered packing Autry's body cavity with salt, like David Livingston's when packed out of the Africa or Augustus McCrae's on Lonesome Dove, but disemboweling his brother? That was out of the question. So he packed more salt around the body and sprinkled the remaining lime over it. He crossed Autry's hands over his navel then sprinkled the remainder of the salt on top.

At the last minute Zachary placed a fresh white washcloth over Autry's face, slipped the plastic laundry bag over his head, and secured it firmly with a cable tie to keep the lime from corroding the face. He folded the three-foot strip of plastic over Autry's body, tucked the ends in, and rolled the remainder tightly around him. With the nylon cord, he secured the plastic near the throat and ankles, then took the cord from the flagpole, wound it around Autry's mummy, and secured it at each end.

•——•⁘•——•

Winter gold, morning light began to slip in under the eaves. Zachary's stomach ached from three days without food. If he hurried, he could still catch breakfast at the Salvation Army then return to move out and finish Autry's burial.

CHAPTER 7

The Christmas schedule and Autry's death had messed up Zachary's sense of time. As he approached the Salvation Army—no cars in the parking lot—he realized it was Sunday. No breakfast today. No food until supper. He shivered then returned to the Villa.

He gathered his personal belongings and moved them to the old shed off Third Street he'd selected for his temporary new home. He took the electric heater—cold helps preserve a dead body, but heat's needed for the living—and good news, the coils purred when he plugged it in. One last time he returned to the Villa, swept the floor with a dry rag, made a mat in the middle of the room with a couple of his own old blankets, and spread the Prairie Star over it.

Reverent, as if Mary receiving Jesus in the Pieta, Zachary lifted Autry's body, placed him on the Pendleton, and wrapped it snugly around him.

Now, one last detail.

Zachary placed the single red rose above Autry's heart.

"Goodbye brother."

He kissed the rose, stepped out, slipped the Salvation Army lock through the latch, and locked the mausoleum.

CHAPTER 8

Quote from the Journal of a Killer:

...life without cause is life without effect.
And I can't allow that to happen.
Paulo Coelho, **Aleph**

MEMORIAL DAY, MAY 28, 2012:

Mercy extends a hand of death to rescue hurting people. At least that's how Zachary Plues perceived death as he watched two uniformed officers lift the plastic wrapped corpse into the medical examiner's van.

The quiet of mid-morning wrapped around him. Rays of summer sun caressed his cheeks and temples, drawing out tension as nimbly as his mother's gentle massages. As he rounded the corner into the First Street alley, blue pulsating lights stung his eyes and disoriented him for a few seconds—an old problem he'd had since fifth grade, caused by strobing or flickering lights.

"What the..." The exclamation slipped from his lips.

A black hole gaped open on Autry's jury-rigged mausoleum. Two Grand Island Police Department vehicles flanked the shed. Blue lights strobed across a handful of homeless people, teens, and business men clustered at the corner of the abandoned Casey's on the north side of the alley. To the south, two men and a woman stood in the garden gate of 1218. Zachary didn't recognize them.

New tenants?

As Zachary feared, the new tenants had apparently broken into the little cement building where he'd laid Autry to rest two and a half years ago.

What a lousy Memorial Day, he thought as he walked away from Autry's now empty tomb. He would miss knowing where his brother was. He would miss the comfort of being able to walk by and remind himself all was okay.

Feeling lousy, he headed down South Locust to visit Joseph Riederhof's campsite. He missed that man too.

Now the sun's rays pricked his skin like a thousand lasers trying to burn off his freckles. The pavement, a virtual solar oven, added to the burns as it reflected superheated rays back toward the sky. Memorial Day was presenting the first sun burnt day of summer. Seemed it liked to alternate. One year cold rain, next year sunburn city.

Still, the walk and the warmth relaxed his muscles. His attitude warmed. His memories slipped back to happier times.

Memorial Days, his mother took him and Autry riding out of Ohio into the Indiana countryside. On the way, Zachary loved the Dayton skyline. As a small boy, he thought all the buildings were fancy hotels, and each year he picked a new one and imagined lying on a luxurious bed, hands clasped behind his head, taking in the fancy artwork of the ceiling and its bracketed supports.

Every year their mother took Perry Street North, and stopped at Emmanuel Catholic Church. To Zachary it was a cathedral. Solemn and quiet as they approached and entered the doors, they passed down a side aisle to candles lit by Saint Joseph's feet.

Zachary loved Saint Joseph. He remembered smiling up at the face of the man who, unlike his father, was holding his son and gently cooing to him. His mother lit a votive candle for each of them. Immersed in mystery, they placed the candles in the rich brown wooden rack then stood silently for a full minute.

Next, they skirted the pews to a beautiful Pieta, Mary holding her crucified son on her lap, and stopped in front of the statue. Zachary loved the blue drapes of Mary's clothes. No one wore clothes like those anymore, which made the ritual more enchanting. His mom genuflected, then they kneeled in a perfect line. Hands folded and resting on the white marble altar rail, knees on the red cushion beneath, they always prayed quietly for the remaining interminable minutes.

When Mom stood, she genuflected again, doing the sign of the cross—the boys never did, they didn't know how—then they left the way they came in…reverent, the boys gape mouthed, Zachary drinking in the beauty of the windows and celestial paintings which stretched down from the vault of the ceiling to ten feet above the floor.

His mother never told them why they stopped at Emanuel Catholic Church, but it was an annual ritual.

After a long drop south and around Cincinnati, they'd cross into Indiana amid the hoots and hollers of the boys when they spotted the Leaving Ohio sign. To them Indiana was a different country. Maybe even a different nation. Zachary loved the hills and beauty of the Ohio River Valley on Highways 56 and 156. He thought the ocean couldn't be much wider than the Ohio at some places.

Their trip wound through the valley all the way to Vevay. Near Vevay, Amish horses and buggies shared the road. The boys stared out the windows wonder eyed. In town, the horses and buggies might be hitched to the rails in front of the store and some homes. Amish kids looked so calm, happy, and handsome. Zachary wanted an Amish life.

Each trip, they stopped at the same little restaurant on the north side of the main drag—Ferry Street. White capped girls served their food while little boys dressed in black with colorful shirts played on the floor by the pastry counter. Zachary's mother always bought them something from that counter—bear claws, cinnamon crisps, or Zachary's favorite, maple sticks.

On their last visit, the Amish girl running the cash register made eyes at Zachary. He returned the favor, but his mother blew into a rage. In the car she chewed his ear till it would have bled if words could make such an injury.

"You have no idea what it means to have an Amish girlfriend," she said. "You have no idea how just flirting can destroy lives. The girl gets shredded by her family. Shunned."

He didn't know what that meant but the way his mom spat it out it had to be bad.

"And if you get her pregnant her life is over. She'd be better off dead."

That day they left town abruptly and drove straight home. No one said a word. In fact, it was only a few days later when his mother abandoned him. Usually they spent the whole afternoon in or near the town.

It would be getting late when they headed up Ferry Street and turned north on Knox Ford Road. "Where's the Ford?" Autry always asked. He thought it meant a special car somewhere. Off Knox Ford they turned down a country lane. More buggies than cars shared this road. At a small white schoolhouse, their mother would get out and go sit on the front step. She called it a stoop or something like that. Zachary and Autry played on the swings and old fashion merry-go-round until dizzy and staggering. Occasionally they checked on their mother. If they found her crying, they laid their heads on her shoulders until she finally looked up and grinned.

Leaving the school, they stopped in an old cemetery out in the woods and his mother would go stand by one gravestone. Zachary couldn't remember the dates on it, but he thought the name, Lengacher, looked hard to pronounce. When he asked his mother how to say it, she just said, "Don't worry about it."

They never stayed long in Amish country. They never spoke to anyone and no one ever spoke to them, not even the waitresses. In fact, the cashier never accepted money from his mother. She always gave it to Zachary and then the lady at the checkout would take it from his hand.

Zachary's mother would slow down by one farm. Her eyes scanned the setting. It was as if nothing else existed. Absorbed in memory, he pictured the white house with its simple lines and many weathered gray barns...

Suddenly he tripped on a raised slab of concrete and looked up. He'd already passed the Best Western Inn and was on the Wood River Bridge. Quickly he backtracked to the McCroskey Building parking lot then froze. Yellow crime scene tape hung across the southwest corner and down into the trees where Riederhof stayed.

CHAPTER 9

Quote from the Journal of a Killer:

"The poor plead for mercy; the rich answer with insults."
Proverbs 18:23 New Living Translation

Laqueta turned to face Stephen as Angelina left. Usually she could sum up a suspect—and most men—with a thirty second assessment, but Stephen Brown proved more complex. After their phone conversation, she expected a mousy little man—though maybe a little belligerent. Her first impression, after a quick visual scan, leaned toward insecure, introverted, or some other softer personality. However, other than an initial tic, during Angelina's attack, he remained calm, unflustered, assertive and quietly in control—nothing hard, careless, or feisty—nothing denoting a person capable of murder.

Laqueta quickly reminded herself that few killers were cut from the same leather using the same die.

"That was something," she said, as she sat in the seat Stephen offered.

He shook his head. "I'm sorry you had to see that."

"You handled it very well. That kind can be difficult. None of us like to be on the defensive."

She noticed a slight flash of satisfaction cross Stephen's face, but he threw his hands up in surrender and replied, "Angelina Abbott, she's always like that. I don't know what her problem is."

"Abbott? Like in Edith Abbott Memorial Library?" Laqueta cocked her head toward the door.

"Yes. Like in the Grace and Edith Abbott Foundation. But Captain says she has nothing to do with the Abbott sisters. Even though she tosses their names around and threatens me with loss of funding, she has no connection to the foundation at all. She's not even related to that Abbott family … But that's not what you came to talk about. How can I help you?"

Laqueta nodded. "If you have a moment, I'd like to ask you some questions."

"Okay." Stephen's posture tightened. "I usually leave at three thirty, but take your time."

"Oh." Laqueta's eyes searched side to side. "What time is it?"

"Three forty."

Her breath stopped short. "I have to pick-up my son by four o'clock." *Maybe I should come back tomorrow. But I need to strike here while it's fresh.* Her deliberate eye contact broken, she felt limp. She'd lost her focus. *Never give the suspect the edge.*

"What's his name?" Stephen's question broke in on her thoughts. She looked up.

"Darren," she replied.

"How old is he?"

"Five."

"Five. You could pick him up then bring him here. I'll hang around. I don't mind." He gave a slight shrug.

Laqueta looked up at the unexpected offer. It sounded good. Having just found Janice Zahn's body, and more Salvation Army clues, she really needed to make progress here. *You're not thinking professionally,* she chided herself.

"We have a playroom down the hall. Captain's wife just came in. She loves to play Grandma." Stephen stood.

Say no, Laqueta thought. *You're supposed to be in control not taking favors from a suspect. This is not right.*

CHAPTER 10

Quote from the Journal of a Killer:

Remember
I'm with you whenever you tell my story
For I am all I've done
I will still be here
As long as you hold me
In your memory
Josh Groban: **Remember Me**

Laqueta shook her head, shot a puff of air from her nose, and reached for Darren as he bounded into Stephen's office just beyond her grasp. He stopped front and center at Stephen's desk, fixed him with dark brown eyes, lifted his chin, and with all the aplomb of an important business man, announced, "Hi there, Stephen."

"Mr. Brown," she corrected him as she caught her breath.

"I prefer Stephen," Stephen replied, as he stood and extended his hand toward Darren, his eyes fixed on the entertaining bituminous spark of coal in front of him.

Laqueta lowered her chin and gave Darren a look that said, "It will be Mr. Brown."

Darren's squinted eyes moved rapidly from side to side as if his little computer brain pinged from option to option. Suddenly they stopped, and he raised a defiant eyebrow. Before she could give a second warning glance, he turned back toward Stephen.

"Hi there, Mr. Stephen." Darren's small hand shot across the desk. "I'm Darren. You got toys?"

"Darren!" Laqueta's cheeks flushed.

"Did I hear a child?" Captain Higgins's wife stepped through the door. "Hi, I'm Captain Marcy." She shook Laqueta's hand firmly.

"Laqueta Ellison."

"I think I know just where you want to go, young man—if it's okay with your mama."

"Is it Mom? Is it?" The kid couldn't keep his feet on the floor.

Laqueta looked up at Captain Marcy and sighed. "If you don't mind." Her shoulders relaxed.

"That's why we have the nursery." Captain Marcy gave a dismissive wave. "And don't worry, I'll stay with him. You won't be interrupted."

"You don't know my son," Laqueta's eyes sparkled as she added, "but I'd appreciate that. Stephen and I do have some business to attend to."

She sat down in the chair Stephen offered a half hour ago and calmly watched Marcy lead Darren away, the latter never missing a beat as he talked. Ready, she turned, lifted her head, squared her shoulders, and established eye contact.

"I have some follow-up questions from our phone conversation," Laqueta said, dry, matter of fact, while she watched Stephen's face.

He nodded his assent, but Laqueta noticed a lift in his eyebrows and the hardened clarity he exhibited when speaking to Angelina Abbott.

"About your relationship with Joseph Riederhof …"

"We didn't have a relationship," Stephen interrupted, "I never spoke to him."

She flinched. Was he correcting her? "Yes, but he attended your meal program."

"According to my kitchen staff, yes."

The response was stiff, so Laqueta waited.

He blinked. "And I remember him waiting for breakfast one winter morning."

She raised her chin. "When was that?"

"Sometime before Christmas. I'd say around December 19th or 20th. That's when my mother's Christmas card usually arrives."

His eyes penetrated hers. She looked down at her portfolio to break the stare, then met his eyes with equal calm.

"Go on…" She nodded.

"Last time you asked me about the green army blanket marked Grand Island Salvation Army?"

"Yes."

"Like I said, one morning I saw Riederhof sitting out front…."

"What time was that?" She moved her pen into writing position. His lock on her face didn't break.

"I usually get here about 6:30 AM," he said.

His piercing gaze still unnerved her.

"Continue..." she said, with an almost imperceptible nod.

"He shivered so hard his body jerked…."

"And you didn't bring him inside?" Even interrupting failed to break Stephen's flat affect. She shifted uncomfortably.

"No, that's against our policy. Everyone was cold. Like I was saying, his body was jerking." He imitated the memory. "So I sent out an army blanket to help keep him warm. I didn't say anything. I saw a need and just took care of it."

Laqueta noted the hint of irritation in his words.

Stephen dropped his gaze. His hands fidgeted in his lap, then he tipped back in his chair and continued, "It was very cold. So that would have been at least November or December. But, I remember it was…I think it may have been the same day I got my annual Christmas card from Mother. No note. No invitation for Christmas dinner. Nothing but an enclosed check...."

Stephen's voice rose as he clicked off the last three phases. A clear scowl lingered. "…with 'buy what you want' on the memo line. It really ticked me off. I decided I didn't want the money. I was about to tear up the check when the picture of Riederhof, cold and jerking, popped in my head, so I decided to use it for him. I bought him the highest rated winter Carhartts …"

Laqueta held her left hand palm up and lifted her right eyebrow.

"Winter coveralls, he explained, "Some fleece lined gloves and some wick-away socks—to keep his feet dry. I stuffed the remaining $45.19 into the chest pocket, then I drove back to the Salvation Army, left the coveralls and a note in the kitchen for Andy, and the next morning staff gave them to Riederhof."

He paused and appeared to study her face. "Mom's card usually arrives around December 19th or 20th, so that's when I gave Riederhof the blanket."

Matter of fact. Non-defensive. Just a period on his explanation. An "end of conversation" statement.

Laqueta adjusted her weight in the chair again then changed the tone of questioning to an instruct-me mode.

"All of that, but he's not on the client list?"

"Yes. True," Stephen glanced up at the florescent light grid and sighed, "I guess you've identified a weakness in our service reports. Usually clients are not added to the list unless they have been in the shelter or had direct contact with me."

"But *you* bought him the coveralls and that's not listed?"

"I considered that a personal donation, not a Salvation Army service," Stephen replied—this time not defensive.

"And meal program clients are served clients, but they aren't listed?"

He nodded. "That's correct. We don't have enough staff to enter the names of everyone who signs the meal roster. Sometimes that's over a hundred people a meal—I think our highest has been three hundred and thirty eight—two times in one day."

"That's a lot of people."

He smiled and nodded.

Laqueta took a quick look at her notes and reorganized her thoughts. "So, when you personally interact with homeless people that's not listed?"

"Yes, but other than a casual 'hi' or 'come see me', I do not interact with clients outside the office. For peace of mind—mental health reasons—we try to keep our personal and professional lives separate. The needs can be overwhelming. We have limited power to address the real or root causes, and never enough resources to do what is optimal to reach all the needs of this population. You will even find homeless individuals we are not aware of because our paths never cross and they don't use the meal program."

"You don't go out looking for the homeless?" She pictured Christ the Shepherd out searching for his one lost sheep.

"No." He looked down into his lap again. "I suppose that's another of our weaknesses. But, like I said, there's not enough money to even do the basics, let alone go out to look for people."

Laqueta gazed down at her notes, then made eye contact.

"So you don't befriend people outside the office?"

"No."

"Never?"

"Never."

She noted edginess again, but couldn't tell if it reflected defensiveness or guilt. She rested an index finger with the pencil against her upper lip and paused.

"Okay, let's talk about the red Pendleton Sioux Star Blanket."

CHAPTER 11

Quote from the Journal of a Killer:

All my experience of the world teaches me
that in ninety-nine cases out of a hundred,
the safe and just side of a question is
the generous and merciful side.
Anna Jameson

That damned Sioux Star Blanket. Stephen's jaw set and he glared at Investigator Ellison. *Time to put an end to that line of questioning.*

Investigator Ellison continued, "I suppose you're going to say that was a private gift as well?"

"No!" He watched the officer wince then continued. "I've been thinking about that blanket. In fact, I researched the blanket just this afternoon. I looked it up on the internet—so I'd know what you were talking about—and that jogged my memory. "I remember thinking 'That's sure an ugly red.' Then I saw one unfolded on the Northwest Museum Store site. It's actually quite beautiful. I wish I had kept it to put on my bed. By the way, that's a great site if you like that sort of thing."

He noted her disinterest.

"But you do know how it got to the murder scene of First Street."

"No." He hated the down tick that formed at the corner of her mouth. It irritated him. "I remember the blanket—or I think I do—but I do not know how it got to First Street...," then for her anticipated next question, "...or who received the blanket."

"But you do remember the blanket?"

The downtick moved to the right side of her mouth as she furrowed her eyebrows and dipped her head.

Pretty cute for a bull. He shook it off.

"I think so." Cold, matter of fact.

She raised her eyebrows.

Finally, a reaction. He wanted to grin.

"Yes?" she queried tilting her head.

Okay, she wants facts. I'll give her facts, but it ain't going to help her.

"If it's the blanket I remember—and I'm not saying it is—I never saw the star inside. I only saw a folded ugly red."

Then Stephen clipped off the facts—flat, stone faced, and emotionless.

"Joseph Running Bear stayed at the shelter. I helped him with treatment. I helped him with a job. I helped him with veterans' contacts, glasses, the Housing Authority, furniture, and household items. And I gave him encouragement.

"He was grateful."

Laqueta raised her eyebrows but he continued.

"Joseph returned with a gift signifying his culture and honor. I received it with due dignity and the honor befitting the giver. But, the Salvation Army discourages receiving personal gifts, so I gave the blanket to the shelter to be given to someone appropriate. The blanket was too big for the single bunks upstairs.

"That was in 2009 or 2010. I didn't look it up.

"I assume one of the night managers gave it to another veteran or some homeless man who didn't qualify for shelter—due to alcohol or being banned for previous bad behavior—some cold winter night because he felt bad about turning him away.

"I don't know when that may have happened. I don't know how many hands it passed through before it got to First Street.

"And I don't have a way to find out."

He emphasized that last phrase.

"Now detective, I have some questions for you." He hardened his gaze. "Who is Janice Zahn?"

"That's confidential." The verbal battering had clearly derailed Investigator Ellison. "It's a new investigation. I was hoping you might know."

"And why would I know?" Too late, he realized his pouty tone.

"Because she had Salvation Army literature in her car."

"Her car?" He furrowed his eyebrows.

"Yes, one of our officers found her dead. He was checking an old station wagon under the pine trees on the Workforce Development property. It's an abandoned building. We don't want it to become a haven for criminals or vandals."

Now the officer sounded defensive. Stephen chuckled.

"The ID said her name was Janice Zahn and she apparently had been living out of the car for some time. Now—that's more than I should have told you already."

"And, because there was Salvation Army literature in the car, you came here to question me about her death too." He bobbed his head up and down.

"Three apparently homeless people found dead in less than a week—yes that strikes me as odd, disturbing—but if that automatically makes me a suspect then I need a new job."

Stephen let out a deep breath, let his shoulders relax, and continued.

"So was she murdered? Maybe she died from exhaust fumes or was overcome by heat."

"The coroner will have to sort that out. Right now we are not sure if it was a murder or suicide. I had not thought about the possibility of an accidental death." Thoughtful Laqueta paused. "Actually, given the evidence, that's highly unlikely."

"What evidence?"

"That's confidential. Chief Greywright would have my badge for what I've already told you." She stuttered and folded her hands in her lap.

Stephen leaned forward, propped his elbow on the desk, and lightly bit his thumb tip. Hardening his stare he continued. "So we have two possible murders, if they weren't suicides or accidents. We have another body with neither a name nor a cause of death and you come to interview me?"

"Yes…" She looked down again. "Like I said I was hoping you could help me."

Stephen turned to his computer, woke up the screen, and said, "I can. I did not kill any of them. So you can mark me off your suspect list!"

CHAPTER 12

Quote from the Journal of a Killer:

A bond is necessary to complete our being,
only we must be careful that the bond does not become bondage.
Anna Jameson

Stephen paused, looked at the monitor. "I looked Janice up while you went to pick up Darren—by the way I really like that kid—that's spelled j-a-n-i-c-e?"

"Yes… and thank you."

"And z-a-h-n?"

"Yes."

Stephen hit enter.

"Nothing … we have no record of services. If you'd like I could check with kitchen staff and get back with you tomorrow to confirm if she was homeless. Maybe she's on our meal sign in sheets."

"I'd appreciate that."

His cell phone chirped.

"Excuse me. I need to take this call … Hey, Gramms."

Stephen felt his smile spread from ear to ear.

"I'm fine, but with someone right now." He turned to face Officer Ellison and chuckled.

"Yes, Gramms. She is very pretty…" He lifted his eyebrows, shot Investigator Ellison a quick look as he shook his head then smiled. "No, I'm still at my office. This is strictly business—you know I don't treat girls like that. Say, can I call you back?"

He paused.

"Okay, I'll call you in a few."

Stephen tapped the end key then explained, "That's my grandmother. She's a character. But she's my rock. Maybe you can meet her someday."

"Mom. Mom."

It was the bituminous spark of coal again.

"I'm sorry…" Breathless Captain Marcy trailed right behind him, "He got away from me."

"Mom. Mom…" Darren took a deep breath. "I missed t-ball."

"Calm down, boy." Laqueta hugged him close. "You didn't miss it. It's tomorrow. We go tomorrow."

Darren's big are-you-sure eyes amused Stephen.

"You play ball?" Stephen said. "I like baseball,"

"Really, Mr. Stephen?" His eyes bugged out. "You play t-ball."

Stephen laughed.

"No, I play baseball—but not this year. Hey, I'd like to come see you play."

"Can he, Mom? Can he?"

"Well…" Laqueta's shoulder twitched. Clearly, she had trouble saying no to Darren.

"I play at the park where the ducks at," volunteered Darren not waiting for permission.

Stephen nodded. "Yes—Pier Park. And what time might that be?"

"Four fifteen," Investigator Ellison replied, defeated.

She stood, took Darren's hand, turned to go then suddenly looked back and took a step to his desk.

"Could you write down your cell number in case I need to get a hold of you tomorrow…" She looked down at Darren. "…after you leave work?"

Stephen pulled a business card from the holder on his desk and wrote on the back, "Mr. Stephen's cell" then his number. Investigator Ellison looked at it and shook her head, her right eyebrow twitched a little, then she quickly slipped it into her pocket.

As she turned to go, she again looked back at Stephen.

"Oh—there's one thing I forgot. Do you know Zachary Plues?"

CHAPTER 13

Quote from the Journal of a Killer:

Seems like sometimes the truly merciful solutions to bad memories require death.
The Journal of a Killer

EVENING MEAL, APRIL 23, 2012:

Zachary Plues surveyed the long rows of folding tables. Where should he sit? With Rainey White? No, not on your life. By the new kid? No. Zachary liked to welcome new people, help them, and, of course, make new friends. But two other people were talking with the kid. Kid used lightly. He was probably early to mid-twenties.

Zachary avoided the drunks and Hispanics when they sat in bunches.

Saybra's alone.

Saybra was forty-eight, not the sixty-eight she looked. Street life did that to you. She appreciated company, but today he didn't feel like listening to an old bag lady cry.

Sit with the shelter guys—no way. Usually they thought they were better than "street people" homeless. After all, they were only "homeless" by federal definition.

Never mind that he didn't live on the street. Nor that his new residence, the White Hall Off Plum, was better than his old Italian

Villa. Or that the Villa had been better than the temporary shack he moved to when Autry died. Never mind that all three of his homes had been heated and kept the rain out while the shelter furnace kept going out and its roof leaked.

He turned his nose up and sniffed at no one in particular. At least he didn't live in a group home like those shelter clients. He, Zachary Plues, lived independently.

Finally, Zachary noticed a new girl, sitting at the end of a row near the wall, partially hidden by a Hispanic family. She did not look up as he approached. When he asked if he could sit down, she made a grunting noise. He could barely hear her response when she spoke her name. When he got low enough to see her eyes, he was stunned. This hunched over shell of cloth folded in on itself hid sky blue eyes, flushed with sunlight, clear, and endearing. Her delight at his attention sparkled in their four corners and revealed a fun loving character despite everything else saying loner, keep back.

Zachary tipped his head down closer to the table so he could look up into her eyes. Reflexively, she smiled.

"Janice who?"

"Janice Zahn."

"Oh—you been here before?" His hand swung an arch around the Salvation Army dining room.

She shook her head no. "I only learned it today."

"I didn't think so. I usually know the repeats. So where did you come from?"

"To here? … Missouri."

She smiled a sort of hangdog grin.

"You liked it there?" Zachary asked. He kept peeking under her eyebrows.

"Yeh. It's real pretty in the spring," she replied, her smile now coy. "I like wild dogwoods and azaleas, everywhere. The Sweet Williams were heavy this time and the flags down there just started."

"Flags?"

"Little irises. I don't much like the redbuds—'cause I don't like peas I guess—but they'z pretty next to the dogwoods. It all so pretty this year. … I missed the pickerelweed by coming here. But its hearts were showing—the leaves," she added when Zachary's eyebrows lowered. "You ever see'd a dogtooth violet? Dem pure white ones?"

"No, just blue and purple ones," Zachary replied and returned her grin.

"Dem's not dogtooths." She sucked in a short breath and ducked her head. Worry wrinkles crept down her forehead and the corners of her mouth turned down. "I'm sorry," she said.

He shook his head. "For what?"

Janice ignored the question and went on. "I see's why they's called dogtooth, white spikes like my Lassie had, but they's so pretty. They should be called fairy skirts."

Zachary imagined Janice twirling through the green grass like an imp on her way to no place in particular—just joy. His smile couldn't resist matching hers.

"So why'd you come here?" he asked.

"Reasons."

"Reasons?" He lifted his eyebrows.

She buried her gaze in her lap. "I had to get out of there."

He wouldn't push. People talk when they're ready to.

"I'm from Ohio. I had to get out of there, too," Zachary said. "But I ended up in North Dakota before I came down here. Too cold up there. When I leave Grand Island, I think I'll head somewhere warm."

"You in trouble?" Janice frowned. Her eyes darkened. "You ain't hurt somebody did yuh?"

Zachary rocked back in his seat his eyes wide as two large buttons.

"Why'd you say a thing like that?"

"Seems the nice ones talk pretty but have a devil heart.... I'm sorry." She began to shrink back into herself.

"Oh, no. No!" He leaned forward to catch her eyes again. "I left 'cause I thought I needed to get away from home. My dad's a jerk and left me and my brother home alone forever. It wasn't right."

"Your mama?"

Zachary nipped the inside of his cheek.

"She left when I was ten. She was high and loud. Came with some scrawny guy to pick up her things and leave. Said all kinds of nasty things about my dad—he wasn't there. Said she never did want kids and didn't want them now. Loud and cursing, she threw things around, emptied the dishes on the floor, stomped on them, and told us to go to hell."

"Wow!"

"Yeah. Turns out she ran away when she was fifteen and never went home. She lived on the street between waitressing jobs and boyfriends and married my father when she was twenty-two 'cause she got tired of roller coaster living. Children were the trade off required to get and keep married. Dad wouldn't marry her till she got pregnant—didn't want to be stuck with a woman who couldn't have kids. Though you'd hardly know he wanted them by the time I left."

"So where're your folks now?" She looked him straight in the eyes now.

"Dad's in Xenia, Ohio—last I knew. Got a little falling down house there. Mom? We don't know where she is or where she went. She could be dead for all I know. Sometimes I say I wish she was. But you know … I miss my mama. A child needs his mama."

Zachary slumped forward looking at the floor under the lip of the table. This time Janice had to duck forward and look up into his eyes.

"My mama died." she said.

He lifted his chin ever so slightly to connect with her eyes. They were flat. Almost grey now.

"I was ten or eleven," she continued. "I don't know. Just remember she died hard. Cancer I think. At home. We had no insurance. She screamed and moaned. Dad kept her liquored up, but even then she moaned and moaned. Worse than a doe that's been shot, but not clean. I remember laying my head next to her on the couch. I wuz kneeling there and had to be careful not to touch her. I wanted to touch. She knows it and sometime she tries to touch me—but it was too hard."

Zachary's lips opened but nothing come out.

"Finally she just sleep'd and moaned then slowly slipped away. Daddy buried her under the tree in the front yard. He didn't know how to live without a wife then. So I became his wife. Actually,

I become his wife before she died. He needed somebody and he would never cheat on Momma."

Still speechless, Zachary shuddered at what that might mean. He couldn't let his mind go there, so they just sat quiet till the kitchen staff came by to wash the table.

"When did you leave home?" Zachary broke the silence as they lifted their trays.

"I was fifteen, my birthday."

"Why not sooner?" He paused. "Cause you were too young?"

Janice ducked her head. "'Cause I thought my Daddy needed me. You know, cooking, cleaning, dishes—not just for comfort. He was my Daddy. What was I supposed to do?"

"You never told anyone? A teacher? A friend? Anyone?"

"I didn't have no friends. Not since fifth grade. And Daddy said teachers wouldn't understand, so be sure not to tell them. I wuz just help'n out my Daddy."

Zachary frowned. It all sounded so unreal, so retarded to Zachary. "What changed? Why'd you leave?"

"'Cause of my Daddy's friends. He started to let his friends take me for comfort. It wasn't the same—didn't feel right."

"They took you to their houses?" His eyes widened.

"No. I gave them comfort at our house. Sometimes in Daddy's bed." She wrinkled her nose and held it, shivered her head and shoulders. "And sometimes they were mean." Her tone hardened. "Sometimes they took their comfort right there on the couch and my Daddy just watched, even if I cried, like he didn't care. Then..."

"Then what?"

She glanced up. "Think we better leave. They's closing up the doors."

When Zachary looked up, he saw Andy standing in the kitchen door a scowl on his face and tapping his foot. Chet was holding the outside door and Susan was heading their way—probably to tell them to go.

He stood and extended his hand to help Janice stand.

"You want to come see my house—where I live? I call it the White Hall Off Plum."

Janice looked at him askance. She pulled back slightly then bowed her head and nodded a yes.

After they settled on the pile of rags Zachary used as a chair, he took her hand and said, "Your daddy let his friends use you? Then … you start to say something but we had to leave. What else happened?"

Janice peered at him warily then continued, "I missed my—you know—my woman thing. That scared me. I could give my Daddy comfort, but it would be wrong to have his baby. And, even if it wuz one of his friends, he'd be mad."

She paused and looked deep into his eyes.

"Then 'bout three months later he asked me, 'Girl, you miss your period?'"

She turned her head away from Zachary and seemed to be starring at the crack where the floor met the wall.

"I lied. I wuz too scared to tell the truth. He might beat me."

"He beat you!" Zachary sat erect.

Janice shook her head. "Not that time, 'cause I lied, but plenty times before. Ev'ry time he got drunk or mad. Most times weren't too bad. But I knew when he found out, this one's gon'ta be a bad one. I just didn't feel like taking it."

Her lips drew in and her eyes narrowed.

Zachary's stomach ached. Its pit turned hard.

"So you left?" He tried to break the tension so she could go on.

She nodded her head.

"Where'd you go?"

Again Janice hesitated and looked up into his eyes.

"Xenia."

"Ohio?" His mouth dropped open. "You went to Xenia, Ohio? That's my home town!"

She nodded.

His eyes widened. "What'd you do there?"

"The trucker dropped me off at that stop out west of town..."

Zachary bobbed his head up and down. "Yeh, the one my Dad used. The one where I ran away." He didn't know if he was shaking his head in encouragement or in disbelief.

"Yah .... Then some old man pumping gas waved at me—you know, like to come over here—asked if I needed some help. 'Course. I needed something to eat. So he took me in the diner, treated me real nice—like'n I wuz his daughter—and fed me real big. Then he asked where I was going to stay. We'd finished eatin'. Said I didn't know. So he said, 'Why'd you come here?' and I said, ''Cuz' I'm pregnant and my Daddy's going to kill me.' So he said to come home with him and I could stay there a few days while I figured things out."

Zachary's neck stiffened as he listened to the story about the old man.

"Where did he live?" he asked. A sharp edge in his voice made Janice wince and look down.

"I don't 'member—Rose Crest, I think." Janice lowered her head. Her eyes dulled and darkened, but Zachary pressed on.

"What did the house look like? Those houses on Rose Crest, they're pretty big."

"Yah, it was big—humongous. Red bricks with a white porch. A big green lawn—huge as a pasture." She paused a few moments, her eyes rolled up under her lashes like trying to read something in her mind. "There wuz a big blue pine tree in front." She walked her hands upward in mock steps. "Up, up, up ... big."

"A blue spruce?" His eyebrows pinched together and his neck tensed. He knew that house. The things they said went on there...

"That's what he called it. ... And there wuz a big pool in the backyard with a fancy shape and cement patios all around.

"My favorite place was the rose garden. It was huge too. Had these boxlike hedges all around. Real private like. You could smell them roses all the time. Roses make people relax and feel peaceful. My momma taught me that. We used to lay out there a lot and he would rub my tummy as it began to grow. He bought me this real nice bikini—but not too skimpy, that would have been weird."

Zachary lifted his chin. "That sounds like the Emil Crawford's place."

"Yah, that's 'is name. I called him Milo," Janice responded with a rare laugh.

"How long did you stay there? Were there other people there?" The questions came out staccatoed.

"'Bout three months. We wuz the only two in that there big house. The maid—she did the cooking but then she went home and the gardener—he come and go when he want—most never come to the door or inside. There's a plant lady brought flowers once a week and always take care of the houseplants. That's about it. Milo said his wife ran off a few years back. He retired early, fifty-five. And they'z daughter she died young. College I think. I never asked. Didn't want to cause no pain."

Janice took a deliberate breath.

"At first he treated me real nice. Respectful like. Said I was his daughter now and he gonna take care of me and the baby. Then...." Thunderclouds crossed her face like a wall cloud then a few drops ran down her cheeks.

"He what?" Zachary said. He sensed she wanted to tell more but he added, "You don't have to tell me if you don't want to."

She sniffled then raised her head. Her eyes focused on the far corner of the room.

"He—he...," she stiffened and continued. "One day he asked me who my baby's daddy was. I said it didn't matter. He wasn't around now. But he got all sad looking and said he'd really like to know. Asked me over and over again. So I finally tells him it might be my daddy's friends or might be my daddy's. Probably my daddy's." She paused. "His face got real dark. He stared at me, his eye gone blank like one of them telescopes looking at a sky with no stars. Then he turned and walked away. That darkness never quite go way. He wasn't as nice after that."

Her pause hung pregnant with terror and Zachary shifted uncomfortably.

"Then one night when the house was real dark, like midnight or something, he came to my bedroom like my daddy used to."

Zachary nearly lurched forward.

"You just know," she said in answer to his unspoken question. "You can tell'z it by the sounds and the quiet and the heavy breathing when they stands in the door.

"He came over to the bed and sat down real close. I feeled his heat and when he start petting me I knowed, so I turned away.

She took another deep breath and let it out slowly.

"He got real angry. Called me—naughty names and started beating me with the glass lamp by the bed. He beat me hard. I don't know how long 'cause I passed out." She let out a soft sob then continued on. "When I woke up there was blood, a big pool of blood on the bed—you know—down by my private parts and the baby laid there—slipped out."

Her shoulders began to shudder from tears held back.

"The cord was cut." She exhaled another long, deep breath. "And when I examined myself they'z a cut up from my female parts all the way to my bone."

Zachary reached around her body to steady her. He tipped his head till it laid softly on hers and just held her.

When the shaking began to stop, he asked, "What did you do?"

After a long time, when her breath came deep and quiet, she explained how she first wrapped the baby in a towel and hid it under the bushes at the side of the house. She nearly passed out from pain, but she didn't want somebody to throw the tiny boy away. Then she went back to her bed and called nine-one-one. When they came she told them whoever did this to her had taken the baby.

The hospital kept her till she could walk on her own and not feel faint. They gave her antibiotics and pain medicine and a drip to replace the blood loss. The doctor told her she almost lost too much to live. It was a good thing she woke up. Milo only came one time. He brought some clothes and the book bag she'd carried from home. Just as Milo stepped in the door, the investigator was asking her, "Do you know who did this to you?" She lied. Said she was asleep and didn't see anybody. That when he hit her she woke up enough to tell it was a man in dark clothes and she thought he had a black ski mask on. Then she passed out from the pain.

At that point Emil Crawford left never to return.

Later, the investigator said she would be coming back again in a few days to talk when Janice was stronger. Maybe she'd remember more then and be able to identify her attacker. But Janice, afraid to make trouble, convinced the doctor to let her go before the investigator could return. She told him she would be going back to Mr. Crawford's and there would be someone to take care of her there. When the nurse had her ready for release, she asked if they should call Mr. Crawford to come get her. Janice said no, just call a taxi. She'd found some money Mr. Crawford put in her backpack. That meant she wasn't welcome back, but she needed to pick up the baby.

Thankfully, no one was at the mansion.

Janice stole a couple blankets then outside she wrapped the baby in a garbage bag to contain the smell. From the garden shed she took a foldaway shovel from the winter emergency kit. Tired, she rested a bit on the living room carpet. She thought about her bed but didn't want too many traces that she had been there.

When she felt a little stronger, she raided the kitchen, called the taxi, and had the driver drop her off at a motel just past the truck stop. From there she walked to one of the bridges over the Little Miami River, crawled underneath, spread out her blankets then passed out from exhaustion.

The next day she awoke real sick and with a bad fever. She sipped a little water from the river, ate one snack bar, lay down and passed out again.

While she didn't know for sure, she thought it was about three days later when she awoke again. She felt parched and hungry, but no fever. Before walking down to the river for a sip of water, she checked her cut pelvic area. It was red—a little infection remained near the cut—but she was clearly out of danger. She bought some water from the truck stop and some lunch meat for protein then rested under the bridge for three more days. Book bag thrown over her shoulder, she then hitched a ride that took her all the way to Missouri from a single woman in her mid-forties.

CHAPTER 14

Quote from the Journal of a Killer:

Living is a sickness to which sleep provides relief
every sixteen hours.
... the remedy is death.
Nicolas Chamfort

TUESDAY MORNING, APRIL 24, 2012:

Zachary woke to light filtered through the narrow basement windows of White Hall Off Plum. Janice had fallen asleep in his arms and soon after, whether from the comfort of a warm body next to him or emotional exhaustion, he also slept. His head rested gently against hers. Embarrassed by his morning erection, he was relieved Janice was still sleeping.

Janice slept through breakfast and though his stomach growled and his arm ached he refused to move. He'd found long peaceful sleeps to be healing and at eighteen Janice had a lot more to heal than he'd ever experienced. Finally, she turned her head and shoulder toward him, glanced up, and smiled. She snuggled up under his chin, relaxed and fell back asleep.

Half an hour later she stirred again and this time looked up then jerked her shoulders away from his body. Her eyes narrowed then popped wide as she looked up at him.

"Where am I?"

"At my place," Zachary responded and slowly lowered his arm.

"No, no…I don't do things like that." Angry darts flashed in Janice's eyes.

"No! We didn't." He pulled away from her and blinked.

Janice looked down at her buttoned clothes.

"No," he repeated softly. "We didn't."

"I 'member now." Janice abandoned fight or flight mode.

"You fell asleep while you were crying. I was afraid to wake you."

"Oh." She blushed and looked down into her lap then peeked up from under her soft brown eyebrows. "Thank you." A bashful smile lifted the corners of her lips. "You make me feel safe," she added then deliberately laid back against his shoulder and snuggled in when he slipped his arm back around her.

Safe! Zachary gazed into her eyes and yielded to the comfort of her body next to his.

Then, suddenly, his muscles jerked and his head snapped back as Janice's fingers cruised over his ribs and hit the ticklish spot below his arm pit.

"You little pixie." He leaned away to escape her roving fingers.

Janice's eyes flushed with delight at his shock and response. They rolled, jabbed, poked, and laughed in unrestrained delight.

His breath shortened into rapid gasps ripped to the surface by this woman who could find more sensitive spots on his body than pits on a hail damaged car. To end the onslaught he seized her upper arms, threw his legs across her lap, and held her firmly, though gently, against the old rags on the floor. They laughed and gasped and giggled till their breathing eased and left them smiling into each other's eyes.

Zachary leaned over and brushed the tip of his nose against hers. Janice grinned and wagged her head side to side to escape. When she stopped, he rested his nose on the bridge of hers and stared peacefully into her eyes then lifted his forehead and brushed her lips with a kiss.

She flinched.

He nibbled her ear then laid a track of gentle kisses down the side of her neck to her shirt collar and up along the line of her jaw to the tip of her chin.

CHAPTER 14

Janice's body went limp.

Resting his nose on the tip of hers, he again looked deep into her eyes' clear blue skies. She let a gentle breath ease across his face and he felt a charge of oxytocin in his brain and its passion coursed to the tip of every cell in his body. He seldom pursued sex with a woman and even less often experienced gentle, narcotic-lined moments that unfolded wings of deep peace and journeyed toward an ultimate passionate escape.

The spike in blood pressure that signals the end sent Zachary rolling to his back taking long, deep breaths. Just as his brain began to clear, Janice's sobs reached his ear.

He rolled her into his arms and lay facing her. The sobs strengthened. Against his chest, the warm dampness of her face turned into a hot torrent of tears. She began to spasm and shook so hard she barely breathed.

He didn't know what was going on so he clung to her desperately. His tightened chest muscles provided a cushion of strength as he rested his chin on top of her hair trying to will the calm and comfort of the night before. He drew her even closer to control the shaking. The skin between his lower lip and the tip of his chin caressed her hair line and he whispered, "Shhh—shhh—shhh..."

Deep and wracking sobs erupted less often replaced by rhythmic breaths. The tears slowed to one large drop at a time flowing down his chest into his armpit. Finally, he sensed a subtle relaxation in her heart rate. His caresses stilled. His grip eased though he continued to hold her.

"It's okay. It's okay," he whispered. "Please, tell me what's the matter?"

A deep sob stuttered up in response to the question so he quickly reassured her, "It's okay. It's okay. You don't have to say anything."

After a long pause she whispered, "I thought you wuz different," and the tears started down his pectorals again.

"What do you mean? Different how?" He tried not to let his muscles tighten.

"All they'z ever want was their comfort—just sex. You'z just like them." Another sob tremored beneath her breasts.

"Who? ... Who?" His temples tensed. His stomach tightened. "Your dad … his friends?"

Angry eyes shot daggers into his.

"Bullies…my cousins an' uncles…everybody. Men can smell a girl is givin' comfort that she don't want to. They'z crawls out of the woodwork and takes what they want." The sobs increased. "Again and again. New ones… old ones. They never stop. They say'z mean things. They say'z sweet things. But they'z all want the same thing—they'z comfort. If you don't give it, they'z goin'ta take it anyway."

He sat silent. Each sob tore at his heart. Each quiver sliced through his brain. His nakedness felt cold like a violation of the warm, sensual body he was trying to comfort.

At last he said, "I—I thought you wanted to. That it would comfort you—I didn't know. I didn't know."

The rhythm of his own breath collapsed. Though with each word his stomach tightened, it still felt hollow. "You relaxed and blew across my face. You seemed to be enjoying it and—I don't understand. I wouldn't have … I don't—I…."

In a near whisper, Janice explained, "I'z learned to do that so they'z won't hurt me. They'z want to feel like it's okay, like I'z like it, or they get mad and beat me, or sad and it hurts when they'z try to hurry. I'z learned to do it to please daddy. I had to do it… I had to."

Rage lined her whispers. Each phrase struck more violently until viciously she pushed Zachary away, vaulted to her feet, grabbed her clothes, and headed up the short flight of stairs.

"I'm sorry. I'm sorry," Zachary called after her. He struggled to slip into jeans and a shirt. "I didn't know. I didn't know…"

The jeans tangled. His body sprawled across the steps as he reached toward her.

"Wait—please wait."

… but Janice smashed the door open and fled naked into the bright sunlight down the railroad berm.

CHAPTER 15

Quote from the Journal of a Killer:

I have always found that mercy bears richer fruits than strict justice.
Abraham Lincoln

Stephen leaned out to watch Investigator Ellison and Darren exit down the hallway. He drank in the deputy's elegant walk. None of the women he had grown up around in western Nebraska could match that mesmerizing gait. None were black, so not one matched her sheer African beauty. As she disappeared from sight he picked up his cell phone and auto dialed his grandmother. That bit of voyeuristic observation and the call to Grams would both come back to haunt him later.

Wednesday morning, the story of Janice Zahn's death occupied the front page of the Grand Island Independent. The article filled in several details—another death by zip tie and, a puzzling piece, an empty bottle of absinthe. At sixty dollars a bottle, why would a homeless person buy absinthe? Stephen would wait for breakfast to finish and talk to Andy and the kitchen staff.

If I don't get that Riederhof article finished, people will assume bad news every time they see a homeless person. He laid the paper on top of the filing cabinet then sorted through the last of Tuesday's mail. Nothing for the residents, just some meeting notices, and junk mail. Tipping back his chair, Stephen thought about Laqueta Ellison.

I wonder if she still thinks I'm a suspect. Incompetent maybe, but not a suspect. His muscles felt on edge. He didn't want Laqueta to think of him that way. Distracted, he looked up at a crack in the wall and considered his reaction when Laqueta stood in the office doorway. Probably Gramms was right. He really liked this lady.

And that Darren, he smiled at the thought of the bituminous bit of coal. What was it about that kid that triggered such warmth in him? Usually pushy kids made him nervous. Stephen pictured Laqueta in his mind again. She didn't wear a wedding ring. Maybe Darren was just looking for a "daddy" figure.

Come on man. That's presumptuous. You're not cut out for that. Besides, he's black. A white man can't be a daddy to a black kid; especially one that's not his own. Still he hoped Laqueta didn't cancel him watching Darren at the ball game.

"Hey, boss! What you doing ogling the woman yesterday?"

Stephen jumped like a guilty boy caught with porn.

Andy.

CHAPTER 16

Quote from the Journal of a Killer:

God did not create death as a punishment.
No, he in the beginning created death as a good gift for man.
I have restored it to its intend use.
The Journal of a Killer

"What are you talking about, man?" Stephen bantered back.

"I saw you ogling that tall drink of Jamaican Coffee—sweet, intoxicating—sets your heart purring doesn't it?"

Glad Andy couldn't read his mind; he tightened his lips and drilled him with icy eyes.

"That was Investigator Ellison from the Grand Island PD," he stated.

"So?"

Stephen blushed.

"Was I that obvious?"

"Yep."

He stood, brushed Andy aside, picked up the newspaper from the filing cabinet, and turned the headline for him to read.

"Did you see this article this morning?"

"Yes?" Andy replied. He looked Stephen in the eyes.

"Do we know this lady?" Stephen asked.

"Yep, that's Janice. She's a regular. Hasn't missed a meal till Monday."

Stephen accompanied Andy and his number ten cans of green beans to the kitchen.

"How long's she been around?" he asked.

"Hey, Susan, how long has Janice Zahn been eating here?"

"I'd say eight weeks."

"First time I saw her was Monday after Easter," Chet piped in.

"Eight weeks on the money." Andy was quick with numbers and dates.

"Do we know anything about her?" Stephen asked.

"She's real shy," said Chet.

"I think maybe she's being abused." Susan looked down. "One morning she came in with bruises on her arm and a cut on her face."

"Did she fall down drinking?" Stephen proposed an alternative.

"Well, you know these people." Andy flipped his eyes to the right and shrugged.

"Not all homeless people are drunks," Susan countered. "She never comes in drunk or high. I talk to her all the time. Even when she hasn't taken a bath, she doesn't smell like beer or alcohol. Besides, the cut and the bruises—I can't see them coming from a fall. She looked battered. Like a classic battered wife. We see plenty of those too you know."

"Yeah." Chet's eyes turned dark, his shoulders elevated. "She never talks about drinking or needing a high and that's really uncommon for single women that come here."

Stephen wrinkled his forehead and frowned. "You keep talking about her as if she's still coming here. She's dead you know?"

A twin chorus of "what" erupted from Susan and Chet. "When?"

"They think last weekend. Her body was found yesterday. The coroner says she'd apparently been dead for two or three days."

Stephen laid the newspaper on the counter. Susan and Chet pored over the article while he surveyed the diners.

"Hey," Stephen interrupted looking off toward the front of the dining room, "Who's Zachary talking to over there? I'm surprised you haven't run them out of here yet."

Andy rolled his eyes.

"Oh," Chet answered. "That's Javier Ruiz-Lobo and his family. He's telling them where they can find food, so I left them alone."

"Oh." Stephen strode over to Zachary and the Ruiz-Lobo family. The parents appeared to be clean, obviously middle class. Three kids all under the age of what appeared to be four. Stephen guessed they might be mid to late twenties.

"We have the food pantry you know," he said to Zachary.

Zachary looked up. "I know." He spoke clipped, defensive. "I told him. But they live out in the woods off South Locust. Besides you don't furnish milk and fresh food ... leastways not enough till they are eligible to come in again."

Stephen ducked his head. "Yeh, I know. Tell them to come see me." Humbled, he returned to the kitchen.

"I think Rainey White hurt her," Susan was saying.

"Who?" Stephen looked back over at the Ruiz-Lobos. He didn't see any cuts or bruises on the woman.

"No, Janice," Susan corrected him. "She complained one day that Rainey'd been hitting on her. He even tried to sell her to Richard Koenig. Said he'd buy her some new clothes and she could clean up at his motel room."

Stephen's right eye twitched. "Who's Rainey White?"

"Some clown that showed up back in March, maybe February." Andy's disgust registered loud and clear. "Word on the street is he forces homeless folks to do favors for him in return for stuff they need. Mainly drugs and alcohol."

"He eats here?" asked Stephen.

"Yeah, everyday," answered Chet. "I hear he forces some of the homeless to turn tricks then takes all the cash. He begs money off people with mental disabilities, too. Sometimes eighty percent of their disability checks."

"And he threatens to turn in runaways, illegals, and people wanted by the cops...you know, blackmail for cash, turning tricks, or just satisfying his own perverted needs." Susan looked up into Stephen's eyes. "Just this morning Saybra asked if there was anything we could do about it. He's been after her almost every day since she got new clothes from him awhile back."

"He's one bad hombre." Andy started to spit in the sink then remembered where he was.

Organized crime. Stephen nodded. "Victimizes the victims?"

"Yeh…" Chet tensed, the sharp knife he'd been washing raised in his fist. "… I'd like to take him out. His kind don't deserve to live." He drove the knife into the wood on the dish window. Everyone jumped.

Wouldn't want to run into Chet when he's angry, thought Stephen as he took a step to walk away.

He stopped. He'd forgotten what he promised Inspector Ellison.

"So we're sure Janice was homeless?"

"Oh, yeah. She lived out of her car," Chet said.

"Do we know anything else?"

Susan looked pensive then stated, "Said she was eighteen. Her birthday was May twentieth. Came here from Missouri, but I don't think that's where she's—she was—from. Maybe up north. Or out east. She mentioned Ohio once."

"The car has Missouri tags," Chet volunteered. "She didn't drive it though. Just moved it once in a while so it wouldn't attract attention—till she ran out of gas. Last time she'd parked under those pine trees behind the old Work Force Development Center."

He abruptly looked up into Stephen's eyes. His face went ashen which made Stephen wonder if and why Chet had been to Janice's car.

CHAPTER 17

Quote from the Journal of a Killer:

Many that live deserve death. And some that die deserve life.
J.R.R. Tolkien, **The Fellowship of the Ring**

No stereotype applied to the homeless. The reasons for their homelessness varied as much as the people—as did their looks. For example, Justin Abreu who now sat on one of the green chairs outside his office door. At first glance this young man looked like a famous model come by to do charity work. His flawless narrow elliptical face with low hanging eyebrows, thin almond shaped eyes the color of apple-blossom honey, long light brown eyelashes, and medium length hair with natural gold highlights made women swoon and men take notice. Stephen smiled at Captain's secretary Sonja's reaction as she walked by.

In reality, Justin arrived in the shelter two days ago. His longtime foster mom kicked him out. Her new boyfriend didn't want kids around. Barely twenty, he attended Central Community College full time and worked part time at the 2nd Street MacDonald's. He could not afford housing, nor could he afford to drop out of class mid-semester. Orphaned at age three, he had no birth family to fall back on. No grandparents. No aunts or uncles. No known cousins. No shirttail relatives. Likewise, he had no criminal record. Justin graduated valedictorian of his high school class and made the Dean's List each semester at the college. So much for homeless stereotypes.

"You waiting for me?" Stephen asked.

Justin's low eyebrows hung like massive wall clouds over the lightening flashing from his golden eyes. His set jaw tightened even more as he stood, stared into Stephen's eyes, and followed him into the office.

Stephen sat down and looked directly into Justin's eyes.

"You've got to do something about that fucking bastard pervert," Justin shot back to Stephen's unspoken question.

"Who?" Stephen asked without breaking his eye lock

"Fucking Rainey White!"

"Tell me about it."

"That fucking clown's a homosexual pervert. He knows I don't do that shit. I turned him down flat. Now he's trying to pimp me."

"Pimp you?"

"Yeh, you know, sell me for sex. Some cougar who can't get it on her own."

Stephen's eyebrows shot up and it wasn't because of the language used.

"He's threatening to get me kicked out if I don't do what he says." Lightning flashed across those golden eyes again. "He's just mad 'cause I won't dick him, fucking bastard!"

"What's he think he can do?" Stephen shrugged. "He doesn't even live upstairs. In fact, I never heard of him until this morning."

Justin furrowed his eyebrows. "Says he knows you. Says he'll tell you he sold me drugs after I came here—and you'll throw me out."

Hard, edgy, laced with anger and fear, Justin's words gouged the air.

"You been using drugs?"

Justin's head shook like a bull marking his territory. "No! I don't do that sh--! Not all us kids do, you know."

"I believe you…." Stephen raised his hand to emphasis the point. "…but I had to ask." He paused then continued. "First off, Rainey doesn't know me. I don't even know what he looks like. So I sure wouldn't take his word for anything. But even if I did, I wouldn't kick you out. I'd just give you a drug test. Don't let him get to you. And, if he tries it while you're eating here, go to Andy. He'll kick him out. In fact we can ban a person for something like that."

He paused again to see if Justin had tracked with him then tipped his head to the side and asked, "Don't you have class?"

"Yeh, at ten. But I knew I couldn't concentrate after that...that deal with Rainey."

Stephen watched Justin's shoulders relax then droop.

"I had to make sure you and I were okay," he said looking down at the floor.

"We're fine. Now, can you it make on time?" Stephen lowered his head, trying to make eye contact again.

"It takes me forty minutes. I have to walk it," Justin answered sounding fatalistic.

"Follow me." Stephen stood and stepped through the food pantry door. "Take one of my bikes."

Justin followed him into the food pantry where Stephen locked up his loaners.

"You know where the bike trail is? It connects right to the college, right near the classrooms."

"Yeah, down at the end of Broadwell. That's how I usually walk to class," Justin replied and took the bicycle by its handlebars.

"If you take off right now, you can make it on time," Stephen said. "I can do it in fifteen minutes. Now get outta here."

What a start to the day.

Stephen turned to the door and sighed. Ten food pantry clients stood lined up more than a half hour early. The sign said ten o'clock, but people always came early.

CHAPTER 18

Quote from the Journal of a Killer:

"Blessed are the merciful,
for they will be shown mercy."
Matthew 5:7 NIV

Stephen hated lines and didn't like the pressure to handle clients quickly. He preferred time for interviews. To get to know their stories and to check on what happened in the lives of repeats.

"What do you do for milk the rest of the month?" he asked Manuela as he handed her two vouchers for one gallon each at Skagway North. It was her second time there.

"Oh, Mr. Stephen," Leticia gushed, "It works out just right! My husband gets paid on the thirtieth and I come here on the twenty-first. That's when we run out of food. Dios te bendigo! You are God's answer to me."

Stephen hated that comment. Yes, God made the Salvation Army possible. But Stephen was just doing his job. He just loved people.

With Leticia's cart rolled out and the boxes lifted into her trunk, Stephen returned to the food pantry then entered his office.

Just as he laid his fingers on the keyboard, the phone rang.

"Stephen?" The voice surprised him. "Laqueta Ellison here."

"Yes, Investigator, I recognized your voice."

"You sure you can make it tonight—Darren's game?"

"Yeh, I'd really like that. You sure it's okay?"

"He wouldn't stop talking about it. I'm afraid he'd be crushed if you didn't come." There was a slight pause. "But that's not why I called."

"Oh, what can I do for you?" Stephen locked his spine straight. His stomach flipped.

"Don't worry. It's not a question about you."

He blew out a sharp breath. I hope she didn't hear that.

"Did you find out if Janice Zahn was homeless? You said you'd talk to staff this morning."

Stephen apologized about forgetting to call. He presented the evidence that the investigator needed then added, "Susan said Janice came in with bruises and a cut one morning. Clearly not an accident. She and Chet both think it had something to do with Rainey White—he's a pretty bad dude."

"Rainey White?" Laqueta paused. "I don't think I've heard that name."

"Me neither, till this morning," Stephen replied. "Apparently he eats here regularly. Janice complained one day that Rainey'd been hitting on her. She said he tried to sell her to Richard Koenig."

"Sell her? To Richard Koenig? Isn't that the City Councilman?"

"Yep. That's what she said."

"When?"

"Didn't say. Just said Rainey promised to buy her some new clothes and to let her use his room to clean up and get pretty. I think they said something about paying for her to get her hair done—I'm probably wrong about that."

"You think this is plausible?"

"Well, I really wasn't sure—but Andy said Rainey forces homeless people to do favors in return for stuff they need or drugs and alcohol. And Chet said he forces people to turn tricks and takes all the cash and he begs money off the mentally disabled. Up to eighty percent of their disability checks."

Stephen took a deep breath. "That all sounded far out but when I got back to my office there was a shelter client waiting for me. He complained that Rainey was trying to intimidate him into turning a trick with some old lady. Said it was because he refused to have sex with Rainey." He paused then added, "Justin's straight."

A moment of silence passed on the phone then Investigator Ellison asked, "What did you tell him to do?"

"Nothing. I didn't know what to tell him." He shrugged his shoulders even though she couldn't see it.

"Tell him to come see me...no...do you still have my card?"

"Yeah."

"Have him call me. My cell's listed."

Stephen smiled. He hadn't noticed that.

"It's pretty hard to catch me in the office."

He heard the investigator shuffle something on her desk.

"How does Rainey do all this?" she asked. "I mean how does he force people to do what he wants?"

Stephen sighed. "All I know is staff said he blackmails them—threatens to turn them in to immigration or the cops or just hounds the person till they can't take it anymore. Justin, he threatened to get evicted from the shelter by saying he'd sold him drugs."

"Had he?"

"No, Justin doesn't do drugs. Never has. He's not an experimenter, just a very focused young man who ended up without a home."

"Did staff mention any other names?"

"Maybe Saybra. I'm not sure. You can come ask them. They work six to ten every morning—well, weekdays—and three to six in the afternoons. Actually Andy comes in at two, but he didn't seem to know as much as Chet and Susan."

"Thanks. One more thing."

"Yes?"

"Do you think Rainey did it?"

Stephen pinched his eyebrows together and rubbed the stubble on his chin.

"Did what?"

"Killed Janice Zahn."

CHAPTER 19

Quote from the Journal of a Killer:

Do not go gentle into that good night.
Rage, rage against the dying of the light.
Dylan Thomas, **"Do Not Go Gentle Into That Good Night"**

Stephen typed Janice Zahn into the search bar. He clicked the link that read, "2 people named Janice Zahn in Ohio | WhitePages."

"Age 65+" and "Age 40-44," too old.

Janice's mother died when she was a young girl so, Stephen tried, "Zahn obituary." This brought up hundreds of obituaries. Men and women from all over the map. He started to click out when he noticed a sidebar that read, "Search obituaries by name, state, and date online at GenealogyBank". Nothing. Just, "Your search for Zahn did not match any items in Historical Newspapers." That couldn't be right. He'd already seen obituaries for Charles Zahn from that time period.

"Harrumph." Stephen jumped and Captain smiled. "You working on the Riederhof article? I got a call from the Independent asking for it. They'd like to use it in the Saturday insert."

"Sorry, Captain. I just got a chance to sit down and was looking for the new victim, Janice Zahn."

"She one of ours, too?"

"Yeah, she was homeless. Andy and his crew knew her pretty well. But, no, she is not on our client served list."

Captain frowned and shook his head. "That's not right. How are we missing these people? We've got to do something to fix that. The most needy of the needy and we're not there for them." He shook his head again and turned to go. "Get on the Riederhof article, okay? Let's try and get it in tomorrow."

Stephen pulled out his notes on Riederhof, stroked his chin, and mentally sketched out the article.

Pretty good, he thought after he'd written his thoughts down. He still needed more on Riederhof's life in Grand Island. *Should've asked Zachary to come see me this morning.* He dismissed the thought. He was too busy. He still needed the Riederhof family's reaction, too. But first he needed to ask if the coroner had ruled Joseph's death a homicide yet.

Don't forget to call Investigator Ellison, echoed through his brain.

"Yes, Captain," he said out loud to himself.

"What's that?" Captain had been walking past the door.

"Sorry Captain." Stephen blushed. "I was just thinking about something you said to me earlier."

He turned Laqueta's card over and dialed.

"Investigator Ellison?"

"Yes, this is Laqueta.... Stephen?"

He smiled at her pleasant response.

"Is something the matter?" Her usual take charge self.

"Not really. I need some information for an article in the Independent."

"How can I help?" A fresh openness edged her voice. "Remind me. What's the article about?"

"Joseph Riederhof."

There was a dull, "Oh."

"Yes, I need to know if his death's been ruled a suicide or homicide."

Her silence made him nervous. Was she reluctant because she still considered him a suspect? Or was she afraid of Chief Greywright? Regardless, he hoped they had ruled it a homicide.

"The coroner called it a suicide." Reluctance still clouded her response.

"You think otherwise?" He queried.

Again, a slight pause.

"What I think doesn't matter." Her reply was cautious. "The official ruling is suicide."

How could a basically quadriplegic man hang himself? He decided to leave it alone. "So the official cause of death is by hanging?"

"Yes, the report says 'self inflicted asphyxiation due to hanging'."

He probed again. "Does that upset you?"

"I'd rather not comment." Cold, flat.

Stephen switched his tone and line of questioning.

"I assume the picture in the paper was the scene of the death—without the body."

"Yes."

A thaw.

"Anything stand out to you that's not readily visible in the photo?"

"I'm assuming this was his home here in Grand Island," Laqueta replied. "There were lots of food wrappers, cups—they all had straws, only a few clothes, and he was still wearing that set of coveralls you bought for him. There were no personal hygiene items and apparently, he kept all his medications on him—in a belly pack. I assumed it was a typical makeshift homeless camp."

"Was there a tent? It'd have to be pretty big for a man in a wheel chair."

"No." She paused. "There were some large plastic sheets. A couple apparently used like a tarp as a roof. Another one looked like it was used over his blankets to keep him dry."

Some how, like the hanging, that didn't make sense. How could Riederhof get under a blanket let alone wrap a sheet of plastic sheet around him? If he could barely use a fork, how could he hold multiple blankets and a plastic sheet in place while sleeping?

"I imagine it kept in his body heat," Laqueta continued, "but, frankly, how did he get them around or even over himself? I just can't see him doing that."

"I can't either," Stephen responded. "Maybe someone helped him. Kitchen staff said Zachary Plues helped him eat sometimes. I know he helped Riederhof put on the Carhartts." Stephen paused to ponder before going on. "He had a catheter with a urine bag, you know. How did he empty that? Did he go into a public bathroom and beg until some brave person helped him?" Stephen turned to face the wall. "By the way, was there any mail in the camp? I'm trying to figure out how he took care of medications and medical supplies. Maybe something from Medicaid?"

"That would be confidential information." She paused, then continued, "Oh well…yes. There was an envelope from Partnership for Prescription Assistance and I believe one from Nebraska DHHS: Division of Medicaid. I don't know what was in them. Even if I did I would not be able to share it with you. Confidential medical information, but you understand."

"Yeah, I understand. But thanks. This really helped. And, actually, that's all the questions I had. Sorry to bother you at work. See you tonight."

"See you tonight. I'm looking forward to it," Laqueta replied.

His eyebrows slid upward and a slight grin curled his lip.

CHAPTER 20

Quote from the Journal of a Killer:

"Death heals."
YouTube: **"Buried Alive: 20 min 'death' heals stress"**

Stephen leaned back in his chair. He'd be lucky to get the article drafted before three-thirty. That left him less than forty-five minutes to change into something more appropriate and drive down to Darren's game. T-ball league would be a hoot. If he took his notes home, right now there was time to make one more call.

He opened the Riederhof family appeal saved on his desktop and dialed the first contact number.

"Riederhof, Castle, and Meyers Attorneys at Law," a pleasant New England accent answered.

Stephen's chest squeezed his heart. "Hello." He fidgeted. "Is Mr. Riederhof available?"

"I'll be glad to check. May I tell him who's calling?"

"Stephen Lanfrie Brown, thank you."

Now why did he give his middle name … because of the formal greeting of the receptionist?

"And what may I say this is about?"

"His son, Joseph."

The line went dead. Stephen looked at his cell phone to see if he was still connected then hurriedly returned the phone to his ear.

"Did you say Joseph? Joseph Riederhof?" The woman's voice finally asked.

"Yes, Joseph."

"My brother?" she said as though not addressing Stephen. "You have information about my brother?"

Adrenaline raised the hair on his arm.

"I presume so." He replied his voice tentative.

"I'm sorry." The woman regained her composure. "I'm Beth Ann Meyers, Joseph's sister. I'm filling in for the receptionist. I'm afraid you have taken me off guard. Dad *is* here. One moment please."

Stephen held his breath, pursed his lips then exhaled long and slow.

"Hello?" The voice resonated deep, businesslike, but pleasant, "This is James Riederhof."

"Hello, sir. This is Stephen Brown from the Salvation Army in Grand Island, Nebraska. Sorry to bother you."

"Grand Island? Nebraska?"

Stephen's full body tensed. What had he gotten himself into?

"You say you have information about my son, Joseph?"

"Yes, sir, he ate in our dining room the last few months."

"Do you know where he is now?"

Stephen's breathing stopped .

"Don't you know, sir?"

Deadly silence —a sinking feeling seized him. *Hang up. Now!* Then reason pierced the emotional fog. The family did not know Joseph was dead.

Stephen's voice quivered. "Has no one informed you that Joseph is dead?"

The answer—two distinct gasps, then silence.

CHAPTER 21

Quote from the Journal of a Killer:

Everyone deserves a good death:
a death that allows the person to die on his or her own terms
relatively pain free with dignity.
The Journal of a Killer

At three forty-five Stephen walked out of the door of the Salvation Army, Riederhof outline, notes, cell phone, keys, and nothing else in hand. He couldn't afford side trips, mental or physical, if he wanted to change his clothes and arrive at Pier Park on time.

Brrrt. The phone. *Now who? Joe? It's too early. The shelter's not open.*

He finished his turn east on Third Street, pulled to the back of the line at the stop light then reached for his phone.

Oh crap, the light's turning. "Hello," he answered the phone and hoped to make it through the light safely.

"Stephen? It's Laqueta." She sounded harried. "Could you swing by and pick up Darren at daycare? We had a robbery at the Cenex Station on Webb this afternoon. I've got about another ten minutes here before I can head out."

Stunned, Stephen shook his head to clear his thoughts then said a quick yes.

"I have his glove and clothes with me. He usually changes in the car but he can change in the bathroom when I get there. There should be enough time."

So much for Stephen changing. At Locust he turned north instead of south. Darren attended school and aftercare at Messiah Lutheran Church at Seventh and North Locust. In the summer he continued in the daycare and participated in the summer school programs. Stephen would be there in under five.

North Locust was lined with cars. He guessed everyone came to pick up their kids at the same time so Stephen turned west on Seventh Street. Even then he had to park a block away.

He moved his papers and things to the back seat and wondered what people would think of a single white stranger picking up a small black boy. It wasn't like Darren could pass for the biological child of a white man. He locked the car and walked toward the church. The mothers' and fathers' eyes turned to look his way then concentrated on the pavement as they hurried—did they actually pick up their pace—to the yard where the children waited. How was it that people could always tell a single man for a man with a child or family? It was uncanny. Freaky.

Stephen spotted Darren, his fingers wrapped through the chain links as he scanned north and south looking for his mother. He raised his arm to wave, but the boy dropped his grip and ran to his teacher yelling, "Where's my mom? Where's my mom? I'm going to be late. I'm going to be late."

Stephen lifted the latch, let himself in, and headed toward Darren and the teacher. Darren had not seen him yet.

Just another white face in the crowd, Stephen thought then shook that prejudiced judgment from his head.

"Mr. Brown's going to pick you up. Your mom just called," the teacher said at the very moment Stephen stepped up.

"I'm Stephen Brown."

Darren's head jerked up, his eyes round a saucers.

"Mr. Stephen! Mr. Stephen!"

Stephen swayed backward as Darren grabbed his legs and clamped them together. He tousled the boys' warm, soft curls.

CHAPTER 21

Darren stiffened into his all business stance and pursed his lips. "You come for me Mr. Brown?"

Stephen nodded.

Then just as suddenly Darren's stiffness crumbled and his bounce returned. With exaggerated jerks of his head he looked back and forth around and behind Stephen's legs.

"Where's my glove? Where's my clothes?"

"Your mom's got them."

"How'm I goin-ta change?"

He laid his hand between Darren's shoulder blades, and began to herd him toward the gate as he explained the arrangement with Laqueta. His eyes sparkled and a warm peace filled his chest.

At the gate Darren automatically reached for Stephen's hand. Stephen's hand swallowed the smaller one up past the wrist. Tentative, feeling awkward, he barely touched Darren's soft warm skin, but that didn't work out too well. Darren's bouncing half-run toward the street required a firm grip.

"Hmmm..." he said and grinned down at Darren who had looked up to see what was the matter.

Across the street, Darren handed him his book bag and skipped ahead. He laughed, skipped backwards and chattered at Stephen all the way to the car. You would think they were best friends.

So this is what I've missed being an only child. No little brother to shepherd around. No nieces and nephews. And what few friends he had, kept their kids a few steps away from single men. *This is fun.*

"Momma. Momma. Mr. Stephen gave me a ride."

Stephen and Darren had sat on the bleachers to wait for Laqueta.

"He's my best friend!" Darren swung Stephen's arm up into the air and laughed.

"Oh, is he now?" Laqueta said with a knowing smile.

She looked so different, even more beautiful, away from work. Her interaction with Darren was relaxed, not permissive, but relaxed and intimate. Stephen never experienced that with his parents. Gramms maybe. Gramms definitely. But not his parents.

Not that they were bad people but they always seemed so uptight, sort of bothered, not the kind who lean in lovingly and talk to a kid like he's a real person. No wonder they moved away when they divorced and rented homes with no room for a son to visit. He was just their "kid" and since he was over eighteen their job was done.

That's it. I was a job not a person. No wonder they weren't intimate with me. A rational responsibility. An accident of birth and an obligation to be met until they could be free again.

If I ever have kids I'm going to be a parent like Laqueta.

"No. I'm not going in the women's bathroom. I'm a big kid now. Boys use the men's room."

Darren's whine caught his attention.

Ah, he's that age...and without a father.

"But you have to get your uniform on. You can't change out here."

Laqueta looked at the men's restroom and then at Darren then back again.

"I'll take him in the men's" Stephen volunteered.

Laqueta looked toward the restrooms then back at Stephen. The crease on her forehead and tension in her eyes showed reluctance.

"He can use the stall. I'll stand watch."

She still looked tentative but nodded okay.

Instantly Darren grabbed Stephen's hand, took off like a road racer pulling him halfway to the ground.

"Come on. We gotta hurry. The game's almost starting."

In the restroom, Darren asked Stephen to tie his waist string, but Stephen said he'd better wait and let his mother do that. Now, the boy pulled hard away from his mom while she struggled to tie the pants. If he just stood still it would go faster. Finally, Stephen reached down and put his hand on Darren's shoulder. In the brief moment Darren looked up, Laqueta tied off the strings. When his mother let go, he took off like a jet.

Stephen and Laqueta looked at each other and laughed. He shook his head and gestured at the bleachers. He followed her to a seat about midway and about half way to the top. A good view behind home plate.

Stephen turned toward her. "Tough day?"

"Not really. The timing was just off. I owe you thanks."

"No problem." He smiled then added, "Your welcome. I love that kid."

"I think the feeling's mutual." Laqueta scanned his face.

"What?"

"You know you two only met yesterday."

"Yeah, but it seems longer." He grinned. Quiet, they paused and looked at each other until "The Star Spangled Banner" erupted out of the speaker system.

First at bat. The coach sat the ball on the batting tee and Darren stepped up, bat dragging on the ground, every joint in his body loose. Coach took him by the shoulders, moved him back a step then told him to put the bat on his shoulder. He arranged Darren's hands on the bat.

"Batter up," yelled the other team's coach to prompt Darren to swing and to get his own team focused on the ball.

Darren drug the bat across his shoulder in a wide soft curve and hit the batting tee.

"Foul," said the opposing coach. League rules stated there were no strikeouts in Grand Island T-ball.

Darren's coach stepped back up put the ball on the tee again. Taking the bat, he demonstrated how to hold it above, but off the shoulder then swing hard. He positioned Darren by the tee and once again arranged his hand correctly.

"Batter up."

Darren swung and just barely knocked the ball off the tee.

"Foul."

Stephen flinched. His shoulder muscles tensed as he tried to will Darren into position and readiness.

Again, the coach demonstrated how to swing and set Darren up for his last swing at the ball.

"Batter up."

"Hit it Darren," Laqueta shouted as he started to swing. He looked up at her then …

Thump. The rubber tee buckled in the middle and the ball fell to the ground.

"Foul three. Next batter," said the opposing coach, his tone gentle and matter-of-fact.

Darren just stood there and stared at the field as another boy shuffled over from the dugout. Coach lowered the bat from Darren's shoulder, gently turned him around, and pointed at the dugout.

"So you uncomfortable with me being here?" Stephen turned and looked at Laqueta again.

"No," she replied, but too softly.

"Because I'm still a suspect?" He lowered his gaze.

She didn't answer just looked down. He knew he'd just pointed to the elephant sitting in the bleachers between them.

"It's okay. You're just doing your job," he said. "Maybe his death was an assisted suicide. In this state that's still murder."

"A Class IV Felony." Laqueta corrected him.

"A what?" Stephen cocked his head. His eyebrows pinched together.

"Under Nebraska State Law an assisted suicide is not a murder or even a homicide, like second degree homicide. It's a felony. A Class IV felony carries a maximum penalty of five years imprisonment, a ten thousand dollars fine, or both. There is no minimum penalty for a Class IV felony."

"Wow! I always thought it was murder unless there were extenuating circumstances then I thought it was at least second degree homicide."

"Most think that," Laqueta replied. "Apparently the law did not attract much coverage when it was written and passed. I can tell you, it feels like a murder when I'm doing an investigation."

"So you still think Joseph Riederhof's death was a murder?"

She couldn't hide her sheepish look.

"And you're still investigating how he died?"

Laqueta glanced at her lap. "Unless someone comes up with new evidence I am forbidden to further investigate the Riederhof case—and Chief made it clear that that someone was not supposed to be me."

"That sounds pretty severe. He trying to interfere with your job...didn't you lay out the reasons Riederhof could not physically hang himself? Did the coroner take that into account?"

Laqueta eyes were empty.

"Yes, both in speaking to the Chief and in conversation with the coroner, I spoke my mind. I also laid it out in my written report which is on file at the Department." She raised her chin. "I even pushed back at them when the final ruling came out. That's probably why the Chief was so sharp with me. And I need this job. I'm not ready to uproot Darren again. Not this soon."

Laqueta stared out to where Darren stood in the backfield.

"Before the letter came out the coroner told me he was going to rule it a homicide. The evidence clearly showed that, according to him. But in the final report it's noted as a suicide with no justification for the decision."

"Didn't you ask him about that?"

"You don't know me, or you wouldn't ask that question." The color returned to her eyes. "Yes, I went to him personally and asked what changed his mind. He said 'politics' then he got evasive."

"That's not right." Stephen furrowed his forehead.

"Like I said, I really can't say more. It's not my place in this department to question the Chief of Police or the Coroner."

The muscles in Stephen's temples tightened. He wanted more answers, but he didn't want to alienate this woman. Not while he was a suspect.

"Tell me, Investigator Ellison..."

"Laqueta's alright."

"Yes ... Laqueta. How did you end up in Grand Island? I don't think you grew up here."

"No, I grew up in Omaha," she replied and turned on the bleacher to face him.

"So that's why you don't have a Southern or Midwestern accent," Stephen nodded his head. He was afraid to say that was why she didn't have an African American accent or vocabulary.

She chuckled. "I suppose. That and I grew up in a middle class family. My father's an engineer. Works for the city, so we had a pretty stable life. And Mom's a registered nurse. We had a lot of the extras most families can't afford."

"And you became a police investigator," Stephen interjected. "Is there a story there?"

"In fact, yes," she answered then her face fell into a frown.

Stephen's shoulders slumped. He closed his eyes. *There I go again.* He opened his eyes; Laqueta grinning at him.

She let out a chuckle. "Stephen, you're trying too hard. Relax! You look like a whipped puppy." She threw back her head and laughed.

"What?" He reared back, eyes opened wide.

"I can't tell if you're trying to not upset me or to impress me. But you keep stumbling over your own two feet and your face gives it away every time." Again she laughed.

"Yeh, Gramms says that all the time. Says I've always been no good at hiding." Laqueta's light laughter and direct manner somehow relaxed him and he smiled.

"You'd like Gramms."

"Yes and my grandmother would like you, too. The two of you would hit it off in high style. Plus she has a great heart for the down and out and the poor. I think you're kindred spirits."

Stephen's mouth hung slightly open like he was about to say something, but he didn't know how to respond. He'd never pictured himself cutting up with a black grandmother though he loved doing so with all of Gramms friends and even the food pantry people. Quite a few of them were in their seventy's and eighty's with limited income. Fortunately, Laqueta rescued him.

"Anyway … my grandfather was a police officer. An investigator to be precise. He'd sit and tell us stories about the various cases, especially ones that stumped him or that were unique. I'd sit with the adults just to listen to him. I'd think about what he would explore next or how the pieces went together. When he was stumped, I'd make up stories in my mind where a new piece of evidence would be discovered or sent to the police then spin the tale forward through the arrest and sometimes trial and conviction, of the perpetrator.

My favorite cases were the murders, especially old unsolved cases. I'd get Grandpa to tell them to me again and again. When we were alone together, I'd ask how different new evidence might affect the case. Always things I made up. We were very close. In fact he's still alive and wants to discuss all my cases when we go back to Omaha."

"Yeh, I loved talking with my Granddad, too. But we talked about the pioneers and homesteading, and nature, and stuff like that. He was a wise man." Stephen smiled at the memories

"Your grandmother's a widow?"

"Yes, for a long time now."

Laqueta gave a sympathetic nod and continued on.

She's such a lady, Stephen thought.

"Well, back to the story. When I first started seeing female black police officers in Omaha—it wasn't always easy to be black there—I knew immediately what I wanted to do. Be Omaha's first black female investigator like my grandfather had been the first black male investigator. Of course, I was too young and someone else had the privilege of being the first."

Stephen leaned back and gave a soft chuckle.

"You were a pretty confident young lady." He smiled. "But then, from what I've seen, you're still a pretty, confident, focused lady cop."

Shocked to realize what he'd just said, Stephen's mouth dropped open. Laqueta mimicked him then laughed loud and long.

CHAPTER 22

Quote from the Journal of a Killer:

We hold these truths to be self-evident, that all men …
are endowed by their Creator with certain unalienable Rights,
that among these are Life, Liberty and the pursuit of Happiness
…and in the absence of these the right to a Good Death.
THE DECLARATION OF INDEPENDENCE
Amended by the Journal's Author

Stephen reached up and caught the ball glove Darren tossed at his mother. The boy raced towards Stephen's car. Darren, way ahead of them, leaned on the driver's side door, arms crossed tapping his foot. Laqueta's spotless white 2010 Chevrolet Impala—every bit as sophisticated and elegant as its owner—was parked two cars down.

"Nice wheels," Laqueta commented as they approached his car. "2011 Chrysler 200 Tour Car." Policewomen had to know their cars.

"Hardtop," Stephen added.

"Darren, you're going home in our car."

"I want to ride in Mr. Stephen's car. It's cool. Not like ours." Darren pushed his lower lip out and stared hard at his mother.

"It's time to go." She gave him the eye.

The boy didn't move, just looked at Stephen and demanded, "Put the top down. I want to show Mom."

Stephen stepped to the driver's door and opened it. Darren tap danced to accommodate the movement outward.

"I put the top down as we drove over," Stephen explained to Laqueta. "He nearly bounced out of the car with excitement." He laughed. Darren's eyes had widened when the top popped loose from the window frame and lifted upward. He'd followed the movement of the lead edge as it moved backward and slowly folded flat behind the rear seat. Total concentration. Darren clung to Stephen's leg and repeated that same intent gaze as the top folded down again. This time with a smile not serious, like before.

When the top clicked into place Darren pushed Stephen into the side panel as he wedged past him. Before his butt hit the seat he grabbed the wheel and rocked side to side like a speeding hotshot about to overshoot the curves on a winding road. Stephen laughed out loud as he joined Laqueta standing in front of the car. She clearly enjoyed seeing Darren happy, even if being a little rebellious.

"Does he ever stop?" Stephen chuckled.

Laqueta shook her head no, smiled wider, and said, "Actually yes, but sometimes I have a hard time remembering it."

They both laughed then she added, "Actually, at home, he plays quietly for hours at a time. I look in his room and there he is sitting on the floor, face all serious, lost in concentration on some new discovery or working on a new design with his building blocks."

They chatted about Darren a few more minutes their eyes fixed on his pretend driving.

"Oh, I almost forgot." Stephen interrupted. "I hate to bring up business again, but I meant to tell you I talked to James Riederhof today."

"James? Who is that?"

Stephen studied her face. There wasn't a clue to her reaction.

"Joseph Riederhof's father. I was working on the article for the newspaper and I figured it would be good to get the family's perspective, their reaction to his death. So I decided to call. His father and sister work together at their law offices in Hartford."

"Hartford?"

"Connecticut."

Laqueta gazed softly at nowhere. "Connecticut? Riederhof's identification showed an address in Indiana. Muncie, I think. How did you find his family?"

"I did an internet search," Stephen replied.

"So did I. I thought I might find a clue or a lead, but there were so many entries for Joseph Riederhof it was useless and the White pages did not show anyone in Joseph's age range." She pulled her mouth tight.

"I know what you mean. When I typed in Riederhof, it gave one hundred and fourteen thousand results. I remember because when I added the name Joseph I got two hundred sixty five thousand results. That made no sense. So I entered the initial E. and that brought it down to five thousand four hundred ... still too many. Finally, I entered missing—I knew from work that sometimes a homeless man is out of touch with his family and so to someone somewhere a missing person—and bingo, on the first entry I hit pay dirt.

"Turns out he was from Rockberg, Connecticut, had a twin brother who was killed in the accident that paralyzed Riederhof, and somehow, though quadriplegic, disappeared from his hospital bed in rehabilitation. His family has been making a public appeal every year in hopes someone somewhere would step forward with information. His story is fascinating though there is nothing available from the last five years. It's a black hole. When you said Muncie that was more than anyone else knew."

Laqueta interlaced her fingers and gazed back into the distance. "That could make a determination of suicide, or at least assisted suicide, more likely."

"I'm not so sure. Anyway—I told the family it had been ruled a suicide by hanging. I didn't give any details. I figured, unless he's a criminal lawyer—and he's not—the idea that someone might have helped Joseph would be even harder to accept. You know, like a triple tragedy instead of a double tragedy. It was hard enough to give a straight answer to 'how did he die.' I couldn't stand making things worse. Besides, I thought they'd already been notified or I wouldn't have called at all. Isn't law enforcement supposed to notify the family?"

He looked at her his eyes begging for an answer and her eyes answered with sympathy.

"In Hall County death notification is the responsibility of the County Coroner. But, you are right, usually we get asked to do it and, when asked, I'm the one assigned to make the contact."

Stephen's eyebrows narrowed. He flipped his palms up and cocked his head. "So why hadn't his family been contacted? Because you couldn't find them?"

Laqueta tipped her head and replied calmly. "Yes...and no. Usually I do an exhaustive search through police records, people searches—more than one—and interviews with anyone I can find who knows the person. Thankfully, most family contacts are relatively easy to find."

"But I found him on the internet. The articles always mentioned support from law enforcement, even a law enforcement contact number. Surely, he was in a police database somewhere."

"Probably. But I didn't do a police database search nor a thorough internet search. Normally, I would search just like you did but..."

"But this was a suicide." His words cut.

Her shoulders tightened as she returned a hard stare.

"No—I handle suicides, too—but Joseph Riederhof was homeless."

"And homeless people don't count?" His face hardened.

"No ... I mean, yes they count. To me they count. But—,"

Stephen could see a battle for words going on in her head.

"Why are you always trying to get me in trouble with my boss?" She looked up at him and grinned. "The truth is I have been told to not waste—she made air quotes—time on family contact searches for the homeless."

"Who told you that?" Stephen felt heat rising up his neck.

Laqueta smiled and shook her head. "I know it sounds ugly, but it was my boss, Chief Greywright."

"What! ...Why?"

"He said with budget cuts we could no longer afford to do notifications for the coroner—in this town the coroner is always the

County Attorney. He said the costs are the coroner's problem." She put her hand up as Stephen started to respond. "I know, I know. I don't agree with it. But he's my boss and as I told you before I don't want to have to move Darren again. At least not now."

"But the homeless are people are—are citizens."

"I know."

"And their families have a right to know."

"Technically, no. But I agree with you."

"It's the humane thing to do."

"Yes." She punctuated her agreement with a nod. Stephen stopped venting and they stood in silence.

Darren had stopped driving and looked dead tired.

Stephen lifted his hands in surrender. "I guess it's another case of homeless people falling through the cracks. Makes me more determined to contact Janice Zahn's family."

"The coroner hasn't ruled on that yet," Laqueta said rapidly.

"Oh, I thought if Riederhof was ruled a suicide then there would be no doubt that Janice would be ruled the same."

"I understand. That's logical. But there is some other evidence that requires a more careful examination. He can't write this one off just because she was homeless. There is a semen trail, partial fingerprints on the zip ties, and a question of whether she was even conscious when the zip tie was placed around her neck."

"I heard she had her hand on the end of the tie—the end you pull to tighten it," Stephen responded his eyes penetrating and questioning.

"Where did you hear that? That information hasn't been released yet."

He saw a flash of panic in her eyes.

"Two places—the kitchen staff, they said some of homeless men from Pioneer Park were talking about it, and Angelina Abbott."

Despite himself, as he said Angelina Abbott, he cracked a smile and Laqueta returned it a knowing sparkle in her eye.

"She didn't happen to say who told her?"

"Yes. Richard Koenig."

"Richard and the homeless men—people at the murder scene when I was doing the investigation." Laqueta sighed.

"So you think it's murder."

He glanced again toward Darren in the car. "Oh, oh. I think someone crashed."

Darren's little body slumped over the console. Stephen smiled as he took in the scene. Poor boy looked so uncomfortable....

"I'm sorry, Laqueta. I should have let you go."

"Yes, it definitely looks like it's time to go."

Stephen leaned over and tipped the boy up into his arms.

"You get the car door and I'll put him in for you. I'm so sorry."

"It's nothing," Laqueta responded, opened her car door, and cleared the belts from the child seat.

Darren snuggled against his neck and grasped it tighter as Stephen leaned over to put him in the car seat.

I could get used to this, he thought as his face softened like that of a father.

"He's such a sweet kid. I could really love that boy," he said as he straighten up and stepped back to let Laqueta fasten him into the car seat. "I sure would like to come see his game again. I've missed these kinds of events since I left Anselmo. They're the community lifeblood up there. What do you say?"

He realized he really was getting assertive. The old Stephen would never have asked.

Laqueta looked thoughtful—that mother-pondering look on her face again.

She still thinks I might be guilty. He pushed aside his lack of self-confidence. *Don't answer for the person. Ask and wait for an answer. The worst you can get is a no.* He rehearsed Gramms' mantra in his head.

"I don't see a problem with that." Laqueta raised her gaze and confidently looked into his eyes. "I'll get you a schedule. Darren will be excited out of his gourd."

For the first time Stephen realized the boy's tiny head was indeed shaped like a fragile gourd. He smiled and turned away toward his own car.

He will be a handsome man, but no bruiser that's for sure.

CHAPTER 23

Quote from the Journal of a Killer:

Merciful death is…helping a person die to stop the pain.
wiki.answers.com

Stephen spread the notes about Joseph Riederhof on the walnut Pembroke table. Heirlooms were meant for passing on and Gramms did not trust her son, Stephen's dad, or his floozy new wife to hold on to them. They'd already sold, or thrown away, the family treasures he'd received after his first wedding. Stephen's Great-grandmother Analissa hauled the table back from Louisiana when her grandmother Euphemie La Branche died. Family legend said it was shipped from France as a groom's gift to his bride by some ancient family member in 1751. True or not, verifiable records placed the table in his family by at least 1818.

His laptop open, Stephen sat not knowing where to begin. The mental block from wanting to interview Zachary Plues kept his brain locked down. So he reviewed the online articles he'd found, looked at the notes from his conversations with kitchen staff, searched the newspaper photo for inspiration then pushed back and, in his mind, replayed the conversation with Riederhof's father and sister.

"Don't you know?"

He remembered his lame response to Riederhof's father and the same sinking feeling washed over him again as he remembered James Riederhof's question, *"Do you know where Joseph is now?"*

His next response must be one of the worst death notifications on record.

"Has no one informed you that Joseph is dead?"

Obviously not or James would not have asked where he was.

But even worse…the two distinct gasps and silence.

Riederhof's sister broke the silence with a sob and "Oh, no!"

"I'm sorry. I'm so very, very sorry. I thought the police had notified you. I'm so sorry."

"No. They didn't." James Riederhof's response reverted back to the lawyer's facade, all business, all demand. "How did he die?"

"We've been dreading this call for over five years," Beth Ann added her sobs under control.

"I—I don't know how to tell you." Stephen replied.

"Just come straight out with it," stated James.

"He was found hanged at the camp in the trees where he lived."

"Hanged!"

Both responded but not simultaneous.

"Yes, sir. The coroner ruled it suicide."

"Suicide! Not Joseph. He wouldn't do that. No, he wouldn't do that. Not Joseph," Beth Ann blurted out.

"Look I'm an attorney," said James. "I can read peoples voices. You don't think it was suicide."

"My opinion doesn't count, sir. The coroner ruled it suicide based on the evidence."

"But you don't believe him." It was Beth Ann this time. "Why?"

"Because I don't think he could physically do it. I don't know how he was when you last saw him, but in the dining room he could no longer lift a fork to his mouth or lower his mouth to the table. One of the young homeless men helped him eat. When he first came to Nebraska, he could still roll his chair slowly and feed himself. The changes happened about a month ago according to my kitchen staff. I just don't think he had the mobility required to hang himself."

"Homeless. Oh my God," Beth Ann responded.

"You talked to him? How was he—mentally?" questioned James.

"I'm sorry.... I never spoke to Joseph directly. I made sure he had winter survival gear back in January. I think he arrived then, but I never spoke to him."

The long silence that followed unnerved him. He frantically flipped the pages of the Grand Island phone book.

"I can give you the coroner's phone number to inquire about the body."

"I want to see where he died," Mr. Riederhof said quietly.

"Let me give you the number for the local investigator, Laqueta Ellison. Perhaps she can help you."

Stephen gave Mr. Riederhof and Beth Ann the two phone numbers and his own cell phone number. "Please, if I can help in anyway, let me know."

"Yes, thank you. But one more question, please, before we hang up," Mr. Riederhof requested.

Stephen's muscles tensed.

"How did you find us?"

"On the internet," Stephen replied his muscles relaxing and his voice lightening, "I discovered this year's article from the Rockberg Times asking for assistance in locating your son. I had just about given up on learning anything about Joseph, but that article filled in a lot of the story and directed me to your family's website where I picked up your phone number. You were the first contact on the list."

"Thank you. We just about gave up on those annual requests, but decided to try it one more time."

Stephen heard the satisfaction in James Riederhof's voice.

"I was the one who said, 'Let's just stop,'" Beth Ann said. "I'm so glad we didn't. Thank you Stephen for finding us."

"You're welcome."

They said their goodbyes and hung up.

CHAPTER 23

Stephen returned to the laptop and typed a sentence. He abandoned the how, what, when, and where approach and opened the article with a story—the story of notifying someone about their lost, homeless son's death and suicide. From there the article flowed freely.

First, the phone conversation with the Riederhofs. Next the briefest review of the discovery of Joseph's body followed by a step back to the car accident and Riederhof's disappearance from the hospital. Compelling, heart ripping reading. He then addressed how Riederhof lived in Grand Island including his loss of ability to eat or move his own wheelchair. That set the article up for the Salvation Army's response: frustration that the most needy fall through the cracks, the importance of the feeding program, especially to people without shelter, and finally his belief that Joseph's death was not a suicide. That at the worst it was a murder, or not much better, a mercy killing or assisted suicide.

He leaned back against the stiff wood of his high backed chair. His eyes watched a speck of dust floating in the air. Sure, Captain could make him remove that last part. That would be clarified in the morning. He'd needed to write it now for his own piece of mind.

Standing up felt like the punctuation on a satisfying sentence. As the mantle clock, a wedding present to his great-grandmother, struck ten, he sank into his favorite wing chair and closed his eyes and dozed.

The phone rang.

He nearly jumped out of his skin. No one called at this time of night, not on a weekday, unless there was an emergency at the shelter. He checked the caller ID. Laqueta.

"Stephen, I hope it's not too late to call?"

"I'm up. Just finished the Riederhof article." He sidestepped her question. Truth was he usually went to bed by nine o'clock. He operated best on eight hours sleep but liked to get to the office between six and six thirty most mornings. "How can I help you?"

"I just got a call from Darren's coach. Darren has an unscheduled game tomorrow at four fifteen again."

Perfect. Another invite to a game. "Thanks. I really do want to go."

"Believe me, Darren really wants you to be there. That's all he could talk about tonight—that and your car. By the way that's a pretty fancy car for a man working at the Salvation Army. Isn't it?"

"If you're asking if I can afford it on my salary. No, I can't. It's Gramms fault." Stephen's grin bled over into his voice.

"It's your grandmother's fault? Like I believe that." Laqueta laughed.

"No. It's true. Gramms is afraid my dad will blow all the family inheritance and leave me nothing, so she's been giving me the important family heirlooms and spends what she can on me before she dies. She said something about setting up a trust fund one time, but I don't know about that. Anyway, she paid for my college—and grad school. When I showed her a picture of that car and talked about how much I liked it—we do that all the time, go through catalogs or magazines together—she called the dealer down in Broken Bow. Then she got the price for one exactly like I wanted, asked the dealer if I could get a loan on it if she co-signed, ordered the car, put seventy five percent down, and called me. Told me to get up there and sign the loan papers."

"She knew how much you could afford?" Laqueta asked.

"Yeah. She's a sly one. Talked about that when we were looking at the magazine. We're always talking about money so I didn't think anything of it. Besides, with seventy-five percent paid it was only pennies left. She wanted me to start building a good credit record—and wanted to give me an out so I could say I bought the car instead of my grandmother bought it for me."

"I think your right. I think I'm going to like this lady. But there's more to why I called," Laqueta said.

Stephen tensed. The worry about being a suspect popped up again so he answered cautiously. "Yes?"

"I know you just helped me out today—okay, and the other day when I came by the office—but I'm doing a presentation at the American Landmarks 4-H Club out in Doniphan at four and can't get back until at least five. Could you pick up Darren and take him to the game again?"

Stephen felt his adrenalin spike. He tried not to sound too enthusiastic. "Sure, I'd be glad to."

"Same as yesterday. I'll bring his glove and uniform by your office. Okay?"

"Okay."

"See you in the morning."

CHAPTER 24

Quote from the Journal of a Killer:

Death is the wish of some, the relief of many, and the end of all.
Lucius Annaeus Seneca

The Riederhof article sat overnight before Stephen began revision. One decision remained. He leaned back in his chair his knee wedged against the desk to keep it tilted and tapped a finger lightly on the keyboard. Leave the personal opinion in or take it out?

No doubt in his mind, Joseph had been murdered. But was it an assisted suicide—technically not a murder. Street people tended to be self-protective and take aggressive action to relieve their stressors. Had the killer believed he, she, or the homeless community would be better off with Joseph dead?

The tasks of emptying the urine bag, removing, sanitizing, and reinserting the catheter—these thoughts made Stephen cringe—changing and washing his clothes, and bathing Riederhof, all created stress. He tried to imagine how or where homeless persons even accomplished this.

"Article ready?" Captain Higgins leaned on Stephen's door casing, briefcase in hand. With a start, Stephen looked up.

"Don't worry. I told you we could turn it in this afternoon. I was just checking."

Stephen shook the tension out of his shoulders as he sat up straight and pressed print.

"Actually, I just sent it to the printer. Want me to bring it down to you?"

"I'll pick it up. The printer's on the way to the office." Captain smiled teasingly. "Did you contact Investigator Ellison?"

"Yes." Stephen wrinkled his nose. *Assertive. Don't grovel.* He resisted the urge to apologize for putting his own opinion in the article. "When you're done, I'll be glad to run it down to the news for you."

Captain tipped his head back in acknowledgement and left the room.

"Was that Captain Higgins?"

Stephen swiveled toward the door at the sound of Laqueta's voice.

"Yeah."

"He's bigger than I expected."

"Yeh, he is a giant of a man." Stephen stood to greet her. "Makes room for a giant heart."

A smile spread across his face and was returned by Laqueta.

"This is Darren's uniform." She handed him the white and blue uniform neatly folded with Mizo Nine Cleats centered on top. "Are you still okay with taking him?"

"Oh, yeah!" He nodded. "I'm looking forward to it. Thought maybe I'd pick him up a little early and work on his swing if that's alright." Stephen watched her eyes for any sign of reluctance.

"Sure." Laqueta glanced briefly toward a chair and Stephen nodded for her to sit down. "That would be fine. He was discouraged last night because he missed the ball all three times." Her eyes sparkled. "He wanted to hit one over the fence like the big leagues."

"I doubt we can get one over the fence." Stephen laughed. "But we can make sure he hits one this time." He rubbed his hands together. "I'm really going to enjoy this...by the way; do you really think you're going to make it back by five?"

"I hope so. This is my first 4-H presentation so I don't know how they work."

A wrinkle crossed her forehead.

He looked directly into her eyes. "Don't worry. Darren and I'll be fine. If you don't make it back, just call when you leave. I'll tell you where to find us." He rolled back a few inches in his chair. "By the way, I still had a question about notifications. You got a minute?"

A shadow dulled her eyes but she said, "Yes."

"When you call another police department, how are notifications handled at the other end? Do they just make a phone call or what?"

"Phone calls are insensitive." She squinted. "People deserve the support and the presence of a trained person when receiving a death notice. It is very uncommon for us to do a telephone notification." She shifted her weight in the chair. "Out of town notification are more difficult, but we still try to ensure a real person gives the notice." She reconnected with his eyes. "When we get requests like that, we send a trained officer to speak to the family—we have several. Most agencies do the same, though some small towns and rural counties might not have trained personnel. Even then some of them ask a local minister to go with them, especially if they know the family and their religious affiliation." She relaxed.

"Does the coroner do the same thing?" Stephen asked.

"Yes, generally. I mean coroners generally ask the police to do the notification." She shot him a knowing smile. "That's why we used to do all the local notifications. Besides, with our local coroner being the County Attorney, the currently elected official may or may not be trained in notification techniques." With a tilt of her head, she asked, "Does that help? ... Did your question grow out of your experience with the Riederhof family?"

He nodded yes then twisted his lips to the side before looking up to ask his final question.

"What if you can't find a family contact?"

"We notify law enforcement at the last known address—often the one on their drivers' license or photo ID. It is up to that department to try to find more information. Locally, that means requesting information from the Drivers' Licensing Office—the address on the license or ID turned in for the newly issued one. If that does not yield a lead, we might request assistance from the local newspaper or, as with Riederhof, contact local agencies which might have provided the individual with assistance. Besides you, I contacted the Saint Francis Emergency Room—the most likely service point for a non-Medicaid disabled person and ..."

Stephen interrupted. "You contacted Saint Francis?"

"Yes—no. Not for notification purposes, but to further my initial investigation, same as I did with you. In this case, the only information they had was a general delivery address and the Indiana address, from Joseph's ID. I struck out with both of your organizations.

"I suspect the same happened when the Grand Island notification went to the Muncie, Indiana Police Department."

"Investigator Ellison, I presume." Captain Higgins stepped into the office. Holding up the article he continued. "Did Stephen contact you about this article—I mean Joseph Riederhof. I see here his death has been ruled a suicide."

"Captain Bramwell Higgins, Investigator Laqueta Ellison of the Grand Island Police Department." Stephen and Laqueta quickly stood.

"Pleased to meet you, Captain." Laqueta extended her right hand and gave a firm handshake. "And, yes, Mr. Brown and I have talked about the case several times."

Captain chuckled. "I hope he hasn't caused you any trouble. I see here he disagrees with the suicide ruling."

Laqueta flicked a quick look Stephen's direction. "Yes, sir. I am aware of that. We discussed that ruling by the coroner and I must say, I, too, question its legitimacy."

Stephen noted her professionalism during the response.

"And no, Stephen has not caused any trouble. He has been gracious and helpful."

"So you agree with this article when we say we believe the death could not have been an unassisted suicide but that it could have been a murder rendered to relieve the homeless community of the burden of Joseph's care?"

Stephen relaxed. Captain said "we" not "he." Laqueta, however, flinched at the end of the question, nor did she answer quickly.

"I do share Stephen's doubt over the legitimacy of the suicide ruling…" Her eyebrows rose again. "… though I am not free to officially say so. In my mind, assisted suicide is the most likely cause of death. His physical restraints allowed nothing less. But I must admit while I've considered the possibility of a mercy killing, the possibility that Riederhof was killed to relieve other homeless individuals from needing to help with unpleasant tasks never crossed my mind. If the suicide ruling should ever be overturned, I will certainly include that motivation in my further investigations."

"You mean you don't object to my allegation of a missed ruling?" Stephen asked the Captain.

"No," Captain replied nodding his head firmly. "Go for it—unless Investigator Ellison here has an objection. The article is well written and I agree with all of your positions."

"I have no objections as long as my name is not mentioned in connection with the Salvation Army's position. I have no right to interfere with your internal business." She paused and gave Captain a demur smile. "In fact I really appreciate your willingness to present that argument publicly...please don't tell anyone I said so."

"Great! It's all yours, Stephen." Captain handed the article back to him. "Run with it. And, Investigator Ellison, we are pleased to be of service." He saluted then smiled with a twinkle in his eye and left.

CHAPTER 25

Quote from the Journal of a Killer:

Life unbreakably chained to the trauma of the past is no life at all.
The Journal of a Killer

A busy morning. Fifteen food pantry clients, three coordinating phone calls, plus a double check with Captain to be sure the article was still okay—*Why do I always doubt positive answers?*

Stephen checked his cell phone. Five minutes late for lunch. *Not that it matters. I don't have any place to go.*

"Brttt," he jumped as the phone vibrated in his hand then rang.

"Gramms!"

"Lunch time?"

"Yes."

"Good we can talk. How's my favorite grandson?" Gramms meadowlark lilt lifted Stephen higher on an already good day.

"Your *only* grandson."

"My only grandson and the sole heir and executor of my will," she pushed back, all business now.

Stephen laughed. "That's not funny Gramms!"

"Who said I'm joking?" she gently rebuked him.

"Excuse me."

"It's official." Gramms business tone continued. "I wrote out a codicil to my will this morning. I'm taking it to the bank box after dinner."

In rural Nebraska, lunch was dinner and dinner was supper. Only city folks got that confused—and the TV and movies.

Stephen's brow furrowed. "Are you sure that's wise? Dad'll be furious."

"Hell yes it's wise, precisely because of your dad. If I hope to pass on this property, I can't leave it to someone who'll just sell it off and spend all the cash."

A curse word and plain speech—no, rough speech—definitely uncharacteristic of Gramms. In fact, Stephen wasn't sure he'd ever heard her use a cuss word before, nor so openly criticize his father. But, her next statement softened a bit.

"You know I don't trust that stepmother of yours. Not that your dad has ever been very wise with money, but that woman, if she has it she spends it, and he can't say no. I think I'm actually being very wise, taking a very businesslike approach to my assets."

"But Gramms, I can't come farm the ground. My life has a different goal. Besides I wouldn't know how."

The truth felt hard, especially not providing the answer to her concerns.

"I know that, Son." It was another of her pet names from when he lived with her. "But, you're smart enough to hire a reliable ranch manager and preserve assets." A half teasing half serious lilt returned to her voice. "Besides, if you own it, I bet you'll come back to it and retire here."

That was precisely what he dreamed. He even worried that his future wife might not be willing to do so. God help him, he'd never marry a woman like that.

"But Gramms...."

"No buts about it. It's what I've done. And furthermore, I'm transferring all of it into a living estate to minimize taxes, with one condition—that all property and assets remain available for my use until my death or such time as I am unable to handle my own affairs. Even then they are to be used to sustain my life in as comfortable manner as appropriate until my death."

"Gramms." Acid burnt his stomach. "You're not going to die… are you?"

"We all have to die sometime." She snickered at him. "But no, I just had a complete physical and the doctor says I'm healthy as a horse. No reason to plan a funeral right away. But, honey, I am old enough to put my things in order in case something unexpected happens."

"But I don't know what to do if you get sick. I can't come take care of you…not that I won't want to, but I can't." *I wish Dad would straighten up. This is his role, not a grandson's.*

"Relax, Stephen." Her voice reminded him of the times she held his head on her lap and caressed his hair. "I've written a living will and health directives with instructions for what to do if you need to intervene. It will be appended to the power of attorney we executed when you were twenty-one. You do remember that don't you?"

"Yes, Gramms."

"And I'm leaving your Dad a hundred thousand dollars cash. So it's not like I'm cutting him out of my will. I think he'll be glad not to have to handle the business end of my estate."

"Gramms?" he spoke gently, calmly.

"Yes."

"Can I ask you one favor?"

"Of course, Stephen, anytime."

"Would you please make someone else your executor—maybe your attorney or perhaps Mr. Crowley's son at the bank. He's young enough. He'll probably out live you."

"Well, if you want. But why?"

"I just don't want to execute a will where I am the primary recipient, especially if my Dad's still living. It might look bad—like I'd been meddling and manipulated your affairs. I don't want that kind of challenge when I'm grieving you."

He paused a few seconds.

"And Gramms, please state that the hundred thousand for my dad will go in whole to his surviving wife—whoever that may be—or to her estate if he has preceded you in death. I don't want to have to deal with any hard feelings on that account either. Okay?"

"Sure Stephen." Gramms' silence meant she was thinking. "Tell you what. I won't go to the bank today. I'll call and get an appointment with the ranch's attorney and take all of this to him. We want to make sure it's all legal, worded properly, and above possibility of being contested."

Stephen let out an audible breath.

"Now, on to the reason I really called." she laughed like a merry turkey. "Did you ask that Investigator to come for your birthday?"

"Not yet Gramms."

Silence.

"I know. I promised." He shook his head in exasperation. "It's only been a couple days, Gramms."

"Yes, but I need to know if she'll come. I've got preparations to do." She inhaled through pursed lips. "You two are getting along okay, aren't you?"

"Gramms, I'm a suspect in her investigation. Two of them now."

"Two!"

"Yes, there's a young girl dead now. She was homeless, living out of her car. Could be foul play."

"Oh, Stephen. The investigator—what's her name?"

"Laqueta Ellison, Gramms."

"Well, she's a sharp cookie. Yes? I'm sure you're not a suspect by now."

If Gramms says it, that settles it. Stephen smiled at her unwavering faith in him.

"Now tell me about this girl. She's from there?"

"She's a woman, Gramms."

"Ohhh."

"And no she's not from here. She grew up in Omaha. Her family's from the South—South Carolina. They sound like good people."

"But how did she end up there?"

"To take the investigator's job."

"And does she like you?"

"Gramms." He tried to sound strong, resistant.

"Well, does she?"

"Are you being nosey, Gramms?" He tried to break her drive by throwing it back on her.

"Well, yes. I'm not one of those gossips." That was true. "And I can tell you've got your eye on this gal. You like her Stephen?"

He cleared his throat but said nothing.

"Well, do you? I'd hate to invite her up here and you can't stand her. But…some little birdie told me you two have been up to more than just business. Am I right?"

He'd been baited worse than a fish on a hook. She knew he wouldn't lie to her.

"Who told you that?"

"Oh, it's just a grandmother's intuition."

He hated expectant pauses, but he hesitated.

"Well, have you?"

Stephen settled back in the chair.

"Yes. I went to her son's t-ball game. In fact I picked him up from school and met her there. And, yes, we had a great time."

"She has a son?"

Why did country grandmothers always worry about that?

"Yes, Darren. He's a pure spark of bituminous coal. Smart. Courteous. But all boy. Just like you like them."

She laughed. "Sounds like you two get along real well. But then you always loved local sports—playing and watching."

"Yeah, I'm picking him up again tonight. Laqueta has a conflict with 4-H so he and I are going to his second game. Think I'll pick him up early and work with him a bit. It was really hard on him last time. He didn't even hit a ball."

Gramms merry chortle rippled through the line. "I can just see the two of you now."

"But Gramms," his tone dropped, became serious, "It worries me."

"Worries you? Why?"

"I'm a single man. I hardly know his mother. And here I am picking him up at school, helping him change into his uniform, and doting over him—I can't help it. I just love that kid. What will people think? That's how perpetrators groom kids for sexual abuse. A single man has to be careful nowadays." The elephant of over thinking a thing was sitting on his chest again. "And Gramms… he's black. What am I supposed to do?"

"Son, just treat him like he's the most special thing in the world and don't worry about what people think. Your actions speak louder than words. If you go getting all cautious and backwards people will think something's up. Don't give them a chance." Confident, she didn't even pause. "And do just what his mother allows. Don't get ahead of her. She's a mom. She knows what's good, what's safe, for her son. Besides, she's an investigator and already scoped you out and got inside your head, if she was worried she wouldn't have asked you to help." Gramms paused. "Are you sure you want to get involved with a woman that can get inside your head?"

She laughed, but Stephen didn't join her.

"But Gramms, she's black. Real black." Why did Western Nebraska men like him have such an issue with that? Seemed like the more comfortable he got around her, the more uncomfortable he got.

By the time Stephen got off the phone and promised Gramms to speak to Laqueta tonight about Gramm's invitation, lunchtime was over. The newspaper's copy of his article sat on his desk so he stepped around, asked Sonja to cover for him then picked up the article and headed off to the Independent. He'd grab something to eat on the way back. But, hey, it had been a good day. It's not like he had shirked his duties.

He thought back to his conversation with Gramms. He thought about Laqueta. Gramms would know what to do. She'd help him.

CHAPTER 26

Quote from the Journal of a Killer:

Sleep is good, death is better; but of course,
the best thing would be to have never been born at all.
Heinrich Heine

MONDAY EVENING, MAY 28, 2012:

Janice Zahn sat at the aisle end second row from the door, an unusual position for her. She repeatedly peeked at Zachary from under heavy eyebrows. Was she signaling come or stay away? After her angry naked exit from the White Hall Off Plum, she'd avoided eye contact for several weeks. Today's signal left him torn.

He picked up his food, retrieved a salad, a drink, and bread from the self serve table, kept to the east side where he could watch Janice then finally walked over and sat in the seat opposite her. Her eyes remained down, but she did not cringe like she usually did when people sat near her.

"You mad at me?" she asked.

"Me? No! You still mad at me?"

"No." Janice raised her head and looked him straight in the eyes. "I'z never mad at you, just at me."

"But I got it wrong!" he said.

"It's water under the bridge. I'z not mad. Never was," she said firmly.

Her sad terrier eyes coaxed him to put an arm around her, but he was on the wrong side of the table and a pang of guilt still lingered in the pit of his stomach.

"You heard about Joseph?" Janice asked.

"What'd you mean?" he questioned, unsure.

"They'z found him dead." A cloud and pout distorted her face. "They say he killed himself."

He nodded but remained quiet, his eyes questioning her.

"Sometimes I think about it." Janice dropped her head.

Zachary tilted his and ratcheted down his eyebrows.

"Think of what?" he asked, but not roughly.

"You know. Killing myself."

His mouth gapped a half inch, but he said nothing.

"How he'd do it?" she asked.

"He was hanged. They found him hanging from a tree, his feet dragging the ground. He couldn't lift himself, you know."

"Duz it hurt?" Janice asked then continued when he looked puzzled. "Hangin. Duz it hurt?"

Zachary leaned closer across the table.

"If it's done right, it snaps their neck and they're dead. Leastways that's what I heard.... Why'd you ask?"

"I'z couldn't do it if it hurt. I'd need to pass out—or for it to be fast." She peeked up at him.

He quivered.

"Do you think he died fast? You knows, didn't hurt himself?" Janice's eyes sank deep in their sockets. "I couldn't do that. I'z couldn't."

"Maybe he had help." Zachary shrugged. "I mean how could he? He couldn't even feed himself. How could he hang himself?"

A blip of fear crossed Janice's face, but then she squared her shoulders and a soft hope replaced the fear. Her words firm, under control, she said, "I'z need somebody to helps me. I'z couldn't do it alone."

Zachary shook his head. "You don't want to die.... Why'd you want to die? You're too young."

"I'z eighteen." Janice bristled. "Old enough to knows my own mind!"

"So?" He shrugged his shoulders again. "That doesn't mean you'd want to die. Why should you want to die?"

Panic built in his chest. He'd never talked to someone who wanted to die—well, that wasn't true—but this was different. She was a girl. Girls shouldn't die young.

"Why should I want to live?" she shot back. "I is too messed up. I is a freak who had sex with her daddy and thought it was okay. I'z damaged and hurt and..." She squared her lips and raised her chin. "... and it's ruined me."

Zachary's eyes grew wide.

"People smell the hurt on me." Her words were clipped, sad. "And men, they smell that I been used like I'm open season or something. And they know they can hurt me. They know nobody will stand up for me. Nobody will think they done something wrong. I'z sick of it. Just sick of it. Why should I'z want to live?"

Zachary fought to keep his mind from going blank. Most challenges gored his stomach or hit like a gunshot—clear, sharp, and loud. But this challenge ate in on itself, ate in on Zachary's mind, ate into Janice herself like a black hole.

"I'll stand up for you," he finally responded. "I'll take care of you. I don't care what's happened to you. I'll take care of you."

"Like you can be everywhere all'z the time," she retorted. "Besides, if I can't even feel safe after sex with you, how could I ever be a wife to someone? Be normal? I'd just cry and go crazy and walk out naked like the dang fool I is."

Her tone shoved any goodness, any hope, away. She didn't mean to. She didn't want to. But...she might as well have shoved a fist inside his chest.

She's right. How can anyone live so messed up?

CHAPTER 27

Quote from the Journal of a Killer:

... their thoughts turned to the rituals of justice
rather than justice itself.
Sharyn McCrumb, **The Ballad of Tom Dooley**

TUESDAY, MAY 29, 2012:

After the conversation about Riederhof on the twenty eighth, Zachary walked with Janice down the John Brown/St. Joe Trail. They strolled along quietly, enjoyed the pleasant air and the beauty of the setting sun's kaleidoscope of colors. To Zachary, nothing matched a Nebraska sunset, the mystic twilight that followed, or the starry canopy of the wide-open prairie sky.

As they passed Railroad Town at the Stuhr Museum, Janice asked, "Did you see'z that story 'bout that lady here in Nebraska that killed her boy then herself with zip ties—in her car? He wuz twelve!"

He had.

"I wonders if it hurt or wuz it like being choked to death. Wuz the boy scared? How could she look in his eyes and watch his terror while death took him?"

Zachary avoided eye contact and watched the movement of his steps.

"What if she'z changed her mind?"

"It wouldn't matter. You can't undo a zip tie. Once it's tight, it's tight."

Janice cringed and walked on in silence till she almost whispered, "I has never seen a zip tie that big."

Zachary thought of the ties in his book bag, but decided not to mention them.

At the junction with the Riverway Trail, they turned left and followed the canal bank. A mystic twilight settled in and fringed the wide open sky.

They splashed water at the Wood River ford and bantered back and forth, even managed a few giggles and a laugh. As they turned north at South Locust, Zachary slipped his hand into hers.

"How duz people help they'z friends or relative die—when they'z want to?"

Zachary shrugged. "With giving them a drug overdose or poison I suppose. I never stopped to read about that."

"Hmmm...," Janice replied.

They walked in silence three or four blocks.

"Maybe they cut their vein then holds them while'z they bleed to death." She made a stroke up the vein on the inside of her arm. "'cause they'z too scared to do it themselves." She paused. "Duz you think that hurts?"

"When you make the cut, I suppose. But not the bleeding out. I think it's probably like going to sleep."

Her eyes raked across his face.

"You could do that for me."

When he chose not to respond, she looked down, her lips pouty.

After a few more blocks her hand relaxed in his and she leaned against his shoulder. The gentle pull of midnight drew them into the White Hall Off Plum. They lay down on his rag mattress and faced each other, their hands clasped between them. He smiled tenderly as his eyes traced the outlined ruins of the fun, loving, gentle, grace she could have been. No one had a right to kill such potential, yet hers was destroyed before it flowered—a life trapped for all of adulthood in the scars of the past.

Gazing deep into her eyes he fell asleep.

The next morning when he woke, she lay sleeping in the same clasped-hand position.

"You feeling better," he had asked when her eyes opened.

And she answered, "No." The deep sadness of the previous evening crept back into her eyes.

"Let's go to breakfast," he suggested.

In quiet they walked the several blocks to the Salvation Army. Neither one said a word as they ate, though they exchanged bemused grins at the conversations around them. Disposing of their dishes, they departed their own separate ways.

When Janice didn't show up for supper that night, Zachary felt with a tinge of fear.

CHAPTER 28

Quote from the Journal of a Killer:

A revenge kill is an impure thrill
that brings sorrow – I feel dirty.
To die will be the pure thrill.
Emily Giffin, **Love the One You're With**

WEDNESDAY, MAY 30, 2012:

Wednesday morning Janice failed to show up again. Nor did she come for supper that night.

Zachary scanned the room every few minutes then stared at the door. He felt like an oil filter clamp had tightened around his head with someone trying to twist off his skullcap. Where was she? Even when they'd stopped talking, she always came to meals. She might bury herself in a dark obscure corner, but she always came.

Finally, compassion, or was it curiosity, overcame the numbness in his head and he decided to find her car. It sat parked under a row of Ponderosa pines behind the old Work Force Development Office between Third and West North Front Street. The drapes were drawn, but between the cracks he saw her lying on the mattress in the back. He dropped his forehead onto the car. His stomach fell. The clamp returned, but as he shut his eyes he heard a sob. Eyes wide he heard another then saw it wrack her body.

"Janice?" he called.

No response. He spoke a little louder.

"Janice. Can I come in?"

He rattled the handle on the rear passenger door.

Through the crack he saw her body go completely still. Not even her chest rose for several seconds. When she finally gasped for air, he called out again.

"Janice?"

And surprisingly, she reached over and lifted the lock.

Carefully, he opened the door and peered in. When she made a slight nod he crawled in. He did not touch her, just sat Indian-style inside the door and stared into her eyes. She accepted his gaze, held it then slowly closed her eyes and lay still a few more seconds. In what seemed like only two seconds more sobs again wracked her body. Hot tears coursed down her cheeks and spattered onto the curtains flung wildly by the convulsion of her body.

Zachary pulled her shoulders into his lap and placed her head against his chest. Her body convulsed again and her head fell into the crook of his arm. He laid his free arm along her back and began to stroke her hair. Finally she slipped into calm soft undulating sobs.

"You okay?"

Instantly he knew that question was inappropriate. *Why? Why do we people ask such dumb questions when we can see the answer?* He paused briefly then simply asked, "What's the matter?" and again stroked her hair.

Janice lifted her eyes toward his. Behind the tears her irises were laced with terror, anger, and a deep hurt, but her body relaxed almost imperceptibly.

She shook her head, no.

"Tell me," he prodded and looked deeper into her eyes. "Please."

"Rainey...," she began then the deep wracking sobs returned. She choked on her own breath and let out a moan like the sound of rocks as they slip past each other in a quake.

"Rainey," Zachary repeated. "What about Rainey?"

His anger rose to rage, but he contained himself so she'd be able to speak.

"What did Rainey do to you?"

She turned, eyes like a deer looking into the face of the hunter preparing to fire a compassionate final shot, shook her head, and pulled the front of her pants and undergarment down.

Horror paralyzed his gaze.

"He burned me," she breathed then gathering strength added, "He raped me and burned me!"

Anger shut down her tears leaving only terror and a murderous rage.

"Tell me," he said.

Janice sat up, steadied herself, and deepened her self control. The story spilled out.

Late Tuesday afternoon Rainey dragged her out of her car, twisted her arm behind her back, and forced her to walk to his motel room. Councilman Koenig sat there all decked out in a fancy suit, a pale blue tie, and an inviting grin. He'd set up a folding table with a linen cloth, fine dishes and silver, candles, a rose, and a full meal—like a fancy restaurant.

Rainey forced her to strip to nothing then put a sleek green gown over her head and arranged her at the table. Like some makeup artist for the movies, he brushed on blush, and lip gloss, a touch of eye shadow, and eyebrow liner then he pulled her hair up and back and fixed it into a high ponytail bun held by a wooden barrette and pin.

She refused to eat, but Rainey forced her mouth open and Mr. Koenig fed her one bite at a time until she gave up and played along with their game—Zachary noted that she had actually resisted, stood up for herself this time.

When Councilman Koenig finished his meal he came around the table, lifted her to her feet, and slowly pulled the gown over her head pawing her body as he went. Rainey pinned her arms to her sides while Koenig, kissed and caressed her, orally violated her, and removed his own clothes. Next, he held her immobile against his naked body while Rainey took his turn then they carried her to the bed, took turns restraining her while each man violently raped her multiple times.

Both satiated and satisfied, Rainey took out his cigarette lighter, a small pliers, and a paperclip and they took turns branding her "mine" on the insides of her pelvis. While she still gasped in pain, Rainey handed back her clothes, forced her outside the door, and bolted it. The two men laughed. She heard them slap high-fives and congratulate each other on a fine evening and a grand time.

The tale completed, Janice lay down, wrapped her arms around herself, and softly moaned. Zachary held her affectionately until she drifted asleep then, laying a zip tie below the window for her to find later, he slipped out of the station wagon and headed to Pier Park to recover.

CHAPTER 29

Quote from the Journal of a Killer:

The death of what's dead is the birth of what's living.
Arlo Guthrie

WEDNESDAY NIGHT, MAY 30, 2012:

Parked cars crowded the lane down the center of Pier Park. Music pumped from oversized speakers. Gangs of high schoolers played pickup games—baseball and hook ups. Loud talk reached from Pine Street to Oak Street. Police cars cruised through in opposite directions keeping an eye on the scene. Sometimes they yelled out their windows. Sometimes they examined car trunks and interiors. Periodically they stopped side by side, window to window to chat with each other.

When a couple of kids abandoned it, Zachary worked his way around to a concrete bench on the north side of the lake. The White Hall would have been quieter but the memories of Janice would have made it impossible to unwind. Some action across the lake distracted him. He blinked to regain focus then the cycle started over again. He couldn't think.

This time the sight of a man half-hidden in a juniper hedge nearby distracted him. He looked Native American with a long straight ponytail. Like a solitary warrior meditating before battle. He guessed the man to be about twenty nine.

After a few minutes, the man took something from the pouch that hung around his neck. He held it up with three fingers. Zachary watched intently as he lifted the object and examined it from all sides with the wonder of a child then laid his hands to his lap. This happened again and again. When the man raised it higher, Zachary realized he was looking at the sky beyond the object. He then removed three more items from his bag and repeated these actions with each item At last, Zachary saw the man's shoulders slump and his head hang down.

When the man started the ritual again, Zachary stood and walked toward him.

"What you doing?" The man definitely was a Indian.

"I'm trying to find the wisdom. To listen to Wakan-Tanka." The man sounded developmentally disabled. Drooping his head and shoulders, he rocked from side to side.

"Wakan-Tanka? Who—what is that?"

"The Great Holy. Mama say my guardian sits with the Wakan-Tanka. He will take care of me 'cause she died."

The sound of wonder and lack of full understanding hung in the air.

"Wakan-Tank love me, take care of me, protect me."

"And you can't hear anything? Is that the problem?"

"Yes. No! Mama say my guardian the Big Bear. My friend Joey call him Big Dipper. I can't find the Big Dipper. The branches in the way."

"Maybe you should move by the water."

"No. No! Hank not allowed to sit by water without Mama. Too dangerous." He looked up and across the lake still swaying from side to side. "Lots of people, too dangerous. Hank not know 'em. Mama say stay away from strangers. 'Specially if they loud and dangerous."

"I can sit with you. I'm not loud. You want me to sit with you?"

"You dangerous?"

"No, I promise. I'm not dangerous. We can sit by the water. Come on."

"No. Mama say no sit by the water." Hank looked up into Zachary's eyes. "My friend Rainey not dangerous. Rainey my friend. He take care of me."

Zachary squinted. "You know Rainey. Rainey White? Was he your mama's friend?"

"No. Rainey didn't know my momma. She died in the earth in South Dakota with my people on the Rosebud. Hank can't stay with Rainey. He takes care of me but I can't stay in his room. Hank's a big man now. Can stay alone. Rainey says, 'Go. You have to stay alone.' Rainey's my friend."

Zachary had been in Nebraska long enough to know that the Rosebud was a Sioux Indian Reservation in South Dakota on the Nebraska state line. Indians who had eaten at the Salvation Army said it was very poor, poorer than the Pine Ridge.

Hank wrinkled his forehead and tightened it a little each time he said Rainey was his friend.

"Why did you come to Grand Island."

Hank opened his eyes wide and looked to be thinking hard.

"When I gone, go find help. She point out our door. Say go till you find help. They put me in home but I don't stay there. I obey my Mama. I go find help. Help picked me up in car. I say I go where they go."

"And they brought you here?"

"They bring me here then open door and say I not go with them no more. They say, 'Get out here.'"

He pointed to the Valeria Quick Stop on South Locust.

"They drives away. Hank no knows what to do. Lady say go eat at Salvation Army. So I go. Rainey finds me there. He's my friend. He say he take care of me." He pointed to a sheet of cardboard tucked deep under the Juniper bushes. "I sleep here. Rainey help me. Mama say go 'til I find help. Rainey help."

Zachary looked Hank over thoroughly. This conversation was going nowhere.

"Why you trying to talk to the Big D—Bear? What are you holding up for him to see?"

Hank opened the beaded deer skin pouch hanging around his neck then stopped with one finger inside and held it up for Zachary to see.

"Mama make this for me. Wakan. Holy. Protect me. Says always keep aroun' my neck to protect me like Mama did. It has holy things in it. Talk to Big Bear through wakan—holy things."

He lowered the bag and dug out a burnt twig.

"This mean Fire. It from big fire at Hot Springs. Mama get it when she a little girl."

He deliberately, carefully returned it to the medicine pouch and pulled out the tip of a turkey feather.

"This Air. Mama say this Air."

He pulled out another object but two came out together and one fell in the grass. Hank got really agitated looking for it and let out an exaggerated sign when he found it.

"This Water."

Zachary could see that it was the head of a dried dandelion.

"Mama and I go find water. We look together and pick it by edge of the water. Dangerous. Hank not suppose to go near water. Mama be mad."

He carefully put the dandelion head in the pouch and held up the final item a small bone.

"This a kn—knuck—knuckle. Belong to my great-great grand-mother. Sitting Bull's granddaughter." His eyes got big and round.

Zachary hoped it wasn't a human bone but it looked like a child's knuckle bone to him.

"This Earth—Fire, Water, Air, and Earth."

He held them up one at a time as he named them again.

"They protect me. They give me life. Mama say, 'Don't lose.' Mama say, 'Lose and lose life.' Not live anymore."

Zachary raised his eyebrows. He'd have to check this out at the library. Right now he needed to get out of here. He flicked his eyes toward the road with the parked cars. His muscles were still tight from holding Janice and his brain ached from talking to Hank.

"I gotta go."

"Potty over there." Hank pointed across the lake.

"No…." Zachary chuckled. "I got to get away from here." He pointed to the crowd parked on the other side of the lake. "I need to go somewhere and clear my head. Hall County Park will be quieter."

He pointed toward South Locust and Hank nodded.

"Hank go with you. Hank scared here. Hank can't see the Big Bear here."

Someday I've got to learn to say no.

"You want to see the Big Bear?"

Hank nodded.

"Hall County Park has lots of stars. I bet tonight you can even see the Milky Way."

The moon had already slipped behind the horizon. At Hall County Park it would be a great night for stargazing. Zachary always liked that word. Had a kind of carry-you-away feeling.

"Milky Way?" Hank had trouble saying it.

"I'll show you. Okay? Let's go." He looked back at Hank and the kid-man got up.

A paved trail existed from Pier Park all the way to the Hall County Park some six miles away. For Zachary six miles went quickly and it turned out that Hank walked just as fast if not faster than Zachary. From their long conversation two segments would stand out later.

First, Zachary asked what Hank was trying to learn from Wakan-Tanka through the Big Bear guardian.

"How you get to the Happy Hunting Ground. Hank want to know how to get there."

"Why?"

"Hank want to be a great hunter. I never learn hunt here. No father. No uncle. No grandfather and now no mother. Big Bear live at Happy Hunting Ground. Mama say his son teach me to hunt. Rabbit, deer, and buffalo—plenty there. Easy hunt. I never be hungry. No more."

"Will you be a great warrior there?

"Hank a great warrior now!" He thumped his chest with his right fist and squared his shoulders. "Mama say Hank great warrior. Mama's great warrior."

Hank also believed his mother was waiting for him in the Happy Hunting Ground and he had to find out how to get there so she would not be lonely.

"And Hank not be sad," he said.

But Hank didn't know the rituals needed to get to the Happy Hunting Ground or to keep his mother's spirit with him until he could go.

"Here no Indian. Hank no learn how."

Hank had elaborate dreams—waking and sleeping—about his spirit quest and his journey to the Happy Hunting Grounds. Sometimes he dreamed he was playing there with the baby who died and his mother was happy in their little house in the great Black Hills where Fire, Water, Air, and Earth take care of them. Protect them. Being left in Grand Island frustrated him because he thought the people were driving him to the Happy Hunting Ground and now there was no one to help. Rainey was a friend but did not know anything about Happy Hunting and wanted Hank to stop talking about it.

Zachary tried to warn Hank about Rainey White but Hank had too much childish innocence to comprehend being raped. Talk about being cut, to become blood brothers, frightened Hank, but then he smiled and said, "Rainey not hurt Hank. He Hank's friend. Hank take shower with Rainey. Tickle. Poke aroun' and laugh."

Zachary dipped his head to acknowledge listening.

"Lady with dem bags do Hank's laundry." He frowned. "Sometime she unhappy, but Rainey make her do it anyway. Give her money for dryer."

Hank flapped his arms, lifted his pant legs, and giggled.

"Hank wear Rainey clothes while he wait. Don't fit."

He lifted his pant legs again, danced around Zachary, and laughed and laughed.

"Rainey poke Hank's tummy and play peek-a-boo."

He crossed his hands over his stomach then over his genitals.

"Pants no fit. No zip."

He folded his hands across his genitals then bobbed and turned like he was trying to avoid being touched.

"Rainey say Hank too big."

He peeked behind his hands.

"Rainey laugh when Hank fall out."

The boy-man raised his eyebrows and sucked his cheeks in. His eyes danced like a child promising to keep a secret.

"Just be careful." Zachary frowned. He realized Hank had no idea what that meant. To Hank being careful was about falling in the shower or on the motel steps not inappropriate child-adult play.

Hank sensed Zachary's frustration. He pouted out his lips then pointed down the trail and said, "In Happy Hunting Ground Hank's mind work right."

The other thing that stuck in Zachary's mind was their conversation about Janice.

Hank remembered the words "clear my head" and in a lull in the talk asked, "Why you need clear your head?" He moved his head side to side. "Got cobwebs o' sticks in there?"

He poked at Zachary's head and did a backward hop scotch dance in front of him.

For such a developmentally simple man he had an acute sense of humor.

"My friend wants to kill herself," Zachary replied when Hank settled down, came back and looked down into his eyes for an answer. "She's very sad and been hurt real bad and wants to die."

"Die in the ground? Like Mama?"

"Yes … and I need to clear my brain so I can think straight about it."

Hank looked at him and moved his eyes and head around trying to figure that out.

"Hank want to die. Hank want to die in ground and join Mamma."

The statement floored Zachary but he didn't let it show. Instead, he stopped, pointed into the sky, and helped Hank find the Big Dipper and identify the Milky Way.

CHAPTER 30

Quote from the Journal of a Killer:

The death of an abused victim is like throwing a pebble in a pond
it makes a small splash and sends out melancholy ripples across the water
but soon all is calm again and the pebble is forgotten.
Such lack of compassion should not be so.
The Journal of a Killer

SATURDAY NIGHT, JUNE 2, 2012:

Each morning Zachary carried a doughnut or a couple slices of bread and a bottle of spring water to Janice's car. At most she took two bites. The rest lay dry and stale. She drank the water, so he brought one after breakfast and one after the supper meal. She left the car door unlocked so he could slide the food and water in and visually check on her. Each time he asked how she was, but the response was always the same—great wracking sobs, no words, him holding her till she went to sleep, and, after straightening her hair, slipping out.

It was time to take action.

For starters, he let Rainey White take pleasure on his body in exchange for a bottle of 150 proof Absinthe Roquette – 1797. He could tolerate Rainey as long as it didn't require anal sex and he needed the absinthe—which the old alcoholics told him sometimes caused mild hallucinations and numbed whatever bothered a person—to break Janice out of her mental impasse. The trick would be to get her to drink it without getting drunk himself. He'd stopped using alcohol or drugs after Autry's death and did not want an excuse to start again.

Around nine PM, he opened the door of the station wagon then flinched. Janice sat cross-legged and stared out the door. Her eyes shone clear and confident. He even detected a hint of a smile.

"Was it quick?" she asked not waiting for him to get in.

"What?"

"Was he dead quick?"

And when he flicked his eyebrows and raised his shoulders…

"Riederhof—did it hurt?"

"I don't think so. Didn't have time to hurt. Why?" His shoulders grew tense.

"I made up my mind. I is gonna do it."

He frowned, shifted his eyes. "What? Hang yourself?"

"Yes," she answered head tilted up then smiled. "Gonna hang myself."

"H-how?" he stammered. "Who's going to help you?"

"You are!"

His body pitched backward as he shook his head. "No!"

"Why not?"

"I can't." He let his head hang forward and down. He knew his words disappointed her, but he just couldn't. He couldn't do it.

"There's other ways," he added. Zachary's pulse started to knock inside his chest. His mind shut down. He wasn't ready for this—not this dogged determination to die.

Janice lowered her chin and focused on his face. "Then how? I'm gonna do it. I'm gonna die. How you gonna help me? I can't do it alone."

For a few minutes they talked about ways to commit suicide—assisted and unassisted. A gun was out of the question. She couldn't shoot herself and cringed at the thought. Besides, many gunshot attempts failed. Assisted suicide by gun, even with the victim's permission, that was murder, pure murder. A drug overdose—choosing the right drug, trying to buy enough of it illegally, the terror many drugs created in the moments before death—too risky. Alcohol poisoning—the same risks. Janice needed a sure, fast death.

She reached over and picked up the zip tie Zachary had laid under the window, hung it around her neck, slipped the tip into the head of the cable, tightened it into a loose necklace then hooked her fingers around the cable and let her hand rest on her chest. Her body swayed in a relaxed arch. Exhausted by her mental struggles, she slid toward Zachary. Legs spread he slid her in against his body and held her.

"I always 'magined it'd be like falling to sleep—but with a little help."

She laid her head on his shoulder and tucked up against him, her blue eyes gazing out the window.

"I'z thinking of those bluebells down in 'souri," Janice said, "I'd like some of them on my grave, but I know they stopped blooming now and 'souri's too far away."

"I'd get some for you if I could—you wouldn't even have die."

He shifted his head forward and smiled at her then rocked her as they enjoyed a few moments of peace—no shuddering.

"I don't really want to be dead," she said. "But I don't want to be alive. Not this way. Not a whole life feelin' dead and bein' hurt."

He didn't reply. Just rocked her.

After some more peaceful quiet he said, "I brought you something. Old Jim says it numbs the pain and clears the mind. Figured you could use that kind of comfort. Plus it's got a lot of alcohol. Enough to put you to sleep."

"Not right now."

Silence…he feeling surprised, she looking thoughtful.

"Zachary, I want you to make love to me."

His heart skipped. He remembered the aftermath last time, but if Janice wanted it, she should have it—with someone who felt safe. He peeked around, gazed into her eyes, and began caressing her hair. For the next hour, they melted into the acceptance, satisfaction, and passion that come slowly and with meaning.

CHAPTER 30

Partially undressed, sitting entwined together, they lay in each other's arms filled with an intense afterglow.

"Okay." Soft spoken, Janice broke the silence. "I'm ready for that absinthe now. I want to hold this moment forever."

But, the spell ruptured by her own words, the old response to sex took over and she began to cry softly. Zachary broke open the liquor and poured a little into a coffee mug. Holding the rim to her lips, he tipped it gingerly. Janice let it slide evenly down her throat. The anise smell calmed him, a gentle aroma therapy.

Janice looked up and smiled at him with her eyes. He poured more into the mug and held it to her lips.

"Nice?" he asked.

She nodded her head then returned her lips to the rim of the cup. He continued to nurse Roquette –1797 down her throat until at last she collapsed in his arms in deep sleep.

Sleep is good, death is better; but the best thing is to have never been born. The misquote going through his mind, he carefully laid her head on the cool pink of a satin covered pillow imprinted "I love you to the moon and back".

I wonder if she ever truly felt that way.

CHAPTER 31

Quote from the Journal of a Killer:

... endings are almost always a little sad, even when there is something to look forward to on the other side.
Emily Giffin, **Love the One You're With**

Straight up three o'clock Stephen stepped into Darren's classroom. He found the class at their workstations reading. Darren was the current reader. He spoke clear and confident with nearly flawless execution.

That's my boy, he thought then mentally rebuked himself and checked to see if anyone was scrutinizing him.

"Very good, Darren," Ms. Weaver-Howard praised him. "Now children, time to put your books in your lockers and get your things ready to go home. Be sure and zip your book bags tight so nothing falls out."

She walked to her desk and picked up a stack of flyers.

"Take this home to your parents and begin planning to come to our Summer Fair next Wednesday."

"Stephen!"

Darren flew across the room and grabbed Stephen around the legs.

"No running inside, Darren," Ms. Weaver snapped.

"Stephen! Stephen!" He jumped up and down and nearly knocked Stephen backward.

"Hey, calm down. Put your book away, then we can go, okay?" Darren had left it on the desk in his workstation.

"God, he's a cute kid," the woman standing next to Stephen commented, "Is he your…?" She stopped mid-question a stricken look on her face and looked down.

It was a dumb question though to be fair three families in Grand Island included coal black sons adopted from Haiti. None attended Messiah Lutheran Church or the school.

"No," Stephen replied, "just friends."

His whole body relaxed as he flashed a proud smile. The dreaded first inquiry over.

"His mother must be gorgeous," the woman said. "How did you meet?"

Nosey. Stephen held his tongue. "It's a long story." He turned away. *Reminder to self—don't marry a nosey broad like that.*

Darren stood stiff as a little soldier his shoulder touching Stephen mid-thigh. He waited quietly while Ms. Weaver-Howard gave Stephen several messages for Laqueta.

"Here, Buddy," Stephen squatted and held out the uniform for Darren, "how about you hand me your backpack and take these to the bathroom." He pointed to the door in the corner. "I'll help tie your shoes when you get back."

"I can tie my own shoes."

"Okay! Sorry man. Go on then."

Stephen shuffled his feet as he waited. He didn't know any of the parents—all women at this hour.

When Darren returned, he poked his belly out and Stephen cinched the drawstring and tied it. Soon they were in the car. Top down. Listening to "Pontoon" both bopping to the beat, fingers poking at the clouds. A look passed between them and they laughed hysterically. *Thank you, KRGI!*

At Pier Park, Stephen set up the batting tee he'd bought at Downtown Sports. Darren swung the bat in tight circles over his head then let the momentum spin him around and around till he fell down.

An object in motion stays in motion. He remembered from physics class. It didn't make any more sense now than it did back then.

"Okay, Buddy. Batter up.

Darren ran over to the batting tee. Standing passive, he let the bat drag on the ground and looked down. His pouty frown made Stephen laugh.

"Come on, Buddy. You can do this. What did coach show you last time?" He bent over to look up into Darren's eyes and softly repeated, "Batter up."

Darren lifted the bat to his right shoulder.

"And your hands?"

He put his left hand on the grip.

"Remember, right over left."

Darren adjusted his grip. The boy swung hard at the tee.

"Whoa, whoa boy," Stephen stepped nimbly out of the way. "Okay, batter up."

Darren just stared at him, lips pinched.

"It's okay," Stephen gave a nod. "You're learning. First you have to learn. Then you work at it real hard. And then, it starts happening the way you picture it in your head."

Darren grimaced.

Stephen walked him through holding the bat correctly and taught him how to approach the plate, line up with the ball, and signal the pitcher he was ready. He noted a flicker in Darren's eyes followed by a full grin as he watched the tip of the bat circling through the air above Stephen's right shoulder. Around and around seemed to be Darren's favorite motion. He talked him through each step several times until Darren's confidence built then set a ball on the batting tee.

"Okay, one more thing today. When you swing, keep your eye on the ball. See like this." He took the bat and illustrated. Each swing he stopped just before hitting the ball showing the bat coming in level and centered on the ball. Darren grew wonder eyed and nodded. Stephen could see the adrenaline begin to pump through his veins. "Now you try it."

"Left hand by the knob.

"Right hand on top.

"Grip it with your finger tips.

"Excellent! Now position it above your shoulder."

The tip of the bat swirled above Darren's right shoulder.

Why am I not surprised? Stephen thought. "Good—Okay. Now keep your eye on the ball and swing." He caught Darren glancing back at his bat, "Don't watch your bat. Watch the ball. One more time now. Without looking, get your bat ready over your shoulder."

The confident swirl returned—even if it was a little over done—then a satisfying thump sent the ball flying. Shocked, Darren's eyes widened. His mouth dropped open. He looked up at Stephen then grinned and started jumping like a jackrabbit dodging bullets. Stephen grabbed the bat to keep from getting hit.

After a few solid hits Darren tired and ran off to the jungle gym to practice his GI Joe moves until the coach arrived.

The game lasted till five-thirty. Darren's last at bat he knocked the ball down the base line to first base. He didn't want play to end.

"Next time I'll show Mom. I'm a pro now." He pumped his fist and gave Stephen a homie bump.

At Lee's Family Restaurant, Darren picked cottage cheese with peaches and sunflower seeds. Stephen couldn't persuade him to take anything green. From the kid's menu came macaroni and cheese. Darren gave it a hard stare when it arrived. Called it slimy. Said at home his Mom baked it.

By the time Laqueta arrived Darren lay curled up, his head on Stephen's leg. He neither flinched nor responded when she called his name. Stephen looked down at his lap and smiled. Didn't matter if they were black and white. They made a perfect picture and the waitress said so when she came by to take Laqueta's order.

"No, thank you," Laqueta replied then to Stephen, "They served hamburgers and fries before we left, cooked by the kids. Really good. They insisted I stay to eat and I'm glad I did. You know, I think Doniphan might be a great place to raise a boy."

He nodded his agreement then asked, "How about a slice of pie? They make the best,"

Laqueta looked at her sleeping son then said, "Okay, I think Darren could use a little more nap before we leave, pie sounds good." Except for her figure as she indicated with hand signals.

Stephen laughed. "Don't look to me like you have that problem." He signaled the waitress.

"What you got for pie?"

She named off seven—blackberry, coconut cream, butterscotch, cherry, apple, peach crumble, and country custard—definitely a prairie menu.

While Stephen ate his favorite, rich homemade butterscotch with four-inch high meringue, Laqueta ate the peach crumble. He filled her in on the practice and the game. She ohh'd and ahh'd over missing Darren's hit to first base then told Stephen about the 4-H meeting.

"It's the first time I've been to 4-H. I always thought 4-H was just for white farm kids, but they were just as big on city related skills as they were on agriculture."

She blushed after the racial reference. Stephen had never noticed a black person's blush before. He almost missed it. Laqueta picked up her napkin and wiped a speck of butterscotch off the corner of his mouth.

"Please tell me about your Riederhof article. I'm interested in how it turned out."

Stephen reviewed the general structure of the article—details of the death, coroner's suicide ruling, the Muncie, Indiana ID, the fact he had been a missing person for five years then the story of his accident, hospital stay, and disappearance."

Laqueta's eyebrows tensed. "I've not heard that information. Can I get a copy?"

"Sure." Stephen nodded his head then looked down to see if he had disturbed Darren. "In fact I have one in the car for you."

"So, you end it with the disappearance? Nothing more?"

"No. I also tell about my shock that the family they had not been notified, and my struggle with being the one to tell them the coroner's ruling, their response—that suicide wasn't possible, and Salvation Army's distress at the gap in our services. Then, I state our position on the coroner's ruling including the evidence that indicates that an unassisted suicide was impossible and present the alternatives of assisted suicide or murder, including murder to remove a burden on the homeless community. But I think you probably surmised that ending from Captain's comments the other day."

Stephen exhaled loudly and let his shoulders slump. Darren's body shifted in response then relaxed again. The table was quiet for a minute. Finally, he continued.

"I know we're directly contradicting the coroner's ruling. That might throw questions back on you. And I know that could be awkward because you don't agree with the ruling. Do you think Chief Greywright will be angry? I don't want to cause you any trouble."

Stephen noted a slight drop in Laqueta's shoulder. A wrinkle at the corner of her eye betrayed the depth of her mental struggle before, poised, she looked at his face.

"First," she replied, "I know you don't intend to cause me trouble, so please don't worry about that." She paused slightly. "As for Chief Greywright and County Attorney Lesig, I suppose their response will depend on whether they receive any inquiries or pressure over the issue. I think I had better give Chief a heads up and put a copy of the article in his hands tomorrow. I'll let him handle the coroner. I've made myself plain and fortunately Chief knows that if I am asked about it directly, I'll give an honest answer. But I have an alternative. I can refer any inquiry back to him or the County Attorney. The exception would be if Chief is present when a question is raised and directs it to me. I don't think he will risk that. He's politically savvy you know."

Stephen nodded. In that instant he remembered James Riederhof's planned visit. "Oh, no...."

"What?" Her eyebrows lifted.

"I forgot to tell you I passed your number to James Riederhof for more details if he wanted them."

"Yes?" There was a slight frown.

"Well, he plans to come to Grand Island to see where Joseph died. Probably bring his wife and Joseph's sister, maybe one of the brothers." He paused to check Laqueta's eyes. "Surely they won't come this quickly." The last was more of a question than a statement.

Laqueta opened her mouth but paused before speaking. "I received an out of town call this afternoon. I was at 4-H. I let it go to voice mail. You said the Riederhofs are from Connecticut. Right?"

"Right."

"Do you remember the area code?"

As Laqueta pulled out her cell phone, Stephen answered, "860 if I remember right."

The area code matched. When Laqueta read the number to him that also sounded familiar. They listened to the message together. He was wrong—the Riederhofs hoped to come to Grand Island within two weeks.

"I'll follow up on the call tomorrow and let you know. But now I've got a sleepy boy to take home."

Stephen slid from the booth Darren wrapped tightly in his arms. After Laqueta fished her keys from her jacket, he followed her to the car and deposited the boy into his booster seat and laid Darren's head to the side hoping it wouldn't fall on the drive home.

"Thanks," said Laqueta.

"Your welcome. I really enjoyed it." He stood erect. "By the way, where's Darren's dad?"

Laqueta glanced down at the asphalt. "That's a thankless subject."

"I'm sorry. You don't have to tell me if it's uncomfortable."

"No, it's okay. His father lives in Omaha."

Stephen cocked his head to the side. "Does he see him often?"

Laqueta's good posture melted. "Dreaux has never seen Darren."

Stephen's eyebrows rose.

"I told you it's a thankless subject. One I'm not very proud of."

"That's okay."

"No, it's not." She gazed down at the asphalt. "It's not okay. I acted very foolishly. I knew better. I always said I'd never let this happen to me and then it did. 'Stupid is what stupid does.'"

She took a deep breath, straightened her shoulders and looked Stephen in the eye.

"I started out right. Won a position as a beat officer at age nineteen then pursued a BA in Criminal Justice and Community

Policing. Held a three point nine grade point average. My first summer on the job, during summer break from University of Nebraska-Omaha, I attended the Police Academy and graduated at the top of my class. I received the Take Down and Marksmanship Awards and the Academic Honors Trophy."

Stephen raised his hand in mock horror. "Remind me to never tick *you* off!"

"I'd even started my Master's of Arts in Criminal Investigation when I met Dreaux Benjamin." A sparkle registered in her eyes. "Dreaux was fresh from Louisiana—sexy, debonair, built, but not a monster of a man. The music in his drawl made me swoon. I do love the sound of a southern black gentleman. Everything about him was jazz and Creole."

Laqueta let out a musical laugh then frowned.

"My mind turned to grits and the next thing you know I'd gotten pregnant. You know the old story. I was just his trophy."

"And a beautiful trophy," Stephen interrupted. "You'd make any man proud."

Laqueta blushed, looked down then continued.

"Well, he didn't want a pregnant trophy! Dropped me like a corn-on-the-cob off a hot grill. My brain's still etched with his sneer. And he gave me one every time he saw me—even after Darren was born."

At that last memory she fell inward into herself.

Note to self. That's Laqueta when she's hurt.

An almost holy silence passed between them. A moment that needed space to pass like a wisp of cloud dragging its skirt across a mountain trail. But, ever irreverent, Stephen's mind popped a memory to the surface. He grimaced then gave a small frown.

"What?"

"I forgot something." *I sound like a gouged CD.* "I promised Gramms I'd ask you something tonight."

Laqueta looked at him with suspicion.

His assertiveness fled. "It's probably not appropriate right now."

"It's okay," she reassured him.

"Gramms wants me to invite you to the ranch for my birthday—the seventh of July. That's a Saturday."

Laqueta's playful grin broke the tension.

"So. Are you asking me?" She dipped her chin all coy like Popeye's girlfriend Olive Oil.

"Yes," he replied all manly; then grinned. "We live on a canyon and have cows and horses and…"

"Horses?" Darren's head came off the seat.

"Quiet son. Go back to sleep."

He laid his head back down and closed his eyes.

"Will you at least think about it? I'd really like that and you could stay for the weekend."

It was late and he didn't want to pressure her. "Please," he added and put on a begging look that made her laugh.

"Of course."

"Of course you'll come?"

"Of course, I'll think about it." She gave him the look.

And if Darren has anything to do with it you'll be there with bells on. But he didn't say anything, just returned the look, wished her a good night, and walked off with a satisfied grin.

CHAPTER 32

Quote from the Journal of a Killer:

Are there limits to what God permits when we rescue a person from a life of misery?
The Journal of a Killer

⁂

AFTERNOON, JUNE 7, 2012:

Laqueta touched her lips. *I wonder how Chief's reacting.*

She rolled back in her chair, worried a button on her jacket, and stood. *Guess I better get this conversation over.*

⁂

When she returned from the Salvation Army, she'd tossed the article onto Chief Greywright's desk.

"I think you'll want to read this." She turned and left.

The Chief had it in his hand, eyes scanning the lines, as she looked back through his window.

⁂

As Laqueta took a step toward her door, the Chief strode into her office, plopped into a chair, and tossed Stephen's article onto her desk.

"What's this guy trying to do—make trouble?" His forehead hardened. "Wasn't he one of your suspects?"

"He's harmless. We can rule him out." She kept calm and controlled.

"The harmless ones make the best murderers," Chief spouted back. "Besides, most people who assist with suicide look harmless enough—those mambee pambee bleeding heart compassionate pricks can't think straight no how."

No wonder our opinions clash. In fact that clash of viewpoint created the only tension she felt with this job. She knew Chief respected and appreciated her work. Protective of his staff and officers, Chief was doubly protective of her. When a joint city-county work group hired her, his supportive statements and firm request sealed the deal.

"I ain't going to let no meddling bleeding heart tarnish your reputation."

He crossed his arms tightly across his chest. His ice blue eyes flashed beneath his blond flip of hair and his blonder eyebrows.

"You know I don't agree with the coroner's report." She lifted her chin. "Stephen and I have talked—several times. In fact he's the one that suggested you might want a heads up on the article and provided the copy. As far as I'm concerned it's Attorney Lesig who's got more to lose. Our department provided the same information to him that Stephen cited in the article."

"Yeh, but I stood behind his ruling. I sort of leaned on him to rule that way so we could close the case—and you know how much I hate having a case reopened. I like to get these homeless things looked at, acted on, and done, period. Nobody cares about them anyway."

"I'm aware." Laqueta didn't break tone. "And you know I disagree on that point. I think they deserve the same thorough investigation and careful deliberation as any other citizen. Looks to me like this one might backfire on you."

Laqueta lowered her chin to peer at him from under determined eyebrows. A quiet moment passed before she continued.

"Actually, I don't think the article will harm you at all. My reports give all the relevant details. Nobody else knows about your conversation with Lesig. I doubt he'd be interested in looking petty by bringing it up. After all, it's the coroner and County Attorney's job to make an independent decision based on pure facts and he's both."

Chief rubbed the light stubble on his chin. "You're probably right—but I still don't like it. And I don't like this Stephen Brown fellow either. Not if he's going to write stuff like this and get people all riled up." He paused then looked up at Laqueta. "After all I'm an officer of the peace, a *peace officer*. I like that," he ended smugly and laughed at himself.

Laqueta barely grinned.

Chief put his hands on the arms of the chair ready to stand. "Handle it," he said, "Okay?"

"Okay. But there's something else you need to know."

Chief's eyebrows narrowed.

"I received a call from Joseph Riederhof's father yesterday. He wants to come to Grand Island to see where his son died."

"I didn't think Muncie had anything on him." Chief's face twisted into a jigsaw puzzle.

"Stephen Brown—" Chief eyes darkened and Laqueta cringed "—researched Riederhof on the Internet and found the family. He wanted the family's reaction for..."

"Oh, that's right. It's right there in the article."

"His was the first word the family received in five years. They told him they planned to come and he referred them to me for information about the death. Now they're coming. If anything's a long shot it's the family. Our greater risk is from the news getting ahold of them, not this article."

CHAPTER 33

Quote from the Journal of a Killer:

There is only one ultimate and effectual preventive for the maladies to which flesh is heir, and that is death.
Harvey Cushing

SATURDAY EVENING, JUNE 9, 2012:

On the year's first one hundred degree day, Zachary's White Hall Off Plum remained naturally cool. He pulled the light blanket over his shoulders and napped away the torrid afternoon. Routine woke him at four o'clock, time to head for supper up at the Messiah Lutheran Church. The railroad tracks and houses moved animated by waves of heat radiating from the bare rail beds. In the mirage, the streets lied about the distance to be walked.

"Chet! What you doing here?" Zachary asked when he recognized the Salvation Army staff person in front of him.

"I come here all the time. Guess you've never seen me. I usually sit back there behind the pillar."

"I thought you cooked at home on Saturday or had a wife to cook for you. Why would you want to come here if you have your own home?"

Chet rolled his eyes. "You mean my hole in the wall. I barely make rent on the pay from my Goodwill work program. Food's usually out of the question and, hey, I know where the free meals are so I take advantage of them. It helps a lot."

Zachary looked at him askance."I just figured these meals were for the homeless and people from the motel apartments."

Chet smiled. "Lots of people here have homes. Even some of the families. They just can't afford food or want to spend their money on something else."

"You mean some of these folks have regular jobs?"

"Sure and most people who eat at Salvation Army work full time too. Maybe another third are on disability or retired. Not a lot of homeless. People get that wrong all the time."

Trays ready, Chet headed off to his spot behind the pillar and Zachary looked around to see where he could sit. Javier Ruiz-Lobo sat near the middle of the room with his three children, Guillermo, Leticia, and Jose. He didn't see their mother, Marta, but never mind there were two empty seats.

"Esta bien—I sit here?" he asked.

"Si. Esta bien." Javier motioned at the chair beside him.

"Donde esta Marta?" Zachary asked reluctant to sit in her place.

"No se." Javier shrugged then repeated in English, "Don't know."

Unsure of his Spanish, Zachary decided not to pursue the question.

"Where you from in Mexico?"

They had exchanged names, explored children's ages—five, three and a half, and twelve months—boy, girl, boy, and Zachary knew that Javier needed a job plus Marta was willing to work. They first came a year ago and lived in a small apartment. That was about all he knew and since then they'd mainly said hello. In passing, Zachary would stop and tousle the children's hair. Guillermo, the five year old, would swat his hand away then reach around to pinch Zachary behind his knee. Zachary would make an exaggerated hop skip to get away and they'd laugh.

"We lived Ojinaga," Javier replied.

"Ojinaga?" Zachary shook his head.

"Presidio, Texas?" Javier was obviously trying to give a location Zachary would be familiar with.

Zachary shook his head again.

"Chihuahua?"

"Oh. Si. Su familia there?"

"Si, mi madre, una hermosa—sister, y mi grandmother. No otros."

Javier dropped his head, a deep sadness visible in his eyes.

"Y su papa?"

"Mi papa and mi brother estan muerta. Shot. Heads..." he made a motion for decapitated, "y sobre bridge." He ended with a throwing motion and grimaced.

Chilling. Just like in the news. "Who?" Zachary asked. "Sinaloa Cartel?"

"No. La Linea!"

They talked—broken Spanish, broken English—until the kids finished eating then went outside so the kids could play on the school equipment.

Javier had received a message to get out or be killed. He was not even allowed to retrieve the bodies of his father and brother. He fled with his family across the river on a day pass, but seeing three of the La Lineas who had kidnapped his father, they fled inland to Notres. There he registered with the Mexican Consulate in Midland, Texas. However, as they came out of the Consulate, another La Linea from Chihuahua was leaning on the building. He called out Javier's name then ginned and cackled at his family's terror.

Afraid the cartel might be tracking it, Javier abandoned his car, hitch hiked, and with the help of sympathetic Chicanos and the Overground Railroad, they ran until they came to Grand Island where he felt safe.

In Grand Island, with help from Saint Mary's Immigration Program, he filed for asylum. Due to some irregularities related to their first few months of flight, the asylum was turned down and now was in appeals. Javier was afraid he would be deported if he filed for a green card before the appeal ran its course. Of course with Javier's limited English and Zachary's limited Spanish, Zachary's understanding of the facts might not have been exact.

The bottom line, Javier was afraid. Afraid of being sent back. Afraid the La Lineas might reach Nebraska. Afraid of "angry Americans"—people angry about him being here, angry about any Spanish speaking person being in their community. Zachary also figured out that the family no longer lived indoors and survived on free meals and clothing giveaways. But Javier was adamant. He wanted to do everything legally.

Exhausted from the bilingual conversation, Javier and Zachary sat in silence on top of the bike rack watching the kids play.

"Mamma?" Jose, the one year old, asked and looked up wide-eyed at his father.

"No esta aqui."

"Where is she?" Zachary asked. "Are you waiting for her?"

"No se."

Zachary had never seen a man look so helpless.

"Que es la problema?"

"Raney…." Javier checked Zachary's eyes. He seemed unsure that Zachary would understand. "Raney?"

Zachary furrowed his eyebrows, tried to figure out what phonetically was going on then lifted them … "Rainey. Rainey White?"

Javier nodded then took ahold of Zachary's arm with both hands and pretended to pull on him like he wanted him to come with him except he didn't move away.

"Marta. Rainey toke…" Javier said and tugged Zachary's arm again.

Zachary's eye widened. *No! No, it can't be!* "Rainey took her away?" Zachary mimicked Javier's pantomime.

Javier nodded. His tone changed to pleading. "Ayuda me? Help me."

"Policia," Zachary suggested.

"No! No! No policia." Javier pulled his three children close to him, terrified. "No policia!"

Zachary lowered his eyebrows and bit his bottom lip. Javier's eyes pled again. The children cowered, scared. But what could he do? Javier was afraid of the police.

"Posible manana," Zachary said and nodded his head once sharply. "I'll talk to Stephen," he added.

Javier looked puzzled. "Stephen?"

"Si. Yo hablo con Stephen manana." Stephen hoped he'd used the correct Spanish phrase.

Terror fringed Javier's squinted eyes.

"Salvation Army. Es un buen muchacho." Zachary nodded his head vigorously to assure Javier that Stephen was a good man. Safe.

"O Estephan. Mr. Stephen. Si you entiendo." Javier nodded his head "Manana...."

CHAPTER 34

Quote from the Journal of a Killer:

If you don't have any fight in you, you might as well be dead.
Scott Caan

"How's the new girlfriend?" Andy asked as Stephen stepped into the kitchen.

"Can't have a new one if he's never had one," teased Chet.

"Who?" Susan raised her eyebrows.

"You know, Investigator Ellison." Andy got a dirty look from Stephen.

"We've been talking about Riederhof. That's all."

"Oh?" Andy raised his eyebrows. "That's why you picked her boy up at Messiah? And that's why I saw you'all come out of Lee's Restaurant that night?"

"What do you know about Messiah? You're working then. Leastwise that's what your time card shows."

"My girlfriend tried to talk to you and you blew her off." Andy laughed. "Nobody blows Laneshia off without paying the piper. Besides she knows who that boy is. She talks to Laqueta all the time."

"Wait a minute," Susan reared back on her heels, "Isn't she black?"

Andy shot her a watch-your-mouth glare while Chet's eyebrows jumped.

"Why Stephen you sly dawg! Wouldn't a thought you had it in you."

"Okay, enough of that." Stephen pointed his chin at the two of them. "You seen Zachary Plues?"

Chet looked out into the dining room. "He was here earlier, but I don't see him now."

"Yeh, I didn't see him either," Stephen agreed, "So, he was here?"

"Why?" Susan asked.

"I need to talk to him. The Independent needs an article on Janice Zahn now. Thought Zachary might know something. Sure can't find her on the Internet." Stephen faced Susan. "Guess I'll have to go look for him."

"I don't think he's working right now. Last job ended and detasseling don't start for another week," Susan volunteered. "Probably be at the library." Somehow Susan always knew where people might be.

"Let me know if he comes back in." Stephen turned and stepped out the back door.

Susan tipped her head up and called out, "You better wait till noon to look for him. He usually does a walk-around in the morning. Hard to find then."

"Thanks." Stephen tipped his head in appreciation and continued out to check on supplies in the Disaster Services Warehouse.

"There you are!"

Angelina's verbal bullet made Stephen jump.

He turned to face his scourge.

"I know you're lazy, but you don't have to advertise it in the paper."

He tried to resist but her deftly thrown shurikens sliced his soul.

Stephen fixed her with acid lined eyes. "What do you mean?"

"This Salvation Army never gets out there and finds the hurting, but you—you have to go and say it right out in the newspaper. You stupid or something? How do you think people will react to that?"

"Well … obviously it upset you. But—for other people—perhaps you're not a good representative. Captain's already had conversations with several potential new donors and the Independent asked us yesterday for another article on that young woman Janice Zahn. Said they'd had forty or fifty good responses to the article and—strangely—not even one of the hate letters they usually get for compassion stories. I don't know about you, but in my book that's a pretty good response. Certainly nothing to be afraid of."

"Humph…" Undaunted, the tip of Angelina's nose curled up like it always did when she set her jaw. Stephen nearly laughed—she looked so elfish. She tossed her hair back, tried to zap him with a tasser barbed stare then blurted on….

"I bet that County Attorney's gonna haul you into court for that challenge to the coroner's ruling."

"The County Attorney is the coroner," Stephen responded.

"I know that!"

Gee, how can her jaw get any tighter? Her head's going to snap off.

A grin crossed his face and a light chuckle slipped out as he pictured Angelina's head snapping clean at the neck and rolling off her shoulder.

"The City doesn't need its dirty laundry hung all out in the paper! It'll just hurt our image."

Yours or the City's? he wondered.

"So you agree. Something seems wrong about that ruling."

"Well, I—I—I…" She shot him a dirty look and stamped out of the donations gate.

CHAPTER 35

Quote from the Journal of a Killer:

It was a time when only the dead smiled, happy in their peace.
Anna Akhmatova

Stephen sat in the window at his apartment and ate a bologna and cheese sandwich on a single slice of multi-grain bread. He needed to get to the "Y". He didn't want his pecs and abs to go soft. Furthermore, he felt emotionally upbeat when he exercised. Exercise also supported his move from a passive person to an assertive responder. This self image stuff apparently worked as well on him as it did the clients.

After Angelina, the morning crept by. Half dozen food pantry clients. Captain approved the Zahn assignment. The secretary needed to review supplies with him before she headed out to Sam's but she left for lunch early. That put his search for Zachary on hold. Stymied, time slipping away; he'd headed to his apartment for lunch.

CHAPTER 35

Bartenbach's Alley lay dead in front of him. Not even a stray car or pedestrian appeared for the whole half hour he watched it. So at a quarter till one he headed to the library anxious to get this Zachary interview done.

Hope the kid isn't high, he thought.

Walking close to the apartment building he stepped blindly into the alley.

"Hey! Watch it."

Stephen pulled up short and looked to his left.

Zachary scowled. "I could've been a car."

"Zachary!" Stephen stepped aside. "I was just coming to look for you. You headed to the library?"

Zachary reared back his head and looked Stephen over.

"How'd you know?"

"I didn't. Susan said you usually go there about twelve thirty every day." Stephen shrugged. "How about it? You want a ride. My car's right over there."

"I don't know. What's this you want to talk about? We don't have any business." His head still cocked, Zachary scanned Stephen's shoes and body before making eye contact. "Actually, I was coming to the Sally to talk to you."

Stephen stood, watched as Zachary gave him a third once over, and waited for eye contact. "I'd like to talk to you about Janice Zahn."

Zachary's shoulders twitched.

"The newspaper wants me to write an article like the one on Riederhof. Did you see it?"

"Yeh." Zachary's eye brightened. "I read that. Pretty cool. I liked it."

"So I need your help writing about Janice. How about it? … Hop in! We can talk at the library. It's quiet there—unless you're afraid to be seen with me."

Stephen chuckled, held opened the door, and Zachary got in.

As he pulled away from the curb Stephen said, "So tell me what you know about Janice Zahn. I hear you two were an item."

"Friends," corrected Zachary.

"With benefits." Stephen said it matter-of-factly.

Zachary grimaced. "It's not what that implies," he responded. "Not with Janice. She was sweet, but sex was hard for her."

"What do you mean?" Stephen asked with a quick glance to his right.

"I don't know," started Zachary, "It was kind of private to her."

"Yeh."

"She had a hard life. You know, raped by her dad and all."

"By her dad?"

"Yeh."

"Say… do you have anything you need to do at the library? Let's catch a cup of coffee at the Chocolate Bar. You ever been there?"

"Never been." Zachary shrugged. "Sounds fine."

Stephen pulled across the left hand lane, swung around the block, and headed back east on Third Street. They rode in silence.

At the café Zachary filled him in on Janice's dad and all the sexual abuse she experienced before she ran.

"So where did she come from?"

"Ohio. Chillicothe. Down US 35 from my town, Xenia. That's where the trucker dropped her off when she ran away."

"So you knew her there?"

"I know the truck stop where he dropped her. That's where my Dad stops and where I ran away. And yeh, I know about the Emil Crawford Mansion where that man made her lose the baby. But I left before she came. It's kind of funny ain't it—she running away to my hometown and me running away from it, both of us running from fathers."

Stephen nodded but he needed to fill in more of the pieces.

"You said some lady picked her up from under the bridge. Where did she take her? Did she stay other places before she came here?"

"The lady took her to Missouri and left her at her momma's house. The momma took real good care of her. Helped her get strong. Gave her her own room and all of that. Janice even worked at the Josephine's Eatery. Said it was real famous. Home of the

Mound Burger. Janice really liked it there. Said it felt like a real home. That's the lady who gave her the car and everything."

Stephen knew that homeless people often stayed at places where they could work and people took good care of them. Treated them like regular friends. With all that going for them, it made no sense when they still moved on.

"So why did she leave? Sounds like her life really came together there."

"Well, one day one of her daddy's friends showed up at the restaurant. She didn't recognize him till she poured his coffee. But he knew her. Said, 'Why if it isn't that sweet piece of ass from Chillicothe. Didn't you ever tell your daddy thank you for letting me fuck you? He'd be real interested in knowin' where you got off to child.'

"Janice screamed, dropped the coffee pot, and it shattered on the floor as she ran. She could hear that fuckneck's crazy laugh. She never looked back, just jumped in the car and came here."

"That's an amazing story." Stephen's shoulders remained straight and his ears alert. "You said sex was hard for her. I can understand why, but what did you mean? You and her had sex, right?"

Zachary didn't duck his head or indicate any shame but he looked at Stephen out of the corner of his eye. Probably trying to be sure he wasn't some voyeur getting his jollies off.

"Yeh. Twice," Zachary shook his head slowly. "The first time she went berserk! Got mad. Cried. Yelled at me and ran off naked."

"You raped her?"

"No man!" Zachary shot him a dirty look. "I don't rape women! If they don't want it, I don't do it. That simple. Rapists need to have their heads cut off and their balls dropped down the sewer."

Whoa!

"I read the signs wrong! She melted in my arms and we had great sex then she went ballistic. Said I was just like all the other guys and all that. When we talked later I found out she always relaxed and participated. She'd learn that made it easier. Besides if she made them mad they'd hurt her. I didn't know it and she didn't either—I mean to her it felt like rape and she didn't know I was trying to comfort her. Comfort. That's what her daddy called it. Makes me so mad." He stopped and looked Stephen in the eye.

"The second time was just before she died. She'd had trouble with Rainey White and was crying. Said she wanted to die—she was tired of being hurt and living on the street. We even talked about suicide and how Riederhof did it then about some lady here in Nebraska who used zip ties to kill her son and herself. Made me real sad. I hate it when people are suffering like that. Anyway, that time she asked me to make love to her so there was no misunderstanding. I couldn't believe after all that that she still wanted comfort for herself from sex. Just holding her wasn't enough. She cried afterwards, but just a soft, cathartic cry.

"That was the last time I seen her alive."

Zachary's chin dropped as he sighed and shook his head.

They sat in silence for a long time then Stephen asked, "You said she's had trouble with Rainey White. What'd you mean?"

A flash of anger did everything but shake Zachary's body.

"That...," he sealed his lips and puffed out his cheeks, "...that no good piece of—" He calmed himself and looked Stephen full in the face. "He raped her then cut her while—while they hit orgasm."

Sounded Ted Bundyish to Stephen.

"In her car? On the street?" he asked.

"No! That coward helps people out. Invites them up to his motel room and gives them favors and such then he hurts them—mostly rape but sometimes more."

The fire in Zachary's bones smoldered white hot.

"He invited Janice to use the shower in his room to clean up. First couple of times he just let her shower. Made a few comments, but left her alone. Course he knew she didn't have no money so one day he asked her if she'd like to earn some. Said he had an acquaintance—that's the word he uses—who wanted a date but was no good at asking women out. Of course, he'd expect sex in exchange of a meal and a movie. Paid for her to get her hair done. Bought her a new dress. You know—took care of all of that. She was desperate and depressed—it was while we weren't talking. She figured if she could do it for her father and his friends she could put up with some stranger too, for a little money.

"Anyway, the guy liked it and asked for her again."

"She know his name?"

"Kening—Conning—K...."

"Koenig?"

"Yeh! Anyway, like I was saying, he wanted her again so Rainey made Janice do it, but she didn't want to. When the guy came to pick her up, she started to cry and the more he tried to comfort her the louder and harder she cried till she started screaming, 'No—no—no!' Rainey threw her down on the bed and ripped her clothes off. Made the man take her right there then crawled on top himself. He had a box knife in his hand. He screwed her and screwed her while she screamed and kept screaming. Then cut her under her right breast as she came."

Zachary spat the words out. His voice had risen. The Chocolate Bar staff stared their way. Things got real uncomfortable, but Stephen remained voiceless.

"You know he did the same thing with guys, too," Zachary said more calmly.

Stephen was afraid to respond, but finally said, "No, I didn't know."

"Yeh. You remember when I used to be drunk and high all the time?"

"Yeh." Stephen cocked his head and raised his chin.

Zachary held his hands up, palms out. "Hey man, I been clean for two and a half years now. How about that?" He laughed. "But I haven't needed a place to stay so I never came to see you."

"Two and a half years." Stephen nodded his head while a thread of a smile grew on his face.

"Yep. I haven't drank—been drunk—since...." Zachary stopped and added, "When I used to drink and use drugs, Rainey would supply them in return for little favors—or cash of course if I had it."

Stephen recalled Susan saying Zachary was between jobs. Apparently, he worked spot jobs or seasonal jobs when he found them.

"At first it would be dumb things like shining his shoes or being the runner on a sale. Then, if I got real desperate he'd ask for small sexual favors—I know—I'm not proud of it."

His body shook like something struck it, but he continued.

"Then he tried to pimp me or pressure me for full out sex. That's when I cut him off. It made me mad. I'm not that kind of person. Not that kind of desperate."

Rage flashed hot across Zachary's face. "Someone really needs to do something about that man." Zachary challenged Stephen with his eyes, but Stephen maintained his calm.

"There were others?" he asked.

"Lots of them. All the homeless. How do you think Rainey can afford that motel and his fancy clothes and all that. It ain't from the drug sales. He's a nickel and dime dealer—not big money."

"Including Riederhof?"

This time Zachary literally spit.

"That's disgusting," Stephen reared back. "The man was paraplegic—paralyzed from the waist down." He wanted to spit, too, and he *didn't* want any more details.

"No kidding—it's dope!" Zachary made a sharp click on the 'd'. "Why do you think Riederhof started talking about suicide?"

"You think Riederhof's death was suicide?" Stephen leaned forward.

"Sure. But of course, someone had to help him. We never figured out a way he could do it himself. He couldn't even drink poison without help."

Stephen tucked away Zachary's words to ponder later.

"And now he's leaning on that Javier Ruiz-Lobo's wife," Zachary continued.

"Rainey White?"

"Yeh!"

Stephen's phone rang, but before he took the call he said, "Tell Javier to come see me. Okay?"

Zachary shook his head.

Stephen clicked on the call. It was Sonja, Captain's secretary. She had been waiting for over two hours and needed him to come back to review the supplies list before she headed out to Sam's. He stood up to signal he had to leave.

"Where can I drop you off?" he asked Zachary.

"The library'd be fine."

As they rode back to the library Stephen's mind processed the information from Zachary, especially about Rainey White victimizing so many people. Somehow Zachary knew all this and he, at the Salvation Army, didn't. With Angelina's rant and lies, this could tip the scale. He might lose his job.

"How is it you end up helping so many people, knowing so much about them, while the Salvation Army misses them? Sounds like we need to fix something."

Zachary gave Stephen a distrustful look and answered warily. "Yeh, you need to fix something. You have too many rules, like you're trying to protect yourself from people, and you make people come to you. You need to get out on the street."

CHAPTER 36

Quote from the Journal of a Killer:

Our lives begin to end the day we become silent about things that matter.
Martin Luther King, Jr.

Next morning when Stephen sat down to write, he found that in his rush he had forgotten some of the key points he needed to put Janice Zahn's story together. Not only that but, while writing, the whole Rainey White situation crept into his mind and threw off his concentration. The status quo was inhumane—an insane way for homeless people to live. Frustrated, he headed to the kitchen.

Andy bowed from the waist and rolled his palms as Stephen walked into the kitchen Tuesday morning. "To what do we owe the honor of your presence two mornings in a row? You just love us so much?"

Stephen flipped his nose at him and stepped up to the serving window behind Chet and Susan.

"You seen Zachary Plues?"

Chet craned his neck to look over the dining room as Stephen looked over his shoulder.

"I haven't seen him yet," said Susan.

Chet plunked a spoon full of grits next to the eggs on the bag lady's plate.

"Nah, he's not out there."

"Oh, you're so sweet," the bag lady blubbered. "You remembered this Southern girl loves her grits. Did you get any Northern takers today?"

"Oatmeal and cream of wheat," Chet responded. They exchanged knowing smiles and she ambled on off.

"Could you keep an eye out for me?" Stephen asked. "I need to talk to him again. Tell him to stop by my office. Okay?"

"Sure," said Susan.

Stephen gave Andy a snooty nose then a grin and walked to his office. He pulled his clip pad from his briefcase and started to list known facts about the Zahn case.

Abused child. Runaway. Rape victim. Kept woman. Baby murdered. Incest. Pretty bleak.

Although he remembered more details than he'd thought, maybe he'd read them to Zachary—check the facts—and ask him to fill in the missing pieces. He knew she lived in her station wagon but any real detail about her life in Grand Island was missing. His mind turned back to Rainey White—something about rape and Koenig. She was cut? He'd ask Zachary to review that again. He noted it and added to his list *–time frame related to death?*

"Senor?" A male voice. Soft, tentative.

Stephen looked up toward the door. "Yes."

A young Mexican man stood barely inside the doorframe. Handsome. Mestizo. Short. Maybe five foot six. Slicked back black hair parted down the middle—common for Hispanic middle or wealthy classes.

"May I help you?"

The man, about twenty-seven he figured, shrugged his shoulder and just stared at him. Broad shouldered. Muscular. His tiny feet reflected the people of his state within Mexico. Maybe Coahuila. As Stephen sized up the situation, a young woman leaned in through the door.

"Hello," she said in a heavy Spanish accent.

A young child rested on her hip and gave him the same wide-eyed look as his father.

Stephen motioned to the two chairs in front of his desk.

"Come in."

The man sat on the left and the woman sat on the right closest to the door. Two other small children followed her clinging to her skirt and then stood at the back of her chair.

"What do you need? Food?"

The man looked puzzled and glanced at his wife.

"Comida," she said, "No, senor."

Stephen noted unexpected emotion in her voice. She blushed deep red.

"You help?" the man asked, his English very broken. "Zachary said you help?"

"I don't know. What's the problem?"

The word "problem" clearly registered.

"Rainey …," he pronounced it slowly, very carefully, "…White."

At Rainey's name Stephen remembered Zachary said something about a Spanish man—Javier?—and his wife, but the phone rang and Stephen had cut him off quick. Perhaps a little too quick.

"Rainey—robar mi wife." Javier stated and then made a pulling action on his wife's arm.

Robbed his wife. That didn't make sense then it hit him. *Stole his wife. Oh God, now what!*

"Nombres," Stephen said to Javier. It was too uncomfortable to go on without names, the subject too sensitive.

"Javier." He motioned toward his wife. "Marta."

"Rainey took Marta?"

"Si, Rainey took wife—two days. Friday. Home Sunday en la manana."

God, I hate those hopeful eyes, Stephen thought. *What can I do?*

"Why? Why take Marta?" Did he really want to know? This was Rainey White.

Javier and Marta flushed deep red and looked blankly into their laps. No fear. No anger. Just shame. He looked at them calmly and let them have the space needed.

"Por un otra hombre. To other man." Javier barely looked up then dropped his eyes again.

Marta tipped her head to look at her husband, again blushed, and hugged the baby in her lap.

Stephen struggled for words they might understand.

"Marta no want?"

"No want!" Javier's words came clear, clipped, and forceful.

Marta glanced at Stephen from under thick eyebrows and shook her head. The sadness in her eyes spoke the language of the rape victims he worked with during his Masters practicum. A sadness that filled in the rest of the story.

"Cut her!" Javier continued, now angry, as he reached to lift the side of Marta's blouse. Before Stephen could shake his head to spare her the humiliation, Javier discretely lifted the shirt enough to expose a one inch cut beneath her left breast, outside the bra line.

Now Stephen blushed, hung his head down, and made eye contact with Marta through lowered eyes hoping it was indeed a universal sign of respect.

"You help?"

"I don't know what to do." Stephen shook his head. "Police help?"

"Policia! No!" Javier became animated. Both of them looked terrified. "No policia."

"No police," Marta said very softly again ducking her head. "Please, senor, no policia."

Probably something to do with deportation. They didn't look like people who had trouble with law enforcement.

Stephen reached for the phone to call Laqueta for advice.

"No! No"! Javier shook his head vigorously and waved his hands in cutting motions across one another for emphasis.

"No," Stephen repeated also using hand signals. "I call police man—no. I call mi amiga. Understand?"

"You talk to your friend," said Marta. "Yes?"

"Yes."

"She policia?"

Stephen nodded.

Javier gave Marta a fearful look, but she shook her head yes with a stiff determination.

"You talk to friend. Okay."

Marta started to stand.

Stephen stood. He understood that Marta did not feel comfortable staying for the phone conversation. He reached across the desk and shook both Javier's and Marta's hands. As he followed them to the door he lightly tousled the children's hair. "Mi hijo," he added in the customary courtesy and honor accorded to children in the Mexican culture.

"Tomorrow," he said to Javier and Marta. "Come see me manana."

They nodded their heads. "Manana." And walked out.

CHAPTER 37

Quote from the Journal of a Killer:

"This very day...the Lord placed you at my mercy."
1 Samuel 24:10 NLT

As he said goodbye to the Ruiz-Lobo family, Stephen spotted Zachary in the waiting area. He'd tried to read Javier and Marta's faces but, by the questioning look shot Stephen's way, he couldn't.

"How'd it go?" Zachary asked.

Stephen tightened his lips for a moment then responded.

"Did I get that right? Rainey is pimping Marta out."

Zachary nodded.

"What's his power over them?"

"Fear of being deported." Zachary gave him a duh look. "If she says no to Rainey, he reports them to Immigration. If she resists, he'll beat her—she showed you the cut? If they go to the police, they get deported. Immigration has their paperwork all screwed up and they're scared to death."

"I think it's more than scared. When I mentioned the police they were terrified. What's producing that extra edge of fear? It's got to be more than going back."

"Don't you know?" Disgust edged Zachary's voice.

"What?" asked Stephen flipping his hands up. "Know what?"

“La Linea killed his father and brother. Decapitated them and hung their bodies over the bridge.” Zachary looked him straight in the eye. “They sent word they were going to kill him next, so they fled.” He shook his head in disgust. “If they go back, they get killed. Deportation equals a death sentence.”

“Dammed if they do and dammed if they don’t.” Stephen nodded.

“Yeh. And they’ve already been threatened with death here. La Linea met them as they crossed the river—U.S. side. Then later found them at the Mexican Consulate and again threatened to kill them. They’re barely safe, even here. And if they report to Immigration or the Consulate to sort out their paperwork...”

Stephen nodded his understanding. “They’re afraid La Linea has people watching.”

They stood in silence a few seconds. Finally, Stephen shook off his helpless stupor and motioned toward his office. “Come in.”

“I’d like to read you my list of notes about Janice Zahn. There’re several details I know I’ve forgotten and you can check the accuracy of the rest.”

“Who cares?” shrugged Zachary.

“I do. Every human life deserves to be honored—even in death.” Stephen stiffened. “And the greatest honor we can give anyone, alive or dead, is to tell the truth.”

Zachary made a flippant gesture with his hand and rolled his eyes toward the ceiling.

“Do you know where Janice was born?”

“Hmmm....” Zachary wrinkled his forehead. “I never asked her. Chillicothe I suppose.”

“Ohio?”

“I guess. That’s the only place she talked about.”

Stephen continued, “Died—June 3,2012. Cause of death—unknown.”

Zachary startled. “No! She was choked to death. I mean she killed herself with a zip tie.”

Stephen's eyebrows raised. "How'd you know that?"

Zachary bit the inside of his cheek. "I was at the car. You know when they found her. That black lady was there and I was curious. She talked to me."

Now it was Stephen's turn to say, "Hmmm." He shook it off and then explained that the coroner's initial report stated the cause of death as unknown but that could change. It could be suicide—which fit Zachary's story yesterday—or murder—maybe an assisted suicide, technically homicide.

"But you challenged his ruling in your Riederhof article. I read it."

Am I being inconsistent? Stephen looked in Zachary's eyes."But Riederhof couldn't have committed suicide. No way he could have pulled that off."

"So you think he was murdered?" Zachary rocked back, his eyes opened wide.

"I'm thinking assisted suicide," Stephen said matter-of-factly. "Anyway—going on—what's the name of your hometown? Janice first ran off to there. Right?"

"Xenia."

"Zinnia? Z-i-n-n-i-a."

"No..." Zachary said with emphasis. "Xenia. X-e-n-i-a."

"Like a Greek goddess?"

"Hell, I don't know. It's just the town I grew up in."

"Okay. Ran away. First stop Xenia where a rich man adopted her. Treated her like his daughter. Then turned violent when she rejected him?"

"Yeh. But he came in to rape her. That's important. I think you should say that after she told him about her father...that's when he made his move."

Stephen wrote down appropriate notes.

"Speaking of her father—he had incest with her. Right?"

"Right."

"It began after her mother died."

"No. It began before her mother died—when she got too sick for sex."

Stephen shook his head in disbelief.

"Her daddy didn't know how to live without a wife. That's why—that's why he made her his wife and why she thought it was okay. She was just helping her daddy. Until he started giving her to his friends and they started hurting her—doing it right in front of him, them hurting her too, and he didn't say anything—that's when she knew it was wrong. That and when he got paranoid about her getting pregnant. What did he think would happen?"

Zachary looked dazed for a minute but his unfocused darting eyes revealed a deeper kind of troubled emotion. From seemingly out of nowhere he said, "Rainey White should be killed," then stiffened as he checked back in and tried to engage Stephen's eyes.

"Because of what he did? I assume you're talking about Janice."

"Yeh. The things he did—they're just wrong. Wrong!" The words guttural, from a deep primordial level. "That bastard just doesn't deserve..." Zachary clenched his teeth and shook his head.

"You're talking about the time he cut her?" Stephen didn't have the heart to state any other details. "Was that the time before she—she died?"

"No. That time was worse. It was on the Wednesday before," Zachary began then noticed Stephen's confusion and added, "... before she died."

"The Koe—Koe-nigger guy decided he wanted another go at her—you know I saw his name in the paper. He's a councilman or something. Someone ought to rip him one too. He—Rainey—came and ripped her out of her station wagon; marched her off to the motel. They had the room all set up like a fancy diner. Koenig—in a fancy suit and tie trying to look sexy—sat waiting. Rainey ripped her clothes off, dressed her in some long slinky dress and fixed her hair up. When she refused to eat he forced her mouth open and Mr. Koenig fed her acting like it was some intimate happy meal."

The details made Stephen disgusted to be a man who liked romantic things.

"Then they raped her multiple times all night long taking turns. When they exhausted themselves, Rainey got a lighter and a paperclip and they burned her. They branded the letters m-i-n-e on both sides inside her pelvis.

"That's when she decided." His words calm, matter-of-fact. "She never recovered."

The hour hand edged one o'clock. Stephen was exhausted. Zachary crumpled, despite his forced posture. But Stephen still needed to ask two more questions. After a short breather, he started.

"So, Rainey raped Riederhof, too?"

"Yes." The voice and face were closed, numb.

"You saw it? I mean the results."

"I had to clean him up. Rainey just sat him in the wheelchair, clothes in his lap, catheter and bag dripping, and pushed him out into the alley. The bag lady—she come got me or he'd have froze to death."

Stephen winced then looked deep into Zachary's eyes.

"And he raped you?"

Zachary's chin lifted abruptly and his eyes blazed.

"No. It was all voluntary."

"But, there were others?"

"Yes. Lots. This Indian kid—retard I think—and lots of women like Marta. They were pimped or shared with another man. The boys—well he liked them young and old, not so much in the middle—but only people he could intimidate or done favors for."

"Thanks." Stephen signaled the end of the interview. "I think I'll talk to Investigator Ellison about Rainey. Don't know if it will do any good since no one's filed a police report. But she needs to know about the connection to people who've died.

"By the way, do you know how long Rainey's been here?"

"He was here when I got here. Gave me drugs my first night."

"I remember that night." Stephen stood. "Again, thanks. It's past lunch. Can I take you somewhere? Get you something to eat?"

"Nah, I usually skip lunch—nothing free at lunch you know. I think I'll just head to the library."

They parted ways at the door. It was after lunchtime, but Stephen had to get away.

CHAPTER 38

Quote from the Journal of a Killer:

It is by dying that one awakens to eternal life.
Saint Francis of Assisi

Over a cup of coffee at the Chocolate Bar, Stephen called the coroner's office and asked for Janice's official cause of death. The administrative assistant, Sally, shuffled through papers then picked the phone back up.

"Here it is. Let's see—cause of death—suicide."

"Thank you. Do you know if her family's been notified? I think it's very important to have the family notified—even for homeless people. By the way who does that now?"

The woman laughed, "Slow down cowboy. One question at a time."

"Sorry."

"No, the notification has not happened. Since the Police Department stopped doing the notifications guess who got the job—yours truly—Sally Kaufman. You'd think I'm the acting coroner under this new guy. We don't have a real coroner you know just the County Attorney, my boss. So, no, the notification has not been made. Not because I don't want to. I can't find them—her family—and I haven't had time to do any fancy research. Mind you, I think family notification is very important, top priority. But

I've no training and my old duties are mandated as priorities not this new task. It's political you know."

"So I've heard," said Stephen. "Would you mind if I tried to see what I can find? I don't want to cause trouble."

"I don't know what you can do, honey, but I suppose—have at it. I already did an Internet search. Useless."

"Yeh, I know. I tried that too. A big zero. But since then I learned a bit more about her story and I'll see what I can find."

"You've learned more about how she died?"

"No, I've learn about her background, her life before Grand Island. Like where she grew up and what happened to her."

"Oh," Sally paused. "When I do the notifications, when I can't find the families, I feel a little sad and wonder what their life was like. No one should die alone. Did you learn why Janice committed suicide?"

Stephen gave her a brief run down on Janice's life before running away, the 'adopted' rich man in Xenia, and the rapes in Grand Island.

"Oh my God!" she gasped when he stopped.

"Yes. Oh my God. By the way, thank you for answering my questions. I'll let you know if I locate the family."

Talking through Janice's story brought structure to the article he needed to write but Stephen was too drained to work on it now … and he still had Darren's game this afternoon.

Relief washed over him as he stepped outside to get his clothes for the game. The sun warmed his tight neck and shoulder muscles. He rotated his arms and did some elbow lifts as he walked. He'd forgotten what a stress relief a little exercise and a regular change of scenery brings.

Speaking of change of scenery, he still hadn't gotten Laqueta's answer for Gramms. He smiled at the thought of showing Laqueta the ranch and maybe taking an afternoon trail ride together. Did black people ride horses? He didn't know. Oh, surely they did. Look how Darren reacted—and he was half-asleep.

He changed in the staff bathroom and returned to his desk. Two forty five. That left an hour and a half. Disenchanted he turned to the computer and typed "need details," shifted down two lines and wrote "what could cause an eighteen year old young woman to consider suicide? and "how does an eighteen year old runaway end up homeless and in Grand Island?"

Next thing he knew, a drafted heart of the article was finished.

"Brrrt…" The cell phone caused him to flinch.

He glanced up at the clock. Four twenty.

"Mr. Stephen, where are you? You comin' aren't you."

Laqueta made a clucking sound in the background.

"On my way, spud. I'll be there in ten. Now run along and warm up...and bud, hit one out of the park for me, okay?"

"Yes, Mr. Stephen! Will do."

He heard the phone change hands as Darren ran off screaming.

"Stephen?"

"Yeh, I'm here. Got caught up writing Janice Zahn's story. Sorry. I'll be right there."

"No problem. Can I read your draft?"

"Sure. Be there in a sec."

CHAPTER 39

Quote from the Journal of a Killer:

Some men are alive simply because it is against the law to kill them.
E. W. Howe

"I'm speechless." Laqueta pointed at the draft of the article. "How did you learn all of this?"

"From Zachary Plues."

The corners of Laqueta's eye creased.

"He said he talked to you at Janice's car. You know—when you were investigating the scene."

"Young guy? Brown hair slightly flipped over the ears?"

"Sounds like him. I had two interviews with him. He hung out with her some."

"I'm impressed." She flashed him a smile. "You should be an investigator. Seems you have good instincts on how to run down information. And, from the detail and insight of this draft, you must have a great interviewing technique. Do you mind if I put a copy of this in my report and share it with the coroner before you go to press?"

"Sure. But why?"

"Because maybe this wasn't a suicide. Both Rainey White and Zachary might be involved in her death. Maybe even Councilman Koenig."

Stephen leaned in and pondered this unexpected response.

Laqueta tilted her head to watch his eyes and added, "Rainey could have come back for her and, when she refused, killed her. There was a zip tie around her neck, but maybe the body was posed to look like she pulled it herself. As for Zachary—it sounds like she pleaded with him to help her find a way to die. Hers might have been an assisted suicide.

"And Councilman Koenig—if something like this got out he'd be ruined. Even if there was no way to prosecute for sexual assault and kidnapping, he has a reputation and a social prominence to lose. You do know he's part of one of Grand Island's founding families?"

"You've had him on your radar before?" Just saying that made Stephen's heart race. "Has he been investigated?"

"You know I can't answer that—if it's true. But no he's not on my radar. Chief Greywright filled me in on who's who in Grand Island last week. The man has a history and a track record of political shenanigans."

"Shenanigans? Whoa—where'd that word come from?" He looked at Laqueta and chuckled. "You're going to ruin your cultured image using words like that."

She joined him laughing.

"So you think I'm cultured. A snob."

"Cultured? Yes. A snob? Definitely not!" Stephen smiled and flicked his eyebrow. "Laqueta, you're one of the most elegant, secure, pleasant, articulate people I've ever met." He blushed.

"Thank you for the compliment. Not often a policewoman gets to hear that,"

Laqueta's cheeks flushed.

"Believe me it's true." Time to close his mouth before he made a fool of himself.

They both looked out at the ball diamond in an awkward peace.

"Why do you want to share this with the coroner before it goes to press?" Stephen asked.

Laqueta squinted.

Cautious, he thought.

"Two reasons. If he sees the possibility of foul play he might request I reopen the investigation. Technically, once he's ruled on the cause of death I cannot do further investigating. The matter is officially closed."

She paused and gave Steve that cautious look again.

"Yes?" he responded.

"Your last article questioned the coroner's job performance. This article might produce the same effect. What I'm trying to say is a preview copy would leave him forewarned. That's a much more comfortable position, especially for an elected official. Remember he *is* the County Attorney and here in Hall County that is an elected position. Am I making sense?"

He nodded. "Yeh, be careful about making enemies."

"Right."

"After what you said about Janice—do you think we have someone killing homeless people?" Stephen asked. "If so why? Or maybe we're having a rash of suicides—assisted or not. I guess it doesn't matter, in either case something needs to be done."

"Like what?" asked Laqueta. "Other than investigate."

Stephen locked his fingers together and put his thumbs into the stubble under his chin. "I don't know." A ball rolled toward the outfield fence. A blur of small legs scrambled after it.

Darren stood frozen at the plate.

The crowd screamed, "Go Darren. Go!"

"Run, Darren run," Laqueta shouted.

Stephen jumped to his feet screaming. Caught up in talking he'd missed Darren's turn at bat. "Keep going. Keep going. Go boy. Go! Take second!"

Darren slowed at second to look for the ball.

"Run!" his coach shouted.

"Go. Go!" the opposing coach yelled to encourage him on.

"All the way!" Stephen turned to slap high fives with Laqueta then back to see Darren. "Way to go son! I knew you could do it!"

Laqueta shot Stephen a surprised look. He blushed.

"That's my boy!" He gave Laqueta a crooked smile. "This calls for a celebration. My treat. What's Darren like to eat?"

"Pizza," she replied without hesitation. "He loves Pizza Hut pizza. And if you want to really celebrate buy him some cinnamon sticks. He'll go crazy."

"And what does the momma like?"

She blushed and looked down.

"Chocolate dunkers."

"Chocolate dunkers?"

"I'll share them with you."

Over pizza, Laqueta filled him in on details at the Janice Zahn crime scene.

The smell of anise and the empty Absinthe Roquette – 1797 bottle drew his attention. How could a homeless person afford that? And why? He asked a few questions about other items a homeless person might have in their nest, especially food and personal care items. Nothing else seemed unusual.

"Were there any letters? Brochures from traveling? Birth certificate? ID?"

"Are you trying to do a family notification again?" The corners of Laqueta's eyes creased. "The birth certificate was from Ohio. Chillicothe. The ID was from Missouri, a driver's license. I suspect after reading your story that the address is that of the lady she lived with. Most likely she sent away for the copy of the birth certificate so she could get the license. And, yes, there were some brochures. But, after reading her story, I see they matched her journey here. Otherwise, there was food stamp application correspondence and a personal letter—again from Missouri, different address. Probably from a co-worker. There was a check stub from her final pay, apparently sent to her via general delivery."

Laqueta cocked her head away from Stephen.

"I'm concerned that Janice never reported her abuse by Rainey White to our office. I'm the one who would have investigated it, you know. Maybe there's some way to let homeless women know that law enforcement—or at least I—am woman friendly in this town."

CHAPTER 39

"Mr. Stephen, Mr. Stephen, when we goin' to see those horses?"

Darren had remained quiet throughout Stephen and Laqueta's conversation. After stuffing himself—first with pizza then with cinnamon sticks—he placed his hands on his stomach, made a little groan, and collapsed against Stephen—he wouldn't sit by his mom.

"Horses?" Stephen laughed and Laqueta rolled her eyes.

"Depends on your mom. She hasn't given me an answer yet." He turned to face her. "Gramms' been asking again."

Laqueta twisted in her seat and straightened her shoulders. Stephen braced for a no.

"Gramms sounds like a charming person," she began calm and serious. "And the ranch sounds enchanting. But..."

She left him hanging, changed her expression saying so you have your answer.

He pursed his lips, shot her a slant eyed look then rose to the challenge.

"So..."

"Sooo...." She drew it out then paused. "So I guess tell Grams we'd love to come for your birthday."

"Yes!" Darren came alive and pumped his fist with Stephen. "You got ponies? I'm pretty short you know."

Stephen loved it when Darren played the serious, in charge little man.

"Nope!" Stephen squared his jaw. "You have to be a real man to ride my horse."

"I am a real man," Darren shot back and stretched his neck as high as he could.

"Well, I guess you are." Stephen nodded. "So I guess you can ride along with your mom and me."

"Whoa..." Laqueta's eyebrows rose. "Who said anything about me riding a horse? I don't think so."

"You don't ride horses?"

"No!"

"Ever tried."

"No! And I don't plan to."

"We'll see!" Stephen challenged her.

"No we won't."

He assayed her face and Darren looked up wide-eyed to see what would happen.

"Well," Stephen said matter-of-factly. "If you're going to be my friend you're going to have to learn to ride horses. After all, someday I'm going to inherit all of them and Darren's not going to be around forever to ride with me."

"Friend, huh?" She smiled and stood. "I like that."

Darren jumped from the booth into Stephen's arms and gave his head a big hug.

"I love you, Mr. Stephen."

CHAPTER 40

Quote from the Journal of a Killer:

The timing of death, like the ending of a story, gives a changed meaning to what preceded it.
Mary Catherine Bateson

Stephen completed the opening to the Janice Zahn article using the information from Laqueta then he revised the middle of the article—Janice's life story.

Now, did he dare put the cause of death as suicide? That was the official ruling. From that standpoint, it was accurate reporting. But what about from the standpoint of his own integrity? Would calling it suicide when he remained conflicted compromise his inner integrity? Would it be a lie?

He ducked the issue of his own indecision and decided on wording that stated the coroner ruled the death a suicide. The article needed to be to the publisher today.

The issue of conclusions remained. What could he say about the missed opportunities to help Janice? To be honest he didn't know if she refused services, was refused by the services, or never knew they existed. He decided to leave the conclusion until he talked to Captain Higgins.

And what of his goal of family notification, his desire to include a family response? Could he bear to speak to Janice's father and treat him like a bereaved parent given all he knew? Did the man even deserve to be notified? To let her father bury her seemed like the ultimate betrayal and the thought of the man putting on a show of grief or caring—that would be total hypocrisy. Time, however, dictated the answer. He didn't have time to wait for notification. Just barely enough time to do a little research and pass the results to Sally.

After a quick proofread, Stephen drug the article into the task bar and pulled up Internet Explorer.

He used Janice's birth date to search for a birth announcement in Chillicothe's local newspaper, The Chillicothe Gazette. Dead end. He clicked the link for paid archives. The cost was not listed. Too risky.

Noting a sidebar entry, he clicked on publicrecords.com. He filled out the information sheet. It did a search, charged a $1.00 fee then brought up a blank report form with a note to check back in three hours to see if more information came available. He didn't have three hours. Besides he doubted a birth record would be considered public records given how hard it was for homeless individuals to get them for identification purposes nowadays. That's when the solution popped into his mind. Laqueta said there had been a birth certificate at the crime scene. It would at least have Janice's father's name.

"Laqueta? Stephen here. Got a moment."

She laughed. "For you? Any time."

"I'm trying to find family contact information for Janice and remembered you said there was a birth certificate. That should have the father's name on it."

"Yes, it did. I checked because I thought she might have a single mother."

"Do you remember it?"

"I think it was Frank—Franklin. Or was that his middle name? Unusual names seem to stick in my memory. Didn't the coroner's office have it?"

Stephen sighed. "I talked to Sally over there yesterday. She said she couldn't find notification information. I assumed she didn't have his name."

"Maybe she overlooked it." Laqueta paused. "No, here's the original. Apparently I didn't send it to her." He heard some paper rustle. "Yes, that was his middle name. John Franklin Zahn. Says Janice was born in Chillicothe, Ohio, her mother in Frankfort, Maine, and her father also in Chillicothe. It gives a street address of 779 North Clinton Road. I wonder if he still lives there."

Someone called out in the background.

"Sorry, I have to go. Chief is calling me."

According to the White Pages, John F. Zahn still lived at 779 N. Clinton Road. Despite the growing trend to cellular, he also still had a landline. The listing showed an age of forty, which pretty much confirmed he was Janice's father. Stephen passed the information on to Sally who was glad to receive it. She didn't like loose ends.

"Sure wish I could get him charged with sexual abuse of a minor and incest," she said. "But I guess it's too late for that. Janice is already dead. It's a sick world."

Ten by the time he got off the phone, he plugged the names of Janice's parents into the article, printed it off, and headed to the Captain's office.

"Come in," Captain said. "Got that article for me to review."

He cleared his desk and Stephen handed him the edited draft.

"It needs a conclusion yet."

A raft of emotions crossed the Captain's face as he read. He marked a couple errors and placed a couple star marks. Other than an occasional uhuh or humm…he held all comments till the end.

"That's a tough story to read."

Stephen nodded.

"You think these stories about Rainey White and Koenig are true?"

"Rainey White—from what I'm learning from others—yes. In fact I need to talk to you about a Spanish couple. He's pimping the wife against her will. As far as Koenig, if the rest is true there's no reason Zachary would have made that up. Doubt if he's had any interaction with Koenig or any fight to pick."

Captain looked solemn. "Okay, but we'll need to take out their names. We can't play judge and jury and we can't afford a liable suit. You can keep the details just remove the names. Otherwise, I like it…powerful. Gets across a different side of homelessness.

"Now, about the ending? What's on your mind?"

"Well, Laqueta thinks this might not be a suicide and I'm undecided. When she read the draft last night she thought it was possible Rainey came back for Janice and killed her when she refused to be a victim again. Or, she said, Koenig might have gotten scared and decided to silence her. That one I'm not so sure of. But, maybe it was an assisted suicide. In that case Zachary would be a suspect, but I just don't see someone with his compassion killing anybody. Anyway, the info has me sort of mentally blocked."

"I understand." Captain was gentle. "But let's put all of that aside. What can we do about a situation like Janice's? How do we want people to react to this story? We may have to tell them how to react."

Stephen nodded and waited for Captain to continue.

"An appeal for money would be an insult—to Janice's memory and to the thinking public—and more than a few of them will read this article."

"We really don't have anything to offer a Janice Zahn." Stephen frowned. "So asking for referrals to us would be a waste of time. The problem is we need a way to find out the life stories of the homeless and we need a way to get homeless victims to come forward to the police."

"See…." Captain gave him a fatherly smile. "You do have some thoughts on the issue though I'd remind you that we do have something we can do for the Janice Zahn's of the world. We can connect them to resources."

"Yeh…," Stephen's pessimism showed. "But who's got the time to dig out the resources or even to draw out the story. I don't have time to build relationships with these people. And this is Grand Island. There's probably not enough need to justify a fulltime worker. Who could do it?"

"Who?" Captain threw the question back at Stephen,

Stephen pressed his lips together, cocked his eyebrows and then, just before he blurted out no one, his face relaxed. His smile returned.

"The public. We need the public to get involved. If people made a habit of saying hi to the homeless. Offering them a bit of encouragement. Asking questions. When the stories come out they could send them to law enforcement or to see me. We need the public to be the eyes on the street. It would change their whole view of homeless people."

"Preach it boy!" said Captain. They both laughed. "Now go write that down. Sounds to me like a perfect ending to the story. Gives people something simple to do. I like it."

Stephen nodded and smiled again.

"Make those few corrections, put in an alias for Rainey White—say that's what you've done—and simply call Koenig a local councilman and I think you've got it. Looks like you can turn it in by noon. You don't need to bring it back to me. I trust you."

CHAPTER 41

Quote from the Journal of a Killer:

Death will be a great relief.
Katharine Hepburn

Stephen picked up a Thai wrap from the Chocolate Bar on his way back from the Independent. It disappeared too quickly leaving him once again staring at a blank computer screen. He caught up the client entries from the shelter and food pantry. There were no grants or contracts to be worked on in June. Thank God! He hated writing grant and contract proposals.

He made several calls regarding donations—mostly food items—and the initial call to Stuhr Museum to coordinate this year's fund raising Prairie Mud Run. Those jobs done, the blank computer screen dared him to click on. But, not to be intimidated by technology, he chose to see Captain about Rainey White.

"Got a minute?" he asked as he leaned his chest on the doorframe.

Captain swiveled from a small desk where he worked on special projects and looked at Stephen expectantly.

"Girlfriend problems?" he teased.

"No! He never knew what this father-figure might ask.

"What about that investigator? Pretty hot."

Stephen blushed at Captain's use of the word hot. "She's black."

"So—so was Jesus' grandmother. You got something against that, Mister Open-Minded?"

"No," Stephen stammered and changed the subject.

"Can we do something about Rainey White? What he does is chilling. You ever experienced something like this before?"

"Unfortunately, yes." Captain's moustache dipped in a half frown. "Once this guy in the food program at Minot started to lean on young men for sex in return for drugs or girls. I called him in and confronted him. Let him know I had two guys ready to file criminal complaints plus the names and addresses of the girls involved. That canned it. At least no one complained to me anymore and he stopped doing solicitation on our property."

"I guess you have."

"Then there's always the occasional guy leaning directly on women for sex. I handled them the same way, though sometimes I had to bluff because the ladies weren't willing to press charges. Homeless women don't usually want to attract attention to themselves. I think they carry more shame for their condition than the men.

"I don't think I've had anybody doing actual physical harm though. Been afraid of it, especially towards teenaged guys and young girls, but this is the first time those crimes have caught up with us."

Stephen leaned back and rested against the opposite side of the doorframe.

"We could ban Rainey from eating here. That might slow things down," he suggested.

"But what would we accuse him of. Usually banning depends on being drunk or high and disruptive. Occasionally there's some rough cob who's picking fights. But I don't recall banning someone because of accusations of criminal activity. Even registered sex offenders are allowed in the feeding program—though that's more because we can't check every diner."

Captain looked up when Stephen paused.

"By the way, have you approached your girlfriend for ideas on anything she can do?"

"She's not my girlfriend…but no, we haven't discussed what law enforcement can do. Remember, all the victims we know of are either dead or unwilling to go to the police. Mostly out of fear."

"Then, maybe that's something we can address. Seems we mentioned creating a comfort zone towards the police when finishing your article this morning. Maybe God's trying to tell us something. Maybe this is one of the answers to what he wants the Salvation Army to do."

"Maybe." Stephen remained unenthusiastic. "At any rate I can see if Rainey's on the sex offender list and discuss options with Laqueta. You know, last night she wondered if there was anything the Salvation Army could do to create a comfort zone toward law enforcement, or at least toward herself. Maybe God is saying something here?

"Thanks, Captain." He turned and walked back to his office.

He considered a call to Laqueta, but for some reason felt uneasy like he was forgetting something. Nothing came to mind, so he decided to do something productive with the last hour of his day. He opened the National Sex Offender Registry search page, typed in Rainey White, and hit enter.

There he was. Rainey White, State of Wyoming, Green River, and a motel address. He checked the supporting pages for the entry and found unresolved charges including failure to register as a sex offender. Time to call Laqueta.

He looked up at the clock. Three twenty two.

Adrenaline jolted him to attention. He'd promised to pick up Darren at half past to go practice batting and catching the ball. No time to change. He'd have to jump in the car to get to the school on time. They could go by his apartment and change there.

CHAPTER 42

Quote from the Journal of a Killer:

Because of indifference,
one dies before one actually dies.
Elie Wiesel

The next morning the National Sex Offender Registry page sat open on Stephen's computer. Rainey was not registered in Nebraska, which explained why he didn't stay in the shelter when he arrived. He was too scared. All Salvation Army shelters checked the national sex offender registry before accepting a client.

Stephen realized he'd forgotten to say something to Laqueta last night.

He decided to check the other tabs under Rainey White before he called. Multiple offenses in California, Las Vegas, and Green River, Wyoming. Recent entries included Deadwood and Sturgis, South Dakota. Nothing in Nebraska yet despite the pattern of re-offending.

Every location, even California where he first came to the court's attention, included failure to register as a sex offender. Short stints in jail for that failure lasted six months or less. With the sexual offenses arranged chronologically, the time between convictions represented how long it took for him to get caught rather than breaks in offending. So far, in Nebraska, no one had stepped forward to file charges so Rainey managed to stay off law enforcement radar.

Next he entered Rainey White into the Google search bar.

"Wow!" The exclamation slid out.

Three hundred listings about Rainey White. The whole first page of sites related to his crimes. Articles and interviews revealed an arrogant sadomasochist—a show off, when caught. How was it possible he spent such little time in jail?

Stephen put the Google responses in time order.

Rainey was escalating. Not that he'd been any less criminally engaged. There were huge numbers of alleged victims from the beginning. But, with so few willing to testify, he'd won acquittals, light probationary periods, banning from schools and churches, and other off the radar sentences. It was unreal. Wyoming featured forcible rape but the witness refused to cooperate after charges were filed. Allegations of nonsexual violence surfaced in South Dakota, but there he disappeared from custody.

On Janice and Marta, he left a distinct personal mark—a classic form of escalation. Maybe he did kill Janice. If so, would Marta die next?

I wonder if Laqueta can do anything—he shook his head—*without an official complaint.*

A string of eighteen families needed food boxes. His arms ached from hauling out thirty two boxes.

He broke for lunch.

Back at the computer Stephen flipped through a couple more pages of Rainey White entries and was just about to shut the search down when a different headline caught his attention—"Local Student Receives an American Academy of Forensic Psychology (AAFP) Dissertation Award."

The muscles across his shoulder blades tensed.

"Award given to graduate students conducting dissertations in applied areas of law and psychology, with preference shown for dissertations addressing clinical-forensic issues."

The award winner was Rainy White. The perpetrator was an expert in the clinical-forensic psychology of serial sexual offenders.

"Sick!"

"You talking to yourself?" Captain stuck his head in the door.

"No, just to anybody who might hear."

"Who's plucked your feathers?"

"This guy's a serial sex offender, but listen to this." He read the award title to the captain.

"You talking about Rainey White?"

"Yes." Stephen read the entry out loud. "Wait, here's another one. 'Doctor Rainey White, UC-San Diego Professor of Criminal Psychology received the American Academy of Forensic Psychology Saleem Shah Award for Early Career Excellence in Psychology and Law!"

CHAPTER 43

Quote from the Journal of a Killer:

Fly on proud bird
You're free at last.
Unknown

SATURDAY NIGHT, JUNE 16, 2012:

Ten fifteen at night. Cedar scented the air where Henry Many Horses leaned against the downspout of the Red Cross Blood Donation Center just beyond the downtown on East Third Street. Hank had a scratched face and his hair puffed out—pulled loose in his ponytail. It looked like Hank had stumbled and hit the wall. But something more than falling down happened. His shirt was buttoned two holes off, his underwear was pulled up to his rib cage, and his pants were twisted. He'd tried to put them on backwards.

When Zachary touched his shoulder, Hank flinched. Hank looked up at Zachary like a toddler in trouble. "Rainey not friend!"

"What do you mean?" Zachary brushed tear-matted hair from the young man's cheek.

Hank lifted his head.

"Rainey hurt me. I take bath and Rainey hurt me!"

Hank pulled his unfastened pants open, tugged the crotch of his underwear aside, and pointed at his torn, bleeding anus.

Zachary removed the hands, straightened and zipped Hank's pants.

"Thank you," the little boy voice said. "Hank have trouble."

"Yes, I see," said Zachary. "Here let me button your shirt. Okay?"

"Okay."

Hank watched as Zachary re-buttoned the shirt and straightened the tails.

"Hank scared. Hank ran away. Hurry too much. Can't get clothes right."

"I know. It's okay."

Zachary had an overwhelming urge to hug Hank, to rock him gently in his arms, but this wasn't a little boy. Hank was a man. A bigger man than Zachary.

"What are you doing here?"

"I lost. Don't know where to go. Zachary help?"

Hank's innocence disarmed Zachary but he had no idea where Hank stayed. Where he might be safe from human predators.

"Okay. What Hank want to do?" It was so easy to slip into baby talk and mimic Hank's own wording.

"Happy Hunting Ground," he replied shaking his head and widening his eyes.

This must be the way little children are, Zachary thought, *always ask for an inch then grasp a mile. Thinking adults can make fantasies come true."*

"Momma say, 'If there trouble, go to Happy Hunting Ground.'"

Hank didn't understand death. He thought the Happy Hunting Ground was somewhere you walk too and then the Big Bear takes your hand and walks you across a shallow place in the water.

"Maybe you have to get ready to go first. Maybe that's why your mother told you to go for help. Sometimes it takes many years to get ready to go to the Happy Hunting Ground."

"Hank want to go now." Those big demanding eyes told everything. "Zachary help me. Hank wash bottom get clean to go?"

Zachary shook his head yes then no and tried to formulate a plan to distract him.

Hank squinted at him, confused.

"You have to go on a vision quest first. Yes."

"Yes. Like big boys in Sun Dance tepee. Boy's bleed. Have vision. Mamma tell me Hank need to have vision. Momma say family help Hank have vision," Hank looked down at the grass. "Hank no have family. Zachary help Hank get new family, yes? Zachary help Hank have vision?"

"Zachary Hank's friend, yes?"

Hank nodded. "Zachary Hank's friend. Rainey no friend no more. Yes?"

Zachary chuckled. "No, Rainey is not your friend anymore." Hank smiled and mimicked Zachary's chuckle. "If Hank and Zachary were blood brothers we'd be family."

"Blood brothers." Hank struggled to say the words and frowned…then his eyes brightened. "Big boys bleed, become brothers. We be brothers. Hank have vision."

How could the mentally handicapped have such insight?

Zachary took Hank's wrist and turned it inside up in his own hand. "Zachary knows how to make blood brothers. But it might hurt."

He looked questioning into Hank's eyes and Hank frowned. "Hurt? Like Rainey. Zachary want to hurt Hank like Rainey?"

"No! No, not like Rainey. Just a little hurt with a knife." He traced a short line across Hank's wrist. "To make us brothers. I cut a little mark on my wrist." He demonstrated on himself. Then I make a cut on Hank." He lifted his eyebrows and look into Hank's eyes.

Hank mimicked with his eyebrows, but concern rounded his eyes.

"We have to share our blood. Then we become blood brothers and Hank has a family again."

"Share blood?" Hank spoke soft and slow.

"Cut." Zachary marked the spot on their wrists again. "Bleed. Then we put the cuts together."

He put their wrists together.

"Then we brothers. Family, yes?"

Zachary lifted a switchblade from his pocket. He made a light cut across the wrist of his own arm. A thin line of blood formed. He turned the inside of Hank's arm up again and rested it in his hand.

"Now Zachary cut Hank?"

Hank pulled his shoulder back, scrunched up his face, and closed his eyes but left his wrist in Zachary's hand. Zachary gripped it tightly, drew the blade across. Blood immediately flowed.

Hank opened his eyes.

"Does it hurt?" Zachary asked.

"No."

Zachary laid Hank's cut across his own then griped their wrists together.

Hank grinned widely and wrapped his fingers around Zachary's wrist. A perfect blood brothers' hold. They both laughed and sat there for a long time with their wrists together satisfied, sharing a moment of life unified while occasional drops of blood floated down into the grass—a moment Zachary dreamed of as a boy.

Finally Zachary relaxed his grip.

Hank touched the dried blood around both cuts.

"Brothers," he said.

Using his other hand, he unbuttoned his shirt and pulled it open revealing his upper chest. He flexed the muscles then reached out with his 'brothers' hand and took the knife into his own hand. Ceremonially he raised it toward his chest touching the tip lightly on his skin.

"Now Hank get vision." He smiled as he looked into Zachary's eyes.

"No."

"Yes," Hank retorted and puckered up his whole face.

"No," Zachary said putting his hand over the knife. "Not that way."

"But big boys bleed here." Hank pounded his fist against his chest. "Blood for vision here."

"Not for Hank," Zachary said firmly.

The defiance weakened in Hank's eyes.

"Hank's blood for vision comes from here." He pointed at Hanks cut wrist. "You have to let the blood run down from here." He hung his own cut arm down till his hand pointed toward the grass.

"Lean back on the wall, close your eyes, and wait for a vision—pictures in your mind. That's how Hank gets a vision."

The boy-man nodded like a young boy claiming to understand what he does not. On a man sized body it looked like full understanding.

"When you see your vision, you put your other hand over the cut." Zachary demonstrated. "Hold it until it stops bleeding. Then when the time is right you'll be ready to cross the big river into the Happy Hunting Ground. Understand?"

"Zachary help Hank. Yes?"

"No. A vision quest has to happen on your own. You have to do this for yourself."

He handed Hank the knife and mimed reopening the wrist wound.

"I'll come back tomorrow to check on you. Okay?"

The deep shadow of a cedar bush would hide Hank through the night. The air was warm, it didn't show any sign of rain. It would not be a problem for Hank to sleep outside while he waited for Zachary to come back.

"We'll find your home tomorrow. Okay?" He stood to go. "Don't forget to stop the blood." As he demonstrated how to apply pressure, uncertainty crept across Hank's face. "What?"

"Hank afraid to make cut. Momma say, 'Don't play with knife. Dangerous.' Zachary cut. Hank stop blood." Henry Many Horses held Zachary's eyes for a long time then, when Zachary did not respond, his chin began to slip toward his chest.

Zachary's eyes hardened. His forehead tightened then he took the knife and quickly sliced Hank's wrist open again. He placed Hank's arm down and watched the blood flow until it pooled in the grass, closed Hank's eyes, clicked the switchblade shut, and walked away.

CHAPTER 44

Quote from the Journal of a Killer:

Watching a peaceful death of a human being
reminds us of a falling star; one of a million lights in a vast sky
that flares up for a brief moment only to disappear
into the endless night forever.
Elisabeth Kübler-Ross

EARLY MORNING, JUNE17, 2013:

The call woke Laqueta at five twenty eight Sunday morning just after she'd slipped into a deep sleep.

Silhouetted against the west wall of the Red Cross Blood Donation Center a young officer spotted a sleeping vagrant. Odd but not uncommon. A pungent spicy smell, not the alcohol he expected, tweaked his nose as he stooped to shake the tall Indian.

No response.

Routine for drunks and vagrants.

"Get up you drunken sot!" he commanded. "Come on."

A steel toed pushed.

Again, no response.

"Come on, you old stiff." The officer leaned in to shake him but straightened without a touch. He checked the sole of his right boot then stepped back from the pool of blood beside his left boot.

"Secure the scene." Laqueta tried to sound authoritative in spite of needing to yawn.

"Yes, ma'am."

She took a quick shower, laid out a clean uniform, had a breakfast shake with a slice of toast and butter, then put on her face while she decided what to do with Darren.

God help me. This is Sunday. Where can I find somebody today? The desk is only staffed one deep. That won't work. Maybe the desk sergeant could help her locate someone.

She gathered toys and clothes for Darren. If he had to wait at the office for someone to come, he'd be satisfied with a breakfast bar and milk from the vending machine. The toys carried to the car, she left the backdoor open so she could easily put a sleepy boy into his toddler seat.

"Momma?" Darren said then laid his head on her shoulder.

"It's okay, honey. You have to go to work with Momma while I find somebody to take care of you."

"Stephen," he said groggily.

"Stephen?"

"Supposed to play ball with Mr. Stephen."

She'd forgotten the play date.

"Stephen?"

He sounded raspy. She almost didn't want to say anything.

"Sorry to call so early but I have to cancel the play date."

"What time is it?"

She heard him jockey the clock.

"What's the matter?"

"I've been called in on an investigation."

"This time of morning? What is it?"

"They found a man dead down by the Red Cross Donation Center. That's all I know so far. But I doubt if I'll be finished before one."

"One of mine?'

"It's too early to know," she repeated. "Look I have to go."

"Wait."

She heard him just before she disconnected.

"What about Darren?"

Oh, please. I don't have time for this.

"I'm taking him to the office. I'll have to find someone from there." Short and firm.

"I'll take him." He paused. "That's if you'll let me. I don't mind."

Silence.

"I can't ask you to do that."

"You're not. I asked you."

He sounded wide-awake now.

"Give me five minutes. I'll come by the office and get him. Okay?"

"Oh. I don't know."

He did not give her even a second to object.

"I'll meet you. He'll be in good hands. I'll even take him to church—your church. See you there."

And like that he hung up.

Laqueta remembered their conversation the first time they met. *He sure has learned to be assertive.* She found herself not knowing how to take it. But, it didn't matter. *God heard that prayer. Thank you God. Thank you for Stephen.*

At the Law Enforcement Center, Stephen was waiting in the parking lot; backdoor open, ready for Darren. He transferred him seat and all and Darren nuzzled Stephen's neck when he reached over to secure the seatbelt.

"What class is he in?"

Laqueta gave him a blank look.

"At Sunday School…what class does Darren attended?"

"Ms. Philip's."

"What about church? Does he go to the nursery or is there a children's church?"

He was so parental and focused. Laqueta smiled.

"I prefer to keep him with me. He's been in big church his whole life. You shouldn't have any problems."

"Good," pronounced Stephen with one sharp nod. "That's the way I like it. We should have great fun. Call me when you're free. Otherwise don't worry. We'll catch a bite to eat. Play ball. Maybe go for a ride in the country. Who knows? Oh, does he still take a nap?"

She nodded.

"What time?"

"Usually about two. If he doesn't fall asleep on his own, on Sundays I put him down for an hour at three. But you don't have to do that. I'll be home by then."

"Call me."

He closed his door and they were gone.

"So, what do we have here?" Laqueta asked the officer at the scene.

"Looks like a suicide. Sliced wrist."

"You the one who discovered it?"

"Yes, ma'am."

"Anything been moved?"

"No ma'am. I started to touch his shoulder to wake him. Thought it was just some passed out drunk. Then I saw that pool of blood by his hand. Almost stepped in it, but I stepped back to here and haven't been any closer till you got here."

"Thanks, Quinn. It is Quinn isn't it?"

"Yes, ma'am."

Laqueta slipped on her vinyl gloves as she surveyed the area around the body. She checked for footprints or signs of struggle in the grass. Nothing. But when she moved closer she found three sizes of shoe impressions near the body. One, about a size ten, looked to be the victim's. Another significantly smaller—say a size six—partially overlapped the ten but still no sign of a struggle and no sign the second person had sat down. The toe impressions of the size six—pointed toward the body—indicated someone stood or squatted by the victim for a considerable while.

On the other side of the body, the officer's boot print was visible just as he said only an inch or less from the dark pool of blood. The blood trailed from a cut above the wrist. She stepped back and took a generous amount of pictures including digital video and close ups of the foot prints, blood pool, cut on the arm, and the face of the victim. Despite the second set of footprints, the initial impressions suggested a suicide.

Laqueta pulled the cell phone from the clip on her belt and located the coroner's number. However, she stopped short of calling. Her gut said she needed more time alone before the disruption of the County Attorney. Lessig's lack of training often got in the way.

She checked the cut. Definitely smooth indicating a well made, well cared for blade or razor. She checked around the body for the instrument but found nothing.

"Quinn, you seen a knife or razor blade?"

"No, ma'am."

"Could you do a search for me—within throwing range. Say sixty feet. But put up the Crime Scene tape first. Okay?"

He grunted.

It was unusual for a suicide victim to throw his blade or razor. But then it was unusual for a male to commit suicide by slitting the wrist. Hanging and gunshot were the two most common means of adult male suicide.

She removed a thin wallet from the victim's right rear pocket. Henry Many Horses. No middle name. The South Dakota ID listed a Spring Creek address. Another document showed he was an enrolled member of the Sicangu Oyate tribe of the Rosebud Nation.

The coroner's office answering service informed her that County Attorney Lesig was currently in Washington DC at training for coroners put on by the National Association of Medical Examiners. Calls were being referred to the Hall County Medical Examiner.

The County Medical Examiner was a contract position responsible for forensic examination of bodies. The contract, held by the St. Francis Medical Center, utilized its own fulltime forensic staff. Dr. Avery Winston, the lead forensic pathologist, usually responded and was Laqueta's contact for today.

"Dr. Winton? Investigator Ellison. Sorry to interrupt your morning."

"That's okay; I just stepped out from early mass. What do we have?"

"Possible suicide by the Red Cross building. But I'm suspicious."

"Okay. Be there in ten."

She turned to watch Officer Quinn finish the crime scene tape then together they searched all areas within an arc sixty feet from Henry's body. They thoroughly searched the branches and upper reaches of bushes in case a blade had lodged there. Nothing found, Officer Quinn called the station and requested a ladder to facilitate checking the roof and gutters. Conceivably the blue and grey grains of the roof could camouflage a razor or small knife. She doubted they would find anything, but investigation protocols demanded thorough consideration of even unlikely scenarios.

"Good morning, officers."

Doctor Winston arrived and proceeded immediately to the body.

"Let us know when you need assistance."

Laqueta stood back about three feet observing and ready to answer questions. She knew that he preferred to investigate the scene for himself first before entertaining others opinions or input.

"Looks like death by exsanguination. Probable cause of death—suicide by cutting the volar interosseous and seriously nicking the ulnar artery causing two streams of blood…" He paused to point to the two blood trails on Henry's arm. "… which joined just above the ulnar making one stream to the pool in the grass. There are actually two cuts."

He rolled back the edge of what appeared to be one large cut.

"The first narrower and less deep but cutting open the volar interosseous, the smaller vein. This cut formed an initial clot sealing off the wound. This is similar to the attention getting cuts made by young people and the cuts made in blood-brother rituals. The second cut—apparently the same blade—cut deeper severing the volar interosseous. It appears to have been made by the tip end of the blade with considerable pressure. That allowed it make a shallow cut in the ligaments here. The pressure caused the tip of the blade to drop down the side of this tendon and catch the ulnar here before being reflected away by the flexor carpi ulnaris. This second cut would have been difficult to self inflict and given the trajectory of the wound was most likely made from above, again an unlikely angle for a self inflicted wound."

Dr. Winston stood and brushed a knuckle across the tip of his nose as if pushing the scent of the blood away.

"That said, I don't think the cutter knew what he was doing. The offending wounds may have been with suicidal intentions, most likely requiring assistance, or a combination of a purposeful initial cut and an accidental second cut.

"The blood pressure in the ulnar artery would have been sufficient to keep a small but steady flow from the ulnar nick and the severing of the smaller artery probably kept it bleeding for some time. The exsanguination was slow and steady with the victim likely passing out prior to death. It is conceivable the victim expected to stop the flow from the second cut but did not recognize the signs that the point of no return was being breached.

"This one's going to be a hard call for Mr. Lesig.

"Did you find the blade?"

"No," Laqueta replied. "I assumed the cut could have been from a razor or a blade, but we found neither."

"A razor you can rule out. Not strong enough. The width of the cut requires a thicker blade."

Dr. Winston looked pensive.

"You didn't find a blade? That's odd. Certainly seems to support a second person involved."

"Maybe a second person stole the knife. From your description of the wound, the blade must have been a quality instrument—hunting knife, precision switchblade. I have foot imprints where a second person sat very close to the body. Probably close enough to remove a knife. A knife of that kind could be pawned for enough to buy a cheap bottle of gin."

She made a mental note to check the pawnshops and local gun shops.

"What about blood samples?" she asked. "You certainly have a big enough pool."

"Yes. And I'll take a generous sample there." He was already removing a vial from his examination bag. But I'm going to take several swabs from around the wounds, especially those dried areas above the cut. If there was some kind of blood sharing ritual I might find multiple DNA there. You got the finger prints you need? I noticed some in the dried blood."

"Yes, I lifted them while you were on your way. Several from the arm around and above the cut and of course the victim's fingers."

"So, you're done with the body?"

"Yes."

"Good. I'm anxious to get started this afternoon. I'll call you if anything helpful turns up. Actually, I'll call you when the DNA tests are done and let you know if we have one or more persons' blood."

By the time Laqueta drove back to her office, processed the evidence, and completed the initial reports it was already two thirty. She had removed all the contents from Henry's pocket after the body was lifted on a gurney and slipped what appeared to be a talisman from around his neck. She'd also removed his boots for further inspection.

George from the Independent called.

"Yes. Officer Quinn discovered the body about five thirty this morning on the west side of the Red Cross Building near the wall. There is not much I can say. We are investigating the death. As usual, no name is being released pending notification of next of kin."

She listened to George's comments and further questions then added, "The cause of death is under investigation. That's all I wish to add at this time." She sidestepped a question about the victim being an alcoholic or homeless. Even if she knew she wasn't ready to go there. Her relationship with George was pleasant. Courteous, but professional.

"Ready to get rid of a little boy?"

Stephen laughed.

"Absolutely not! We're having a load of fun."

"Where can I find you?" Actually, she'd rather go home.

"Down at Stolley Park. Darren fell asleep on the bench watching soccer. I decided not to move him."

Laqueta hoped he'd stay asleep.

"Hey," Stephen said, clearly alive and energetic. "We gotta buy this boy a soccer ball. Armando brought one over while the other guy's were playing and kicked around a few balls with him. The sprout loved it. He fell asleep with the ball in his hands. By the way, have you eaten yet?"

"No." Laqueta sighed. "I just finished my paperwork and I'm walking to the car right now."

"Let's go to Freddie's Steak Burgers? I could meet you there."

"You know. I'd rather just go home."

"You want me to keep Darren a while?"

"No. I just want to get home and back to a normal Sunday. I'm mentally exhausted."

She was thankful for the momentary pause before Stephen responded.

"Tell you what. I'll swing by and pick up dinner from Freddie's Burgers and meet you at your house. You go on and get settled in. We'll exchange burgers and boy and you can get on with a quieter afternoon."

Laqueta was in the shower when Stephen arrived. Awkward.

When she didn't answer the door quickly, she heard him push it open and call out, "It's Stephen. Where shall I put Darren?"

"He can lie on the couch," she called down. "Sorry, I'm in the shower."

"You want me to wait till you come down?"

He sounded nervous.

"No. It's alright. Just lock the door so Darren can't get out. Okay?"

"Sure—I'll set the burgers on the island in the kitchen."

She heard footsteps then quiet. The door closed and Stephen's key from the morning turned in the dead bolt.

CHAPTER 45

Quote from the Journal of a Killer:

Do not stand at my grave and weep,
I am not there, I do not sleep.

When you wake in the morning hush,
I am the swift, uplifting rush
Of quiet birds in circling flight.
I am the soft starlight at night.

Do not stand at my grave and weep.
I am not there, I do not sleep.
Do not stand at my grave and cry.
I am not there, I did not die!
Do Not Weep by Mary Frye

What next? Stephen wondered as he unlocked the north door of the Salvation Army building. After eight hours with Darren, Stephen couldn't stand going home alone. He felt jumpy, adrenaline charged—like trying to shut down midgame after an injury. In the office quiet, he'd unwind and clear up the miscellaneous paperwork on his desk.

When the volunteer workers arrived at three thirty to prepare the Sunday evening meal, he headed into the kitchen.

"Hey, Joe," he greeted the team leader. Maintaining motivated happy volunteers required face time as well as phone calls. "How's it going?"

"Well…"

Stephen tried not to stiffen.

"Seems we've pissed off Andy again. Guess we're not supposed to use Salvation Army silverware or milk. That man's crazy. Plastic flatware won't work for home cooked meals and he's never complained about milk before."

Stephen addressed the communication issues then circulated to speak to each of the other fifteen volunteers present. When his cell phone rang, the caller ID read Laqueta Ellison so he excused himself and took the call.

"Thanks Stephen. I really appreciated your help today. My usual on call sitter's out of town the next two weeks. On the weekend, there are no personnel at work who can help."

She sounded refreshed, her voice that of a friend not an on duty investigator.

"The pleasure's mine.'" He smiled remembering vignettes of his time with Darren. "You know I love that kid. And eight hours together didn't spoil it."

Laqueta's relaxed laugh was thanks enough.

"I hope you don't mind. I used the key to take him home before church to get his Sunday clothes. He wanted 'the right clothes' to wear. Awfully set in his ways for a small boy." He laughed before continuing. "You should have seen his eyes when he woke up and saw me. He was in my arms in a heartbeat. Did I tell you how much I love that kid?"

"Yes. Only about a hundred times a day and a dozen already in this conversation." She laughed out loud.

"Sorry about the shower," she said.

"Hey—that's okay. You should expect privacy in your own home. I had my arms full so felt for the knob and came on in. I'm sorry. I was just thinking about getting Darren laid down."

"And I'm used to the door being locked when I'm in the shower." She gave a self-conscious chuckle. "Actually, I left the door ajar so you could get in without waking him. It's my own fault and you were the perfect gentleman."

"You just didn't see me blush and hide my eyes," he teased and they laughed again.

"By the way, was the victim one of ours—a homeless man?"

"Who said it was a man?" She half teased. "Yes, it was a man, about my age. Native American I think. Actually, I'm pretty sure. He's a registered member of the Rosebud Tribe, so Sioux I suppose. He had one of your cards in his pocket so I suspect he was homeless."

Stephen couldn't remember giving a Native American his card recently, but he didn't mention it.

"Can you describe him? Maybe I've seen him at breakfast. I'm trying to get in there on a regular basis and start meeting the people. You know, do a little prevention work."

"The ID said five nine. Slim built but broad shoulders. And for what it's worth he had large feet. There was a little talisman around his neck...."

Stephen interrupted her. "...long silky black hair? Classic Indian ponytail but no headband? A medicine pouch beaded—several rows of mostly white beads—with a deerskin cord?"

"I take it you've met."

"Not yet. I saw him at a couple meals, that's all."

"The meals confirm he's homeless, I suppose. Nothing on him to indicate why he's in Grand Island. No money in his wallet just a faded picture of him with his mother, I think, a twist of pine needles tied with red thread, a flat thing—I think it's a porcupine quill, and some paper with scribbles on it. More like a child's wallet than that of a twenty nine year old man.

"Oh. And thanks for the Freddie's Burger. That little bit of food really brought my energy back and helped emotionally too. I've never had a Freddie's. It was very good. Again, thank you. You'd think you were my mother the way you take care of me—but you're the wrong color."

"And the wrong sex if you haven't noticed!"

She chuckled.

"I won't keep you longer. Just wanted to say thank you right away. By the way, Darren's still sleeping. I think you wore him out. Oh, my phone just beeped—it's the medical examiner."

CHAPTER 46

Quote from the Journal of a Killer:

Live life, if you can, with dignity and meaning.
When you can't ask for assistance
And if you must, to restore dignity and meaning,
Let the honor of death restore your soul
And bring you a new life
The Journal of a Killer

The information about Henry Many Horses piqued Stephen's interest. He sensed another interesting article. He turned his chair and faced the computer screen. Surely a name like Henry Many Horses would be on the web. The first entry—"Local man missing from reservation."

On www.rosebudsiouxtribe-nsn.gov, the home page asked for help locating Henry (Hank) Many Horses who had walked off from a Memorial Day celebration at the Indian cemetery in Spring Creek where he had also visited his mother's grave. Before leaving the adult care home where he lived, he told staff several times that his mother had said when I am gone, go find help. She'd pointed out the door of their house, so Henry kept trying to walk away from the care home, always walking south—the direction of the door at his mother's house.

A thorough search of roads leading south turned up nothing. Announcements on the radio stations in Rapid City, Valentine,

Chadron, and even O'Neil, Nebraska, yielded no responses. Current efforts concentrated on stretches of open land populated by trees along creeks on the Rosebud Reservation and south into Cherry County, Nebraska. A search of the Samuel R. McKelvie National Forest was occurring even while Stephen read the computer article.

Hope of survival remained high. Hank was a healthy sturdy male and water was easy to find in the search areas. However, Hank's extremely limited mental capacity placed him in extreme danger. The search had to be conducted as if for a three year old child.

Anyone with possible information was asked to call the Rosebud governmental offices.

Stephen dialed the numbers.

A woman answered.

"Little Willow speaking. Cante waste nape ciyuzapelo!" (We shake your hand with a good heart!)

"Do you know Henry Many Horses?" An awkward question.

"Yes! We are family. Everyone in the tribe is family, but I am his mother's first cousin. Do you know where he is?"

The excitement in Little Willow's voice made Stephen's stomach drop. He'd forgotten he would be giving a death notice.

"I'm sorry. Yes."

He paused to let her prepare.

A deathly quiet settled over the other end of the signal.

"He's in Grand Island, Nebraska. We found him this morning beside a building downtown—I'm sorry, but he's dead."

He heard Little Willow weep.

"Did he starve to death?" The words were choked by tears.

"No. I work at the Salvation Army and he has been eating in our dining room every day, so he did not starve to death."

"Then how did he die?"

Stephen hesitated. "I really can't say. The medical examiner and Investigator Ellison are exploring that right now so the cause of death has not been determined."

"Was it a violent death?"

"I don't think so, but again I don't have all the details. Tell me," he continued, "Did Henry have any close relatives? I see from your article that his mother died and he was staying at a care home."

"Yes, his mother died a little more than three weeks ago. Her memory is very alive with us still. We cousins are his closest blood relatives but in the Sioux culture everyone in your tribe is family. We all care for each other, especially our vulnerable ones. Can we come get his body?"

"That, I'm afraid will be up to the County Coroner. Again, I'm sorry. I did not call to notify you of his death. I was just exploring his life so we could put an appropriate article in the paper. I didn't expect anyone to be in the office on a Sunday. I can give you the coroner's number and, if you wish, the number of the investigating officer. Okay?"

"Oh, yes, please. Thank you."

They continued talking about Henry's life. What happens next—in the mourning and burial customs—fascinated Stephen. The information would really round out the article. He gave Little Willow the contact numbers and she gave him her office number again as well as her cell phone number. He reassured her he would pass them along to Laqueta and Sally. Despite the accidental death notice, this was definitely better than miscellaneous paper work—at least closer to what gave his heart satisfaction.

He hung up—*I wonder who will be next*—and immediately dialed Laqueta.

CHAPTER 47

Quote from the Journal of a Killer:

We all need the freedom to die noble in a life
that has been unworthy of us,
being subject to sin and emptiness.
Sorin Cerin

"Isn't Javier Ruiz-Lobo the Mexican refugee you talked about?"

It was Laqueta's second call to Stephen that Saturday.

First, at two PM, she called to see if he could help entertain Darren—almost déjà vu from a week ago. She'd promised Darren a trip to see the Kool-Aid display to the Hasting Museum, Darren was all pumped to go, but as they walked out the door she got a homicide call.

Of course Stephen said, "Yes. We'll have a great time."

In fact they were still in the museum. She heard Darren oohing and aahing at the native animal dioramas.

"Yes, Rainey White's been pimping his wife. He marked her with a cut under her left breast like Janice." His voice tightened. "Why?"

"Javier's today's murder victim." She realized that was the last thing Stephen needed to hear.

This week had been crazy with reporters and television cameras, a whole media circus. The Janice Zahn article started the ball rolling. Two homeless suicides in a small town like Grand Island got picked up on the wire. Two suicides that might be murders was beyond belief.

The coroner's office had been ravaged by negative attention and savaged in the op-ed articles being called everything from incompetent to participants in a conspiracy to deprive the homeless dead their full right to a thorough investigation. The fact one victim was male and disabled and one an abused female sent the media mining for more. Laqueta's office was inundated. At least their media spokesman provided her a partial buffer. She felt sorry for Sally over at the coroner's office.

Henry Many Horses' death on the same day the Zahn article appeared brought triple coverage. Henry's death, another apparent suicide but possible murder, brought international attention. Then when the reporters discovered the unnamed victim found off First Street speculation ran wild and the media created the Homeless Exterminator title for the supposed serial murderer of homeless people in Grand Island.

Broadcast vans remained parked at the Law Enforcement Center over the weekend. One created a permanent site at the Salvation Army. Only a restraining order kept them out of the feeding program so that clients could eat in peace.

"The media followed me to the murder site, not far from where Joseph Riederhof died. Fortunately, the responding officers set a perimeter at the sidewalk to the east, across the business parking lot on the north then about a block to the west and south.

"The site includes trees along the Wood River. The smell of the body, which permeated a full block away, had already led to speculation of another homeless murder.

"No one's calling the deaths suicide anymore. Not even the coroner."

"Does it look like a suicide again?" Stephen asked.

"No, Javier's death is clearly a murder. Throat slit deep, the head hanging backwards fastened to the body by only the unsevered spine. However, there is no sign of struggle. Toxicology reports will be important, but the media aren't going to want to wait to hear back from those."

CHAPTER 47

Laqueta, while stressed, spoke with confidence, professionalism, and poise.

"What about Marta and the children? Do they need help?"

"There's no sign of them. Their clothes are folded, stacked neatly in the tent. There are a few toys scattered around, but it looks like they've not been here for a few days. All their tracks are partially eroded from Javier and someone, or more than one person, having walked over them. From what the family told you, do you have any ideas where they might be?"

"Well, it's too late to be at the food program at Messiah Lutheran. And I doubt Marta has the children. Rainey keeps her captive from Friday afternoons through Sunday nights. Hopefully, he left her alone this week, but based on what happened to Janice I doubt it."

Laqueta made a soft whistle.

"What?" he asked.

"Maybe he killed her?" She paused. "Oh, Stephen, do you think he might have killed her? But if so where are the children?"

The implications of Rainey being involved were mind numbing.

"Maybe the La Linea found him." Stephen speculated. "Or maybe he saw someone associated with La Linea and sent Marta and the children into hiding."

He didn't sound very convincing.

"That would fit the type of wound, but there's no sign of struggle. Something doesn't add up. Anyway, I'm not asking you to solve the case. I only needed to confirm that Javier was the same individual. His history gives me a place to start. I'm sure you'll be getting calls and people standing outside your apartment building waiting to see if there's another homeless connection."

Laqueta drew a deep breath.

"I'm really glad you and Darren are out of town. If you want, you can take him to my house when you return. The media won't be looking for me and if this turns out to be late you'll be able to put him in his own bed. Clean pajamas are in the top drawer. He usually puts them on after taking a bath or a shower."

"I hear you. Don't worry about us boys. We'll be okay."

She turned back to processing the scene.

CHAPTER 48

Quote from the Journal of a Killer:

"In your great mercy, you sent them liberators who rescued them from their enemies."
Nehemiah 9:27 NLT

Darren spent two hours in the Wildlife Dioramas going back and forth to his favorites and then exploring little details like the seven striped ground squirrels in the Bison Display and the burrowing owls in the coyote case. He backed up to the gigantic free standing Polar Bear to compare his size. Stephen whipped out his cell phone and started snapping pictures. Darren spent several minutes posturing and measuring himself by the bear's various features. Of course the bituminous little spark did plenty of clowning for the camera. Stephen even managed a few shots of them together.

Every ten minutes or so Darren went back to the diorama with two wolves—one black and the other a silver wolf—set in a night scene. The play of the moonlight off the black wolf mesmerized him. Stephen couldn't tell if it was because the animal was black or because its fur reflected with a deep luminescence. Perhaps it was both.

To avoid potential reporters at a Grand Island restaurant, Stephen took Darren to Bernardo's Steak House in Hastings. The boy ate a whole baked potato with sour cream, an eight once fillet mignon, some vegetables, and a piece of coconut cream pie. The only thing Darren turned down was the lettuce salad but the rest made a balanced healthy meal for a youngster. Not surprising, he fell asleep with his head on Stephen's lap so Stephen sat there nursing his own peach pie with ice cream for a good half hour more. The waiters asked the usual questions about a black boy with a white man followed by the usual discussions concerning a child and then Stephen's work. Stephen found this father role deeply satisfying, not to mention fun.

Finally, he scooped Darren into his arms and exited the building.

"Stephen Brown."

The voice was sharp, cutting, and coming from behind him. He turned to be courteous but Angelina Abbott marched right into his personal space and fixed him with those disapproving eyes he used to dread.

"Mr. Brown. I have a bone to pick with you."

Her swagger was unbecoming in a woman.

"Good afternoon to you too, Angelina. What brings you to Hastings?"

"Sunday dinner with friends, but don't get me distracted." She puffed up her determination. "Why are you glorifying these homeless no accounts who commit suicide?" She propped her hands on her waist. "I've been reading your articles in the paper!"

"And you have an objection? I don't understand."

Stephen shifted Darren's weight on his shoulder and changed his stance. Angelina would have her say before she'd let him go. For the moment she just stared at him.

"I believe that every life deserves to be honored—regardless of its handicaps, or failures," he added. "The stories of Joseph Riederhof, Janice Zahn, and today, Henry (Hank) Many Horses are hardly offensive and, personally, I do not believe any of the three were suicides. But, even if they were, the very tragedy of suicide means there is a story that needs to be honored, a cause observers need to hear before they judge unfairly."

"But they are just homeless. Nobody cares!"

Stephen grimaced.

"Perhaps if someone had cared they wouldn't have been homeless. Perhaps if someone built a relationship with them after they came to Grand Island, they could have been rescued."

"Oh, get real Stephen. That's a bunch of liberal-leftist crap and you know it. If they didn't get everything free they'd get over themselves and get to work."

He knew he shouldn't argue, but more needed to be said.

"So Mr. Riederhof, paraplegic and deteriorating, should have gotten a job and everything would have been alright!" He shook his head. "Janice, who worked most of the time since getting the courage to flee abuse and incest, should have had an immediate job here—by the way she was working as a night shift maid at a motel and had been accepted to work for the Chicken Coop at minimum wage—then she wouldn't have been raped and branded by a sadist and one of our own fair councilmen!"

Angelina gasped.

"And Henry Many Horses, who lacked the mental, emotional and social skills to take care of himself should somehow get a job and place to live and his developmental disability would have gone away. Ms. Abbott, I think your whole position on this is ignorant and wrongheaded."

"Well, I never!" She spun to go. "I will certainly have something to say about this to Captain Bramwell." And she started to march off.

"His name is Captain Higgins, ma'am. Captain Bramwell Higgins. And I am quite confident he supports what was written in my articles. He read and approved them before submission to the Islander."

She stopped to look defiantly at him.

"But I have one more thing I want to say. I do not believe any of these three individuals committed suicide any more than the unidentified young man found over Memorial Day could have been suicide."

He punctuated the sentence with a determined lift of his chin which upset his balance with Darren, so he shifted his burden again.

"But the coroner declared them suicides—you need to quit making trouble for the coroner. He's the County Attorney you know. If he said it's a suicide, it's a suicide." Dug in and stubborn as usual.

Stephen wanted to laugh at her reasoning and her exaggerated body language.

"I believe the evidence says different."

"What do you mean?" she demanded.

"Riederhof could not move his own wheelchair. There was no way he could have tied a knot, thrown a rope over the tree branch, or moved his wheelchair far enough to snap him out of the chair and break his neck—and his neck was broken.

"Janice had so much alcohol in her system that she could not have remained conscious enough to pull that zip tie and cut off her own air supply. Don't forget she had been raped and branded and neither of the two men involved could risk being caught and prosecuted. Yes, she wanted to die. I don't dispute that, but there is enough evidence to raise a question about who assisted her.

"And Henry Many Horses—according to the medical examiner—could not have made the cut that nicked his artery and resulted in him bleeding out. Additionally no weapon was found at the scene raising a question about whether someone else was involved. Evidence points to a blood brother ritual and the presence of one other person at the scene before he died.

"None of the victims left a suicide note. And the coroner appears to have ruled them suicides for political reasons."

He paused and glared at Angelina.

"Do I need to go on?"

"Well," she answered and prissed herself up, "I'm sure the coroner took all of that into consideration. No one would make a death ruling based on politics. This is America for God's sake. It just wouldn't happen."

CHAPTER 49

Quote from the Journal of a Killer:

Death is a delightful hiding place for weary men.
Herodotus

When Stephen and Darren got back at her house, Laqueta was not yet home. So they watched "Bridge to Terabithia" on the Disney Channel then tried to blast planes and bombs out of the sky on the games channel.

Darren needed some mom time and started getting antsy.

About seven thirty Laqueta called to say she expected to be home in about an hour.

"Tell you what, buddy. Let's go get an ice cream." It was a bribe and Stephen knew it. Parenting by bribing, an ancient art.

"Dairy Queen! Dairy Queen!" Darren jumped up and down. I want a peanut butter blizzard," he announced. "Large." And he measured out an eighteen-inch cup with hand signals.

Darren's peanut butter dream turned out to be a Reese's Pieces Blizzard in a medium size cup served with no reporter present. Stephen ordered himself a small butterscotch sundae—too much indulgence for one afternoon already—skipped the nuts.

A short warm bath followed the cold ice cream and readied Darren to nod. It was Stephen's first time giving a young boy a bath. He guessed he did okay. Darren seemed to be comfortable. He wrapped him in a super-sized bath towel and carried him to the bedroom where Darren chose Cars pajamas and went whroom, whroom as Stephen gently tossed him onto the bed.

"Read me a book," he demanded so Stephen picked up a copy of *The Little Engine That Could* from the bed stand. Even though Darren held it and tried to turn the pages, he was asleep by the bottom of page four.

"I think I can. I think I can." Stephen said then laid the book aside and tucked him in.

A lock clicked.

Stephen rolled over on the couch and looked up at the clock under the Celtic wall cross.

Eleven o'clock.

The key turned in the second lock now and he heard Laqueta gently open the door and close it behind herself.

"You okay?" she asked when he sat up. "Sorry it's so late. I really thought I'd be here by eight thirty. This investigation has so many angles to cover and contacts to make—all due to Javier's status as an asylee waiting for a residency permit. Tomorrow will be even more trouble with notification of the Mexican Consulate and beginning contact with law enforcement in Chihuahua. The cartel's involvement with the family is tricky. We don't want to trigger reprisals against his sister or mother.

"Then there's the whole matter of the missing wife and children. I haven't even started on that."

She sighed and sunk onto the couch in deep exhaustion.

"You okay? You going to be able to sleep?"

If she were his girlfriend or wife it would have been appropriate to draw her into his arms and hold her, but of course, at the time that would have been presumptive and uninvited.

"I'll sleep. A hot shower and bite to eat usually distracts me enough to settle down. And, yes, I'm okay. This media presence and so many murders in such a short time demands extra duty. In the city we'd have five or six investigators working on this, but in a town this size there just aren't those kinds of resources—usually isn't a need for them." She allowed herself another sigh. "But tomorrow I'll be back in early. I hate to ask, but could you take Darren like you did last Sunday. I hate to miss church, but he seemed very comfortable with you there."

"Who says you have to go in early? You expect a call from the Consulate or something?" Stephen tried to sound nonintrusive.

She nodded. "Yes, I'm expecting a call from Immigration at eight—maybe last about an hour. Then there are all the other angles that have to be explored. I guess I figured I might as well get a jump start on them before the Riederhof's get here Monday."

Mental exhaustion showed on her face as she spoke. Stephen figured the jump start was more a want to than a need, so he again risked being intrusive.

"Why don't I come at seven? I'll cook a hot breakfast." He cracked a smile. "Load you up on the carbs for the day. Then I'll get Darren ready and we'll go to Sunday School. I really like the class pastor leads on the book of James—great for today—for things we're dealing with right now.

"I suggest you join us for worship to recharge your mental and spiritual batteries before a quick sandwich meal at Jimmy Johns and we'll send you back to work. You'll have a more productive day if you do."

God, he was sounding like Gramms now. But it was true.

Laqueta pondered his suggestions for at least a full minute.

"I don't know…"

"Come on. You'll thank me later."

She looked up into his eyes—his heart fluttered—she smiled and acquiesced. "You better get out of here and get some sleep yourself then," she said.

They exchanged brief good-byes. He took her hand.

CHAPTER 49

"See you in the morning. If you need me call." The hand was warm and soft. He didn't want to let go but he gave it a gentle kiss then slipped out the door.

It double latched behind him.

CHAPTER 50

Quote from the Journal of a Killer:

Sex is a weapon that has enslaved
more lives to perpetual fear than those who have found relief.
May I be an instrument of their peace.
The Journal of a Killer

Stephen quietly unlocked the door off Laqueta's kitchen and placed two arm loads of supplies on the counter. Soon the smell of vanilla hazelnut mocha wafted up the stairs and brought down a bleary-eyed boy in Cars pajamas.

"Mr. Stephen." Darren came over and held on to his leg. "Can I have some?"

"I'm sorry sprout, that's coffee. But I brought you some hot chocolate." He lifted him onto the barstool at the center island.

"Sit here a minute and I'll make it for you."

Chocolate and hazelnut blended in the air. Stephen put the steaming cup under Darren's nose and he immediately took a sip.

"So what you think?"

Darren's eyes sparkled. "What's for breakfast, Mr. Stephen?"

"Let's see." He laid out the cooking supplies. "Pancakes, eggs, bacon, and butter, syrup, milk, coffee, and chocolate." He tousled the tyke's hair.

CHAPTER 50

Soon the smell of slow cooking bacon overpowered the coffee and chocolate. Scrambled eggs kept warm on a back burner. Stephen whipped up pancake batter.

Darren laid his tired head on the counter as he waited, watching every little move Stephen made.

"How's a girl supposed to sleep with all these enchanting smells drifting into her bedroom?" Laqueta stood on the bottom step in a rose pink chenille robe.

"Hello, sleepy eyes. Time to rise and shine. You got work to do!"

"Oh, I don't have to rush in this morning. That Immigration Officer called me last night right after you left. I didn't want to call you at midnight when we finished."

"Yah, yah. You just wanted someone to make you breakfast. I know how that works."

She offered a quiet smile and eased onto a stool beside Darren. His hair got tousled again. "How's my man?"

Darren leaned his head on her arm and smiled. "Mr. Stephen makes a mean cup of Joe." He lifted his cup in salute as Stephen set a cup of steaming coffee in front of Laqueta.

"Does he now?" She took a sip. "What is this flavor?"

"Vanilla hazelnut mocha—same as the sprout's chocolate. Do you need cream or sugar?"

"No, thank you. This is good the way it is. I usually drink mine black with lots of sugar. Learned that from my Gramps when he taught me to drink coffee. My mom had a fit."

"Yeh," Stephen said. "Grams taught me. My dad threw the fit."

"Okay, pancakes up! Dollar cakes for Darren and six inchers for mom. Eggs? Bacon? Or both? What's your pleasure?"

He sat real butter and maple syrup on the counter.

"Yeah! I want bacon." Darren bounced on his stool.

"And a scoop of eggs," his mother added with a glance and a raised eyebrow.

"And for you my lady?" Stephen asked as he placed Darren's plate on the counter.

"Some of everything please."

Stephen lifted two six inchers from the griddle and lined them with eggs and bacon.

"Enjoy!"

He made himself a similar plate and leaned on the counter opposite Darren and Laqueta.

"A woman could get used to this."

"And gain fifty pounds in a week."

Laqueta gave him a disgusted smile.

"I mean having a man around to cook breakfast every morning. For a single gal this is pure luxury. You could fix healthy meals or diet meals, but it would still be pure luxury." She closed her eyes in dreamy contentment.

"Uhh...don't count on it! I'm not usually a morning person. At my house it's cereal, milk and coffee, and sometimes I forget the cereal."

They laughed together.

"I'll clear this up and head on home," he added. "You and the sprout don't need me now."

"Not on your life," replied Laqueta. "You're already dressed for church."

It was true. He'd been cooking in a jacket, shirt, and tie, but wore an apron to keep flour damage to a minimum.

"Besides, I still need you for the afternoon. Wasn't that the arrangement?"

"Sure was lady," Stephen responded businesslike. "I'll get Darren ready and you can relax and take your time."

"Good thing. I'll have to be extra picky about what I wear since I'll have a man on my arm this morning." She shot him a cool sultry look and her laughter tickled his ears.

Every morning should be this enjoyable, he thought.

Laqueta grabbed Stephen's elbow as they walked up the center aisle to four pews from the front. Some bemused smiles followed them, but no one seemed to have a negative response.

The pastor surprised Stephen when he spoke about the deaths among the homeless in the city. "We need the public to get involved.

People need to make a habit of saying, 'Hi' to the homeless. Offering them a bit of encouragement. Asking them leading questions."

Stephen and Laqueta exchanged glances.

"Then we can encourage them to go to the police, the Salvation Army, or the other resources in town. No, we need to take them to those resources. Be their friend—their advocate. Can you imagine how intimidating it is to be in need, or abused, or a victim of criminal actions having to get up the courage to go see some strangers so they could ask you questions? Wouldn't it be easier if you went with someone who already knew your story?

"We Christians are Christ's hands and feet. We need to be where he was, on the streets with the people in need of spiritual, mental, emotional, and physical help. It would change your whole view of homeless people. It could change the experience of homelessness here in Grand Island.

"Imagine what might have happened if someone had gotten to know Joseph Riederhof. What if some matronly woman, like the one in Missouri, befriended Janice Zahn? What if we had discovered Henry Many Horses was a missing person? We might have saved their lives. They might be here with us today. Henry might be back on the Rosebud, alive, surrounded by his family and tribe."

Stunned, Stephen could remember little else about the service.

Captain would be amazed.

CHAPTER 51

Quote from the Journal of a Killer:

There is no real ending.
It's just the place where you stop the story.
Frank Herbert

At the risk of a brush with reporters, Stephen took Laqueta and Darren to Jimmy John's Gourmet Sandwiches. They huddled around a small rectangular table and ate their subs.

"I don't like Billy Blisterman." Darren squinted.

"What?" asked Laqueta. "Why'd you say that? That's mean."

"Ms. Cunningham said we have to love everybody—like homeless people, but I don't like Billy Blisterman. He's mean."

"But he's not homeless," replied Laqueta.

"Is too," said Darren.

"How do you know?" Stephen lifted his eyebrows.

"He lives in a car!"

"Yes," said Stephen. "A big van with his mom and dad. Do you know why?"

Darren shook his head no.

"They lost their house when his mom got sick. Sick for a whole year."

Stephen looked at Laqueta and added, "Evicted by the bank because they didn't have enough money to cover her loss of income. It was cancer."

Laqueta covered her mouth and closed her eyes.

"What's evicted?" Darren struggled with the word.

"It means to be forced to move out of your house," Stephen said.

"Is that why Billy lost all his toys?" Darren's eyes reflected his deep thoughts.

"I suppose so," said Stephen.

"But what about Hope Harbor? Can't they help?" Laqueta leaned forward and put her sandwich down.

"Billy's father has two felonies from his twenties that disqualify him for life." He was referring to Dan Blisterman's sex offenses.

"And that disqualifies him from public housing, too, I suppose."

"Yes. He'd have to give up his family so they could have a home. He's not willing to break up the family. I wouldn't be either."

Laqueta nodded her head in agreement and turned to Darren.

"Darren, maybe he's mean because he needs a friend. Maybe you could be nice to him."

"Not on your life. He's mean. He be mean before he lived in a car. In pre-school. 'Fore his mom got sick." Darren squared his shoulders and his lip slipped out further.

"That's about the ugliest look I've ever seen." Stephen bugged his eyes out at Darren making him laugh then turning to Laqueta said, "Seriously though, I loved that sermon. Right off the front pages today."

"And right from your homeless article," said Laqueta a hint of pride in her voice.

"But you know that sermon also bothers me. It's almost word for word what I've written and what Captain and I talked about." He looked down at the table top. "But how can the Salvation Army promote that vision of homeless relationships throughout the whole community? How do you change the expectations, the actions of a community?"

"Mr. Stephen," Darren interrupted, "can we go see the horses today?"

He shook his head. "No. It's too far. Gramms lives up by Anselmo about two, three hours from here."

Darren began to pout, but perked up. "What color are dem horses?"

"Them," his mother corrected.

"Them," Darren echoed.

"Well...," Stephen drawled like a old farmer. Darren laughed and giggled. "I guess there's an Indian pony, an old sorrel mare, old Black Jack, some gorgeous Appaloosas, and maybe twenty or thirty more of all kinds. I reckon there's some fine colts by now, but we'll just have to go and see them for ourselves."

Darren's eyes rounded as the list went on and on.

"Can we ride all of 'em—them?" Darren's shoulders moved up and down like John Wayne riding some big old gelding in a western movie.

Stephen shook his head. "No, some of them aren't tame. They'd buck you off."

"I can break 'em." Darren puffed out his chest. He tucked his thumbs behind the seams of his shirtsleeves. "No problem, pardner."

Stephen and Laqueta let out hardy laughs. Eyes throughout the restaurant turned their way then also lit up.

"You know, pardner, I think it's time we git." Laqueta stood. "Come on."

As they walked out the door, Stephen saw Laqueta nuzzling her son.

Mothers and their boys. Stephen could watch them all day. The warmth and intimacy had been something he'd missed out on when little. Gramms made up for it as much as she could, but watching Laqueta and Darren made his heart ache for an experience he could not go back and make up.

I hope the mother of my boys is like that.

"Stephen!"

Stephen jumped at the sound of the sharp voice. He'd failed to see Councilman Koenig come up behind him. He rolled his eyes when he saw Angelina Abbott glare at him from behind Mr. Koenig's shoulder.

"Yes, Councilman?" He could feel his forehead furrow.

"When are you going to stop bashing the County Attorney?"

"Excuse me?"

"Those articles in the Independent. When are you going to stop questioning the County Attorney's death rulings? He's an elected official. Have some respect!"

Stephen tightened his jaw. "I write the facts, that's all. If the facts suggest a different cause of death then let the facts speak."

Laqueta had gone on to the car. Stephen glanced toward her vehicle. He wished she was here to back him up.

The councilman caught the direction of Stephen's eyes and raised his eyebrows.

"So that's your angle," he crooned. "Sleeping with the enemy are you?"

Stephen took a shallow breath and grabbed control of his emotions. "No, Mr. Koenig. Investigator Ellison and I are just friends. No romantic relationship like a certain councilman with a taste for rough sex, branding, and Janice Zahn. Perhaps you should be more concerned about your own affairs." He glared, trying to blaze a hole through Koenig's heart.

Koenig's eyes turned hollow and his face paled.

"Laqueta helped me write accurately about the crime scenes and I assisted her with details of the victims' lives."

"Victims!" Angelina spat. "Since when are suicide victims victims? These people messed up their own lives. Of course they kill themselves. Even they can't live with themselves. They do us a…."

Stephen added the unspoken words. "A favor? Why Miss Abbott. I thought you had a soft spot for the homeless."

Her eyes shot daggers at him. "Someone has to keep them off the street. For God's sake, this isn't India. Anything to keep them out of the way of the public the better."

Wow! That lays it out there, he thought.

Richard Koenig grasped control of the argument. "That's exactly my point. Look at the damage you've done to this fair city with your articles. And all these media people running around speculating about the coroner's competence. You just stir up trouble."

"My articles are not what brought the media circus here. Four homeless murders brought them. My articles just saved everyone some difficult investigative reporting. Now, if you two will excuse me, Ms. Ellison has a homicide from yesterday to investigate and Darren needs a babysitter. Good day."

CHAPTER 52

Quote from the Journal of a Killer:

Real isn't how you are made.
It's a thing that happens to you.
Sometimes it hurts.
It doesn't happen all at once.
You become.
That's why it doesn't often happen
to people who break easily,
or have sharp edges,
or who have to be carefully kept.
Once you are Real you can't be ugly,
except to people who don't understand.
Once you are real you can't become unreal again.
It lasts for always.
Margery Williams, **The Velveteen Rabbit**

"Thank you for meeting us." James Riederhof offered his hand and Stephen shook it. Joseph Riederhof's sister, Beth Ann Meyers, older brother Raymond, and mother Beverly Sue Randolph-Riederhof stayed by the baggage carousel to grab their luggage. "That idea to send an email photo works well. I'll remember that the next time we travel on business."

"Beth Ann's gone to pick up our rental." Raymond had stepped over. "How about we drive past your office, to see where we will meet later, then follow you around to the Kirschke House Bed & Breakfast."

Stephen nodded. "Actually, the Kirschke house is only three blocks from the Salvation Army. I'll be glad to take you around. I hear the hostess is terrific."

James' phone rang and he turned away to answer it.

"Did the meeting with Inspector Ellison work out?" Beverly asked.

"Yes." Stephen thought he heard James Riederhof say, "You'll be arriving when." "Laqueta could not join us this afternoon for introductions but she will catch up with us for dinner at the Texas Roadhouse. Salvation Army's supper meal begins at four fifteen. I have arranged for volunteers to complete the serving so you can meet the kitchen staff and get a taste of Joseph's life here in Grand Island. They interacted with Joseph the most. But a dinner offsite will be quieter and allow more privacy for talking with Laqueta. Will the new Texas Roadhouse be okay?"

"Sure. What do you think, Mom?"

"That'll be fine. What do you think, dear?" she asked James who looked distracted.

"Yes." His response sounded rote. "That'll be great." He turned to Stephen. "This is a hard trip for me. I'm used to being in charge and this whole deal with Joseph leaves me feeling helpless."

"Dad. That's not true," Beth Ann and Raymond said. Beverly Sue slipped an arm around his broad shoulders and said, "The car's ready."

CHAPTER 53

Quote from the Journal of a Killer:

Do not fear death so much but rather the inadequate life.
Bertolt Brecht

"Compared to the statistics on your website this facility is quite small," stated James Riederhof at the end of the facility tour".

"Compared to the size of our town the statistics are disturbing," replied Captain Higgins. "The tragedies of homelessness and poverty know no boundaries."

"I understand the needs in rural areas, including per capita numbers, remain high," said Raymond as he inspected the ceilings and corners of the room. "The more remote the more desperate the needs."

"You've done some research?" asked Stephen.

Although about Stephen's own height, Raymond with his blue pin striped suit, light olive silk shirt, and olive and blue tie, portrayed wealth and power not compassion or interest in homelessness and poverty.

Raymond met Captain's eyes then glanced at Stephen.

"In my sociology of economics course," he explained, "I did research on poverty and homelessness in America. My mother has always had an interest in poverty especially homelessness. It's ironic that Joseph became part of that system. But then, I always supposed he was dead so I never thought of how he might be getting by."

Raymond's inspection of facility details reflected his work as an engineer specializing in public buildings—government and non-profit. His face and conversation registered a quest for improving nonprofit functionality and public perceptions by subtle upgrades in facilities.

"So, I'm interested in where Joseph lived," said James.

"Laqueta will show you Joseph's nest tomorrow," Stephen said.

Eyebrows shot up all around.

"Nest?" Beth Ann queried. "You mean the place where he died?"

"He lived in the woods?" asked Mrs. Riederhof. "Not in a building?"

Stephen nodded.

The mother's head slumped forward; deep sadness replaced her curiosity. "I just wish we could have found him before it came to that." She paused. "Do you think Joseph had a death wish? He blamed himself for Jonathan's death."

"It's common for survivors to believe they should be the person who died," Captain Higgins responded. "And yes, sadly, they often carry a death wish for the rest of their lives." His eyes sought to connect with Beverly Sue. "But, statistically, few act on it. It gets expressed in deteriorating emotions and unwise choices that place them on our doorstep."

"So, you're saying he might not have committed suicide?" James Riederhof's shoulders stiffened and his neck muscles tensed. Resentment burned from his eyes.

"I—I...," Captain stammered.

"I don't think so," Stephen said with greater confidence than he felt. "At worst his death might have been an assisted suicide. But my gut says that doesn't add up. I can't explain why or how, but I think his death was an accident or possibly an outright murder. Maybe when we talk with Laqueta tonight some little piece will fall into place. But, no, I do not think Joseph committed suicide."

"I read your article," Beth Ann said. "By the way it was very good. Thank you. You really pointed out the inconsistencies of the coroner's ruling."

Stephen ducked his head slightly. "Yeh, I sort of got in trouble for that."

Beth Ann chuckled. "I suppose so—questioning a government official and all that. But what I was going to say was, based on the other articles you've written, I go for the possibility that Joseph was murdered. It looks to me like you have a serial killer on your hands."

"And I want him caught!" James Riederhof's aggressive personality accentuated by his anger caught even his family off guard.

"Speaking of..." Stephen replied, "It's about an hour and half till we sit down with Laqueta to learn the details of her investigation. Perhaps you'd like to go back to the Kirschke to freshen up and rest. I'll come by and knock at the Carriage House about five. You can follow me out to the Texas Roadhouse."

"Texas Roadhouse?" asked Captain Higgins raising his eyebrows. "What kind of damage is my junior staff trying to do to the Salvation Army—taking our guests to a roadhouse?"

Everybody laughed.

* * *

"In your article you said Joseph couldn't lift a fork to his mouth," Beth Ann said as she settled into Stephen's car. She and Raymond had requested to ride with Stephen. "When he disappeared from the hospital, Joseph was able to feed himself so something changed."

"Yes," said Raymond, "the doctors warned us that without further treatment and careful monitoring, over time, Joseph might lose function. We wanted to get you alone to ask if you knew anything more about his physical condition. The whole thing just makes Dad mad."

Stephen shook his head. "I wish you could have talked to Susan and Chet. They'd assisted your brother ever since he came to town." His forehead creased as he went on. "I know your brother was unable to change his clothes. One of the homeless men—a possible suspect if this was a murder—used to take him to his motel room, clean him up, wash his clothes, and dress him. A young homeless kid named Zachary drained his urine bag and helped changed the catheter. My understanding is that Joseph was doing these things himself until the last month or so. Same with the feeding. Plus, for the last month someone had to wheel him wherever he went, also a change from when he arrived."

"If he could do it earlier, that was a gain over when he left the hospital." Beth Ann smiled. "That's good to hear. Sounds like most of the losses happened after he came here. "I wonder where he lived before."

"Yes," said Raymond. "At rehab Joseph needed assistance to stay upright in a chair. The day before he disappeared he lifted himself onto the bathroom stool and changed his catheter but he wasn't able to lift himself from his chair to the bed and was just beginning to be able to change his clothes. Tell us more."

"I noticed Joseph slumped forward more than when I bought him the Carhartts last winter."

"Carhartts?" asked Beth Ann.

"Winter coveralls," said Raymond. "They're designed for spending lengthy times outdoors like hunting or line work."

"Oh."

"Yes. That's why I bought them. He was shaking so bad that first morning it made my muscles ache. Chet helped him get them on and Zachary got them to work around the catheter and urine bag. Oh, and by the way, at the last he had to wear an adult diaper and be changed. Not a pleasant job."

Both Raymond and Beth Ann lowered their heads.

"He was almost quadriplegic then," said Raymond quietly. "Makes the possibility of an assisted suicide make more sense now. I can't imagine Joe being that dependent. It drove him crazy back in the hospital."

"And it's why it might have been murder. He'd really become a burden on the homeless population. One of his caretakers could have decided enough is enough," Stephen added.

Beth Ann nodded.

"But," Stephen continued, "murder by hanging doesn't make sense. There are a lot of easier, quicker ways. Even less painful ways. Rainey—the guy at the motel—is a drug dealer. An overdose would have been easier or slipping him something to knock him out then suffocating him. Almost anything would have been more compassionate.

"Assisted suicide makes more sense of the hanging, but Joseph never mentioned a death wish to staff or to Zachary. Neither did Zachary mention Joseph saying he wanted to commit suicide. That leaves only an accidental hanging. But that doesn't make sense either."

"Maybe," Raymond lifted his chin, "Joseph was always curious—about everything. I could see him asking what it would take for a man in a wheelchair to hang himself. He was that kind of crazy. Always solving problems that might, but didn't, exist. And I agree I can't see a wheelchair bound person trying to commit suicide by hanging. There are so many other ways."

"Sociology class?" Stephen glanced at the passenger and raised an eyebrow.

"No," Raymond replied and laughed.

"But seriously," interrupted Beth Ann, "I could see Joseph trying out some hanging theory. He liked to be hands on and there are multiple ways to keep a mock hanging from becoming a real hanging. Something would have had to gone wrong for it to be an accident. But you know, I can see that accident theory. Dad will never go for it. He's locked in on the murder idea. And these other so called suicides look more like murder than they do accidents or suicides."

"I agree," said Raymond, "I picked up a paper over at the main house. This weekend's homeless death was clearly a murder. That fired up Dad. I want to ask Inspector Ellison if she sees any connection between the former deaths and this one. It just feels different."

Stephens's heart raced. Murder and suicide were a long way from his first interest—family notification and telling the victims' stories.

CHAPTER 54

Quote from the Journal of a Killer:

Having brought peace to one,
ushering the others into that
balm becomes easier.
The Journal of a Killer

At the Roadhouse, James Riederhof changed the meeting location to the dining room. He dictated the seating order. Eight o'clock sharp, wait staff centered six separate appetizers on the table: an Onion Blossom, Rattlesnake Bites, Grilled Shrimp, Tater Skins, Killer Ribs, and Boneless Buffalo Wings. Stephen's face lit up, but Laqueta's turned dubious—department policy and weight.

They found out James had preordered for everyone and asked for the table for six under the moose head. When the waitress took drink orders, no one ordered alcohol. Stephen wondered if that was in deference to the Salvation Army or a lifestyle choice. A second waitress came to ask how they'd like their Texas T-Bones grilled.

When the drinks arrived Mr. Riederhof lifted his glass and said, "I thought we'd make this meal a wake for Joseph. To Joseph!"

"To Joseph," they echoed punctuated by tinkling glass.

Staff shifted into place on the dance floor.

"And now for the entertainment," James bellowed to the embarrassment of his whole family. Stephen and Laqueta raised their eyebrows.

Beverly Sue Riederhof inspected Laqueta's hair, face, and clothes. "How did a beautiful woman like you decide to be a police investigator?"

Laqueta blushed. No one but Stephen seemed to see her discomfort.

"My grandfather was an investigator with the Omaha Police Department," Laqueta began. "We were very close. He'd share old cases with me and I would make up a new piece of evidence then we'd explore what effect that might have on the case. He's still alive but now he probes me for opportunities to discuss my cases."

"Have you discussed Joseph's case with him?" asked Beverly Sue.

"I bet he calls it murder." Mr. Riederhof remained truculent.

"No," Laqueta replied. She relaxed her shoulders as she smiled at James. "My grandfather thinks there is a missing piece to the investigation. His gut tells him it was an accident."

"An accidental hanging? That's bull crap!"

"James!" Beverly Sue cast him a sharp look.

"Okay. Okay." He backed off his pugnacious tone. "That doesn't make sense to me."

"Me neither," Laqueta answered quickly. "But, like Granddad, I still think something important is missing. Something that would clarify my conclusion that this was actually a murder."

"You've ruled out assisted suicide and mercy killing?" asked Raymond.

"It's not mine to rule on the cause of death. That's the coroner's duty," Laqueta replied.

"Like any of us agree with that man." James again.

Laqueta continued, "Personally, I don't see it as an assisted suicide. The marks of a suicide are missing—fresh trauma, disabling depression, a note or final message, those things are typical facets of a suicide. Besides the more I hear about Joseph, whether from you or Stephen, suicide does not fit.

"Mercy killing also doesn't fit. His caregivers had the option of walking away. Abandoning him. The only kind of mercy killing that makes sense to me would be an individual who thinks he's doing Joseph a favor by putting him out of his misery." She blushed again. "I'm sorry that sounded harsh. But again, if the motivation was compassion or mercy why the choice of hanging? Hanging is hardly associated with mercy or compassion and the on-scene evidence makes hanging uniquely cruel."

"What do you mean?" asked Beth Ann.

"I'll show you more clearly tomorrow—at the site. But the rope was relatively long for a hanging. The noose was most likely placed around Joseph's neck...." She looked at each family member and paused to read their eyes. "Do you really want me to go on with this?"

"Yes." Mrs. Riederhof said her voice shaky. The other three nodded affirmatively.

Laqueta shot Stephen a quick look, took a deep breath, and continued. "The tracks at the scene indicated that someone walked backwards pulling the wheelchair by its arms. The distance and Joseph's final position indicate the use of considerable force. My guess is that Joseph's body was lifted upward out of the chair until the tension on the rope snapped him backward—the chair was lying on its back—and the weight of his falling body separated the vertebrae in his neck severing the spinal cord. His legs extended out over the ground, but his seat and main torso hung suspended above the ground."

It was the most detailed account Stephen had heard to date. Everyone sat solemn for a few seconds.

"My point," Laqueta said, "is that the scene has no sign of mercy or compassion. It's pretty messy to be an assisted suicide. I can't imagine Joseph submitting willingly to the cruelty of how this happened. But then again, we don't know of anyone with the personalized punitive anger expected if this was a pre-meditated murder. Something must be missing. Neither my boss, Chief Greywright, the coroner, nor my grandfather have been able to identify the missing element. So far no one has suggested another way to look at the scene."

The faces around Stephen told different tales. James Riederhof was clearly locked down, stiff, almost paralyzed. Tears drifted down Beverly Sue's cheeks. Beth Ann's horror demonstrated the lock Joseph's hanging body had on her thoughts. Raymond's exsanguinated cheeks and taunt neck muscles bespoke a wish to deny that any of this had happened.

Raymond shook himself first. With fearful eyes he asked, "Do you have a picture of the body still hanging?"

Laqueta's jaw tightened, but she nodded yes. "I brought a copy with me. I thought one of you might ask for it. But I have to warn you, it's grisly. His body shows severe decomposition."

Raymond winced and he set his jaw.

Stephen's temples popped from long held tense. Grief formed a palpable presence as if the table sat within a bubble all its own. Laqueta handled these scenes without emotionally breaking. How? He couldn't.

Again Raymond broke the silence.

"I'd like to see it," he said, "but hopefully you have it in an envelope or folder so I can choose when I'm up to it."

Laqueta pulled a five by seven manila envelope from her valise. "I made a glossy print so you could study it for detail if you wish. Please, be sure you're ready before you open this. I suggest you have a neutral person with you to provide support as you adjust to the reality you will see. Someone emotionally strong."

He took the envelope from her outstretched hand. "Thank you. I'll do that. This isn't the time to…." His voice broke as tears began to glisten at the corners of his eyes. "Yes. Thank you."

"James," Mrs. Riederhof's head remained down as she addressed her husband. "I—I need to go home now." He stood and gingerly helped her to her feet. Once standing she collapsed into his arms. As he held her, the rest of the party stood.

"The tour to Joseph's…" Raymond didn't know what to call it. "…is at nine? Right?"

"Could we make it nine thirty?" Beth Ann choked back emotion. "I may need a little extra time to be ready. I—I don't want to feel rushed."

Laqueta nodded.

James slipped an arm around his wife's shoulder and nudged her toward the door. Everyone followed without a word. Stephen picked up the tab.

CHAPTER 55

Quote from the Journal of a Killer:

Make me a channel of your peace;
where there is discord, may I bring harmony;
where there is despair, may I bring hope;
where there is sadness, may I bring joy.
Saint Francis of Assisi

"Stephen," He didn't even get in a hello. "Are you near a television?"

"I can be."

"Riederhofs called a news conference for eleven thirty this morning. It's being covered live by Channel 11."

Stephen heard Laqueta take a breath before she continued. His clock read eleven twenty eight.

"Chief got a call from one of the national networks. They want a local response. I'm about three blocks from your office. Perhaps we can watch it together."

"Sure." He headed upstairs to the television in the Men's Shelter. "You remember those metal steps on the back of the building."

"Yes."

"Come up there. Knock on the window. I'll let you in."

He dialed the Salvation Army land line and Sonja answered.

"Sonja, I'm upstairs. Riederhofs called a news conference for eleven thirty. Could you please let Captain know? This might be bad news."

By the time Laqueta arrived, Captain and Sonja had joined Stephen upstairs in the shelter lounge. Live coverage streamed from Channel 11. He recognized several news reporters and cameramen. Chief Greywright stood plastered against the back wall and the mayor beside him.

The Riederhofs were just arriving. An escort steered them through the crowd and stepped to the microphones.

"Good morning. This is Linda Abalada from WFSB-TV 3 Eyewitness News reporting from the Holiday Inn-Midtown in Grand Island, Nebraska, where the family of Joseph Riederhof is about to make a statement and take questions from the media.

"Before we begin, I want to thank the Midtown for hastily providing space for this news conference, Joseph's grandmother Cynthia Ann Wilcoxson, for alerting us of this opportunity, and James Riederhof, Joseph's father, for consenting on Monday to address the media today. James...."

"Thank you Linda. And thank you for flying out so quickly to arrange this news conference. You certainly made better connections than we did." He turned to his prepared notes.

"My wife Beverly Sue, daughter Beth Ann Meyers, and Joseph's older brother, Raymond join me in thanking you for your coverage nationally of the tragic deaths of our son Joseph and the other homeless victims of murder in Grand Island. With your help perhaps something good can come from our sorrow that will help save other lives here and elsewhere in our great nation.

"Homelessness remains a national tragedy in the United States. Though my wife and family have been familiar with homelessness and tried to help alleviate the problem in our home area of Hartford, Connecticut, we never dreamed that one of our own, our son Joseph, would become homeless and apparently trapped in that lifestyle. Despite our work with the homeless, we remained painfully isolated from the sordid underbelly of tragedy and crime that Joseph's death has so clearly unmasked.

"Truly these individuals have been treated as second class citizens, often blamed for their own condition, and cruelly victimized by our local citizens and society in general. Many of the homeless, and I understand this is true of the five murder victims in this small village, could be helped if we had the individual and corporate will to do so. Like my son Joseph, they each have a personal story that contains the details needed to assist them in receiving care and recovery services that could restore them to a safer life and, in some cases, to their families.

"We wish to specifically commend Stephen Brown from the Salvation Army for his dedication to quizzing out Joseph's story and that of the other victims here. We owe a debt to his dedication to putting a human face on each of these tragedies and his drive to honor their lives in writing and through locating their families. If it had not been for Mr. Brown, and the assistance he has received from Investigator Ellison, we would not be here today, nor be able to provide our loving son an appropriate burial next to his brother and grandfather. Without these two individuals' persistence our family would have been consigned to limbo not knowing if our son was alive or dead, healthy or suffering."

James took a deep breath then continued.

"Joseph became a paraplegic following a tragic accident in which his identical twin brother was killed. We believe that he blamed himself for his brother's death and ran away from his family—and needed medical services—as a means of punishing himself and to deflect the shame that often overwhelmed him in our presence. Not that we believed there was any shame to be had nor that he was in any way remotely responsible for his brother's death.

"How Joseph got out of the rehabilitation hospital and the means by which he fled our town are as unknown to us as are the places he has lived in the five years since. Of that time period we only know that he ended up here in Grand Island where his health began a sharp decline and where he was murdered before his time.

"My family and I urge you each and everyone, media and listeners across this great country, to personally make it your goal to become a friend and listening ear to at least one of the homeless among us. Perhaps you will be the one with whom they may share their story so that you can help agencies like the Salvation Army, local health services, especially mental health agencies, law enforcement, and others to set them on the road to normalization. Thank you."

"Well, that's not what I expected." Stephen spoke into the silence.

A chorus of "Mr. Riederhof, Mr. Riederhof" erupted from among the reporters.

"I'm a bit surprised," added Laqueta. "James was agitated at the crime scene this morning and critical of the local situation. I figured his statement would be a full blown tirade."

Ms. Abalada stepped to the microphone to coordinate the media's questions.

"The gentleman from ABC, please."

"So you believe your son was murdered?"

Stephen heard Laqueta draw a sharp breath.

"Yes. He would not have been able to hang himself. It's just physically impossible." James' hard edge set in.

"Are you saying the coroner's report is wrong?"

"Yes," James visibly took a deep breath, frowned, and continued. "I believe the local coroner has to be a complete idiot to think a near quadriplegic man could commit suicide. And it is my understanding that he possessed abundant evidence and advice to the contrary."

"There rolls my head," said Laqueta under her breath.

Captain patted her shoulder.

"Perhaps somebody assisted him," another reporter speculated.

"That's just cruel," said Sonja. "Reporters are such a pack of piranhas."

"I do not believe my son committed suicide—assisted or otherwise." James's voice nearly cracked and Beverly Sue was clearly on the edge of tears at the direction of the questioning. So, of course, the next reporter targeted her directly.

"Mrs. Riederhof," she began, "I'm sorry for the loss of your son."

"Thank you." Beverly Sue forced a smile.

"Do you agree with your husband?"

Sonja let out a snort.

"I do," Mrs. Riederhof replied while stepping to the mic. "From what we learned from a young man who was caring for Joseph..."

"A young man caring for him?" said Stephen cocking his head,

"… and what I saw at the place he died, I do not believe my son committed suicide nor desired to commit suicide. He required more help now, but not help dying. Besides, there were many other less traumatic and more efficient ways for him to end his life if he so desired."

"She is one strong lady," commented Laqueta.

Just like you. Stephen gave her an admiring look.

"Mr. Riederhof, Mr. Riederhof…."

"You in the grey jacket," Ms. Abalada pointed to a man midway to the back of the room.

"Mr. Riederhof, do you believe this town provided sufficient services to your son?"

James Riederhof paused before answering.

"No. There were no wheelchair accessible men's shelter beds here."

Captain Higgins's teeth clicked.

"Not at the Salvation Army?" the reporter followed up.

"No. Their men's shelter is not handicap accessible. Someone in this town needs to get off their ass and fix that."

This time Stephen sucked air.

"Surely someone in this town has the resources needed to help make the Salvation Army shelter accessible," James clarified.

"They were very apologetic about that," Raymond cut in.

"But it's too late for Joseph," Mr. Riederhof emphasized.

"You indicated five murders of homeless people locally," began another questioner.

Stephen gasped. It was Richard Koenig.

James opened his mouth to respond but Ms. Abalada cut him off.

"I believe that is a question for the local police and coroner, sir," she said flatly sending Councilman Koenig a piercing glare. Then she raised her hand and said to the others, "Ladies and gentlemen, I'm afraid that was our last question, thank you. The Riederhofs are running late for their flight and must go." She turned her back to the reporters. Spoke briefly to the family, expertly shuffled them through the crowd, and they disappeared from camera range."

CHAPTER 56

Quote from the Journal of a Killer:

Perhaps it's more merciful to forget the dead
instead of remembering them.
Jose Bergaman

THURSDAY MORNING, JUNE 28, 2012:

After breakfast, Zachary peeked into Stephen's office, checked to see if anyone was watching, stepped in, snatched some business cards, and hurried out.

"Hey, bitch!"

Zachary flinched when he saw Rainey White tucked up against the payphone and looked to see who Rainey was addressing.

"You bitch! You...." Rainey stared at him hard. "You been talking around like you know something. But let me tell you, bitch, you don't know nothing!"

Zachary looked down and across his shoulder. "Who stuck your pig? I ain't done nuth'in."

"Don't get cute with me kid! That black bitch came by. Tried to nail me."

"I don't know any black bitch around here," Zachary sneered. "Wouldn't send a hog's ass your way if I did."

Rainey stepped forward.

"I'm talking about that lady cop. She came to my door with questions about Janice Zahn." Rainey sneered. "You remember that pretty little piece of ass don't you?"

Zachary gritted his teeth and lifted a fist.

"Thought you were sweet on her." Rainey's eyes sparkled over a twisted grin. "I don't like attracting the cops. I got a good thing going here and I ain't interested in leaving town."

Zachary shrugged. "So, what she want?"

"Said she heard I'd been spending some time with the little bitch. Messing around a bit."

"And?"

"And—said they'd matched my DNA to the semen inside her." Rainey's eyes penetrated Zachary's cold stare. "Anyway, I said, 'So, lots of guys been inside her.'" He glanced down at Zachary's genitals.

"Then that lady cop said, 'I know. We found three people's semen in her and one of them's probably her killer—I thought the bitch killed herself—anyway she asked, 'You got anything you want to say to me?'I said sure. We had sex a couple days before she died, but that didn't make me a killer."

"And this has what to do with me?" asked Zachary.

"Well, I figured the third guy must have been you. That'd make you the killer."

"You bastard!" Zachary's face flushed and his temples tensed. "I'm not the one who raped her then held her down for that Koe—Koenig guy. And I didn't brand her. I didn't cut her breast and sell her. You damn pimp. I ought to…."

"You ought to what?"

Zachary shut up but his breath whistled through his teeth. "Guess Janice's story about the two of you raping her was true." He looked down his nose at Rainey. In return, Rainey perused his body from top to bottom.

"You know, if three guys raped me in as many days, I might commit suicide, too." Rainey laughed raucously. "Nah … I'd have thought it a treat." He tilted his head down then up. "Anyway, then she started talking about Marta Lobo. Suggested I killed her because she wasn't a very cooperative slit then offed her old man when he made a fuss.

"Now, that talk had to come from somewhere else. Last I knew the spick just up and disappeared. They don't have a body—there wouldn't be any of my semen in it anyway—and I know she never went to the cops. She and the old man were too scared." Rainey was right up in his face now. Crowding him, their jeans brushing each other. "So, I figured somebody's been talking and it seems like all the questions were coming from people you're friends with. If you value your balls, you better not be saying anything to the cop lady about my contacts. That's my business and you better butt out except when I need you—and you better believe I'll be asking. You're too good a fuck and you owe me now. Big time."

Rainey bumped Zachary as he pushed past him.

Die cocksucker!

CHAPTER 57

Quote from the Journal of a Killer:

The only disability in life is a bad attitude.
unknown

BREAKFAST, JUNE 27, 2012:

"Mind if I sit here?"

Zachary looked at the skin headed man as he threw a brawny thigh up over the chair, slid his butt down to the seat, smirked, and said, "Don't mind if I do."

Zachary scanned him from top to table. The man's smell stung his nose.

"Name's Flynn. Cornelius Flynn. People call me Corny." He reached across the table to shake hands.

Ignoring the gesture, Zachary lifted a fork full of eggs to his mouth, and grunted. He didn't often take an immediate dislike to people.

"From Carter, Illinois," the man chatted on. "Been in this hell hole goin' on a week now. This place kicked me out Friday night. Can you believe that? Man's stuck in town for court 'cause they have some asshole of a judge and the Salvation Army kicks me out after three days. Where the hell they think a man's supposed to stay with no money?

"Passed out under them pine trees out there. Cops came around about three, woke me up, and told me to get moving." He snorted. "I'm smarter than those pigs down here. Walked around the block; laid back down. Not even the damn trains could wake me."

Zachary laid his fork down and gripped the sides of his tray with both hands.

"Wouldn't be here if that bitch hadn't tried to cut me off on the interstate. Hit the side of my trailer. Sent herself flyin' all the way across two lanes of traffic. Serves her right. Government shouldn't allow dumb people on the roads. They just get hurt. It's stupid, man. Plain stupid."

Zachary recognized Flynn from the news photos. Cornelius Flynn—the trucker who killed six people on the Interstate three weeks ago. Witnesses said the van was passing him on the left, halfway down his vehicle when he whipped out into their lane and spun them across the median into the path of another trucker on the other side. His alcohol level registered .12. An empty Tullamore Dew bottle lay tossed behind the driver's seat.

"You're lucky you're not sitting in jail," Zachary snarled. "Why'd they kick you out?"

"What?" Flynn raised his brows.

"Salvation Army. Why'd they kick you out?"

Flynn sneered. "Failed their fucking breathalyzer three nights in a row." He grunted. The pig-like sound irritated Zachary. "Those things don't work right. Probably calibrated wrong."

"How much?"

".199."

"You should have been passed out with that much alcohol in you." Zachary stiffened. "You killed six people. Why aren't you in jail?"

"She was an idiot, I tell you. Shouldn't...."

Zachary cut him off. "Paper said they put you in jail."

"Insurance paid the bail." Flynn shrugged his shoulders.

"On six murders? Gotta've been something more."

Flynn nodded. "Yeh...yeh, the kids. My old lady lit out for Montana or some wild place and left me with two boys—six and ten. What's a trucker supposed to do with two kids? ... My lawyer, the truck line's lawyer, got me out. Judge said to go home and take care of the kids."

Zachary pictured himself and Autry abandoned at home about the same ages. His anger roiled. "Then why are you here?" Zachary squared his shoulders. "And…?"

"Hey man. It's the damn company's fault! They came and pulled my truck leaving me stranded. How'm I supposed to get back to Illinois? I don't got no money left."

"Yeh, drank it all up like my dad."

Corny raised a threatening eyebrow. "Those boys can take care of themselves. They do when I'm out on the road. I don't see no difference."

Eyes flared, Zachary shot up; grabbed Flynn by his top button. The man's chair crashed as he jerked him half out of his seat. Zachary's right fist cocked above his shoulder before he caught Chet's raised eyebrows out of the corner of his eye. He dropped Flynn, shoved his tray clattering down the length of three tables, spat into his face, and literally stormed out the door the face of his own dad fresh and raw in his mind.

Somebody should kill mother-effers like that. Someone else could use that oxygen. He smacked a tree as he passed and winced with pain but kept truckin'.

CHAPTER 58

Quote from the Journal of a Killer:

Dying is easy; it's living that scares me to death.
Annie Lennox

"Stephen!" He heard the sob catch in Laqueta's throat. "I'm going to get fired."

His neck muscles immediately jerked taunt like exercise bands. "What…what's wrong?"

He'd always been the one to panic. *Breathe Stephen. Breathe.* That's what Gramms always said.

Laqueta sobbed.

"Breathe, Laqueta. Breathe."

He heard a deep sharp breath. She held it an unbearable minute before it slipped back out. "That's right." He sounded like Gramms. "Now, tell me what's up." He heard another deep breath but this time Laqueta exhaled quietly.

"I've been called to appear before the City Council. Chief said they want to review the homeless deaths. Are they murders or suicides?" Again she choked on a tear.

Stephen's hands signaled stop. Useless, she couldn't see through the phone. "Breathe."

"Chief thinks I crossed the County Attorney too many times. Probably a response to that Riederhof interview. Oh Stephen, I don't want to be cross-examined by the County Attorney. Lessig's ruthless. No friend of line cops. What can I do? I'm being invited to an inquisition, and on national TV." She took another deep breath.

Way to go, he encouraged her telepathically.

"Do you know if it was the County Attorney who called the meeting? Could it just be Chief reacting in fear? I imagine he's been called to appear, too." Stephen's calmness surprised him.

"Yes…" Control crept back into her voice. "He said we both had been requested to appear, in person, before the City Council at seven PM, July third. The Council Secretary made the call." Suddenly she stopped. He heard her neck pop—must have tilted it back. "Come to think of it, Chief did *not* mention the County Attorney when he quoted the call. Wait. The fax copy just came in."

Stephen heard the crackle of paper.

"No, it doesn't mention Lessig, neither as county attorney nor coroner." There was a shuffling of papers. "Look. Here it says this meeting has been called at the request of Councilman Richard Koenig and community activist Angelina Abbott. Oh, God…."

He knew Laqueta well enough. That was not swearing—just prayer.

"Stephen. What am I going to do? How do I prepare for *that*?" She talked on without a pause. "I know. Relax. Breathe. Lay it aside and let the mind digest it. You don't have to say it. Thanks for listening."

"No, I don't have to say it. You're the one who practices it better than I do. And you're welcome."

There was a salient pause. "Stephen? Would you come over tonight? I think I need someone to be with me."

His heart skipped. "I'll be there."

Captain Higgins slipped a fax in front of him.

His breath caught—his request to appear!

CHAPTER 59

Quote from the Journal of a Killer:

The quality of mercy is not strain'd,
It droppeth as the gentle rain from heaven
Upon the place beneath: it is twice blest;
It blesseth him that gives and him that takes.
William Shakespeare
The Merchant of Venice

"Ms. Abbott may I remind you that your testimony regarding these homeless deaths needs to be confined to the facts not gossip or innuendo."

Angelina Abbott stood hapless at the lectern as City Council President Bailey Brown chastised her.

Stephen chuckled inside at her comeback.

"But how can Investigator Ellison pretend to be objective when her boyfriend works for the Salvation Army?"

"Unless you can present factual incidents of Ms. Ellison's personal life compromising her job duties then I must ask you to refrain from personal attacks on a city employees' job performance. This council has been gracious enough to convene to review the accuracy of the coroner's rulings, the negative accusations made by Mr. James Riederhof and the media, and the potential damage to the community from the recent rash of homeless murders—I believe I am quoting your and Mr. Koenig's written request—please limit you testimony to those three issues."

Angelina bridled. A bit of rose colored her cheeks, but she remained defiant. "I'm just saying."

Stephen checked the reactions of the other Council Members then studied the faces of the ten Grand Island residents in attendance. The national media, confined to the rear of the council chambers, remained out of his vision range. Laqueta maintained disconnected professionalism. Not even a glance his way. Chief Greywright frowned, set his jaw, and looked down at the investigative reports and coroner's letters lying in front of him. A twinkle sparkled in Captain Higgins's eye and there were suppressed grins on the faces of the mayor, city manager, and Chamber of Commerce president. The reporter from the Independent sat with raised eyebrows but an otherwise placid face. And Zachary Plues....

Zachary Plues? ... What was he doing here?

"I just want to say," Angelina continued, "calling these suicides murders is a stretch. They're only homeless people for God's sake. We can't let their personal tragedies define who we are or cast shame on this fine, upstanding, godly, and compassionate community.

"We at the Salvation Army—she glanced at Stephen and Captain Higgins—do all we can to keep them off the streets and out of sight—meals, referrals to mental health, and clothes, so that they can look decent when seen. These allegations of murder—after the coroner has actually ruled otherwise—and Mr. Brown's sob stories in the paper cause nothing but trouble."

"You are aware aren't you," Councilwoman Staulker interrupted, "that the most recent death—she shuffled the papers in front of her—Javier Ruiz-Lobo has been ruled a homicide?"

Angelina shrugged and shot her a so-what look, but Councilman Bryant cut her off before she could respond. "Allegations of murder, Ms. Abbott, always warrant further investigation whether or not the individual is homeless. Isn't that right Chief?" He focused piercing eyes on Chief Greywright who shifted uncomfortably. "In fact I have some questions for Chief about that after you are finished—which I hope will be soon."

He peered at Angelina over black half frame glasses.

Angelina's gaze lowered to the podium top. "I believe my comments are finished. Thank you." She was clearly subdued. Who wouldn't be given the hostility of the council? thought Stephen.

"Councilman Koenig, do you have anything to add?" asked the Council President.

"Yes, indeed," he answered. "But first let me say that I find this council's treatment of Ms. Abbott reprehensible! She is a fine upstanding citizen of this community involved in many civic activities and highly valued for her work on behalf of the homeless citizens of this town continuing in the footsteps of her aunts Grace and Edith Abbott to whom this city owes an immeasurable debt."

He glanced down at some notes in front of him. "First, I want to address the recent comments of Mr. James Riederhof, father of one of the victims. I believe Mr. Riederhof's allegation that these deaths—the coroner's report of Ruiz-Lobo didn't come out till after he left town—represent the ruminations of a desperate grieving father unable to accept the truth that his son committed suicide.

"May I interject here that Mr. Brown's conjectures—he shot Stephen a withering look—are simply attention grabbing ploys to enhance fundraising and donations."

Stephen's eyebrows shot up. He glanced toward Captain Higgins.

"The coroner's job is to weigh all the facts and competing theories. Our County Attorney is certainly more highly trained and competent to do that than a mere civilian.

"The tragedy of the Riederhof family though its final resolution occurred here neither warrants national news coverage nor reflects negatively on the character of our fair city. His emotional appeal to his family's history of work with the homeless back east may not even accurately reflect reality for all we know.

"Mr. Riederhof's mean spirited statement that homeless persons are treated as second class citizens reflects badly on the volume of homeless services rendered locally and denigrates the work of our fine police force. He could not possibly have sufficient basis to call all five deaths murders and allege a cover up. Neither can we be blamed for the failure of homeless persons to accept the restorative services available to rescue them from their condition. And who in their right mind would spend personal time with such raggedy, smelly, disgusting people—sorry, Captain Higgins."

Captain Higgins nodded. Councilman Koenig probably took it as agreement, but Stephen recognized the dismissive I-hear-you nature of the movement.

"As to the value of Mr. Brown's stories, I completely disagree with Mr. Riederhof. The emotional tone of his writing and the stories themselves do nothing of service to this community. I believe their sole purpose is to increase donations—not to, as Mr. Brown alleges, humanized and honor the homeless. That's an absurd statement.

"Finally, Mr. Riederhof's name calling—calling our County Attorney slash coroner a 'complete idiot'—was rude and certainly inappropriate. And, in a similar vein, Mr. Riederhof's allegation that the investigation clearly proved his son's death was murder does a disservice to Chief Greywright—with whom I understand Mr. Lessig spoke at length before issuing his ruling—and to this sweet young woman sitting there, Investigator Ellison.

"I respectfully called this special council meeting to urge you all—he paused to look at each council member individually—to issue a statement of support for our local coroner, a commendation of our community's support of homeless services, and an affirmation of the professionalism and work of Chief Greywright and his assistant, Investigator Ellison."

Stephen folded his arms and rubbed his biceps. Laqueta glanced at him and gave a supportive nod.

"Members of the public," began Council President Brown, "are there any additional public comments on this issue?"

There were negative shakes of heads, but otherwise no response.

"Then, Council members, I open the floor for your questions or concerns."

"Investigator Ellison...." It was Councilwoman Philomena Cortez-Rios speaking. "Do you believe these homeless deaths were suicides or murders?"

A portable mic was passed to Laqueta who stood to answer.

"Ms. Cortez-Rios," Laqueta began, "first I want to state that in the latest death, Mr. Javier Ruiz-Lobo, all evidence points toward homicide and I am certainly in agreement with the coroner's ruling. As for the other deaths, the evidence remains less decisive. It is not my duty as a law enforcement officer to comment one way or another on a coroner's ruling unless additional evidence has come to light."

"Yes, I understand, Ms. Ellison," the councilwoman replied then looked askance at her, "but I am asking for your personal opinion." She raised her chin holding Laqueta's eyes in focus. "Do *you* believe the other four deaths were suicides or murders?" She softened her gaze. "And, yes, I know this puts you in an uncomfortable position in relationship to the coroner and possibly your boss."

"Well, ma'am," Laqueta squared her shoulders. "We are assuming that the young man found in the garage on First Street was homeless. Notwithstanding, like the case of Javier Ruiz-Lobo, the evidence leads to the conclusion that he was killed by a second party. That said, I do not personally believe that Mr. Riederhof, Ms. Zahn, nor Henry Many Horses committed suicide. Henry Many Horses' death may have been a mercy killing. Mr. Riederhof's I now believe was accidental. As for Ms. Zahn, I do not believe, despite the placement of her hands, that she committed suicide, but as to the nature of her death I am not sure."

"Have you shared those opinions with the Chief of Police or the coroner, Ms. Ellison?" Councilman Bryant took up the questioning.

Stephen noticed her shoulders slump when she looked toward Chief Greywright.

"Yes, both verbally and in the investigative report."

"And is it true that the Chief and the coroner discussed the final ruling as to cause of death?"

"Councilman, I suggest you ask the Chief directly, but based on conversations with him I believe that is true."

Masterful thought Stephen with a satisfied smile.

"Chief?" asked Councilman Bryant.

"Yes, that is correct."

"Ms. Ellison," Councilwoman Dinsmore joined the conversation, "why do you believe Mr. Riederhof did not kill himself? The coroner's report—she lifted the paper in front of her—says he died from a separated spinal cord caused by hanging with a polyester cord."

"Yes, ma'am, I found him hanging by a polyester cord that had been thrown over a tree branch. A severed spinal cord versus suffocation indicates a fall caused the fatal separation. However, Mr. Riederhof's recent physical deterioration left him unable to move his wheelchair or feed himself. A person in that condition could not throw a rope over a tree branch nor make a knot or roll a wheelchair far enough to create the drop that jerked him from that chair. That is why I do not believe Joseph Riederhof committed suicide. The method of death—it's messy and potentially mentally terrifying—and the apparently quick abandoning of the body show lack of compassion or a sense of fear at what had happened. For those reasons, I do not believe his death was an assisted suicide or mercy killing. I realize that leaves many questions unanswered, especially since evidence indicates the death involved at least one other person."

"And you shared his inability to commit suicide with Chief Greywright and in your report?" asked Councilwoman Staulker.

"Yes, I shared it with Chief Greywright. No, I did not make that direct statement in the investigative report. However, I did make that direct statement to Mr. Lessig in a verbal conversation about the report."

"And yet they chose to rule it a suicide?" Councilman Echemendia joined the conversation. He sounded incredulous. "Do you know why they would do that?"

"Sir, I would rather not speculate."

"Chief," Councilwoman Hornaday turned to face Chief Greywright as she addressed him, "I have some serious questions for you, but first..." She turned to face Stephen. "Stephen, why did you write those articles? That first one plainly questioned the coroner's ruling."

Laqueta handed Stephen the mic and signaled him with her eyebrows.

"Lillian—Councilwoman Hornaday..." He found it difficult to be formal with someone he knew from the Salvation Army and church. "I wrote those articles because I believe all human beings have equal worth and that worth needs to be honored for these homeless victims." He pressed his eyebrows together. "And, yes, the first article directly questioned the coroner's ruling. The error of the ruling was just too plain."

"So, do you also disagree with the coroner's other rulings?"

"Yes, ma'am." His words a clear, sharp staccato.

"Please explain."

"My reasons regarding Joseph Riederhof are the same as those presented by Laqueta." His left eye twitched. He should have addressed her by her formal title. "*I* believe his death was accidental."

"Because you've been sleeping with the enemy," Richard Koenig said under his breath but his mic picked it up with enough volume for everyone in the room to frown or raise an eye brow.

"Janice's hand was on the zip tie around her neck, but her blood alcohol level according to the medical examiner was 0.31," Stephen continued, "High enough to kill some people and certainly to render most of us unconscious. I don't believe she was physically able to yank that zip tie tight enough to kill herself. I believe she wished to die just not that she killed herself."

"And on what do you base that?" Richard Koenig demanded.

"Her background of incest, severe sexual assault, and her miscarriage—caused by a severe beating—made her fragile to begin with. The rapes, cutting, and branding she experienced through one of the local pimps and one of you city council members added enough trauma, in my opinion, to push her over the edge."

Loud gasps filled the room at the mention of a city council member followed by a loud twitter from the media at the back. Councilman Koenig shot him an evil eye. In his periphery vision Stephen noticed Zachary Plues had slipped out of the room.

"Order please." Council President Brown rapped his gavel loudly. "Are you saying one of these council members raped Ms. Zahn before her death?"

"Yes, sir. I am." He maintained unbroken eye contact with Richard Koenig. "And that same councilman branded her 'mine' on the inside of her pelvis."

Again, audible gasps. Silence followed.

Most people, including Captain Higgins were looking at their laps, but Laqueta examined his face.

"Ms. Ellison," President Brown waited till her eyes were focused on his, "Is this so? I assume it is listed in the medical examiner's report."

"Yes, sir," she replied, "There were two brands 'mine', one on each side inside the pelvis. I believe you have a copy of the medical examiner's report in front of you. You will find it on page two near the middle of the page."

Ten sets of papers rustled on the council members' dais. Chief Greywright also riffled through the packet on his lap.

"And did you investigate these brands?" Councilman Federico Echemendia asked alarm in his voice. "Branding is considered torture. It casts this suicide in a different light. That is if it was a suicide. Someone who brands a person might equally be able to kill that same individual."

"Are you saying someone on this council might have murdered Ms. Zahn?" Councilwoman Dinsmore asked Federico her eyes round with terror.

Laqueta without pause answered Councilman Echemendia.

"Sir, I tried to further investigate the marks on Ms. Zahn's body. Semen from three individuals was found in her vagina—one a known sex offender, the other two not listed in any of the national databases. I interviewed the sex offender. He stated that he and Ms. Zahn had consensual sex but claimed no knowledge of the marks on her body. He asserted that the brands were not there when they had sexual contact. With Ms. Zahn dead, there were no direct witnesses to what happened and no way to refute the suspect's claims. Likewise there was insufficient evidence to search his room or to otherwise connect him to the brands."

"Then how do you know what happened? Do you have any evidence that one of these councilmen was involved?"

Lillian Hornaday was addressing Stephen again.

He held his confidence.

"Janice related the events of that night to one of her friends. He saw the brands. As a source for much of the information in my articles, I have found his information to generally be verifiable—leastways that which could be found in my background investigations and family notifications."

"And his name?"

"I'm sorry Lillian. I'm not at liberty to share that information."

"And you were acting off of Stephen's information?" Richard Koenig challenged Laqueta.

"No, sir," she responded equally quickly. "My investigation was founded only on the facts in the coroner's report and my investigation of the scene, specifically the semen that was identified as Mr. White's. You will find my report makes no allegations regarding the parties involved in the branding, the cut under her breast, or the nature of the sexual contact. Mr. Brown's information, for investigative purposes, is intriguing but falls in the category of hearsay."

"I see," Councilman Koenig replied with a crooked grin. "So there is no basis for Mr. Brown's allegations."

"There is insufficient basis to warrant further investigation," corrected Laqueta. "His statement may be true or inaccurate. However, the information and detail Mr. Brown provided when he shared that information with me matched point by point the medical examiner's report and my own visual inspection of Ms. Zahn's body."

It was Stephen's turn to sink into relief. Captain Higgins' nod helped buoy him up.

"One more thing Ms. Ellison," Lillian Hornaday continued. "Are you and Mr. Brown an item?"

"No, ma'am. Just friends. I have interviewed him several times related to these cases and found his information helpful, but insufficient to completely solve them. I have provided some details of the cases, things that are public knowledge, to help complete his articles accurately."

"I see." Lillian nodded and pulled her glasses down from her forehead to further examine the reports in front of her before continuing. "Before I ask you my question, Chief Greywright," she looked at him over the top of her glasses but addressed Laqueta, "Ms. Ellison, are the investigations on any of these cases still open?"

"Only that of the unidentified body from the garage, but we currently have no further leads to follow. All the others, no."

"Why?" Lillian shifted her gaze to Laqueta.

"Once an investigative report on a homeless person is submitted to the County Attorney, coroner, the investigation is closed."

"And what would it take to open it?"

"A request from the coroner or an unexpected major piece of new information."

Ms. Hornaday returned to her withering fixation on Chief Greywright before asking Laqueta one last question.

"And is this the way non-homeless deaths are handled?"

Laqueta dropped her gaze. "No, ma'am."

"Chief Greywright." Councilwoman Hornaday began. Everyone knew tension had marked their relationship for some time. "So, you personally review these cases with the coroner before he makes his ruling?"

"Yes, Councilwoman."

"And do you discuss with the corner what ruling would be most appropriate?"

"Yes, ma'am. He always asks my opinion, my recommendation."

"I see." She tilted her head toward the Chief. "And all of these rulings—she held up the copies of the reports—reflect your opinion?"

"Yes, Ma'am."

"He wrote what you recommended?"

"Yes, Ma'am."

"Then why, with the excellent work of your chief investigator, Ms. Ellison, are all of these—except Ruiz-Lobo—listed as suicides when these investigative reports—she held up a second stack of reports—give evidence that they most likely were not?"

Chief twisted his hips, looked off toward the corner then straightened up and sighed.

"Because this Department does not have sufficient funds to justify further investigation of the deaths of homeless individuals, especially those for whom we have no family contacts."

"What?" Councilman Echemendia responded one eyebrow lifted. "You do not have family contacts on any of these individuals? Wasn't this meeting called because of the negative press following Joseph Riederhof's family's news conference? Enlighten me."

Again Chief took a visible deep breath and let it escape audibly. "At the time the rulings were made there were no family contacts known."

"And whose responsibility is that?" Council President Brown cut in.

"The coroner's office."

"Then why, in the past, did your office make the notifications to my father's family members?"

"Because identifying surviving family members was a part of the investigative process back then."

"And it isn't now?" asked the president addressing Laqueta.

"No, Sir."

Councilmember Elmer Maas, who had sat quietly throughout the meeting, began to scratch his scalp during this current line of questioning.

"Excuse me, Mr. President," he said. "Chief, why has your department stopped locating next of kin? And when? Also, is this the policy for homeless deaths or all deaths handled by your department?"

Typical Elmer, Stephen thought. He followed that same pattern during the Salvation Army board meetings—quiet listening followed by a series of probing questions. But he was a great guy and Stephen appreciated a quiet man who nonetheless was an effective leader and successful businessman.

"Well, Elmer," Chief began, "the Police Department stopped locating next of kin, and doing notifications of next of kin, when this Council cut our budget three years ago. For years we did both as a courtesy to the coroner's office, but according to the county's governing documents both notification of next of kin and locating next of kin is a function of the coroner's office. My understanding is that the Police Department took up that function when the Council combined the office of coroner and the office of the County Attorney many decades ago. With your cuts to our budget, we can no longer provide unfunded services. And, yes, this is the policy for all deaths handled by the department both homeless and otherwise."

There was a slight pause then Ms. Hornaday slowly tilted her head toward the side and asked, "So your department handles homeless deaths and crimes against the homeless with the same in depth work?" Though she had been looking at the Chief she suddenly turned toward Laqueta. "Ms. Ellison?"

Laqueta flinched. She paused for an awkward moment before answering.

Stephen's heart pounded in his chest. He knew the answer and it was a deep seated point of disagreement between the Chief and Laqueta. If he could have he would have answered for her.

"No, Councilwoman Hornaday, we do not," she said in a careful, measured manner.

"No?" Councilwoman Hornaday exhibited shock at the unexpected direct answer.

"Are you telling this Council that you handle homeless cases different than those of other citizens?" asked Council President Brown.

"Yes."

Stephen noticed Laqueta had skipped the formal address.

"And why, Investigator Ellison, do you do that? May I ask?" he followed up.

"Because I have specifically been instructed to do so by my supervisor Chief Greywright."

CHAPTER 60

Quote from the Journal of a Killer:

A dying man needs to die, as a sleepy man needs to sleep, and there comes a time when it is wrong, as well as useless, to resist.
Stewart Alsop

"I don't think Chief understands how damning his statements were," Captain Higgins said to Stephen after the City Council withdrew into an Executive Session. "It goes to character and judgment on his part and neither looks good when a Police Chief admits his department treats homeless individuals like second class citizens. Makes me glad you wrote those articles. Family notification might not have happened if you hadn't."

"And I'm glad, too."

Stephen and Captain turned to the woman who spoke from behind them.

"I certainly didn't know how to dig out the things you found or have the time to do it. Besides, the stories make the people real. Makes me feel my job is about the living not just the dead."

"Hi. You must be Sally." Stephen beamed.

"That's me," she replied with an easy laugh.

"Captain, this is Sally Henson from the coroner's office."

Captain extended his broad hand. "Captain Bramwell Higgins. Pleased to meet you."

"Ladies and gentlemen..." Council President Brown rapped his gavel once on the dais. "...can I please have your attention. Councilman Bryant, I believe you have a motion."

"Yes. Thank you, Mr. President. I move that we adopt the following:

> We, the Grand Island City Council, do hereby direct the Chief of the Grand Island Police Department and all of his officers and employees to ensure that all matters pertaining to homeless individuals in this city are given the same attention to detail and timeliness of action afforded to all of our citizens. In order to facilitate this policy we do authorize the addition of $50,000 to the budget of the Police Department for law enforcement and investigative services."

"Ladies and Gentlemen," President Brown declared, "This proposal is hereby opened for public comment or questions."

After one full minute with no responses, he continued, "I hereby close this period of public comments. Ladies and gentlemen of the Council do I have a second to this motion?"

Councilwoman Staulker seconded it.

"All those in favor please raise you right hand ... Let it be reflected in the minutes and statues that this motion has been unanimously approved without comment.

"Now, Councilwoman Hornaday, I believe you have a motion to offer."

"Thank you, Mr. President. I hereby move that we approve the following in response to issues and concerns raised related to the recent rash of homeless deaths in the City of Grand Island:

> The City Council of Grand Island, Nebraska, formally requests that the Hall County Coroner officially reopen and review the cause of death rulings on Joseph Elias Riederhof, Janice Abigail Zahn, and Henry Many Horses as related to the validity of the current rulings of suicide.
>
> Further, the City Council of Grand Island, Nebraska, also instructs Chief Zane Greywright to reopen the above named

> cases plus those of the unidentified victim of May 28, 2012 and Javier Ruiz-Lobo with such cases remaining open until such time as the perpetrator or perpetrators of said deaths can be determined and, where appropriate, brought to trial."

"Ladies and Gentlemen." President Brown picked up his gavel but laid it down again. "This proposal is hereby opened for public comment or questions." Then after one full minute with no responses. "I hereby close this period of public comments. Ladies and gentlemen of the Council do I have a second to this motion?"

"Second."

Stephen wasn't sure who offered the second.

"All those in favor please raise you right hand.... Let it be reflected in the minutes and statues that this motion has been approved by a majority vote of the Council without comment and with one abstention."

Richard Koenig abstained, but when Stephen inspected his face, the councilman maintained a blank affect with no telltale body language.

"At this time ladies and gentlemen I believe we have one more motion to entertain. I have asked Councilman Echemendia to present it on my behalf. Councilman...."

"Mr. President. I do hereby move that the following statement be adopted:

> We, the members of the Grand Island City Council do commend Grand Island Police Department Investigator Laqueta Charity Ellison for her professionalism in performance of her work duties and in her deportment and communication. We especially wish to honor her for her dedication to and the thoroughness of her investigations into the deaths of the unnamed victim of May 28, 2012, Joseph E. Riederhof, Janice A. Zahn, Henry Many Horses, and Javier Ruiz Lobo. We do recommend and direct that this commendation be placed in her personnel records and be considered in all future opportunities for promotion and for appropriate salary increases.

> Additionally, we commend Investigator Ellison for work above and beyond her duties in assisting Mr. Stephen Brown with compiling accurate life stories for the above victims and assisting Mr. Brown in understanding the workings of the Grand Island Police Department and such points of law as appropriate to his endeavors.
>
> This Council wishes to express our warm appreciation for Mr. Brown's work humanizing and honoring the recent homeless victims of death in this community and wish to encourage him to continue such work from time to time when appropriate occasions arise. To further this work, and in light of his excellent evaluation of the facts in the above mentioned cases, we hereby request that Mr. Brown officially assist Investigator Ellison in seeking to solve the above crimes including helping her to develop the evidence and contacts needed to press forward her investigations whenever such information will not compromise confidential sources or his working relationships with our homeless citizens."

Stephen glanced at Laqueta then looked down at his hand. Just how did the Council think he could assist in a murder investigation, let alone five of them?

The commendation passed with a verbal "I do not support this action" from Richard Koenig, and a dirty look from Angelina Abbott. President Brown invited Stephen and Laqueta to his office—a smoke screen for getting them out a rear entrance in order to avoid the national media. They ducked out the back door and headed up Bartenbach's Alley to his apartment. Their cars would be retrieved after the media wolves settled into their dens for the night.

CHAPTER 61

Quote from the Journal of a Killer:

"A beautiful death is for people who have lived like animals to die like angels."
Mother Teresa quoted by Kathryn Spinks

Gramms surveyed the briefcase, notes, portfolios and writing utensils spread across the terracotta table in the solarium off her country kitchen.

She topped off all their coffee and passed Laqueta some hazelnut cream.

"Yes, Gramms. We needed a relaxing place to work on these murders and I thought getting away from the city might help us get a new perspective," Stephen said. "That's why we came up early."

"I really thought Chief Greywright would object." Stephen smiled at ease with which Laqueta inserted herself into the conversation. "After the Council Meeting, I figured he'd be furious, make me work the holiday and all weekend, too."

"Maybe that's why he didn't object to you coming, honey," Gramms said, a glint in her eyes. "To get you out of his sight for the holiday and weekend. Besides how could he say 'no' to a pretty thing like you?"

"Ms. Brown…." Laqueta gazed down and her face flushed.

"Call me Gramms. That's what all Stephen's friends do. I'd like that very much…. And what's more, this fine young man—a sleepy eyed Darren had just shuffled to the kitchen doorway—needed to get away from the city; don't you think? This is a great place for a young man to run wild."

His head tipped down Darren came over and leaned on Stephen's shoulder.

"Where's the horses?" he asked.

"Didn't you drive past them on your way in?" Gramms looked into his eyes and smiled.

"Dem's all yours," Darren said wide eyed. "Aren't they wild?"

"Well, some are. But I try to saddle up the skittish ones and ride them for a few minutes every day."

Darren tilted his head and watched her squint-eyed, as she stepped into the kitchen for a glass of orange juice.

"But you ancient."

"Darren," reprimanded Laqueta.

"Oh, it's okay honey." Gramms tousled the boy's hair. "Five year olds think like that." She picked him up to eye level by his shoulders. He leaned back saucer eyed. "You'll see it different when you're 'ancient' like me."

The next couple hours Stephen and Laqueta filled Gramms in on the latest cases. Gramms, always inquisitive, asked a lot of questions. Darren busied himself playing with Stephen's old toys kept in a toy box against the solarium wall. Then, after a Jeep tour of the ranch—Darren went wild when they drove among the horses, they enjoyed a lazy glass of ice tea in the dining room.

"So you went and upset Angelina again?" asked Gramms.

"Enough for her to haul me before the City Council," Stephen replied. "I don't know what she thought they would do. Spank me?"

They laughed together while Laqueta looked down sheepishly.

"I'm sorry honey. Sometimes Stephen and I aren't so well behaved. But it helps us get the tension out of our systems. Then we get serious. And you, you must have been terrified being hauled before the Council with your boss' policies on the line."

"She was afraid she'd get fired," Stephen said. "But if there is one thing I know about this lady she's always honest and she tries to answer all questions directly. Just like you taught me. By the way, who's that black lady in the old tintype up there on the mantel? I don't remember seeing that before."

"She's your great, great, great grandmother, Amelia Brown."

Stephen's eyes popped wide. The strain of a question flushed his cheeks. "But she's black." He blurted it out but immediately realized how racist it sounded.

"Stephen," Gramms rebuked him. Stephen blushed. "That's what he said when he first told me about you," she added turning toward Laqueta. "I could tell right away he was sweet on you."

Stephen leaned into his finger tips. "I'm sorry, Gramms. You know I'm not racist. Why, we're even relatives of John Brown. We've always had sympathy for the black cause."

"Stephen! That's tacky." Gramms looked down into the skirt on her lap.

Laqueta caught Stephen's eyes. Her look was sharp, concerned, but not judgmental.

"Black is not a cause," she said firmly. "It's a race. I am not a cause. I'm a person."

"Truth is we come from plantation stock," Gramms elaborated, "down Louisiana way. My grandmother and both of Stephen's great grandmothers were southern belles. In fact, until I married his grandfather, I was a southern belle—a more modern kind but still a southern belle. When I think back to those days in the south, I'm none too proud of it. But truth is that's the way it was. Thank God it's changing.

"Anyway, Amelia was a slave on the Lanrfreniere Plantation which the Browns had owned for I don't know how long. When the Civil War ended, lots of planters' sons married black women. Mostly they'd grown up friends and were celebrating their freedom to love who they wanted. Amelia was a gorgeous girl, kind of like you. Her momma ran the plantation house so she grew up cultured and was included in most of the family activities.

"Stephen is right. The Browns were not as arrogant as some white owners. In fact there is no record of the Lanrfreniere Browns' ever selling one of their slaves. The tale is told that they often bought their slave girls lovers so they could securely live together and raise their families without fear."

Gramms paused and looked up at the tintype.

"Well, Ezekiel Brown had his eye on Amelia for quite some time. When he came back from the War, he asked her to marry him. That picture was taken on their fiftieth wedding anniversary.

"Since his brother Edward, the first born son, inherited the family plantation, Ezekiel Lanfrie Brown struck out for the West and homesteaded here near Anselmo in 1865. In 1872 he filed for a pre-emption and a timber claim which together equaled eighteen hundred and forty seven acres of land. That's how come we have so much room for all them horses.

"And yes, Amelia experienced plenty of hate from the white pioneers on these plains. Both from easterners come west and European immigrants.

"As people abandoned their homesteads due to hardship, Grandpa Ezikiel purchased or filed pre-emption claims on additional lands. Then during Theodore Roosevelt's presidency, he relocated his farmstead in order to claim another land grant of six hundred and forty acres.

"Of course we've bought more land over the years."

She paused and looked at Stephen and Laqueta. Both sported inquisitive looks.

"My husband, William Lanfrie Brown grew up on the original homestead until his parents inherited this place. The same happened to the two of us after we married. This ranch headquarters sits on that six hundred and forty acre land grant. And this house, though it's been expanded and updated several times—thank God—is the original one Grandpa Ezekiel Brown built with his own hands." Gramms looked without focus at the mantel clock.

"Seems my own son's not interested in ranching—and actually I'm glad cause he's a fool with money—so I manage the place with the help of John Kinchloe, my foreman. I've arranged for Stephen to inherit all of this when I'm gone. It'll be up to him whether to live here or manage it through a foreman."

She looked down. "My how an old lady's rambled on."

"Oh, no. I've enjoyed it," Laqueta reassured her. "I've never understood just how homesteading helped build this state. My family didn't come this way till my grandfather brought his kids and wife here after World War II. And then we've only lived in Omaha. I'm the first to move away.

"About race, Gramms, there's actually a lot of white blood in my family. Maybe more than there is black."

Stephen cocked his head. Now this was new. He noticed Gramms had the same reaction.

"But you're dark as midnight," he said. "I don't mean no disrespect—and you're the most beautiful elegant woman I've met of any color—but I don't understand."

"It's genetics—pure genetics. We experience it more visibly than you white boys." She laughed as she gave him that little dig. "My great, great, great grandfather, William Ellison, was an infamous slave owner."

"I'm sorry," said Gramms. "I take it he was a plantation owner?"

"He was. In fact he owned several plantations. But he started out as a slave—very light skinned with three generations of white fathers and grandfathers. He bought his own freedom and that of his wife and children. Considering all of his mothers and grandmothers were house slaves and thus most likely mixed race themselves, William may have been nearly pure white. But in those times, a lot like today, he was still considered black.

"As a free black man he became one of the largest landholders in South Carolina. But that's not why he was so hated. You see, he was a slave breeder." She blushed. "At the beginning of the Civil War he held more slaves than any other slave owner in South Carolina and he was no more interested in them being freed than any white man.

"I am black, but I'm in no position to throw stones at the white landed aristocracy." She paused. Stephen felt a bit of burn on his cheeks as she assessed his and Gramms responses.

"And, as far as John Brown, who knows, we may be related. My mother's name is Ojetta Mason Brown, from a long line of slaves tracing their ancestry back to Cornelius Brown. I've never thought to trace John Brown's family tree to see if he had any southern cousins, but my mother's first free grandfather, being light skinned, was rumored to be Cornelius Brown's slave son."

Gramms stood to pick Amelia Brown's picture off the mantel and handed it to Laqueta. "Seems you two have more in common than one might think. Now, Stephen, I want to know when you're going to do something about it!"

CHAPTER 62

Quote from the Journal of a Killer:

Life is hard. Then you die. Then they throw dirt in your face.
Then the worms eat you.
Be grateful it happens in that order.
David Gerrold

Darren leaned back against Stephen as they approached the cedar grove near the canyon's rim.

"Mr. Stephen, are there Indians down there?"

Stephen tilted his head to peer around the grove of cedars. "I ain't seen one in thirty six years, but anything's possible."

Darren mimicked his stare and Laqueta laughed.

"You two," she said, "What am I going to do with you?"

After coaxing, and lifting, Laqueta took to riding like a pure country girl. She even asked to go explore the canyon with Darren and Stephen Friday while Gramms headed off to town—the city girl wanted to go horseback riding instead of shopping.

"I'll take you by the old teepee rings down on the river," Stephen said to Darren. "Maybe we can find an arrowhead or broken pot scraper."

Appreciation and love set in his dark brown eyes, Darren looked straight up into Stephen's. What more could a man want—well, except for an equally loving relationship with a good wife?

The surefooted horses climbed down the steep trail to the canyon floor five hundred vertical feet below. The sheer beauty of this entry to the canyon compelled silence and the horses seemed determined not to break it. They trailed quietly along the canyon bottom side by side in mirrored strides.

"Do you think there might be one lone killer?" Stephen asked.

"Possibly," Laqueta replied. "But the level of violence in Javier's murder breaks the pattern. Besides, what common motive could there be?"

"Some vigilante trying to clear the streets of homeless and undocumented Hispanics?" offered Stephen.

"Mr. Stephen! What was that?" Darren pointed to a branch bouncing lightly off to their left.

Stephen reined in his horse and nosed it toward the Ponderosa pines searching for other movements or hidden colors. About twenty feet out he stopped and pointed to a branch six feet above the one that moved.

"See that?" he asked quietly. "Up next to the trunk on that branch with a little curlicue."

Darren and Laqueta both leaned forward in their saddles.

"Look Mom!" Darren whispered his hand and arm paralleling Stephen's. "What is it, Mr. Stephen?"

The animal moved its head to peer out at them with glowing eyes.

"A bobcat," said Stephen. "You see it?" he asked Laqueta. "There." He shifted his arm to the point she was concentrating on then lowered it toward the wild cat. "Must be about ten years old. I'm surprised he's letting us see him."

"Oh, now I see," said Laqueta excited.

"Old Mackey probably traps ten of them a year in the canyons around here."

"I want to trap him," Darren said with a loud gasp that caused the bobcat's ears to point straight up.

"Shush," cautioned Laqueta but it was too late. The bobcat stood deftly on all four legs then reached up, pulled himself to a branch three feet above, leapt to another tree about fifteen feet away, and disappeared into the pine cover.

CHAPTER 62

After they got back to the ranch and cleaned up—Stephen didn't like smelling like a horse—Stephen fetched a roll of butcher paper from the hall closet and spread it out on the ox yoke table in the dining room. The smell of bison roast escaped the kitchen. Gramms and Stephen had started a small herd about five years ago. Just enough for butchering every year and selling as breed stock.

"So how shall we chart them?" He asked referring to the five homeless murder cases.

"Let's make columns for name, date discovered, coroner's date of death, gender, age, coroner's listed cause of death, means used—like rope, alcohol, zip tie; there might be more than one—personal history, known contacts, and possible suspects."

Laqueta's penmanship outshone his so she did the writing. For possible suspect they listed Rainey White by the entries for Janice, Hank, and Javier. At Stephen's insistence they also wrote Councilman Koenig by Janice and La Linea after Javier's name. They had precious little evidence linking anyone to the death scenes. Actually, that wasn't true. The same fingerprints were found at each location, but they were not in the national data bases. And there were the three semen specimens in Janice with one match—Rainey's. Laqueta had arrested him for failure to register as a sex offender, but at arraignment the judge released him pending a court hearing.

"Any insights?" asked Gramms.

"Not a lot yet," said Stephen with a frown.

Gramms, reading upside down, perused the chart then returned to the means of death column and studied it from the top down.

"If these deaths are related," she began, "I see a progression here. A sophistication in means and method. More efficient. But what was the motive?"

"Yes, we need a column for that," said Stephen, "though I'm now sure we've identified one."

"I've been noticing all of these victims—except the unidentified boy—were victims themselves or had other significant problems besides homelessness," said Laqueta. She rested her finger on each name as she continued. "Grieving paraplegic losing all control; incest, rape, and sexual abuse; developmentally handicapped and lost; terrified immigrant…hmm."

CHAPTER 63

Quote from the Journal of a Killer:

"So they were completely destroyed without mercy, as the Lord *had commanded..."*
Joshua 11:20 **New Living Translation**

FRIDAY, JULY 6, 2012:

Rage roiled through Zachary's veins. His stomach burned every time he saw Rainey White. When Rainey tried to pimp him out on the 4th that took the cake. With detasseling money, he bought fifty feet of half inch manila rope, a bottle of Intimate Kisses aphrodisiac oil, some handcuffs, and a silky green oriental scarf. However, when he found the machete—blade sharp as a razor—the method of death came together.

"Rainey!" He beat on Rainey's door. "Rainey!"

It took six sharp raps repeated five times to elicit a response. Figured Rainey had someone in there. Thought he heard a child's voice. His stomach wrenched.

"Hold your horses," Rainey yelled.

Zachary heard the bathroom shower door open and close but no sound of running water.

CHAPTER 63

"Whad'u want!" Rainey opened the door and peeked through the crack left by the door chain. "Oh, you. You change your mind?"

"No! But I felt bad about how I treated you the other day. And—you know—for the lady detective hassling you. I want to make it up to you." Zachary tried to sound his sweetest and most sincere.

"The Councilman's not interested any more. I don't have anybody right now wanting a boy. Sorry, I can't help you." Rainey started to shut the door.

Zachary braced his foot against it. "Wait! I told you. I'm not interested in that."

"Then whad'u want?"

"I told you. I want to make it up to you—the hassle you got by the lady detective. I know you like getting into my pants. I know you like things rough. And I heard you like to play outdoors so I've planned a little outdoor feast for you."

"You. On me?" Rainey's eyes lit up.

"With nothing in return?"

"Nothing in return."

"Where?" Rainey let the pressure off the door and Zachary moved his foot.

"In the woods on the corner at Third and Plum across from the railroad tracks. The whole north side of that block is deserted. Nobody should bother us."

"Okay," Rainey sounded cautious but excited.

"Tonight. Around eleven. But don't come early. I need to get everything set before you get there." He flicked his eyebrows to make it sound intriguing.

"Okay!" Rainey almost slobbered on himself. "See you around eleven fifteen. But, I'm not sure you *can* be ready for *me* boy."

Zachary walked out to the Western Edge on Highway 281 and bought a fancy red bandana then headed home for a balled up pair of socks. He carried all his supplies across the street to the empty lot and double checked for evidence of any recent traffic. Nothing.

He spread a quilt—made by the Salvation Army Sewing League—under a large hackberry tree and set out the socks, bandanna, oriental scarf, a pair of fuzzy handcuffs, and massage oil in neat order. Next he made a perfect noose from the rope. He'd studied up on it in the library and practiced several times with a piece of polyester cord. He tossed the noose over a limb about fifteen feet up and tied the loose end to a nearby tree. As an afterthought he went back to the house for a length of polyester cord. He might need it to hold Rainey's body against the tree. Some of what he had planned wouldn't work with a body dancing around on its tiptoes.

His plan came off without a hitch.

Rainey showed at eleven fifteen and got real excited at the candle luminaries in brown bags that cast a dreamlike glow over the clearing under the trees. Zachary secured Rainey's arms behind his back with the fuzzy handcuffs. Silently he blindfolded him with the scarf then muted him with the rolled up socks secured by the rolled red bandanna. When he placed the noose over Rainey's head, the man got super aroused, excited about aphrodisiac effect of being choked right at the moment of climax. Zachary shortened the rope which lifted Rainey onto his tiptoes. He gave Rainey a flute of champagne, took a sip off the other side. In choreographed movements he unfastened Rainey's pants button and lowered the zipper. Slowly, deliberately, he removed Rainey's shoes then each article of clothes until he hung like one of the nine human sacrifices of a Swedish Fröblot.

With a hand behind Rainey's head, he gently fed him another glass of the champagne. As he waited for the roofies to take effect, using the Intimate Kisses he started massaging Rainey's legs, upper body and buttocks. It worked like a charm. Rainey was out in less than five minutes.

With his switchblade, he skinned Rainey's arms then trimmed the meat away from the bones and laid it out in a semi-circle around him. Next, doing his best to keep it in one piece, he skinned the rest of the body, again going back to cut off the various muscle groups. These he cut into chunks and added them to the circle of meat. A perfect butcher shop display..

CHAPTER 63

His rage swept away, Zachary looked around. On the grass and dried leaves, raw meat waited to be packaged, sold, and its nutrients passed on to another. But no human deserved ingesting the evil of the vermin that had inhabited this carcass. Just as no one could escape the message. This man deserved to die!

Zachary pulled a business card from his shirt pocket and tucked it in the hip pocket of Rainey's jeans, the top edge showing. His only regret—he could not summon the vultures and other birds to pick clean the flesh before the body was discovered.

With utter calm, he grasped Rainey's genitals and with one swift cut removed this last reminder of the open wound Zachary had discovered when he washed Autry's body. He dropped the bloody remainder into the storm drain at Second and Plum.

He walked home to White Hall keeping to the shadows between the elevated track and the grove where he'd killed Rainey. His adrenaline slowed, the fresh meat seemed like gore rather than victory. He smiled though at the trap he'd set.

CHAPTER 64

Quote from the Journal of a Killer:

I have killed to protect the innocent. Such killing cannot be called murder. If you think it is murder, you've led a sheltered life, and I envy you.
Dean Koontz, **Odd Apocalypse**

MORNING, JULY 7, 2012:

Zachary woke from a sleep of the dead about four PM tired and sore as when he went to sleep. Hunger gnawed his stomach. He checked for telltale blood then headed to the Messiah Lutheran Church and supper.

As Cornelius Flynn walked up to the table, Zachary sat erect, eyes glazed, and emotionless.

"What's the matter, kid?" Corny sat down. He was the last person Zachary wanted to engage with today. Corny lowered his eye to Zachary's face then rapped him on the head. "Kid, you in there?" Corny's raucous laugh irritated Zachary. "You young boys sure know how to take care of yourselves.... Too many girls?"

This creep of a man who left his own young boys, six and ten, to fend for themselves though the judge specifically instructed him to go home and take care of them made Zachary see double—the face of his own father superimposed on this piece of shit. His rage uncorked. He bolted to his feet knocking his chair back. "You a-hole," he snarled. Red Kool-aid splattered down the length of the table. But the red that coursed through Zachary's brain was neither blood nor Kool-aid.

"Here," Flynn said roughly as he handed Zachary the fallen cup.

He ignored the cup, rewarded Cornelius with a distorted glare, spun on his heel, and dumped his untouched plate of food in the trash. Dishes flew as he slammed the tray into the dish window startling the church volunteer, spun again, and stomped out of the building.

CHAPTER 65

Quote from the Journal of a Killer:

Sometimes the greatest mercy is to remove the source of the hurt.
The Journal of a Killer

NIGHT, JULY 7, 2012:

Zachary tugged on the gate at the Salvation Army. Locked. As he fussed with the padlock the second story light in the commons area blinked off and all the room lights went dark. He kicked gate post then pounded a large nearby commercial trash bin with his free hand, leaned his head forward, and pouted.

The light click brought his face around. A light smile brightened his eyes.

Anticipation heightened, he watched as Flynn sneaked out of the shelter, slipped a brochure between the door frame and the lock, without a noise, exited down the metal stairs, flicked his lighter, and lifted it to his cigarette.

"Flynn." The whisper caught the man mid-light. Zachary lifted the bottle of Royal Crown Whiskey and a red plastic cup above his head and signaled for Flynn to come over.

The man tried the pedestrian gate. It was locked. So he skirted around the fenced area.

Zachary moved into the black area where the fence skirted a large Ashcraft storage building. As he waited for Flynn to round the last corner, he dropped a half dozen roofies into the cup then held it up so Flynn could see the golden whiskey pour into container. He could see the sparkle of anticipation in Flynn's eye as he swirled the liquid in the cup and taunted him.

"You want some?" Zachary lifted the lip of the cup to his mouth and sneered.

Flynn grabbed it. "Damn right you aren't going to drink that." He drained the cup in one smooth gulp and held it up for more.

"What makes you think it's for you?" Zachary raised the bottle and held it behind his head.

"You're the one that asked me to come over," Flynn growled and grabbed the arm.

"Okay, okay. Hang on there. A little patience my man." Zachary sneered again but poured a shot. "To your health." He raised the bottle and took a small sip.

Flynn nursed the drink this time. "What's the occasion? You don't strike me as the kind that stands around drinkin' with old men."

Zachary's chin tipped up. "I don't mind. I just wanted to apologize for how I treated you earlier. That just wasn't right."

The older man nodded but clenched his eyebrows. "So, what was that about?"

"Ah," Zachary ducked his head and spoke softly. "I had some bad run-ins with my old man. Left us and went off trucking. Cost my brother his life."

This time Flynn's eyebrows shot up. "His life…"

"Yeh. Dad was a trucker just like you." He scowled at Flynn. "Left us home alone, no money, nothing. So my brother ran off. Some jerk out on the highway raped him then dumped his body on the side of the road."

"Won't happen to my kids," Flynn chortled. "They're smarter than that."

Zachary's shoulders tighten, but he kept a placid face. *Those roofies should be kicking in soon. Come on. Come on.* "You're right. It won't happen to your kids. I've already taken care of that."

Flynn stared at him a few seconds then leaned up against the chain links and held his cup out again.

Zachary pushed out pouty lips and shook his head, but poured the gold anyway. A silence passed between them for several minutes, then Flynn lifted the cup but struggled to hold it up.

Zachary whipped a zip tie from his pocket. Grabbed Flynn's right wrist and zipped it tight to the fence above his head. Couldn't have Flynn falling. Drugged, Flynn tried to launch a left hook, but Zachary pinned that wrist to the chain link fence, slid it up high, and fastened the man secure just as his body began to slump. *Faster.* He needed Flynn at least partially conscious.

Wide eyes stared up at his face.

"Yu, yu, yu…" The man couldn't talk

Zachary curled his lips. "You piece of trash. Autry and I…your boys deserve better that this." He spit then slashed the length of the dominant veins on each of Flynn's arms wincing as the blood spurt into his face. "I'm gointa watch you die nice and slow the way your boys are."

With his free left hand, he seized Flynn's crotch. "Watch this you lousy trucker. The real payback." His knife sank deep into the groin carving a wide arc up, down, and around. An animal shriek pierced the air. Flynn's body went limp dragging the knife to a stop on a stubborn tendon and propelling a flap of clothes, skin, and bloody genitals against Zachary's left arm. Startled he jerked backward inadvertently ripping loose the spermatic cords behind the testicles.

He reeled backwards. Gasped at the bloody mass lying in his hand. Green bile blocked his throat.

CHAPTER 66

Quote from the Journal of a Killer:

Everything we love will be taken from us, everything, last of all life itself....
Dean Koontz, **Odd Apocalypse**

NEAR MIDNIGHT, JULY 7, 2012:

Zachary stumbled to the edge of the Ponderosa pines and wretched. He stood paralyzed in the silence between trains—emotions suspended between heaven and earth. Heaven—the rescue of two young boys from the suffering he and Autry endured. Earth, or was it hell—the bloody result of his uncorked rage. Blood stuck his fingers together. Twice he tried to wipe them on his shirt then his pants, but both attempts resulted in more blood smeared on his hands.

He failed to plan Flynn's elimination. He had no clothes to change into and the Salvation Army had no outdoor faucet. With blood on his hands and clothes, he didn't dare go shower at Hall County Park. Too many miles. Too many questioning eyes on a Saturday night.

Minutes later, he dropped down from the railroad tracks into the shadows along the chain link storage behind White Hall. The whiff of rotting flesh shot up his nose, caught him off guard. He covered his mouth with his bloody shirt and pressed on hoping the smell had not crept into his basement. However, opening the south facing door, a blast of hot pungent air knocked him back. He dry heaved again.

Inside the smell permeated every corner. Not even shower water kept it away. Given his rage and these unpleasant reminders, he decided to leave Grand Island and pursue that warmer winter climate he'd often talked about—somewhere over the mountains. Somewhere with cool nights, warm days, and fresh air.

CHAPTER 67

Quote from the Journal of a Killer:

Where in the process a dividing line is drawn between life and death depends on factors beyond the presence or absence of vital signs.
Wikipedia

In Anselmo, all three adults rose around five, made their way to the kitchen for coffee. Laqueta then wandered into the dining room and surveyed the chart.

"I wish Granddad was here. Maybe he'd see something we've missed."

"His experience undoubtedly would help," Gramms said. "During the night I thought about these cases." She ran a finger down the list of names. "Every victim had problems, especially traumas, in their life. Right?"

Stephen and Laqueta nodded and scanned the type of history column.

"Of course all of them were homeless?"

They nodded again and shifted to Gramm's face.

"Most likely they knew each other and may have all known their killer, if he or she is also homeless. He or she probably knew their stories. Somebody with a tender heart."

"But the method of death seems to be progressing," stated Laqueta.

"Could be he or she is just getting angrier. A friend of mine worked in Chicago with Bosnian refugees. He said something that made sense to me. His mental health staff carried around the entire traumas they listened to while the clients carried only one. Staff, even he himself, developed vicarious PTSD or something like that.

"If the killer was a victim of trauma then he added other stories on top, maybe he popped a cork. Decided they shouldn't have to suffer anymore. Perhaps a sense of mercy became an excuse for murder."

Laqueta frowned then said, "Maybe the progression in methods is an issue of efficiency, quickness of death." She chuckles. "If we had you and Granddad here together, we'd have this case solved and prosecuted today."

Laqueta's phone at Stephen's elbow rang. He jumped six inches off his stool.

"It's the desk," she said with a frown. "Yes... Uh-hu ... When? ... Where? ... Actually, I'm out of town right now, but, yes, I want to be there before the scene is disturbed. I'll call the coroner and medical examiner when I get there. Give me about two hours."

She looked at Stephen for affirmation, but Stephen's phone rang sending him off the stool again.

"Hello.... Yeh, Dave. What's up?" His eyebrows lifted. "Wait. Go over that again. Give me more details if you can."

He listened a long time. His face a puzzle of responses. He began to pace. "The police are there, so let them take the lead. I'll give you Captain Higgins's number." He looked at Laqueta and tipped his head back to signal he needed her attention.

"Tell Captain I'll be back in about...How long did I hear you say?"

"A couple of hours."

"A couple hours. Now, do I have this right? It was Cornelius Flynn. He was zip tied to the fence, throat cut, and ... well I won't say that right now ... a couple of women here."

CHAPTER 68

Quote from the Journal of a Killer:

A man who won't die for something is not fit to live.
Martin Luther King, Jr.

The sand in Gramm's driveway clogged the luggage rollers. Stephen carried Darren and Laqueta's luggage the rest of the way to the truck.

"Got it all?

"I think so," Laqueta replied. "Darren, where are those chaps and boots Gramms bought you?"

His eyes widened—typical Darren. "In the barn!" He ran off like a jack rabbit and reappeared in under a minute, boots and chaps in hand. Stephen laid them on top of the luggage and closed the trunk.

"Ready." He turned toward Gramms who stayed home from church to see them off.

"What! Leaving on your birthday?" Gramms winked at Darren and tousled his hair. "I suppose birthday cake was fine for breakfast, but you didn't get your birthday surprise."

"Wasn't the surprise the photo of Amelia on the mantel?" asked Stephen.

"Oh no." Gramms shook her head. "There's somewhere important I wanted to take you before this old lady kicks the bucket."

"Oh, Gramms. Quit being so dramatic. You're not going to kick the bucket anytime soon. I still need you. ... So what was it?"

"You'll have to wait." She turned to Laqueta. "You bring him back soon. Okay?"

In the awkward silence that followed, Darren looked at Stephen then at his mother.

"I will," he piped up his chin raised. "'sides Snowy needs me to ride him. Right, Mr. Stephen?"

"You bet, son."

Stephen shot his I-did-it-again-stepped-out of-line look to Laqueta with lifted eyebrows and made a fake clench of teeth. "Now, mount up cowboy. Time to roll."

An hour and a half later as they turned onto Highway 281 north of Saint Paul, Laqueta's phone rang.

"Just turned to come into Saint Paul," she said. "So about thirty minutes. Maybe twenty the way Stephen's driving. Don't tell the Highway Patrol." She nudged his direction with her elbow.

"What?" Her eyebrows lifted framing concern and surprise.

Now what? Stephen thought. His face matched hers.

"Where's this body? ... That's over by the Burlington tracks above Second Street isn't it? Any idea who it is?" She raised her eyebrows and looked at Stephen who was having a hard time keeping his eyes on the road. "Yes, I know Rainey White. I went to his motel a few weeks back. He's our prime suspect in the homeless murders. Did you say he was dismembered?" She winced. "Dismembered and hanged," she said to Stephen then back on the phone. "Could you please secure the site until I get done at the Salvation Army? We're short of bodies this weekend and I already have the backup officer standing by at the Flynn murder site."

Stephen hit the edge of the shoulder.

CHAPTER 69

Quote from the Journal of a Killer:

Because I love you, I have turned you over to death.
The Journal of a Killer

After reviewing multiple headlines, Stephen cringed. Maybe homeless perpetrators didn't deserve to have their stories told, especially when the story humanized them despite the evil they did. On the news clips he watched, the Rainey White at the University of California-San Diego came from a totally different planet. Orphaned at eleven. His father taught Philosophy and Ethics at Marymount University in Calvert City, California. His mother a forensic psychologist. Young Rainey was present, their murder-suicide followed a history of violent verbal fights.

Neither the police nor the Department of Social Services succeeded in finding any living relatives. After a traumatic physical and sexual assault by the uncle of one of his foster parents, the San Diego Child Advocacy Center tried, but again failed to locate any family.

Publicity of the assault, however, produced one positive result. Rainey's final two foster placements took place in the homes of academics. Both sets of foster parents taught at the University of California-San Diego. Rainey changed homes only because the first two professors took teaching and research posts out of state. Other than a scrape with the law at seventeen nothing remarkable happened until his arrest for statutory rape and sexual predation while a professor at the University.

"Statutory rape? That's absurd. Dr. White is a fine award winning professor of Criminal Psychology." That sentiment echoed the responses of a half dozen other colleagues. "He recently received a major award for his work with and research into the dynamics of serial sexual offenders. Single professors get accused of rape all the time" Single professors and single women were as much a staple of the university as they were on television and in the movies. Nothing in the charges seemed unusual except that the charges were filed on behalf of a male student, not a female.

And on videos of student interviews he heard, "Rainey Brainy! Awesome classes though that sex stuff makes your skin crawl. Did you know Ted Bundy was actually a serial rapist? For him the kill was all about the sex.

"Dr. Brainy helped students find drugs, smoked weed with us, loved sex parties—generally all round great guy. Sure, I heard he pressured students to provide things he wanted, but that was jealous talk—somebody didn't get what they wanted or failing a class. They envied him. He was a free spirit."

"Sounds like classic victim grooming," stated the interviewer.

"Grooming his victims? Oh, you mean getting close to them and all that. We studied that in class. Wicked stuff. Twisted thinking. Nah, I don't think Rainey was like that. He was the Sex Crimes teacher for God's sake. Probably just joking around. I tell you man, it's just wannabe students and married men jealous of a cool single guy. Throw them in jail. The perverts."

Unsettled, he shook his head. *Sure would like to have Zachary's input before I complete the article.*

He dialed the kitchen. "Anybody seen Zachary today?"

Chet answered. "Negative chief. He's not here and no one's seen him today."

"Did I hear Susan say she didn't think he'd been here since Monday?"

"Yeh, I think she's right, though that would be kind of unusual. Maybe he headed down towards Santa Fe. He always talked about it, but I didn't figure he'd do that till next winter."

Stephen hung up and massaged his eyebrows.

Had Flynn to do yet, too.

CHAPTER 70

Quote from the Journal of a Killer:

I hope and trust the infinite, the eternal, and merciful and loving God. I worship Him and feel no guilt in my heart before him for what I am going to do.
Alex Campbell

Sonja laid a fax on Stephen's desk. Test results from Flynn's blood samples. *Alcohol and flunitrazepam. Roofies. That's odd.* He called Joe, the shelter night manager.

Joe stammered around then came clean. "Yeh, Corny blew a .003 Friday night. I was doing randoms, an everybody blows night. Kicked him out. Told him if he came back clean Saturday night I'd let him stay 'til I talked to you Monday morning. It was only .003."

"It don't matter now. Go on…"

"I did the follow up test Saturday night and he was clean. He laid down about eight o'clock. I didn't even realize he'd gone back out. So, alcohol might make sense. Trying to get one over and all that. But roofies? Corny was straight, definitely straight."

Yeh, that didn't make sense, Stephen thought as he hung up, *unless someone was planning to rape Flynn. But by then Rainey was already dead.* He let out an exhausted sigh. Called the kitchen staff. Again no one had seen Zachary. *Wonder if he will show up dead next.* He shook it off then called Flynn's contact number in Illinois. A ladies voice on the answering machine. Maybe he'd call the Salvation Army in Santa Fe. But instead he called Flynn's line a second time.

"We're sorry this phone has been disconnected or is otherwise out of service. If you believe you have reached this message in error please contact the operator for assistance." He dialed again. Same results. Strange.

His phone rang.

"Laqueta. Glad you called. I'm hitting a brick wall on Cornelius Flynn. So far I have found two children, apparently still in the home, and a former spouse, location unknown. This stinks.

"Oh, ... and I found his home phone number—matched the one in our records—but nobody answered then when I called back the number had been disconnected." He frowned as he stopped talking.

"Let me stop you there." He noted stiffness in Laqueta's response. "We called the police department in Carter--to help with notification-- and ran into a surprise. They said you notified them on Sunday and the Department of Children and Family Services picked up the boys. You said they were being abandoned at home like your dad did with you when he went on the road. Anyway, the boys were out of food and scared. The Carter Police Department wanted me to thank you for bringing it to their attention."

"Wow. But I didn't call."

"I know." She sounded colder. His muscles began to tense. "The call was made Sunday morning around six thirty. It couldn't have been you. We were drinking coffee and eating toast with your Gramms at that time."

Your Gramms. That sounded odd to Stephen.

"But that's not why I called," Laqueta continued, "Chief and I are looking at the chart and we need you to come over."

"Right away?"

"Right now."

CHAPTER 71

Quote from the Journal of a Killer:

At my hands, dear lord of life and mercy,
please grant my friend release from life and an easy death.
The Journal of a Killer

JUST AFTER MIDNIGHT, JULY 8, 2012:

Zachary dug out his duffle bag. A move meant leaving many things behind. He hated it, but early on he'd learned to roll clothes to maximize the contents in his duffle. Still, he envied guys with huge hiking packs and their all weather sleeping bags on top. Selections made, he hitched the bag's strap over his shoulder. No bus left town before 11:30 AM but it was impossible to sleep in the putrid air in his White Hall Off Plum. Standing outside the door, he gagged but at least he didn't puke. The air still concentrated the stench of Rainey's rotting body parts at ground level. He'd have to put some distance between them and himself in order to sleep.

Hank's cardboard under the bushes would make do on a cloudless night. Plus, Pier Park was over halfway to the bus stop at the Regency Inn Motel.

CHAPTER 71

"How far will two hundred dollars take me?" Zachary had counted his cash on hand when the sun rose. While he had four hundred twelve dollars plus change left from detassling, he decided to limit travel to two hundred.

"Depends on where you're going," the clerk said. "Got some place in mind?"

"Santa Fe's always sounded nice."

No bus stopped in Santa Fe, but the clerk checked the fare to Albuquerque, New Mexico, the nearest stop. One hundred fifty two dollars and fifteen cents. A seventeen hour five minute ride—he could stand that. Especially to go to somewhere he'd dreamed about. If he sweet talked the driver, he could probably get let out in Santa Fe along the way. He'd keep his duffle on board.

A young kid in a rose colored hoodie and baggy pants waited with Zachary for the bus to Denver, Zachary's first stop. A hoodie in July heat was insane. But fashion trumped heat for high schoolers or at least some of them. "You heard about that murder over at the Salvation Army?"

"What are you talking about?"

"On my Walkman." The boy slipped it out of his pocket and lifted it up for Zachary to see. "That's the second time this morning it's been on the news."

"Any details?"

"Yeh! They found this guy chained to the fence with zip ties, neck slit, balls removed. How gross is that? Police investigator said he was nearly decapitated. Machete they think."

"Must have ticked somebody off," Zachary replied and smirked.

"Yeh, and they don't have a suspect. Asking the public for any leads. Damm cops are useless in this town."

The kid started bopping to the music again and Zachary laid his head on the back of the chair. He couldn't get out of the town fast enough.

CHAPTER 72

Quote from the Journal of a Killer:

"Show no mercy to wicked traitors."
Psalm 59:5 NLT

Laqueta and Chief sat in the small conference room at the Law Enforcement Center, the chart, still attached to the roll of butcher paper, spread out in front of them. A phone lay by her right hand.

"Stephen." Laqueta noticed him first. "Please sit down."

She motioned to a chair across from her and the Chief.

He wrinkled his forehead and glanced down. Something was changed on the chart.

As if she read his mind, Laqueta said, "Chief requested that we add the business cards to the chart—and the messages from the backs."

"What business cards?" Stephen asked.

Chief stood and turned the chart toward him, but Stephen remained standing so he could see the whole chart clearly. Two new columns followed each victim's name.

CHAPTER 72

Name of Victim	Card	Message
Unknown	Yes	At last relief from fear and freedom from the past and future
Joseph Riederhof	No	
Janice Zahn	Yes	Sister, you'll never be raped and used again. Hold your head high. I didn't know or I would've been gentler. I never would have taken your flower if I knew your past.
Henry Many Horses	Yes	Finally! Unchained from your mind, happy buffalo hunting, Hank.
Javier Ruiz-Lobo	Yes	Sleep now with happy memories of your family. I have spared you the ruin and trauma of my own past.
Rainey White	Yes	Go to hell you cruel bastard! Now the world is free of your freeloading, pimping, and preying on the homeless.
Cornelius Flynn	Yes	You bastard! Your family deserved better. Hah, hah! I liberated them before you died.

Stephen looked down at Laqueta who looked away. His name had been added to the list of suspects in a third person's handwriting.

"Your cards, Mr. Brown," Chief Greywright picked up a small stack of business cards. "Don't you recognize them?" he demanded in a harsh rub-your-nose-in-it got-you tone of voice. "Those are your messages, aren't they?"

"No sir." His neck stiff, his breath shallow, Stephen only slightly shook his head to accent the negative reply.

"Look!" Chief slid the small pile of cards toward Stephen and fanned them out. "These are yours aren't they?"

"No sir." Stephen regained some composure as his neck loosened.

"That is your name isn't it?"

"Yes, sir. But …"

"And you work for the Salvation Army don't you?" Chief interrupted pointing at the logo on the cards.

Stephen nodded. "But…"

"And you knew all these people."

"I …"

"So admit it! These are your cards. You know, Stephen, things will go better for you if you cooperate. Just tell the truth." Chief slapped the edge of the desk.

Stephen stared at the chart for a few seconds. He could barely feel his heart beat.

"Yes. These are my cards..."

"So you admit it," Chief declared.

"Yes. These are my cards." Stephen thumped the cards with the knuckle of his index finger. "Lots of people have my cards. Other providers—people who knew these individuals—have stacks of my cards for referrals and contact information. Most homeless people have my cards. Sometimes, they take several at a time to give to employers, family, and even other homeless people. These are my cards." He paused to turn the cards over so the messages were visible. "But these are not my messages. This *is not* my handwriting." He pointed at the two entries on the chart which he, not Laqueta, had written. "If my guess is right, Laqueta—I mean Investigator Ellison—already did a writing analysis when I was a valid suspect."

Laqueta ducked her head and nodded.

Stephen pointed at the dates of the last two murders followed by the dates the bodies were discovered. Shifting his focus to Laqueta, he stated firmly, "I could not have committed these two murders. I was with you at Gramms on both of those dates. Furthermore, we were at Gramms together when Cornelius Flynn's body was found and we were together in the car on the way home to GI when Rainey's body showed up."

He fixed her with a lifted eyebrow and eyes that begged a confirmation.

"That's right, Chief," she began softly then broke from his gaze and looked at the Chief. "We were together when all four of these events occurred. I guess I was so caught off guard by your insistence to add Stephen to the chart I didn't think that far."

"Humph," Chief snorted jerking his head back, still looking defiant.

Stephen looked directly in his eyes. "Who put you up to this? Richard Koenig?"

The words surprised even Stephen.

Chief spun on his heel clips and strode around the table and out. He muttered to Laqueta, "Have it the Council's way! But I tell you, you better keep an open mind about this guy." He shot Stephen a dirty look.

A tinge of fear creased the bridge between Laqueta's eyes.

"What was that about?" Stephen asked. "When's the other shoe going to drop?"

Her eyes were pleading. He realized she was afraid.

They both turned to the window to watch Chief exit the parking lot.

The next morning, back at the Law Enforcement Center, Stephen leaned over and propped a hand on either side of the writing on the chart as he and Laqueta worked on reconciling the business cards with the rest of the information on the chart.

"Look. These last two messages have a different tone. A different motive. We may still have at least two killers."

"But they're in the same handwriting," Laqueta pointed out.

"My bad," said Stephen. "After Chief's accusation, I'm now the one a little off kilter." Scanning the list again, he frowned. "That would mean the John Doe was also killed by the same perp."

"If it was murder."

Stephen stopped to look at his watch. "Oh no! I forgot about the articles on Flynn and White. They were due to the newspaper an hour ago."

CHAPTER 73

Quote from the Journal of a Killer:

Death is always, under all circumstances, a tragedy,
for if it is not then it means that
life has become one.
Theodore Roosevelt

At his office, Stephen pulled up the two articles he'd put together Thursday night. *Rough! Something's missing. Sure wish I could talk to Zachary before I finished up.*

He stood and headed to the kitchen.

"Seen Zachary yet?"

Susan scratched her head. "No."

"Hasn't been in all week," Chet added.

"Well...." Stephen frowned. "Thanks." *No body's shown up. Maybe he went to Santa Fe.*

It was a long shot, but back at his desk he called the Santa Fe, New Mexico, Salvation Army.

"Hi. This is Stephen Brown, Director of Social Services at the Grand Island Salvation Army."

"Major Browning here. Say, isn't Grand Island in Nebraska?"

Stephen said, "Yes," Then explained his mission—to find Zachary Plues. Spoken out loud his reasons sounded foolish, probably inappropriate. Thankfully, Major Brown didn't seem to question them.

CHAPTER 73

"Yes, Zachary Plues checked into our shelter Monday night. I can ask him to give you a call. What kind of message do you want me to give him?"

"Just ask him to call me. My cell number is (308) 938-2217. Say it's about Rainey White and Cornelius Flynn."

"Rainy White and Cornelius Flynn. Got it. I'll give it to Zachary when he comes in to supper tonight."

Even so he couldn't wait. The articles were overdue. He quickly finalized them, got Captain's permission to proceed—they were pretty innocuous, and headed to the Independent. From the car he called Laqueta. He wanted to go to the Riederhof death site to see if there might be any further evidence to support an accidental death. Riederhof 's was the only body without a message card.

CHAPTER 74

Quote from the Journal of a Killer:

I pray there is really a purgatory.
Not because I want a second chance
but so these bastards will have to suffer longer
on their way to hell!
The Journal of a Killer

Stephen read the back of the business card they'd found at Riederhof's camp, "Go ahead. Fly away from your wheel chair, catheter, and pain. Now you've paid the death penalty you wanted."

"Maybe Joseph's death wasn't an accident. Oh, by the way, since we're here, I'd like to see Javier's camp. Maybe there'll be another clue there too."

"Will you ever be satisfied?" Laqueta peered at Stephen over the top of her horn rimmed glasses then she stepped south onto the path leading to Javier's camp.

He loved her way of challenging him and charming him at the same time. He loved those horn rimmed glasses. The way her melanin rich black skin brightened the browns and beiges of the frames enchanted him. Even more, he loved the glistening brown eyes they framed. When she stepped into a nest of scraggily bushes, he accelerated his pace and pushed through the last of the red stemmed gray dogwoods.

CHAPTER 74

"Javier died over there." Laqueta pointed to a rotting stump off to the left.

Stephen nodded and surveyed the site. "Still neat," he commented, "except for windblown trash, someone could reset the tent pole and move in. "

"The kid's clothes are still here—sizes twelve months, three and five—if I remember correctly. All folded neat and stacked inside." In the beige rain streaked tent, neat stacks peeked out beside what appeared to be men's work boots.

"Are Marta's clothes still here, too?"

"Yeah. Some pretty things. Lace. Ribbons and bows and the like. Nice bright colors. But come on. I'll take you up to the main homeless encampment. It's this-a-way."

As the path led deeper into the woods, Stephen detoured to inspect a doll lying behind a cottonwood. It looked kind of large, but maybe it had belonged to one of Javier's kids. He poked its hooded head with his toe then jumped back.

"Laqueta ..." he called. He felt dirty.

The skull measured little more than three inches from side to side. Dark brown patches of hair clung to dried skin. Stephen's eyes blurred.

Laqueta peered around the tree. Her body stiffened. Instantly the cell phone was in her hand.

"Step away from the body."

Total professionalism now.

"Look's to be about 12 months old." Cool, calm, she spoke into the phone. "Pretty much intact, looks like some animal damage, probably a mouse not likely a rat."

It's probably Javier's child. Neither one said it. It just sort of sat there, an unspoken agreement between them. In fact they didn't speak at all. Not to each other.

⁂

Later, when Laqueta dropped him off at the Army, Stephen didn't go in. He didn't want to be alone, but he couldn't wait to be home, his home.

CHAPTER 75

Quote from the Journal of a Killer:

To assist in death of the hurting is to usher them into peace.
The Journal of a Killer

THURSDAY EVENING, JULY 12, 2012:

Zachary sat in the lounge of the Santa Fe Salvation Army Shelter his feet curled up in front of him.

How'd he find out? Why else would Stephen call to talk about Rainey and Flynn? He examined the back side of his eyelids and rocked back and forth. *Maybe that's not it.*

"Yeh, I figured you for a big baby." The big man in front of him grunted. "Come to daddy boy." He leered at him. "I know what to do with a wimp like you." Richard Bruiser, that was his name, let out a roar.

Looking into the nothingness of his own thoughts, Zachary merely frowned. Bruiser was unfinished business. A Rainey White and bully wrapped into one. Strong enough to take what he wanted, he terrorized other homeless for the sheer fun of it. *Glad I slipped that machete in my pack. Have to show it to him tonight.*

Yes, that's what he'd do. Take care of business before calling Stephen and facing whatever wild card that entailed. *Let the pieces fall where they will!*

CHAPTER 75

First he slipped around to his bunk where he wrote out what to say to Stephen—if asked about the murder of Rainey White and Cornelius Flynn—then put a change of clothes in his backpack and slipped his machete down the back of his shirt. Zachary double talked, describing the machete to Bruiser with a hint that it might be something more human, more flesh and blood. The big bruiser salivated the whole way to the back of the Senior Citizens Center—one of those out of the way places for sexual dalliance or other malfeasance.

Bruiser tested the sharp edge of the blade and offered Zachary a taste of his blood.

"There's more where that came from if you like it. I like it rough," he half barked, "ruff" punctuated with a raised eyebrow and suggestive smile. Eyes blazing, he swept downward sending Zachary hopping over the machete like a kid playing skip rope. The brute roared. That seemed to be his favorite sound.

Zachary pulled two half pints of whiskey from his pack offering Bruiser one strongly laced with roofies. In no time the man slid to the ground against the block building. Zachary's own swig of whiskey burned down his throat. He shattered the bottle against the wall disgusted that he'd almost broken his sobriety.

The machete slipped easily from Bruiser's grip though he let out a gust of air as Zachary leaned him forward away from the wall. The man's massive chest collapsed against his belly. Machete raised, Zachary stepped backward. The blade flashed as it sliced through a ray of sun. In the glint of light, Richard Bruiser's brawny arm caught Zachary's wrist mid-fall spinning him flat on his back. His head cracked on the cement slab.

CHAPTER 76

Quote from the Journal of a Killer:

Nobody ever did, or ever will, escape
the consequences of his choices.
Alfred A. Montapert

Stephen grabbed the first page of Zachary Plues journal off the fax machine as it came through from Santa Fe. He read the list of eight names written in chronological order. The first, Autry Plues, identified the body of the unnamed victim. The last, Richard Bruiser, according to Major Browning the missing resident from the Santa Fe shelter, read, "You big bruiser—stopped you!"

The pages journaled Zachary's thoughts and activities in Grand Island, each entry dated and carefully worded. A pit formed in Stephen's stomach. He didn't know whether to be excited or wary. The name Janice Zahn caught his attention and he pulled the sheet out dated June 2, 2012. He stood spellbound by the details of Janice and Zachary's last hours together, so involved he nearly upchucked at Zachary's swift cinch of the zip tie and Janice's body going limp in his arms.

"No! Not Zachary!"

CHAPTER 77

Quote from the Journal of a Killer:

The world is littered with the lives of victims
in need of a permanent mercy.
The Journal of a Killer

"Investigator Brown?" Laqueta peered around the doorframe. "You were right. Zachary's in Santa Fe. But I just talked to the Santa Fe County Sheriff, Zachary's been murdered. One of your cards was found on the body."

The fax machine shifted gears to begin printing the next sheet.

Emotionless Stephen handed Laqueta the Janice Zahn entry. She scanned it then looked up with questioning eyes.

"Zachary Plues' journal." He pointed at the stack of papers in the print tray then handed her the first page.

Her eyes widened. "That's a list of all our murder victims! Where did you get that?"

"Major Browning down in Santa Fe. He found it while clearing away Zachary's personal stuff."

The fax machine went quiet.

"Major agreed to send me a copy before he turned it over to the Santa Fe County Sheriff."

Laqueta examined the list again while Stephen continued.

"My guess is Zachary went to kill this Bruiser fellow, met his match, and became the victim instead."

"The Sheriff's looking for Richard Bruiser right now," Laqueta stated but paused. She was examining his eyes.

"What?"

"You just solved the murders in two towns. Why so down?"

CHAPTER 78

Quote from the Journal of a Killer:

Dying caused them no anguish. They suffered no pain.
I am convinced that at the moment their hearts stopped beating,
they were happy. Is there a more beautiful death?
Jan-Philipp Sendker, **Art of Hearing Heartbeats**

Stephen looked up at the cross above his desk. At least he'd been right about Riederhof's death. It was an accident. He leaned back in his chair. But then, as Laqueta had said, he already had the card prepared. The same was true of Javier. He found him dead, but he already had a card prepared.

Despite the weekend, he couldn't wrap his head around Zachary being a killer. *In many ways Zachary had a richer life than I do,* he thought. *In many ways he was more engaged in the lives of the homeless, especially the hurting, than I have ever been. Damm that journal.*

Then there was the last entry in Zachary's journal—the conversation they'd never had. Zachary was right. *"I don't think you can understand. Even Rainey and Flynn were acts of mercy."*

Brushing melancholy aside, he drove out to the Law Enforcement Center.

Laqueta laughed lightly then lifted her eyebrows as he came in. "Oh, I forgot to tell you. The detailed descriptions of the rapes by Councilman Koenig, the branding, and the cut by Rainey White were enough to get a search warrant for Rainey's old motel room. The search turned up the dress, paperclip, and other evidence from the dinner, plus blood—Janice's—and semen—Rainey's plus one unidentified specimen. Based on her letter tucked in the back of Zachary's journal, the County Attorney secured a warrant for a DNA sample from Richard Koenig. They arrested him last night during City Council Meeting on charges of rape, torture, and kidnapping. It may not stick, but at least the community's been served notice of his true character."

"Laqueta." Chief Greywright frowned as he leaned in the door cell phone in hand. "I think you better take this one. A small Hispanic child just walked out of Richard Koenig's house. Asked the neighbor to help find her mama. Says her name's Leticia Ruiz-Lobo."

EPILOGUE

Quote from the Journal of a Killer:

"This is what the Lord of Heaven's Armies says:
'Judge fairly, and show mercy and kindness to one another'."
Zechariah 7:9 NLV

AUGUST 16, 2014:

"Ari-Lee Ojetta Brown," Stephen crooned as he stroked the tiny hand of the newborn while Dr. Brimm cleaned her preparing to return her to her mother. "You're the most beautiful little girl in all the whole world."

How can something so precious come out of my body, be so different and so me! It was the thought of so many fathers when gazing at their child and especially keen in first time dads.

Dr. Brimm laid Ari-Lee, wrapped secure in a warm nursery blanket, into the cradle of Stephen's elbow. All the poking, prodding, pricking, and measuring done, she looked up wide eyed into her daddy's face. He brushed her tiny lips with a fingertip.

"Look at all those soft honey colored curls," he said to Laqueta as he transferred Ari-Lee to her mother's arms then stood there looking down in wonder. He sat on the edge of the gurney with an arm around Laqueta's head and fingers reaching down caressing Ari's hand. Reverence seemed the appropriate response so they sat there lightly cooing, staring down at their daughter's face and tiny hands.

"You look as beautiful as ever," he said and bent down to kiss Laqueta's forehead. Her smile still sent shivers through his heart.

Two years ago they'd driven over to the Alley Rose in Kearney to celebrate solving the seven homeless murders. It seemed right to get out of town away from the context of the murders to celebrate.

"So you still lookin' for a man?" Stephen asked over Tea Smoked Chicken appetizers.

Laqueta blushed and looked down.

You fool! Stephen chastised himself, but it didn't stop his curiosity. "I'll take that as a yes." He moved his head to where he could look in her eyes. "So, what are your criteria? There are not a lot of options in Grand Island."

"More than you know," she raised her head to look into his eyes.

"Well then, how do you sort out the possibilities? What are you looking for in a man?"

"Well," she caressed her lower arm then continued, "Let's see. I don't usually think too much about it, but—let's see—tall, dark, and handsome. I'm not too much into those honey colored boys who think they're all that."

They both chuckled.

"And I want a man whose at least as intelligent as I am, understands my passion for investigation, loves Darren. I prefer someone who's a little creative, with whom I can talk easily, who knows how to laugh, a bit of a romantic—I like warm cuddling, evenings just sitting in each other's arms—and he better be a gentleman. I'm not into bad boys. Never was. Of course I don't need a man like Dreaux who was all those things, but with a one line agenda—sex and run."

Stephen's face became serious. He watched as she noticed his change then lifted her chin and gave that demur smile of hers.

"And you?" She returned the challenge.

He pressed his lips into a thin line then puckered them.

"I want a woman who's tall, dark, and handsome." His eyes sparkled but Laqueta shook her head.

"You men! I swear. You want a straight vulnerable answer then hide behind ridiculous words."

"Nailed me, but what's it matter?" He shrugged. "I'm not your type any way. Wrong color."

Laqueta didn't usually let her negative emotions show, but that got him a dirty look.

"I'll be the judge of that. Now, as you western boys say, 'Time to pony up!'"

Stephen leaned back in the chair and stretched one leg forward. "Well," he started, "I want a woman tall enough to lay her head on my shoulder as I hold her—whether standing or sitting. She's beautiful and elegant and has smooth silky skin with a bluish tint. Because of Gramms I suppose, I have an eye for a woman who handles herself confidently."

At that phrase, Laqueta gave him a suspicious look.

"And she's black as a moonless Nebraska night, but glowing with the luster of the stars."

She blushed.

He frowned and refocused. "She needs to not let color get in the way and—if she's willing—I'd like to count tonight as my first official date with her."

"Here." The nurse lifted Ari-Lee from Laqueta's hands and laid her back in Stephen's arms. "I think there's a little boy out there anxious to meet his sister."

And two sets of grandparents and great grandparents by now, he thought. It felt like too big a crowd to him. Okay, the anxiety was over the too clear difference in their races. He really needed to get over that.

"We'll wheel Laqueta into her room and get her settled in then I'll come get you."

Stephen smiled, turned, and walked out.

The next few minutes with Darren—he loved that kid—and his sister were ones he'd waited nine months to share. A daddy and his own kids.

ARE LABELS HOLDING YOU OR YOUR ORGANIZATION BACK

Is your organization papering over people with labels?

Labels are only designed to describe, but unconsciously we import value judgments, presupposed scenarios, characteristics, etc., that do not actually apply to the humans behind the labels.

The result is:

- Labels stand in the way of open, effective and forward movement.
- Labels prevent companies from becoming unified workforces.
- Labels prevent us from reaching out holistically in social actions.

We lose credibility, effectiveness, and even monetary value.

What about your moral judgments?

Are labels holding back you, your service organization, your church/religious organization, or business from fulfilling its intrinsic mission?

A Certain Mercy demonstrates how our Salvation Armys, our Sheriff's offices, our Angelina Abbotts and Councilman Koenigs, and our communities paper over peoples' lives and legal rights with labels.

I want to help your organization, your community, or you personally stop misusing labels.

Contact me at:

wayne.anson@gmail.com.

Or let's talk at 308-227-3221

ABOUT THE AUTHOR

William L. Silvaneus's total life has centered on human services, mostly with disenfranchised individuals and trauma victims – the homeless, refugees, immigrants, the poor, the addicted, and disenfranchised. Under his given name, Wayne Anson, he developed and opened a transitional shelter/social service center for homeless veterans, teamed with other providers in developing homeless services coalitions throughout South Carolina, and served as a shelter manager at the Salvation Army in Grand Island, Nebraska. He serves as the Immediate Past President of the Nebraska Writers Guild, a three hundred-fifty-member organization with members in sixteen states and one foreign country. He has published articles in the "International Association of Residential and Community Alternatives Journal," "International Association of Justice in Action," and "Bosanski Most;" sold a children's story to "Discoveries," a publication of the Nazarene Church; and spent fifteen years writing adult curriculum for Barclay Press. His other interests include watercolor painting, creating ornamental egg decorations, writing poetry, and loving his four children and thirteen grandchildren.

57999323R10205

Made in the USA
Columbia, SC
17 May 2019